"The Challenge" As some fools do. But do

"The Man Who Photographed Beardsley ꞏꞏꞏꞏꞏ ꞏꞏꞏꞏꞏ pictures from life – or was he simply impatient?

"The Cyprus Shell" There are some you can eat, while others have their own pick-me-ups.

"Clean Slate" If you're in debt to the Devil, don't mess with look-a-like sisters.

"The Deep-Sea Conch" Some species build nests; while others are much like the cuckoo....

"The Ugly Act" But what's a pimple or two – if there's only you?

"Irving's Story" Her downstairs knew best, every time.

"The Running Man" It may be true you can run – but as for finding a place to hide...?

"Somebody Calling" The only way she could. He simply had to listen harder.

"Vanessa's Voice" Both beautiful ... and deadly!

"The Vehicle" Some might think of him that way, others as a dyadic personality?

"Mandraki" Take care who you lie down with ... and where!

"Two-Stone Tom" Yes, except he was an entire science heavier than that!

"The Long Last Night" Was it just a myth – or a Mythos?

"The Weird Wines of Naxas Niss" A wizard's stolen potion is another man's gateway to Nirvana...maybe!

"Stealer of Dreams" Always remember, once they're gone they might stay gone!

BRIAN LUMLEY'S THE BEST OF THE REST

EDITED BY
BARBARA ANN LUMLEY

Copyright Information

Contents

Introduction

This pretty much is what the title says. Many of the stories/novellas here will have only been done in limited print runs; such as in Fanzines, Magazines, Pamphlets, Special Editions or on-line magazines.

It's a mixed genre of stories and these are what Brian considers the best of the rest of the stories in his body of work. We've got 111,000+ words in this collection so that means lots of enjoyment in what is likely the last collection coming from Brian.

Please Note: There are a few stories that Brian has decided he does not want to see published in any format anymore as he doesn't feel they are good enough, so I haven't forgotten anything substantial.

We hope you will enjoy this as much as I enjoyed putting it together for all the avid Lumley readers throughout the years and for those still to come.

This collection will also be done in audio format.

Barbara Ann Lumley
Torquay, Devon 2023

PART 1

The Stories

The Challenge

As some fools do. But do you dare? Yes? *Well Don't!*

The supernatural? Anyone who knows me will tell you that the supernatural and I have no common ground—not in real life, at least. Fiction is something else: it's my *business* to tell weird tales. Other than fiction, however, my feet are firmly planted. Oh, I know that strange things do happen, but I also know there's generally a reason for them. Sometimes we can't figure out what the reason is, that's all.

And yet, having said all that—having decried ghoulies and ghosties and long-leggedy beasties—still you won't find Mrs. Lumley's child messing around with Ouija boards or tarot cards or fortune-telling, or any of that sort of thing…not in real life.

But on the other hand I have plenty of time for UFOs, and Fortean stuff has always fascinated me. I mean, if the universe is as big and as old as they say it is, and if Planet Earth is just one more little mudball among many, many *billions* of mudballs, surely it's entirely feasible that aliens have visited, and are maybe visiting us even now? We would have to be helluva big-headed to imagine—to *continue* to imagine, even without the Inquisition or The Thought Police threatening our imaginations—that we are the center of the universe, the be-all and end-all of intelligent life.

The fact is we just don't know what's out there. Scientists aren't able to tell us, only to predict. And in the main they seem to be predicting that we are not alone. (If they're not, then why are they sending messages to the stars and patiently waiting for the answers?). Myself, I hope that when the postman eventually comes the envelope will have SWALK written on it—and that it's not a "by hand" delivery, and that the parcel isn't ticking or making slobbering, hungry noises…

Very well, that's it on looking outwards. That's it on science and the as yet unfathomed mysteries of space and time. But what about looking inwards? For or course by definition the supernatural precludes science—except perhaps the science of psychology? Or the dubious science of parapsychology? And apart from the latter, what has any of this to do with Ouija boards and what have you, and my cautionary (or precautionary) avoidance of all such…?

———

It was 1974, and I don't remember it too well. Not because of all the time that's passed between…but just because. You'll see what I mean. And you'll perhaps learn from it. I did.

I was in the Army, just posted to Edinburgh Castle as the Company Quartermaster. So they sent me on a Q's course to Aldershot. In the barracks at Aldershot, I had a nine-by-six room (or cubicle, or broom closet) on the third floor at a corner of the building looking out on thin air. My room had a window half as wide as the room itself that opened outwards: good. For of a night, even a cold night, I like to breathe fresh air. The room also had a steel, six-foot locker for my uniform, kit, and personal valuables or other lockup-able stuff, and an indestructible steel-framed Army bed, a chair, and small table for my typewriter. Ceiling height was about eight feet. And that's it. Throw in my mattress and bedding, and that sets the scene.

The typewriter was for any homework during the course, and if I got any spare time I would work on a story Ramsey Campbell had requested for his upcoming anthology, *Superhorror*. In fact I didn't have much homework and so got on with my story. It was called *"The Viaduct"* —and it wasn't supernatural. I mention this in order to confirm that my thinking wasn't as yet under threat from ghoulies and ghosties. Not as yet.

So far so good. I *think* all of this is fact. I *believe* I'm telling it the way it was …

The course lasted two weeks, so right in the middle came a weekend. Time to do a little writing, studying, relaxing. There was this movie going the rounds, and I wanted to see it. It was showing in Aldershot. *The Exorcist*—my kind of picture, obviously.

Well of course it was a stunner. It didn't "frighten" me; I'm not the sort (the first and last time a film frightened me it was George Zucco in *The Flying Serpent*, when I was eight or nine years old. And I "got a kick" out of *Night of the Demon*: the twittering ball of lights in the trees, like something out of Lovecraft, and the nameless whistling in the shimmery corridor). So *The Exorcist* didn't scare *me*, but the three senior ranks I was with were a little bit twitchy, oh yes…

Back in the Mess we had a couple of drinks, and I told a handful of "true" spooky stories. (Hey, it's my business…I was testing out some stuff, that's all). Okay, so maybe *those* stories weren't true—but this one is.

Anyway, the point I make is that we had a *couple* of drinks. No one was drunk, and certainly not me. As a Military Policeman there are things you do and things you don't. If you are intent on getting drunk you do it in your own Mess, *not* while visiting someone else's. *Exemplo Ducemus*, and all that…

My colleagues and fellow students—mature students, you understand, for no one on the course was younger than thirty-or-so years old—were accommodated on the same floor as myself. About midnight we trooped upstairs, showered, sacked. And in my room I threw open the windows, lay on my back on my bed, looked out at the stars. They were very bright against a darkness that was very dark. I could hear one of my friends in the next room bumping about a bit, and more faintly the door next to his slamming as another friend went to bed.

Which was when the practical joker in me whispered: "Well, why not?"

So I let them get settled down for the night, then crept out into the corridor and stood between their doors, spread my arms and put my nails on the door panels…and *scraaaatched*!

Oh-so-slowly scraaaatached!—then paused and did it again, before fleeing back to my room, closing the door quietly behind me, slipping between my sheets and commencing to snore. A count of ten and they

5

were there. Door bursting open, light switched on, a pair of irate faces glaring into my blinking, astonished, oh-so-innocent eyes.

"Geordie bastard!" said one.

"Fucking redcap!" said the other.

"Eh? Wha—?" said I.

Maybe I convinced them of my innocence, maybe not. Anyway, they went back to bed, and I got up and *locked* my door. That's important— this is a "locked room story", yes. And I took the key out of the lock and put it on the table with my typewriter. At least I think I did, but everything is vague.

Then, in bed, I lay on my back and grinned, and looked out of the window at the night and the stars. The supernatural? *The Exorcist*? The Great Big Horrid Unknown? Me, I don't believe. In fact I was…what, contemptuous? Yes, I suppose I was. And I was very secure in my contempt, my disbelief.

So looking out at the night I said to myself *and to anyone else who might be listening*, "Hey, You! You out there—if you are out there—why don't you come on in and try it on me? What are you, a stray thought? A wisp of smoke? A beam of moonlight? A niggle in the night? A shiver that fell off someone's back and lost its way? A ghostie, ghoulie, or nasty smelly demon? Oh, dear me! I'm really scared! Well, I'm just flesh and blood. But I'm big and I'm solid while you're just so much wind. So by all means go and rustle some leaves or moan in the eaves, but whatever you do don't fuck with me!"

I said something like that to myself, anyway. And despite that I said it silently, I said it very firmly, very "loudly". Do you know what I mean? Like a challenge.

And then I fell asleep…

…And dreamed. But the only thing that I remember about the dream is one *very* frightening scene.

Something came. Something big. Awesome strength. It stank. It burned. It crouched on the sill of my open window. It's outline blocked out the stars. Big and black, it came in. And it looked at me, cocked its head on one side, and said, "*Unbeliever*?" Or if it didn't actually say it, it wondered. And I sort of heard it wondering.

Which is why I said, "Please, don't…"

And I *think* it smiled.

•

———————

Next morning…it was like waking up into a different world. Thank God it was the weekend. I had forgotten about the dream (now you just *think* about that); or rather, I wasn't bothered? (Think about that, too). But God, the state of my room…!

As I have said, a room like that is tiny as a nest, with space for just one bird at a time. That's why you keep it neat and tidy. Get something out of place, there's no room left for you. And that morning…*many* things were out of place.

The bed was sideways. The steel locker was standing on its head (you can picture what my kit was like inside it). All my sheets and blankets were knotted together in a big ball. A pillow had been shredded and feathers were everywhere, and there were fist-sized lumps of gum, or black jelly, or shit?—but never *human* shit—all over the place. Only the small table was where it should be, but it wasn't *how* it should be. Because someone had pissed on my typewriter. Drenched it. Well, God help his insides, whoever he was, because his piss had dried like so much glue. Later, I got it off with alcohol (and you're probably thinking I'd got it *on* with alcohol, too, and I don't blame you), and disguised the nasty smell with many a liberal splash of Old Spice.

———————

Then I did nothing. Well, I *did*; I cleaned the mess up. Tossed the large gumballs out of the window, untied the incredibly *intricate* knots in my bedding, emptied my locker—it really was *that* heavy—so that I could turn it the right way up. Oh, and I put my bed back the right way, too, because now it was *across* the room: a six-foot bed fitting snug in a space that only just accommodated it. And I had been *on* that bed; I had woken up on that mattress, with no sheet on me and no sheet under me!

7

And all of this had been done in absolute silence, in darkness, while I slept. And the door still locked, and the sticky key to my room still on the sticky table beside my sticky typewriter. But apart from cleaning everything up I did nothing at all, said nothing to anyone…

And that, my friends, is the frightening bit. I didn't give any of this a thought—not a single *thought*—except to put it right and so return to my own mundane universe, the world with which I was familiar. I didn't accuse anyone, probably because I suspected that no one had done it, or that I'd done it to myself. Oh really? I had made water on my beloved typewriter…?

———————

Four days went by and it was the middle of the week. My work hadn't suffered; I was going to get an "A" on this course, no problem. Then one morning I woke up and noticed that my window was closed — noticed it for the first time since the incident: the fact that I now kept the window closed. And I smelled the stale air…and I suddenly remembered. I remembered *something* of all this, anyway, but can't honestly say if it was the same story I've just told. For I've never been able to fix it in my mind.

It's as if I wasn't *supposed* to think about, talk about, or worry about it. As if I wasn't supposed to blow my top immediately this thing happened, but that the message should be allowed to get through to me in its own sweet time. As if someone had said to me: "Hey, take this as a warning. You did something wrong. You *invited* a confrontation. So don't do it again, okay?"

That day at lunchtime, I walked the lawns around the outside of the accommodation block. I couldn't find any snotballs. It had rained and they'd melted or been washed away. Or they'd never been there. I could never get my typewriter to work right from that time on, and I soon scrapped it. Ramsey Campbell used my *un*supernatural story, *"The Viaduct,"* in *Superhorror.*

And six or seven years later I wrote another story, *"The Unbeliever,"* which gives a fictional and far more horrific account of the "facts" of the thing. By which I mean *"The Unbeliever"* is a fictional development of this *true* story …

———————

Of course there's an explanation, perhaps more than one. Maybe my mind was more susceptible to suggestion than I used to think it was. Maybe it was the booze. (What booze? Two or three shots of brandy, when I might easily have sunk half a bottle?). Or maybe it was *The Exorcist*? What, without George Zucco or the Twitterer in the Trees? Or someone(s) had got into my room…wreaking all that havoc and leaving alien crap behind without waking me? Let me tell you that I've always slept light. All it takes is a creaking floorboard and I wake up.

And over the years, more than twenty of them, it has faded away until I can't any longer be sure of anything. But like the grin on the face of the Cheshire cat in *Alice*, a certain smile remains where almost everything else has vanished. That darkest of dark smiles that something smiled at me on the night I said, "Please, don't…"

Oh, I still meet things head on; an ex-soldier, I'm still into confrontation, certainly on a mundane level. But then I'm a Geordie after all, and a Sagittarian to boot…not that I *believe* in any of that stuff. And yet you won't catch me denying it, either. Not any longer. Or if I do, it'll be because I think I've found an explanation for it. A scientific reason.

But until then I won't be messing with Ouija boards, tarot cards, fortune-telling or anything of that nature. And you can believe me when I tell you I don't even feel tempted to experiment. Not me. I won't be putting out challenges to anything I don't understand. No sir. You've got to be kidding.

I'll tell you something: I've even had to find a way, when I'm lying in my bed at night just about to go to sleep, to put it right out of my mind. So that I don't do anything inadvertently, as it were. It's not a pleasant thought, but I'm fairly sure I *could* do it again—in error, of course. That I *could* say the wrong things to the wrong Thing.

And I feel sure, too, that whoever he is, he'd be listening…

The Man Who Photographed Beardsley

They should have been pictures from life—or was he simply impatient?

Gentlemen, my very own darling boys in blue. If as you seem so determined to avow, there has been about my work an element of the grotesque and macabre ('criminal' I simply *refuse* to admit) and if, in order to achieve the perfection of ultimate realism, I have indeed allowed myself to become a "fanatic" and my art an "obsession"…Why! Is it any wonder? I find in these things, in your assertions, nothing to excite any amazement or stupefaction. Nothing, that is, other than the natural astonishment and fascination of my subject matter.

And yet, in his own day, Beardsley's work excited just such—yes, horror! "His own day!" An inadequate cliche, that, for of course he had no "day"; his work is as fresh and inspiring now—and possibly more so, as witness the constant contemporary cannibalization of his style and plagiarism of his techniques—as when first he put ink to paper. His art exists in a time-defying limbo of virtuosity that will parallel, I am sure, the very deathlessness of Tut-ank-hamen as glimpsed in the gold of his funerary mask.

Times change, my dears! Does Aubrey Vincent Beardsley's art excite any such powerfully outraged emotions now? Except in the most naive circles, it does *not!* Admiration, yes—delight and fascination, of course—but disgust, revulsion…horror? No. Nor, I put it to you, will *my* art fifty years hence. No, certainly not in the finished, perfect article; neither in that nor in the contemplation of its controversial construction. I would think it likely that there will be controversy; but in the end, though my name be vilified initially, I will be exonerated *through my art itself!* Yes, in the end my art must win.

I digress? My words are irrelevant? My apologies, my dears, it is the genius in me. Genius, like truth, will out.

I started, in what now seems a mundane manner, void of any airy aspiration or ambition other than that of exercising my art to the best of my ability, by selling pornographic photographs to the men's magazines. Now: I say "pornographic", and yet even the most permissive of my pictures—so erotic as to shock even, well, Beardsley himself—were executed with a finesse such as to abnegate any prohibitive reactions from my publishers, and they were undeniably the delight of my public.

Came the time when I could afford to be more choosey in my work, when I commanded the attentions of all the first-line publishers in the field, and then I would accept only the choicest contracts. Eventually I was sufficiently established to quit working to order completely, and then I was able to give more time and energy to my own projects. To my delight, my new photographic experiments went down well, better in fact than even the best of my previous works. Pornography became a thing of the past as I grew ever the more fascinated with the exotic, the weird, the outré.

Following the Beardsley Project I had plans for Hieronymus Bosch, but—

Pardon? I must try not to wander? The Beardsley Project?… Once more I apologize. Well, gentlemen, it came about like this:

I had long been disillusioned with color. Colors annoyed me. Without motion they somehow looked untrue, and they certainly did nothing to enhance the sombre quality of my more sepulchral pieces. Oh, the greens and purples were all right, when I could get just the right lighting effects—Rhine Castles and Infernal Caverns and so on—

but as for the rest of the spectrum I couldn't give a damn! And yet Beardsley had ignored color without sacrificing an iota of feeling, in perfect perspective, with the result that his black-and-whites are the wonders of intricate design that they are. But if I was to take a lead from Beardsley in tone, why not in texture? Why not in my actual material?

It was then that I began to photograph Beardsley.

At first there was no pattern in my mind, no plot as to the development of my theme; I simply photographed him the way I found him. My *Venus Between Terminal Gods* became an instant success, as was *The Billet-Doux*. Indeed in the latter picture I actually beat A.V. at his own game! The absolute intricacy of my work was a wonder to behold. The delicate frills and ribbons of her negligee, the art nouveau of the headboard, the perfect youthful beauty of the girl herself…

Ah, but *The Barge* was my piece de resistance. Oh, I was already well on the road toward that type of success I craved, but *The Barge* made me. It took me six days to set the thing up, to get the studio balcony absolutely *right*, to have the costumes perfected and find the perfectly skeletal gent (profile) to match the young woman (the girl from *The Billet-Doux*) with the great fan. And the *wigs*, my dears, you'd never believe the trouble I—

But there… I mustn't go on, must I?

That was when Nigel Naith of *Fancy* asked me for a series. A complete series, prepaid and entirely in my own time, and I literally had carte blanche. The one stipulation Nigel did make—and it made me really *furious*—was that there should be color. *Well!*…

I determined to do the entire series on Beardsley the Weird, commencing with *Alberich!* The trouble I had finding just the right shape of ugly, shrunken dwarf! I went on to *Don Juan, Sagnarelle, and the Beggar*—and it must be immediately apparent that my difficulty in obtaining a decent beggar was enormous. In the end, to obtain a skull of such loathly proportions and contours, I turned to a local mental institution with the tale that I was preparing a photographic documentary of the unfortunate inmates of such refuges.

Fortunately the custodians of the place did not know my work; eventually I was allowed to borrow one Stanley, who was allegedly quite servile, for my purpose. And he was absolutely ideal—except that he didn't like having to dress in rags. I had to beat him, and it was necessary to dub the two normal models in for they simply refused to pose with him; and moreover he *bit* me, but in the end I had my picture.

Pardon? Well I *know* I'm taking my time, sweetheart, but it's my story, isn't it?

Yes…Well, the first real difficulty came when I was working on the last picture of the set. Yes, *that* picture, *The Dancer's Reward.* Now the costumery and props were fairly easy—even that wafer-thin, paint-pallet tabletop, with its single supporting hairy leg—but I knew that the central piece, the head, was going to give me problems. Ah, that head!

And so I looked around for a model. He or she—I'm not fussy, my darlings—would have to have long black hair, that much was obvious. And I would like, too, someone of a naturally pale complexion…. Naturally.

Eventually I found him, a young dropout from up north; long black hair, pale complexion, rather gaunt; he was the one, yes. And he was short of money, which of course was important. I managed to get hold of him on his first day in town, before he made any friends, which was also important. That first night he stayed at my place, but it worked out he wasn't my type, which was just as well in the circumstances. I mean, well, I couldn't afford to get emotional about him, now could I?

The next morning, bright and early, we were up and about. I took him straight downstairs to the studio, unlocked the door, and let him in. Then I lit the joss sticks, sat him down in a studio chair, and went out to get the morning milk from the doorstep. That was so I could make us both a cup of coffee right there in the studio. Coffee steadies my nerves, you know?…

When I got back in he was complaining about the smell. Well, of course, that put me on my guard. I told him I liked the studio to smell sweet, you know, and pointed out all the air fresheners I had about the

13

place and the sprays I used. And I explained away the joss sticks by telling him that the smell of incense gave the place the right sort of atmosphere. He had me a bit worried, though, when he asked me what I kept in the back room. I mean, I just couldn't *tell* him, now could I?

Anyway, I set up a three-minute timed exposure on my studio camera and then kept one eye on my watch. While I was waiting I took a few dummy shots of the lad against various backdrops; getting him in the mood, you know? Then I had him lean over the workbench with his arms wide apart, staring straight ahead. He was getting fifteen a shot—he thought—and so he was willing to oblige; you might even say overjoyed. I took a few more dummy shots from the front, then moved round to the side.

So there we were: me clicking away with my little camera, and no film in it and all, and him all stretched out over the workbench staring ahead.

"That's it!" I kept saying, and "Just look in front there," and "Money for old rope!" Stuff like that. And click, click, click with the empty camera. And I moved behind him and got the cleaver from behind the curtains, and his eyes had just started to swivel round when—

I got him first time, and clean as a whistle, which was just as well for I didn't want to mess the neck up. Believe me, it was quick. You've seen the groove in the bench? And still a full minute to go.

On with my wig, with all its tight little ringlets; and the costume, all pinned up just so. Then over to the table with its hairy leg and ornate band. The blood slopping; the head tilted back just so; my left hand held thus and my right holding his forelocks; the slippers in exactly the right position. And, my dears, his mouth fell open *of its own accord!*

Beautiful!…

And that was when I realized that in my excitement I had made a dreadful mistake. Such a silly little thing really: when I brought in the milk I forgot to lock the outside door. The studio door, too, for I'd been distracted by the lad's complaints about the smell. And that, of course, was all it took to undo me.

14

The Man Who Photographed Beardsley

It was the new postman: a nosey parker, just like the old one. In through the studio door he came, waving a pink envelope that could only contain a letter from Nigel Naith; and when he *saw* what lay across the workbench!—*And* what I had in my hand—

Well, I couldn't let him get away, now could I, my dears? No, of course not.

But he did get away—he did! Oh, I managed to grab the cleaver all right, before he'd even moved. I mean he was still standing there all gasping and white, you know? But damn me if that costume of mine didn't let me down! Halfway across the room I tripped on the thing and went over like a felled oak; at which the postman seemed to come to life again, let out one *terrific* scream, ran for it.

And so there was nothing left for me to do but read Nigel's letter while I waited for you dears to come. Poor Nigel: when was I going to send him the goodies, he wanted to know? Ah, but there'll be no more of my work in *Fancy*, I fear.

What's that, my love? The back room? Yes, yes, of course you're right. The joss sticks? Yes, of *course*, my dear. And the—thing—on the bed? Ah, but now, I really must protest. That was a *model* of mine! "Thing," indeed!

Yes, yes, a model, something else I was working on. The theme? Why, *Edgar Allan Poe's Illustrators*, my darling. Harry Clarke was the artist, and—

You do? Why you clever boy! Yes, of course it was *Valdemar*, and—

Who was he? Why, the old postman, who else! The first one, yes. Of course he still had another week or so to go to reach a proper state of—

You've got all you wanted? Well, anything to help the law, I always say. But isn't it a shame about Nigel—I mean about him paying me in advance and all?

Tell me: is the *Police Gazette* a glossy?

15

The Cyprus Shell

There are some you can eat, while others have their own pick-me-ups.

The Oaks, Innsway
Redcar, Yorks
5 June 1962

Col. (Retd) George L. Glee MBE, DSO
11 Tunstall Court
West H. Pool, Co. Durham

My Dear George,

I must extend to you my sincerest apologies for the inexcusable way I took myself and Alice out of your excellent company on Saturday evening last. Alice had remarked upon my facial *expressions*, my absolute lack of manners and the uncouth way in which, it must have appeared, I dragged her from your marvellous table; and all, alas, under the gaze of so many of our former military associates. I can only hope that our long friendship—and the fact that you know me as well as you do—has given you some insight that it was only a matter of extreme urgency which could have driven me from your house in such an extraordinary manner.

I imagine all of you were astonished at my exit. Alice was flabbergasted and would not speak to me until I gave her a solid reason for what she took to be lunatic behaviour.

Well, to cut things short, I told her the tale which I am about to tell you. She was satisfied as to the validity of the reasons for my seemingly unreasonable actions and I am sure that you will feel the same.

The Cyprus Shell

It was the oysters, of course. I have no doubt that their preparation was immaculate and that they were delicious—for everyone, that is, except myself. The truth is I *cannot* abide seafood, especially shellfish. Surely you remember the way I used to be over crabs and lobsters? That time in Goole when I ate two whole plates of fresh mussels all to myself? I loved the things. Ugh! The thought of it…

Two years ago in Cyprus something happened which put an end to my appetite for that sort of thing. But before I go on let me ask you to do something. Get out your Bible and look up Leviticus 11:10, 11. No, I have not become a religious maniac. It's just that since that occurrence two years ago I have taken a deep interest, a morbid interest I hasten to add, in this subject and all connected with it.

If, after reading my story, you should find your curiosity tickled, there are numerous books on the subject which you might like to look up—though I doubt whether you'll find many of them at your local library. Anyway, here is a list of four such books: Gantley's *Hydrophinnae*, Gaston Le Fe's *Dwellers in the Depths*, the German *Unter-See Kulten* and the monstrous *Cthaat Aquadingen* by an unknown author. All contain tidbits of an almost equally nauseating nature to the tale which I must relate in order to excuse myself.

I have said it was in Cyprus. At the time I was the officer in command of a small unit in Kyrea, between Cephos and Kryenia on the coast, overlooking the Mediterranean, that most beautiful of all oceans. In my Company was a young corporal, Jobling by name, who fancied himself something of a conchologist and spent all his off-duty hours with flippers and mask snorkelling off the rocks to the south of Kyrea. I say he fancied himself, yet in fact his collection *was* quite wonderful for he had served in most parts of the world and had looted many oceans.

Beneath glass in his billet—in beautifully made 'natural' settings, all produced by his own hands—he had such varied and fascinating shells as the African *Pecten irradian*, the unicorn-horn *Murex monodon* and *Ianthina violacea* from Australia, the weird *Melongena corona* from the Gulf of Mexico, the fan-shaped *Ranella perca* of Japan and many hundreds of others too numerous to mention here. Inevitably my weekly tour of inspection ended in Jobling's billet where I would move among his showcases marvelling at the intricacies of Nature's art.

While Jobling's hobby occupied all his off-duty hours it in no way interfered with his work within the unit; he was a conscientious, hard-working NCO. I first noticed the *change* in him when his work began to fall off and had had it in mind for over a week to reprimand him for his slackness when he had the first of those attacks which eventually culminated so horribly.

He was found one morning, after first parade, curled on his bed in the most curious manner, with his legs drawn up and arms curled about him—almost in a foetal position. The MO was called but, despite treatment, Jobling remained in this inexplicable condition for over an hour; at the end of which time he suddenly 'came to' and began acting quite normally, seemingly unable to remember anything that had happened. I was obliged to relieve the man of all duties for a period of one week and he was obviously amazed at this, swearing he was fit as a fiddle and blaming his lapse on an overdose of Cyprus sun. I checked this with the MO who assured me that Jobling's condition had in no way corresponded to a stroke but had been, in fact, closely related to a trauma, as though the result of some deep, psychological shock...

The day after he returned to duties Jobling suffered the second of his withdrawals.

This second attack took exactly the same form as the first except that it lasted somewhat longer. Also, on this occasion, he was found to be clutching in his hand a book of notes relating to his shell collection. I asked to see these notes and while Jobling, still dazed, was taken off to the hospital for an examination, I read them through in the hope of finding something which might give me some insight into the reason for his strange affliction. I had a hunch that his hobby had much to do with his condition; though just why collecting and studying shells should have such a drastic effect on anyone was beyond even guessing.

The first two dozen pages or so were filled with observations on locations where certain species of sea-snail could be found. For instance; *"Pecten irradian* — small — in rock-basins ten to fifteen feet deep. Etc., etc...." This section was followed by a dozen pages or so of small drawings, immaculately done, and descriptions of rarer specimens. Two more pages were devoted to a map of the Kyrea coastline with shaded areas showing the locations which the collector had already explored and arrowed sections showing places still to be visited. Then, on the next page, I found a beautifully executed drawing of a shell the like of which I had never seen before despite my frequent studies of Jobling's showcases, and which I have seen only once since.

How to describe it? Beneath it was a scale, in inches, drawn in to show its size. It appeared to be about six inches long and its basic shape was a slender spiral: but all the way round that spiral, along the complete track from mouth to tail, were sharp spikes about two inches long at their longest and about one inch at the narrow end. They were obviously a means of defense against oceanic predators. The mouth of the thing, as Jobling had coloured the drawing, showed a shiny black operculum with a row of tiny eyes at the edges, like those of the scallop, and was a bright shade of pink. The main body of the shell and the spikes were sand-coloured. If my powers of description were better I might be able to convey something of just how repulsive the thing looked. Instead it must suffice to say that it was not a shell which I would be happy to pick up off a beach, and not just because of those spikes! There was something nastily fascinating about the *shape* and the *eyes* of the thing which, taking into consideration the accuracy of the other drawings, was not merely a quirk of the artist...

The next page was a set of notes which, as best as I can remember, went like this:

Murex hypnotica?
Rare? Unknown???

2nd August...Found shell, with snail intact, off point of rocks (marked on sketch of map) in about twenty feet of water. The shell was on sand in natural rock-basin. Pretty sure thing is very rare, probably new species.

Snail has eyes on edge of mantle. Did not take shell. Anchored it to rock with nylon line from spear gun. Want to study creature in natural surroundings before taking it.

3rd August…Shell still anchored. Saw most peculiar thing. Small fish, inch long, swam up to shell, probably attracted by bright pink of mouth. Eyes of snail waved rhythmically for a few seconds. Operculum opened. Fish swam into shell and operculum snapped shut. Have named shell well! First funny fascination I felt when I found shell is obviously felt to greater extent by fish. Thing seems to use hypnosis on fish in same way octopus uses it to trap crabs.

4th August…Cannot visit shell today—duty. Had funny dream last night. I was in a shell on bottom of sea. Saw myself swimming down. Hated the swimmer and saw him as being to blame for restricting my movements. I was the snail! When the swimmer, myself, was gone I sawed at nylon line with my operculum but could not break it. Woke up. Unpleasant.

5th August…Duty.

6th August…Visited shell again. Line near shell slightly frayed. Eyes waved at me. Felt dizzy. Stayed down too long. Came back to camp. Dizzy all day.

7th August…Dreamed of being snail again. Hated swimmer, myself, and tried to get into his mind—like I do with fish. Woke up. Awful.

There was a large gap in the dates here and, looking back I realized that this was the period which Jobling had spent in hospital. In fact he had gone into hospital the day after that last entry had been made, on the eighth of the month. The next entry went something like this:

15th August…Did not expect shell to be there after all this time but it was. Line much frayed but not broken.

Went down five or six times but started to get horribly
dizzy. Snail writhed its eyes at me frantically! Felt that
awful dream coming on in water! Had to get out of sea.
Believe the damn thing tried to hypnotize me like it does
with fish.

16th August…Horrible dream. Have just woken up
and must write it down now. I was the snail again! I've
had enough. Will collect shell today. This dizzy
feeling…

That was all. The last entry had obviously been made that very day,
just before Jobling's new attack. I had just finished reading the notes
and was sitting there bewildered when my telephone rang. It was the
MO. All hell was on at the hospital. Jobling had tried to break loose,
tried to get out of the hospital. I took my car straight round there and
that was where the horror really started.

I was met by an orderly at the main entrance and escorted up to one
of the wards. The MO and three male nurses were in a wardroom
waiting for me.

Jobling was curled up on a bed in that weird foetal position—*or was
it a foetal position*? What did he remind me of? Suddenly I noticed
something which broke my train of thought, causing me to gasp and
look closer. Froth was drying on the man's mouth, his teeth were bared
and his eyes bulged horribly. But there was no movement in him at all!
He was stone dead!

"How on earth…?" I gasped. "What happened?" The MO gripped
my arm. His eyes were wide and unbelieving. For the first time I
noticed that one of the male nurses appeared to be in a state of shock.
In a dry, cracked voice the MO started to speak.

"It was horrible. I've never know anything like it. He just seemed
to go wild. Began frothing at the mouth and tried to get out of the place.
He made it down to the main doors before we caught up to him. We
had to *carry* him up the stairs and he kept straining towards the
windows in the direction of the sea. When we got him back up here he
suddenly coiled up—just like that!" He pointed to the still figure on the

21

bed. 'And then he squirmed—that's the only way I can describe how he moved—he *squirmed* off the bed and quick as a flash he was in the steel locker there and had pulled the door shut behind him. God only knows why he went in there?' In one corner of the room stood the locker. One of its two doors was hanging by a wrenched hinge—torn almost completely off. "When we tried to get him out he fought like hell. But not like a *man* would fight! He *butted* with his head, with a funny *sawing* motion, and bit and spat—and all the time he stayed in that awful position, even when he was fighting. By the time we got him to the bed again he was dead. I...I think he died of fright."

By now that hideous train of thought, broken before by the horror of Jobling's condition, had started up once more in my mind and I began to trace an impossible chain of events. But no! It was too monstrous to even think of—too *fantastic*...And then, on top of my terrible thoughts, came those words from the mouth of one of the nurses which caused me to pitch over suddenly into the darkness of a swoon.

I know you will find it difficult to believe, George, when I tell you what those words were. It seems ridiculous that such a simple statement could have so deep an effect upon anyone. None the less I *did* faint, for I saw the sudden connection, the piece in the puzzle which brought the whole picture into clear, horrific perspective...The nurse said: "Getting him out of the locker was the worst, sir. *It was like trying to get a winkle out of its shell without a pin...*"

———————————

When I came to, despite the MO's warning, I went to the mess—I had not met Alice at that time and so was 'living in'—and got my own swimming kit out of my room. I took Jobling's notebook with me and drove to the point of rock marked in red on his map. It was not difficult to find the place; Jobling would have made an excellent cartographer.

I parked my car and donned my mask and flippers. In no time at all I was swimming straight out in the shallows over a few jagged outcrops of rock and patches of sand. I stopped in about ten feet of water for a few seconds to watch a heap, literally a *heap*, of crabs fighting over a dead fish. The carcass was completely covered by the vicious things—it's amazing how they are attracted by carrion—but occasionally, as the fight raged, I caught a glimpse of silver scales and red, torn flesh. But I was not there to study the feeding habits of crabs. I pressed on.

I found the rock-basin almost immediately and the shell was not difficult to locate. It was lying about twenty feet deep. I could see that the nylon line was still attached. But for some reason the water down there was not as clear as it should have been. I felt a sudden, icy foreboding—a nameless premonition. Still, I had come out to look at that shell, to prove to myself that what I had conjured up in my over-imaginative mind was pure fancy and nothing more.

I turned on end, pointing my feet at the blue sky and my head towards the bottom, and slid soundlessly beneath the surface. I spiralled down to the shell, noting that it was exactly as Jobling had drawn it, and carefully, shudderingly, took it by one of those spikes and turned it over so I could see the pink mouth.

The shell was *empty*!

But this, if my crazy theory was correct, was just what I should have expected; none the less I jerked away from the thing as though it had suddenly become a conger eel. Then out of the corner of my eye, I saw the *reason* for the murkiness of the water. A second heap of crabs was sending up small clouds of sand and sepia from some dead fish or mollusc which they were tearing at in that dreadful, frantic lust of theirs.

Sepia! In abrupt horror I recoiled from my own thoughts. Great God in heaven! *Sepia*!

I wrenched off a flipper and batted the horrid, scrabbling things away from their prey—*and wished immediately that I had not done so.* For sepia is the blood, or juice, of cuttlefish *and certain species of mollusc and sea-snail.*

The thing was still alive. Its mantle waved feebly and those eyes which remained saw me. Even as the ultimate horror occurred I remember I suddenly knew for certain that my guess had been correct.

For the thing was not *coiled* like a sea-snail should be—*and what sea-snail would ever leave its shell?*

I have said it saw me! George, I swear on the Holy Bible that the creature *recognized* me and, as the crabs surged forward again to the unholy feast, it tried to *walk* towards me.

Snails should not walk, George, and men should not squirm.

Hypnotism is a funny thing. We barely understand the *human* form of the force let alone the strange strains used by lesser life-forms.

What more can I say? Let me just repeat that I hope you can accept my apologies for my behaviour the other night. It was the oysters, of course. Not that I have any doubt that their preparation was immaculate or that they were delicious—to any *untainted* palate, that is. But I? Why! I could no more eat an oyster than I could a corporal.

Sincerely,
Maj. Harry Winslow

Clean Slate

If you're in debt to the Devil, don't mess with look-a-like sisters.

He snapped back into consciousness not knowing his name, how he came to be here, or anything of his previous life. There wasn't even a darkness prior to this, or if there was he wasn't aware of it. It was something like being born again, but without all the struggling and pain. And of course he was full grown. However, there was a stink, much like cordite but slowly fading, and the instinctive knowledge that he was different.

But...even the not-quite-cordite smell could be his imagination: his senses rebelling against the sudden presence of auto-reek, steamy basement exhalations and subterranean maintenance systems piping their grey-steaming exhaust fumes out into the darkening city streets. But it wouldn't get night-dark for a while yet; a few shops were still open, even a bank. In the windows of the latter, silhouetted by the street lighting, he examined himself. Perhaps in so doing he hoped to gain some clue as to his identity. Whatever, this is what he saw in the night-reflective plate glass:

A young man maybe twenty-eight or -nine years old, or maybe a thousand, for he had that kind of face, certainly: those all-knowing nothing eyes, pale, hollow cheeks, dark hair slicked back from a high forehead, and lips as red as if they were rouged. He was tall and slim in a dark, unfashionable suit, and those strange, young-ancient eyes of his were very worried where they stared back at him. Other things about him:

There was a small pain in his left thumb where a tear of blood welled from a fresh, V-shaped puncture, and his heart was beating very quickly to match his respiration. He felt like he'd been running, but at the same time he was sure he hadn't. And something which was very obvious: he was one hell of a cool customer. He had to be, else the shock of all this must surely have unnerved him.

He went through his pockets: an unrewarding task for there was nothing in them. But when he ran his long, slender fingers through his hair, brushing it back over his delicately shaped ears, his hand touched and *clinked* against a ring of gold in the lobe of his left ear. And he observed on the central digit of his left hand a second, heavier golden ring which, still frowning, he stared at for long moments. For without knowing how he knew, still he was aware of the meaning of the finger ring; (patently this knowledge was also instinctive). The ring was the sigil of his darkling nature: its crimson gemstone was shaped like a tiny bat in flight, and if he removed the band from his finger he knew he would find an inscription—or rune-script—graven widdershins around the inner circle.

An through ears of memories he didn't even know he had: "*Never utter that spell out loud,*" a voice hissed, causing him to start, it sounded so close, real and immediate. But of course there was no one there, only the effortlessly conjured, now fading memory of a voice; "*If circumstances are dire—the very direst—then and only then use it. And good luck to you, for* HE *lusts after us before all others…*"

The young man—a stranger even to himself—looked again at his finger: at the tiny V-shaped wound, a fresh drop of blood forming there even now.

Blood?

And…he was hungry…

He was hungry for…blood?

Yes…yes he was! (He trembled with a strange yet strangely familiar excitement.) Hungry for someone else's blood! Human blood! And now he knew *what* he was if not who. And knowing what he was, he also knew what he must do.

Clean Slate

This place was...America! It had to be. He recognized it from...from what? Books he supposed. From television? Newspapers? So strange that he should know about such things without remembering the least thing about himself. Or rather, without remembering anything of his past. In any case, this wasn't his country — but that wasn't important either. Blood is blood regardless of colour, race or creed. Some things are ever constant. Like night and darkness. And sunlight! Night was drawing in, true, but after night would come morning; the sun shines even in the city, and its rays must not be allowed to find him up and about. He needed a place, any safe place — a shelter however temporary — for tonight at least.

The bank was almost empty now. Slipping the ring from the lobe of his ear, he entered and approached a weary, yawning teller behind her counter and reinforced glass screen. She smiled at him and he showed her the ring. "Gold," he said, softly. "It is quite heavy. You have scales? I would trade this ring for money."

The smile passed from her face, was replaced in turn by a puzzled look, then a frown. "I'm sorry, sir," she said, not cold but merely efficient, "but we don't trade money for gold. Do you have an account with us?"

He shook his head. "No, no account." And he insisted: "In Germany, Hungary — *Bucuresti* — I could get money for my gold."

"Here, too," she answered, her voice turning cool now, "Almost anywhere, but not in a bank. I'm sure there are plenty of dealers in precious metals in the directory. But now I'm afraid I really..."

"...Afraid?" he repeated her word, cutting her off. "*Not* to be afraid!" And he held her with his eyes.

"But I...I...eyes!" She couldn't look away from his burning gaze.

There was something about this girl. It was her skin, her blue eyes, golden hair. It was her beauty, her purity. Oh, she was not innocent — she had known a man, possibly men; she had lived something of her life, at least — but she *was* pure. In heart, in thought, in being. Her blood was pure. She was the one, and he knew he had to have her. Tonight!

It was strange…she *reminded* him of someone else in time gone by, *long* gone from him now. But how could that be when he could not remember anything else that had gone before? Perhaps it was simply that she was of the type he could never resist. It was strange…

But…he glanced quickly over one shoulder, then scanned casually left and right. No one was close, no one looking.

"Your money, yours," he said, his voice dark as bloodied earth, pulling on her mind like a magnet. "Some of your money, for my ring. What is its value?"

"I…I don't know," she whispered, unable to look away, seeing only his eyes. "Eighty dollars, a hundred…"

"Give me eighty," he instructed; but as she reached for her purse he changed his mind. "No, not your money—the bank's. I don't want your money. I want…you!" His smile was a fearsome thing. 'You are free—tonight?'

She passed him three twenties and two tens, automatically taking the bills from her till. "No, I have a date."

"Yes—with me!" Affronted by her attempted refusal, his monstrous smile became a scowl and his upper lip momentarily drew back from eye-teeth like small curved daggers. Then: "Your address!" he snapped. "Quickly, tell me your address!"

She couldn't refuse but simply gave him directions to her apartment.

"Now forget me," he commanded, "until tonight. As for this…date, which you say you have: you will not go out. You will wait at home for me. Now say it!"

"I will not go out but wait at home for you."

"Good! Until tonight…"

She blinked…blinked again and he was gone. And in her hand a ring of gold. She looked at the ring and frowned, then slowly shook her head. But eventually, wonderingly, worriedly, she put the gold band in her purse.

Then it was closing time and her supervisor came to close down her till, and shortly after that she was walking home through the darkened streets. And hurrying through those evening streets, she shivered without knowing why...

Normally, at home, she would eat. She would buy food on the way home, prepare it, eat and watch the news on television. Tonight it would have been the merest snack, for she had a date. But she had not bought food and she did not eat. There were simple things in the apartment which she could eat if she wanted to, but she didn't' want to. She *wanted* to go out on her date, but could not. She wasn't sure why, but she couldn't go. And when she looked at herself in the mirror, they were not her eyes but someone else's which gazed hypnotically back at her.

She gasped and clutched at her throat when she saw those alien eyes, for though she couldn't be sure, suddenly she suspected that the horror was about to happen again!

Galvanized, she phoned the number she'd been given: it rang and a gravelly, disinterested voice said, 'Inspector Grodescu?'

"This is...is...Helen Gardner," she managed to gasp the words out—just as her doorbell rang! And at that she dropped the 'phone, which struck the cradle and broke the connection. But not before she'd heard the Inspector's answering gasp.

And leaving the 'phone dangling there, turning on its flex and buzzing, she walked like a zombie to the door...'

For Grodescu it was becoming something of a vendetta. He'd investigated the Anna Gardner case and that of Paula Gardner, and now it was the turn of one of their younger sisters.

With Anna it had been close: a neighbour had reported a prowler. Grodescu had been in the vicinity; he'd chased his quarry into one of the city's parks, cordoned the place off while his men searched the wooded area from one end to the other. They had a couple of dogs on the job, too, who had complained bitterly, nervously about the whole deal...like there was a tiger in there or something!

Grodescu had been *sure* they'd find the guy, had *known* someone was in there, hiding. But no …nothing. Just the hot reek of something which had been there but now was gone. And later poor Anna's body had been found in her apartment. It wasn't a vampire, of course not, just someone who *thought* he was a vampire. But what odds?—the result was the same.

Grodescu was from homicide. He'd attended the funeral because crazy killers like this sometimes show up to pay their last respects. No luck in that direction, but at least he'd got better acquainted with Anna's identical sister, Paula, and with their two-years-younger sisters, (also identical twins, it ran in the family,) Helen and Marie. And just a few days later he'd met Paula again…in her flat…also dead. And again the air had held a suspicion of that same hot stink, gradually fading…

It had been almost a replay of the first time: the guy across the corridor from Paula—who had fancied her himself, in his time, and so kept something of an eye on her—had reported a stranger lurking outside her door. Perhaps he'd hoped to queer some unknown rival's pitch. A prowl car had been in the vicinity; its crew, together with two men from the local Crime Watch Committee, had broken in the door…and discovered Paula's body. At which they'd called for Grodescu.

A day or two later and the lab reports had come in; he'd matched up the two crimes. The same man, definitely—if it was a man. Certainly it was something with human semen, anyway—and copious amounts of it, at that! But there were other things in those reports, things which caused Grodescu to revise his initial notion. Sharp teeth had made the punctures; very little blood remained in the bodies; no blood had been spilled.

And then the Inspector had remembered again certain boyhood stories from the Old Country, and certain ways they still had in remote parts of that Old Country. Oh, it was true that his parents had sent him to America when he was a child in order that he'd grow up in a land free from such dark fears and superstitions (also in a land which was itself free) but…

Clean Slate

Twin-sister victims seemed just too much of a coincidence; and what about the younger twins, Helen and Marie? The newshawks hadn't been informed about those two; it would be asking for trouble to tell a lunatic world—and a certain monster in that crazy world—that there were third and fourth innocents ripe for the taking. But privately Grodescu had offered Helen and Marie a little advice—strange advice, stuff which never would have gone down with the boys in the precinct. And also, privately, he'd put himself on their case. If that damned it-can't-wait job hadn't come up in the office, why, he'd probably be keeping an eye on one of them—maybe even Helen—right now! Except...that damned it-can't-wait job *had* come up!

And the devil of it was that this wasn't the first call he'd had tonight concerning Helen Gardner; half an hour ago her boss at the bank had called him: something about her takings not balancing out. Eighty dollars on the light side, apparently.

"You don't suppose she's taken it?" he'd asked the anxious bank manager.

"No, of course not. I've always placed her above that sort of suspicion. A girl of real character. No, it has to be a mistake. It's just that you asked me to keep an eye on her—report anything peculiar—and like that. Well, I find this very peculiar, that's all..."

The tough Inspector from Homicide hadn't found it at all peculiar, a simple error at worst; certainly there'd be no way he could connect it to a vampire. But ...then she herself had called...

Now, speeding through the city with his siren howling and roof light flashing, Grodescu glanced at the leather bag of tools beside him on the front passenger seat. His police special lay on top: a real stopper!—*if* you were dealing with your everyday, run-of-the-mill, common-or-garden mugger, rapist or murderer. But Grodescu had come to believe that this one wasn't like that, and he also suspected—indeed dreaded—that he'd be too late. The way Helen had put the 'phone down on him, it could mean that the bastard was already with her!

He cornered in a controlled skid and narrowly missed a car trying to traverse the junction, tore through red lights and sent a crowd of youths on a pedestrian crossing scattering for their lives, straightened up on the last stretch of road between him and the end of his journey. She lived—or by now lay dead—just a half-mile down this road.

And again Grodescu glanced at his bag. Under the gun, a bundle of short, sharp, hardwood stakes, and a mallet—and a razor-honed, long-bladed hatchet! If the guys at the precinct had seen this lot, or known what was on his mind…

But then, the guys at the precinct hadn't come from the Old Country.

The Inspector switched off his siren and slewed against the high kerb, popping a hubcap and grinding his wheel rims. Then he'd snatched up his bag and was out of the car, leaving the door flapping behind him as he ran across the shadowy street and into the electric glare of the building's foyer. *God grant I'm not too late!* he thought, punching at the elevator call button. But in fact he knew that God had very little to do with it: Time was the only imponderable here. Helen's call had been broken off all of twenty minutes ago.

Behind him as the elevator doors closed on him, the night clerk came yelling and cursing from behind his desk. Grodescu ignored the man's hammering on the doors as the cage begin to lift…

————————

A little less than twenty minutes earlier…

Inside the apartment the vampire felt uncomfortable. There was something decidedly wrong here but so far he couldn't put his finger on it. Perhaps he'd be well advised to give it more thought, but the girl was a distraction. He was in her bedroom and under his hypnotic control she was undressing. He had told her to do it slowly, and commensurate with the removal of each garment, so his distraction increased.

First, because she was beautiful, he would take her. And because he would demand it, she would not be able to hold anything back. Then (because by then he would be even more hungry) he would…take her again. *Take* her: her blood, her soul. Which would make her his, would add her to his list of stolen souls, and provide him with a place to live until he had worked things out and was ready to be rid of her.

All very basic, very simple.

And yet something continued to disturb him. Something…about the girl herself? He could swear he'd known her before. More than once? But how could that be? For if he'd know her before—even once—then she wouldn't be here now.

The memory of a smell—burnt gunpowder stench?—briefly returned, causing him to wrinkle his large, dark nostrils. And again the thought came to him: *something is not right here!*

The prick in his thumb irritated him and he looked at it. It had almost healed now, that V-shaped puncture; but there was one other small scar on his thumb, a white scratch in his pale flesh. And it, too, was V-shaped. What did it mean?

Helen Gardner was completely naked now; she crossed slowly to her bed and lay down upon it, her eyes never once leaving his eyes. The vampire went to her, his movements liquid, languid, belying the need which was building in him. He lay down beside her, grunting in anticipation of great pleasure, gazing at her warm, inviting flesh, the throb of blood coursing in her neck—and frowned…

So, he had known girls like her before…what difference did that make?

Then he saw the scrapbook.

It lay open on her bedside table, with newspaper cuttings pasted into its large, coloured pasteboard pages. The cuttings included photographs—of her!

This was important. He knew it, again instinctively. He reached out, slid the scrapbook from the table and onto her flat stomach. Her flesh shivered a little from the cold touch of paper. And he read these items which she had collected.

The girls in the photographs, they had been identical twins. And he read of the first sister, Anna, cruelly murdered. And of Paula, a second *murder macabre*. The first had died a fortnight ago on the other side of the city, the second a week ago just three blocks away. So *that* was where he'd know her (no, them) before! Not Helen but blood relatives, almost duplicates of her—her older sisters! And apparently he'd had both of them!

"GROTESQUE Vampire Murder!" the headlines shrieked. "BLOOD-LUSTING Lunatic Stalks City Streets!"

Well, and now he was stalking again. And he'd chuckled darkly to himself as first he sated his enormous lust on the girl, then his monstrous thirst. Twenty minutes was all it took, and then she lay cold and dead in his arms...

Dead? But he hadn't intended that. To enslave her would have been sufficient. Except...his needs had been too demanding. Still, no use crying over spilt...whatever. And at least he would have the use of he apartment for the night. But as he unhurriedly dressed:

What was that?

His vampire senses warned of imminent danger! A pursuer—an avenger—close by. Running footsteps in the corridor outside. He extended his thoughts, searched the intruder's mind—and recoiled as if burned! One who knew, who was equipped, prepared!

As the first rain of demanding blows fell like thunder on the outside door, the vampire finished dressing, sprang to the bedroom window and drew back its curtains—then leaped frantically backwards, away from the window box visible beyond the glass. Garlic! And the recently installed wooden bars on the window forming the hated cross of the Christ!

Hissing his frustration—his fear—the murdering thing rushed through the apartment checking the rest of the windows. They were all the same: cursed with that hideous cross. A fire escape out there, but useless to him for he could never pass through those windows or over that damned garlic.

And now from beyond the exit door a strong authoritative voice was raised in concern, in warning, in anger: "Helen, open this door. This is the police, Inspector Grodescu. Whoever is in there, open the door at once or I'll break it down!"

Police! And that name, Grodescu: a man of the Old Country.

The vampire thought to challenge him, perhaps destroy him—then thought again. Others were coming even now; he could sense their presence; also, the man Grodescu knew what he was about.

In a frenzy of frustration the vampire rushed back to the bedroom, and through it to the girl's bathroom. But in there…hated mirrors on every wall! And his grotesquely distorted, red-glistening face reflected in every one of them, reminding him of what he was?—and how he could be made to pay!

He returned to the bedroom, locked the door, listened with a hammering heart to the shuddering and groaning of the outside door. There was nowhere to run! And the memory came from nowhere: *it was like this in the woods, with the dogs closing in.* That had been after he'd taken Anna Gardner. But…why should it suddenly spring to mind now? *And in Paula Gardner's flat there had been no fire escape.*

But no more than that: only half-memories, really, emerging from the desperation of his situation. He was trapped; panels were splintering in the outside door; the bedroom door was less sturdy; this bastard Grodescu would come through it like a bull!

The vampire groaned. There was only one way out. His ring. *"If circumstances are dire—the very direst—then and only then use it.'* He slid the ring from his finger, held it up and read the widdershins inscription—to himself. It was enruned, but he knew it anyway: his vampire instinct, of course.

"And good luck to you, for HE *lusts after us before all other sinners…"*

HE: Satan! The Devil Himself! The Dark One! Lord and Master of all vampires. Of course HE lusted after vampires, for who else of all manner of creatures upon the earth had the power to steal or convert human souls? Only the vampire, for the vampire's victims are not truly dead—they are undead!

Chains were rattling now in the main room. Grodescu's hand groped into the room through a shattered panel, removing the bolts. Behind the locked bedroom door, the vampire read the rune—out loud!"

Satan came in a belch of yellow-tinged smoke, stood tall, serene, totally evil…and handsome as the Devil, of course! He appeared with a quill pen in one hand and a contract in the other, and the vampire knew it was a contract not only for his own soul but for all the others he'd cursed with undeath. And Satan smiled:

"Ah, you again! Well, I can't say I wasn't expecting it." His voice was deep and dark as his eyes. He raised an eyebrow, curled his lip. "And I see you've left it somewhat late again."

"Again?" the vampire snarled, backing into a corner as Satan stepped closer. "No games, Lord of Hell, I need your help. I have three wishes, and when they're used my soul is yours."

"Not much of a mathematician, are you?" said Satan, frowning; and all the time the trapped vampire was aware of the sound of rending timber, and finally gunshots as Inspector Grodescu gave up on the last stubborn bolt and blew it free from its screws. "You have one wish left," Satan continued. "And you'd better make it snappy before whoever that is gets in here."

"*One* wish?" the vampire hissed. "Only one? It's well known that you're a liar, and that you'd cheat hell itself if you could, but—"

"One wish," Satan cut him short, shaking out the contract in front of him. The thing was all small-print, signed in blood, twice, with sufficient room remaining for just one more signature. But … both of the signatures already scrawled on the parchment were his: Paul Szoleski! So that now he also remembered his name, but still nothing more than that.

There were questions he would ask, but no time in which to ask them. Grodescu was in the apartment, flitting cautiously through the rooms, his weapons ready. And other men were outside forming a rearguard. There would be no way through them.

"What's it to be?" said the devil.

"Only get me away from here!" Szoleski panted. "Anywhere in space or time—anywhere on Earth, that is—but away from this place. I need a fresh start."

"A fresh start?"

Clean Slate

"A clean slate, yes."

"Agreed," said the devil. "Give me your left hand."

Szoleski held out his hand—and Satan stabbed at his thumb with the sharp point of the quill!

"What—?" said Szoleski. This was all very wrong and he knew it.

But Grodescu was outside the bedroom door night now; the knob was given a cautious, exploratory twist; there was no more time. "Sign!" said Satan. And trembling, the vampire signed his name in his own blood—directly underneath the other two signatures!

"No imagination whatever," said Satan, sadly shaking his head. "But very well, now I remove you from this place—and wipe your slate clean…"

The door shuddered massively—and again—then slammed back on tortured hinges…

———————

He snapped back into consciousness not knowing his name, how he came to be here, or anything of his previous life. It was something like being born again, but without all the fuss. And of course he was full grown. There was only a hot reek, quickly fading, and the sure instinctive knowledge that he was different.

Following the girl, he paused where she paused, ostensibly staring into a jeweler's window but continuing to watch her out of the corner of his eye. She was very beautiful, the sort of girl he'd never been able to resist. Ignoring the small irritation of pain in his left thumb, he continued to trail her as she started off again through the night streets.

Behind him, unseen, followed a squat, heavily built man in a dark overcoat. He had one hand in the pocket of his overcoat; in the other he carried a leather bag much like the ones fancied in bygone times by village doctors. But his eyes never blinked, never strayed for a moment from their fixation with the back of the vampire's head.

A little way behind Grodescu walked another, jauntily, and smiling sardonically. He wore a hat and twirled a stick and his shoes were oddly shaped and seemed rather short. Also, if anyone had been close to him, they would certainly have noticed the not quite cordite smell of brimstone…

The Deep-Sea Conch

Some species build nests; while others are much like the cuckoo....

11 Tunstall Court,
West H. Pool,
Co. Durham
June 16th, 1962

Maj. Harry Winslow,
The Oaks, Innsway,
Redcar, Yorks.

My Dear Harry,

What an interesting tale that letter of yours tells. Hypnotic gastropods, by crikey! But there was no need for the apologies, honestly. Why, we all of us thought you must be ill or something, which you were as it happened, and didn't for a moment consider your actions "inexcusable!" If only I'd known you were so, well, *susceptible* to shellfish; I would never have had oysters on the card! And for goodness sake, do put Alice's mind at rest and tell here that there's nothing to forgive. Give her my love, poor darling!

But that story of yours is really something. I showed your letter to a conchologist friend of mine from Harden. This fellow—John Beale's his name—spends all his summers down south, "conching," as he calls it, in the coves of Devon and Dorset; or at least he *used* to. Why! He was as keen a chap as your Corporal Jobling (poor fellow) seems to have been.

But it appears I must have a stronger stomach than you, Old Chap. Yes, indeed! I've just been down to The Lobster Pot on the seafront for a bite and a bottle, and I couldn't resist a fat crab straight out of the sea at Old Hartlepool. Yes, and that after both your story *and* this tale of Beale's. Truth is, I can't make up my mind which of the two is the more repulsive—but I might add that neither of them appears to have affected *my* appetite!

Still, I've just got to tell you this other story—just as Beale told it to me—so, taking a chance on further offending your sensibilities, here we go:

Now you'll probably remember how a few years ago a British oceanographical expedition charted the continental shelf all the way up from the Bay of Biscay along the North Atlantic Drift to the Shetland Isles. I say you'll probably remember, because of course the boat went down off the Faroes right at the end of its voyage, and it was in all the newspapers at the time. Luckily, lifeboats got the crew of *The Sunderland* off before she sank.

Well anyway, one of the crew was a friend of this Beale chap and he knew he was keen on shells and so on. He brought back with him a most peculiar specimen as a present—for Beale. It was a deep-sea conch, dredged up from two thousand seven hundred fathoms beneath the Atlantic two hundred miles west of Brest.

Now this thing was quite a find, and Beale's friend would have found himself in plenty of hot water had the professors aboard ship found out how he'd taken it from the dredge. As it was he kept it hidden under his bunk until the boat went down, and even then he managed to smuggle it into a lifeboat with him. And so he brought it home. Of course, after a month out of the water—even had it survived the emergence from such a depth—the creature in the conch would be long dead.

You'd think so, wouldn't you, Harry...?

Anyway, as soon as Beale got hold of the conch he stuck it in a bowl of weak acid solution to clean up its surface and get rid of the remains of the animal inside. It was quite large, nine or ten inches across and four deep, tightly coiled, and with a great bell of a mouth. Beale reckoned that once he'd got the odd oceanic incrustations off the thing it ought to be rather exotically patterned. Most deep-ocean dwellers are exotic, in various ways, you know?

The next morning, Beale went to take the conch out of the acid— and as he did so he noticed that a great, thick, shiny-green operculum was showing deep down in the bell-shaped mouth. The acid hadn't even touched the incrustations on the shell, but it had obviously loosened up the dead snail (is that what you call them?) inside the tight coil. Which was where the fun started.

Beale took a knife and tried to force the blade down between the green lid and the interior of the hard shell, so that he could hook out the body of the snail, d'you see? But as soon as the knife touched the operculum—*damn it if the thing didn't withdraw!* Yes, it was still alive, that creature—even after being brought up from that tremendous depth, even after a month out of water and a night in that bowl of acid solution—still alive! Fantastic, eh, Harry?

Now, Beale knew he had a real curiosity here, and that he should take it at once to some zoologist or other. But how could he without dropping his friend right in it? Why! The deep-sea conch looked like being the best thing to come out of that entire abortive expedition….

Well, Beale thought about it, and a week later he finally decided to get a second opinion. He asked his oceangoing friend (a Hartlepool man, by the way, name of Chadwick) up to Harden where he brought him up to date before asking his advice. By then he'd bought an aquarium for the conch and was feeding it on bits of raw meat. Very unpleasant! He never actually saw it *take* the meat, you understand, but each morning the tank would be empty except for the great shell and its occupant.

Beale's chief hope in asking Chadwick for his advice was that the fellow'd tell him to hand the conch in. He hoped, you see, that Chadwick would be willing to face the music in the "interests of science." Not so. This Chadwick was simply an ordinary little Jack tar, and he feared the comeback of owning up to his bit of thievery. Why

41

couldn't Beale (he wanted to know) simply keep the thing and stop worrying about it? Well, Beale explained that his hobby was conchology, not zoology, and that he didn't fancy having this aquarium-thing smelling up his flat forever, and so on. At which Chadwick argued why couldn't he just kill of the snail and keep the shell? And Beale had no answer to that!

He's not a bad chap, this Beale, you see, and he knew very well what he really ought to do—that is, he should hand the conch over and let Chadwick take his medicine—but dame it all, the fellow was his friend! In the end he agreed to kill the snail and keep the shell. That way he could get rid of the smelly aquarium (for the conch did have quite a bit of a pong about it) and live in peace and quiet ever after.

But Chadwick had seen Beale's initial indecision over the conch's destiny, and he decided he'd better stick around and see to it that his pal really did kill the snail off—and that's where things started to get a bit complicated. That night, by the time Chadwick was ready to get off back to Hartlepool, they still hadn't managed to put the damn thing out of its misery. And believe me, Harry, they'd really tried!

First off Beale had taken the conch from the aquarium to place it in a powerful acid bath. Two hours later the deposits on the shell had vanished, allowing a disappointing pattern to show through. Also, the surface of the acid had scummed up somewhat—but the hard, shiny-green operculum was still there, tight as the doors on the vaults at the Bank of England! Now, remember, our friends knew that the snail could get along fine for a least a month without food or water, and it looked as though the lid and the hard shell were capable of withstanding the strongest acid that Beale could get hold of without any great difficulty. So what next?

Even after his friend had gone off home Beale was still puzzling over the problem. It seemed an altogether damned weird thing this, and he was feeling sort of uneasy about it. It reminded him of something, this shell, something he'd seen before somewhere…at the local museum, for instance!

The Deep-Sea Conch

The next morning, as soon as his sailor friend turned up, they went off together down to the museum. In the "Prehistoric Britain" section Beale found what he was looking for—a whole shelf of fossil shells of all sorts, shapes, and sizes. Of course, the fossils were all under glass so that our pair couldn't handle them, but they didn't really need to. "There you go," said Beale, excitedly pointing out one of the specimens, "that's it—not so big, perhaps, but the same shape and with the same type of markings!" And Chadwick had to agree that the fossil looked very much similar to their conch.

Well, they read off the label describing the fossil, and here, (as best I can remember from what Beale told me, though I'm not absolutely sure about the thing's name,) is what it said:

Upper Cretaceous:
(—?—SCAPHITES, a tightly coiled shell from Barrow-on-Soar in Leicestershire. Flourished in Cretaceous oceans 120 million years ago. Similar specimens, with more prominent ribs and nodes, occur frequently in the Leicestershire Lias. Extinct for over 60 million years…

…Which didn't tell them very much, you'll agree, Harry. But Beale jumped a bit at that "extinct" notice—he had reckoned it might be so—and once again he asked Chadwick to turn the thing in. Why! It was starting to look as good as the coelacanth, at least to any conchologist!

"No hope!" Chadwick answered, perfunctorily. "Let's get round to your place and finish the thing off. For the last time, I'm not carrying the can for doing you a favor!" And so they went back to Beale's flat.

There waiting for them in the kitchen, was the conch—still in its bath of acid, and apparently completely unharmed. Well, they carefully drained off the acid and sprayed the conch down with water to facilitate its immediate handling. Chadwick had brought with him from Hartlepool a great knife with a hooked blade. He tried his best to get the point right down inside the bell of the shell, but always there was that incredibly hard operculum, all shiny green and tight as a cork in a bottle.

This was when Chadwick, having completely lost patience with it all, suggested smashing the conch. Suggested it? Why! He had the thing out on the concrete landing before Beale could get his thoughts in order. But the latter needn't have worried; I mean, how does one go about smashing something that's survived the pressure at two thousand seven hundred fathoms, eh?" Chadwick had actually flung the conch full swing against the concrete floor of the landing by the time Beale caught up with him, and the latter was just able to catch it on the bounce. It wasn't even dented! Peering into the bell-shaped mouth, Beale was just able to make out one edge of the green operculum pulling back out of sight around the curve of the coil.

Then Chadwick had his brain wave. One thing the conch had *not* been subjected to down there on the bed of the ocean was heat—it's a monstrous cold world at the bottom of the sea! And it just so happened that Beale had already made inquiries at the local hardware store about borrowing a blowtorch to lift the paint from a wardrobe he wanted to do up. Chadwick went off to borrow the blowtorch and left Beale sitting deep in thought, contemplating the conch.

Now, I've already mentioned how Beale had had this strange, uneasy feeling about the shell and its occupant. Yes; well by now the feeling had grown out of all proportion. There seemed to the sensitive collector to be a sort of…well, an *aura* about the thing, that feeling of untold ages one has when gazing upon ancient ruins—except that with the conch the sensation was far more powerful.

And then again, how had the conch come by its amazing powers of self-preservation? Was it possible?…No, what Beale was thinking was plainly impossible—such survivals were out of the question—and yet the mad thought kept spinning around in Beale's brain that perhaps, perhaps…

How *long* had this creature, "encased in the coils of its own construction," (Beale's words), "prowled the pressured deeps in ponderous stealth?" But extinct for 60 million years…

The Deep-Sea Conch

Suddenly he dearly wished he had some means at his disposal of checking the conch's exact age. It was a crazy thought, he knew, but there was this insistent idea in the back of his head —

In his mind's eye he saw the world as it had been so long ago — great beasts trampling primitive plants in steaming swamps, and strange birds that were *not* birds flying in heavy, predawn skies. And then he looked beneath those prehistoric oceans — oceans more like vast *acid baths* than seas such as we know them today — at the multitude of forms that swam, spurted, and slowly *evolved* in those deadly deeps.

Then Beale allowed (as he put it) an "unwinding of time" in his mind's eye, picturing the geologic changes, watching continents emerge hissing from volcanic oceans, and coralline islands slowly sinking back into the soups of their own genesis. He watches the gradual alteration in climates and environments, the bombardment of meteorites and volcanoes, and the effects such changes had on a majority of their denizens. He felt the most remote forbears of the conch altering internally, building a resistance to the tremendous pressures of deep seas; and, in various other disasters, as Nature killed off so many other prehistoric creatures, sank into even deeper, darker abysses and developed their unique longevity to ensure the continuation of species.

Beale told me all this, you understand, Harry? And God only knows where his thoughts might have led him if Chadwick hadn't come back pretty soon with the blowtorch. But even after the sailor got the blowtorch going — while he played its terrible tip of invisible heat on the coils of the conch — Beale's fancy was still at work.

Once, as a boy, he had pulled a tiny hermit crab from its borrowed shell on the beach at Seaton-Carew, to watch it scurry in frantic terror in search of a new home over the sand at the bottom of a small pool. In the end, out of an intensely agonizing empathy for the completely vulnerable crab, he had dropped the empty whelk shell back into the water in the soft-bodied creature's way, so that it was able to leap with breathtaking rapidity and almost visible relief back into the safety of the shell's calcium coil. It is death for this type of creature to be forced from its protective shell, you see, Harry? That's what Beale was telling me, and once out such a creature has only three alternatives: get back in or find a new home—and as quickly as possible—or die when the predators come on the scene! Small wonder the snail in the conch was giving them such a hard time.

And that was when Beale heard Chadwick's hiss of indrawn breath and his shouted, "It's coming out!"

Beale had been turned away from what he rightly considered a criminal scene, but at Chadwick's cry he turned back—in time to see the sailor drop the blowtorch and fling himself almost convulsively away from the metal sink unit where he'd been working. Chadwick said nothing more, you understand, following that initial cry. He simply hurled himself away from the steaming conch.

Quick as thought, the flame from the fallen blowtorch caught at the kitchen tablecloth, and Beale's first impulse was to save his flat. Chadwick had burned himself, that was plain, but his burn couldn't be all that serious. So thinking, Beale leapt over to the sink to fill a jug with water. The torch was still flaring but it lay on the ceramic-tiled floor where it could do little harm. So Beale thought, but its searing flame was already scorching the wooden base of the sink unit. Avoiding both the blazing table, and its several inflammable contents, Beale was aware as he filled his jug that the overspill moved the conch—as though the shell were somehow lighter—but he had no time to ponder that.

Turning, he almost dropped the jug as he saw Chadwick's figure stretched full length half-in, half-out of the kitchen. Dodging suddenly leaping flames and flinging the jug's contents futilely over them, he crossed to where his friend lay, turning him onto his back to see what was wrong. There was no visible sign of a burn; but quickly checking for Chadwick's pulse, Beale was at once horrified at his inability to detect one!

Shock! Chadwick must be suffering from shock! Beale pushed his fingers into the other's mouth to loosen up his tongue, and then, seeing a slight movement of the man's throat, he threw himself face down beside him to get into the "Kiss of Life" position.

He never administered that kiss, but leapt shrieking to flee from the burning flat, down the stairs and out of the building. He told me that apart from that mad dash he can remember nothing more of the nightmare—nothing, that is, other than the *cause* of his panic flight. Of course, there's no proving Beale's story one way or the other, the whole block of flats was burned right out and it was a miracle that Chadwick was the only casualty. I don't suppose I'd ever have got the story out of Beale if I hadn't met up with him one night and showed him that letter of yours. He was almighty drunk at the time, and I'm sure he's never told anyone else.

Fact or fiction?…Damned if I know, but it's true that Beale doesn't go "conching" any more, and just suppose it did happen the way he told it?

What a shock to a delicate nervous system, eh, Harry?

You can probably guess what happened, but just put yourself in Beale's place. Imagine the heart-stopping horror when, having seen Chadwick's throat move, *he looked into the sailor's mouth and saw that shiny-green operculum pull down quickly out of sight into the fellow's throat!*

And that's it, the whole story. That's the whole story, Harry…

The Ugly Act

But what's a pimple or two—if there's only you?

No one should be born as ugly as Hesch Blarzt; so ugly that at first sight they believed the placenta hadn't bothered to wait its turn. And certainly no one that ugly should also be unlucky enough to live. Indeed if Hesch had been born just a couple of decades later he wouldn't have been *allowed* to live, but in 2129 the Ugly Act hadn't yet been introduced. The Ugly Act, as its either beautiful or extremely rich proponents could have told you, was designed to get Old Mother Earth all nice and green and tidy and unpolluted again—which meant doing away with anything that was likely to clutter the planet up or make it look unpretty. Like, for instance, Hesch Blarzt.

2247 was the year of the Ugly Act—which forced the big industrial combines to bury their trash under forests of giant GM ferns that grew and sucked out all the rubbish and turned it into purple tendrils and huge smelly red flowers, leaving nothing but a soft gray ash behind that made a damn good fertilizer—but at the time of which I write all of that was still eighteen years away, and that was when Hesch Blarzt was born.

His parents took one look at him, denied all responsibility, put Hesch in a home and ran off to the moon to grow low-grav tomatoes. Five years later the moon got atmosphere and the Blarzts looked like living happily ever after…except Hesch.

Of course, if people had looked close enough they would have seen that he was a mutant, the result of three generations of Blarzts working in experimental hydroponics, which involved a degree of proximity to certain industrial radio-actives. His was a classic case of jelled genes.... But nobody looked that close. Few could even bear to.

By the time Hesch was twenty-one and ready to be kicked out of the orphanage where he'd been trained to fuel furnaces (which particular work would keep him more or less out of sight in the bowels of the city, tending to the central heating), the Ugly Act was more than forty years old. Moon tomatoes had fallen through when people discovered they could eat giant flowering ferns, but Hesch's folks had got out of moon farming early and were doing great in Darkside nickel-iron and uranium.

And so, down in the sweaty, dirty, dark environment of the city's basest basement, Hesch grew to manhood...which, being a slow starter and all, took him another three years.

Naturally—what with all the murders, muggings, riots, gangbangs and what have you—few self-respecting young women would dream of going out at night in the city; they only very rarely went out in daylight! And that left Hesch in kind of a hole. For he was beginning to feel the sap rise (in fact it had been rising for—oh, for twenty years or more—which accounted for his many pimples), and no satisfactory way to tap the sap.

He'd tried the whorehouses, certainly, but the androids were too mechanical, and real live whores were too expensive. Also, where the latter were concerned...well, Hesch wasn't growing any prettier. The only live one he ever had, he'd had to pour a half-bottle of fern wine down her neck before she'd even look at him, and even then she'd made him wear a handsome mask first.

You see, Hesch wasn't just ugly. He was *ugly!*

In the mid-twentieth century he would probably have gotten along okay; lots of people were very unlovely in those days. But since then, why, man and womankind just kept getting prettier. So anyone who was seventy seven inches tall, awkward with it, large-pored, hook-nosed, bowlegged, coarse-haired, *and* warty to boot simply didn't stand a chance in the AD 2290s The people at the home had done Hesch a real favour putting him in furnace-stoking: there were campaigners "up top" (meaning on the surface levels) who were all for extending the Ugly Act to include anyone below a Grade Three Pretty—which wasn't far short of devastatingly beautiful!

The world was kind of crowded—even the moon was getting that way—and natural disasters and small country wars just weren't doing their bit to keep the numbers down. For the last decade or so the population explosion had been more a nova. Of course, most of the people who wanted a law passed to "put down"—the soon-to-be-legal extermination of—something like thirty six-percent of the world's population were all very rich; rich enough that if they weren't beautiful already, they could become beautiful very, very quickly.

Plastic surgeons were rich, too, and getting richer every day as the Ugly Act tightened its grip. And yet they were still poor compared with some. Anybody who owned a quarter acre, for instance, was a billionaire in an age when you could walk houseboat decks from Long Island to New Haven. And so, since men were having trouble settling the planets—and since flowering fern and quahog chowder didn't taste half so good as sweet and sour pork—naturally the with-its were looking for a way to *do* away with the withouts and the Pretties wanted rid of every Unpretty...and Hesch Blarzt fitted both unwanted categories perfectly.

Saturday afternoons and Sundays, when he wasn't working, Hesch would put on a handsome mask and walk the lower levels of the city. His size kept the muggers away. Now and then he would catch a glimpse of a girl, usually as she turned to run. They'd run if anyone looked at them twice, what with all the crime and what have you; but someone as tall as Hesch, who also shuffled...that was just too much. Now and then some overzealous cop would stop him and whip out a gun, ram the barrel up one of his large nostrils under his handsome mask and yell, "Hey, you, Grot! You never heard of the Ugly Act?"

Of course, the Ugly Act didn't apply to Hesch—not just yet, but it was very worrying anyway. Pretty soon now...well, he reckoned he had about a year left, two at the outside. And it was probably this sort of anxiety that brought to light the other side of Hesch's mutation: his ability to zoop. It happened this way:

He was sitting in his little cell (his so-called flat-let; but since furnace stokers didn't rate very high in the social order, it was the size of a small cell) watching this obscene minitele show one night, when suddenly a startling, incredibly silly thought occurred to him: how it would be quite splendid to own an uninhabited island. And later, lying in his bunk in the darkness, the thought returned; he saw a detailed picture of the island in his mind's eye. And it was very beautiful.

Now, uninhabited islands were nonexistent. Every habitable piece of real estate on the entire planet was simply crawling with people, so obviously Hesch's little bit of escapism was simply, well, escapism. Except he'd been wishing very determinedly, and—zoop!

Just like that, the darkness of his cell turned to bright sunlight on the golden sands of a wonderful uninhabited island! An island with palm trees and a fresh, clear stream bubbling down from a central hill and a sky bluer than Hesch had ever dreamed of, without a trace of smog. And no people, not a one, except Hesch. Which soon proved to be the one big drawback.

Night came on and the stars came out, amazingly bright in the smokeless atmosphere, and Hesch lay on his back on the hill beside the little stream, and there was no Ugly Act and everything was very wonderful.

Except that he was lonely…

———————

In the morning Hesch had a coconut for breakfast then went for a swim. The water was cool but not cold; fairly large fish swam in small schools; there wasn't the slightest hint of a current or even a tide. It could have been the Mediterranean a couple of hundred years ago, but he knew it wasn't. An island such as this couldn't possibly have escaped humanity's explosion; and beside that, the stars hadn't been right when he'd gazed up at them in the night. No, this place Hesch had zooped off to was other than mundane.

He spent three days there, living on fish, nuts, fresh clean water like none tasted on Earth since immediately after the last ice age, then zooped back to his cell. There he sat and thought about it for a while, then put on a handsome mask and went for a walk in the city. He got a lot of funny looks, saw perhaps half a million people in half an hour — of which total maybe fifty were women — was threatened three times by policemen, then returned to his flat-let.

Four hundred and ninety-nine thousand, nine hundred and fifty men were forgotten as soon as the door closed behind him and he was alone — but not the fifty women. And not the three policemen...

It was getting bad and Hesch knew it. It seemed the only thing people were talking about was the Ugly Act, to which he would surely become subject and soon. If only there was a woman on his island. She didn't have to be a Grade One Pretty, (hell, could he afford to be choosy?) Just as long as she —

But what was he thinking about? If he could zoop himself, mightn't he be able to zoop someone else? Like maybe the prettiest god-dam Pretty in the city?

Taking an elevator up sixteen levels, Hesch went out again onto the city's evening streets. But even as he left the elevator a policeman grabbed his right arm, bending it up behind his back. "Are you Hesch Blarzt?" the cop asked, making it a statement of fact.

"I am he," Hesch answered in his deep, croaking voice. "Is something wrong?"

"Yeah. You stopped working."

"Is that a crime?"

"Yeah. Everybody contributes, Grot. We've all got to keep working as efficiently as possible to help the ecology, to help Nature balance it all out, and to comply with the Ugly Act."

"You are brainwashed, fellow," answered Hesch. "Man ruined his environment decades ago. The world is dying; it is poisoned and recycling its own poisons. All the Ugly Act will do is slow it down some, but never enough. The corpse will only support so many maggots before it falls apart, and soon we'll have to move on. And by the way, you are hurting my arm."

"Hey, you're not only really grot, Grot," said the cop, "you're also stupid! I don't know if anyone ever told you, but really ugly buggers like you aren't supposed to mouth off. Did you know that? What happened anyway—you forgot your handsome mask or something?"

He twisted Hesch's arm very hard and smiled up at him with white teeth that flashed in his young, naturally handsome face. It was almost angelic, that face. Hesch couldn't understand why a crud like this deserved a face like that.

"I did forget my mask, sir, yes," he answered, pain twisting his features into even less lovable lines. "Do you—uh!—swim?"

"Swim?" Such an abrupt change in the mood and direction of the conversation took the cop by surprise. "What are you trying to accuse me of? They're making pools illegal, even you should know that. There's no excuse for waste of that magnitude. What, water to swim in? Water's for drinking, Grot."

"I learned to swim at the orphanage, in a static—uh!—water tank."

"So what?"

"So that gives me the—uh!—advantage."

"Yeah? You think there'll be a deluge before I can get you to the station?" The cop opened his mouth to laugh, and several pints of salt water rushed into it. Hesch had zooped the two of them onto his island. Well, he'd zooped *himself* onto it, at any rate. The cop he'd zooped into the sea.

Hesch stood on the golden beach massaging his arm and dispassionately watching the black-uniformed man drowning. Then, in a moment of remorse, he quickly zooped the cop back to his own world. Alone again, he stared at the concentric ripples on the surface of an otherwise still ocean, and grinned hideously—which was the only possible way someone with his looks could grin. He could imagine the scene as a thoroughly soaked, half-drowned cop suddenly arrived out of nowhere into the crowded evening city.

Then the grin slipped from his face as he realized that he didn't have too much time now. Next time, he'd probably be shot on sight. And holding that thought he zooped back to his little cell and put on his handsome mask.

He took a different elevator to a recreation level. In one of the halls a frenzied crowd was watching a bleedie, relieving their pent-up hatreds, anxieties, and frustrations by screaming obscenities at the 3DV stage. One act showed an ugly man, almost as ugly as Hesch, throwing himself into a steam driven blender. It was all very explicit, and the mob went wild when grey, simulated (well, possibly) brain matter and purple-veined entrails rained down on them from concealed ducts in the ceiling.

Looking up, Hesch spotted a couple in a private box. The woman was very beautiful. Hesch zooped her onto his island and approached her from a safe distance along the beach. She saw him coming and put a trembling hand up to her mouth.

"'Lo," said Hesch. "This is my island."

"How…how did I get here?" Her voice trembled.

Hesch offered a shrug (why should he go into details?) and croaked, "There's plenty to eat here—and I can teach you how to swim."

Something of the horror of this impossible thing that was happening to her sank in, and with a little shriek she fainted. Hesch carried her into the cool shade of a palm, where he propped her with her head against the rough bole. Then he prepared a coconut, caught some fish, built a fire and sat back waiting for her to wake up.

When she came to, he had a line already worked out.

He didn't know how they came to be on the island, he told her, but they were in the same boat together. They would simply have to make the best of it. He was a man, she was a woman…there was plenty to eat, and he would teach her how to swim.

When she started to cry he put on his handsome mask and went for a shambling walk along the beach. An hour later when he came back she was still sobbing her heart out. She hadn't touched the coconut and the fish were black and smoking where they hung over the fire.

She looked up at him through her tears and said, "You did this to me, didn't you? You brought me here for...something. How could you?" She was a nice young woman, and suddenly Hesch felt ugly and unclean. He was used to feeling ugly but the uncleanliness was something new.

"Uh—sorry!" he said, and zooped her right back to the city. Then, after a short period of dejection and a shorter one of considered thought, Hesch had an idea. Zooping himself into a whorehouse he asked for a live one. The madame sniffed doubtfully, but took Hesch's money anyway—his total life savings, maybe enough to buy synthetic groceries for one for a month—then gave him the key to an upstairs nest.

As he climbed the stairs, Hesch told himself it made no difference: a woman was a woman was a woman. At least a prostitute shouldn't be too awkward about...things. After all, he had a whole lot to offer, really.

He let himself into the nest and closed the door. Behind a curtain of beads a figure stirred languorously. The light was only poor, so that when she parted the beads she couldn't quite see him at first. "Hey! A really big boy!" she cooed, then got close up. "Ow!" she exclaimed then, drawing back. And: "What a Grot!"

"I own a whole island," said Hesch, "and—"

"Out, you ugly bugger!" she told him. "There are certain things even I don't do. And you're one of them."

"Listen," said Hesch, "I am quite desperate, and I really do have a very lovely—"

"Out!" she yelled.

So Hesch zooped her onto his island, which he'd intended doing from the start. It stood to reason she'd be more amenable to persuasion there. "This is my island," he told her, as she sat down abruptly in the golden sand and stared in amazement at the sea, the sky, the waving palm trees.

"Your lovely island," she repeated him faintly.

"Yes, and there's plenty of fresh food here. And, er, if you would like to learn to swim, I—"

"Swim?" She jumped to her feet and attacked him furiously, slapping his face while he put up his hands to protect himself. "I don't want to fucking swim! I want to go back home!"

"Home?" Hesch held her off and shook his head sadly. "To the whorehouse? How long do you think that will last? The Ugly Act will soon do away with the brothels—the common or garden sort, at least—and you'll all be outlawed and erased, along with all the sick 3DV bleedies. Prostitution is ugly!"

"Oh, you think?" she came back. "Well, you're right about the bleedies, "but they're doing well enough."

"The bleedies are a diversion," said Hesch, "designed to take the public's mind off the Ugly Act on the one hand, while preparing for it on the other. Believe me, the end is also nigh for the bleedies. And that time is coming fast!"

She was looking more closely at the island now, big-eyed and curious, thinking to herself that Hesch was probably right. She saw the huge ripe nuts on the palms, fish jumping in the sea, the sparkling stream. She felt the sun warm on her skin, not hidden away behind poisonous clouds, and felt strangely caressed by the warm breeze that oh-so-gently moved the palm fronds.

"You own this place?" she finally said. "I mean, you? So where is everybody?"

"There's no one else here. Just we two," Hesch answered, moving closer.

She took another look at the island and decided that she liked it. In fact, there seemed to be only one thing wrong with it. Long ago she'd had her fill of men, if not quite literally, but a girl has to eat. Here, however, she could eat without men. And she could definitely eat without Hesch Blarzt. Indeed, his absence would be a positive incentive to eating; without a doubt it would help in keeping the food down.

The Ugly Act

She reached up and put one arm around Hesch's neck, but as he bent to encircle her waist she drew out a long straight pin from concealment in her belt. Out the corner of his eye, at the last moment, Hesch saw silver flash in the sun as she aimed the deadly pin at his side. He zooped her away as hard as he could, without direction, and heard her rapidly diminishing scream, an echo that vanished into emptiness. She hadn't gone back to the whorehouse, nor anywhere on Earth, Hesch was aware of that. He wasn't exactly sure where she'd gone, and he didn't much care. She hadn't been worthy of his plan after all, and he was angry with himself that he'd ever believed such a thing might work.

Then he heard something; something so unexpected that at first he failed to recognize the sound. It was a splashing from along the golden sands. Someone was bathing in the sea, singing in a low, cracked—female?—voice. Hesch squinted his little eyes and looked along the beach. A sun-browned figure splashed noisily at the edge of the ocean. Hesch moved warily along the beach wondering how this could possibly have happened.

He knew that he hadn't zooped this unknown woman onto his island, so who had? Or maybe this was only one island of many; maybe this was an entire world, populated but thinly, and maybe this woman was only visiting the island. He at once looked for a boat but couldn't see one.

He felt a little disappointed on the one hand, excited on the other. If this was some other world he'd zooped himself onto, and not a parallel dimension as he'd suspected...well, it seemed most unlikely that the inhabitants of a planet like this would have an Ugly Act. And if there was no Ugly Act, and nothing but a handful of friendly, happy people, why—

—How did you get onto my island?" she asked in fractured, grunting tones, staring at him squint-eyed from the blue sea.

Hesch was astonished. "Your island?" he said. "But this is *my* island."

"Oh, really? Is that so?" Her voice took on a definitely amused if somewhat gravelly tone. "And just how did you get to be the owner?"

"Why I...I just zooped here! It's a thing I do, a means of getting about, and I—"

"And since no one was here, you took it upon yourself to assume ownership," she finished for him.

"Er, yes."

"Turn your back, I'm coming out," she said.

Hesch turned his back and she left the water and shrugged into a worn dress. "Okay," she told him. "You can turn around now."

Hesch did so and looked at her. And in a little while he said, "I think I get it now. You zooped here too, just like me, to escape the Ugly Act."

"Right," she answered.

He studied her more closely. Apart from her squinting eyes which were dissimilarly coloured—her hair was tangled, her shoulders sagged, and her legs were too short. She was a mess. And yet, strangely, there was a kind of kindness about her.

"Well," he said, "since we're both strangers in a strange, empty land, I guess that makes us joint owners."

She shook her head. "No, *I* own this island."

"And what gives you the right of ownership?"

"I made the island," she said, grinning lopsidedly.

"Oh, come now—" Hesch began, but stopped short when he found himself floundering in the sea. The island had shrunk to a cartoon-sized beach with a single palm tree. She sat beneath the tree while he swam slowly back and forth.

"I made it," she said again, "and I can unmake it whenever I want to. If I fancied I could just zoop off elsewhere, taking my island with me and leaving you right here."

"I would zoop back to Earth," Hesch countered her threat, but still felt alarmed.

"Back to the Ugly Act?" She cocked her head on one side.

"I could maybe find some other island to zoop to...some other planet even."

"There are no other islands," she said. "I didn't make any others. As for other planets...you want to try? I've tried it already. There are worlds you'd freeze to death on in a matter of minutes, and others that will fry you black in half as long. There are planets where the atmosphere is so poisonous your insides would melt in as much time as it takes to tell; also where acid rain falls on semi-molten continents. But as shitty as it is, there's no place like Earth."

"There's this place."

"Yes, but I made it. It's a place in my head, and it will only exist as long as I exist."

"Perhaps," Hesch considered aloud, swimming to and fro in the crystal sea, "perhaps I can also, er, make an island. Er, another island, that is."

"Go ahead and try it," she answered. "I wish you the best of luck. For it must be obvious that there's no room for you on my island."

"Don't concern yourself," grated Hesch. "I wasn't planning on staying—not with you here. You remind me too much of the Ugly Act."

"Now you're being deliberately cruel," she said, enlarging the island until Hesch stood on dry land, dripping salt water. "Perhaps it'll help you concentrate if you don't have to swim."

"Concentrate?"

"You need all the concentration you can muster in order to make an island."

So Hesch concentrated as hard as he could, but no island. "No good," he finally admitted defeat. Then he brightened. "So maybe I can get you to make one for me?"

"No chance." She shook her head. "It's enough of a problem keeping this place going. Two islands would be twice as hard."

"Well, all right," said Hesch reluctantly. "So I…I guess I'll be going, then."

She nodded, but he made no attempt to go. And she seemed equally uncertain about making a move. So for a long time they simply looked at each other. And it was a funny thing, but the longer they looked the less ugly each appeared to the other.

"What do you intend doing, er, when I've gone?" he asked her.

She blushed furiously, which strangely enough improved her looks—well, a little. But Hesch only noticed her confusion.

"I…I…well, I—" she stuttered and stumbled.

And Hesch cried, "Well I'll be damned! So that's it, eh?"

"What is what?" she asked, reddening more yet.

"They didn't want you, did they?"

"Who?" she asked. "What are you talking about?"

"All the men you've zooped to this island," Hesch answered. "All of the Pretties you brought here. Everything you had to offer, still they didn't want you. Hah! The same thing happened to me."

She began to cry. "All of my life," she sniffled brokenly, "I have dreamed of a handsome prince of a man who would love me like none other; and yes, I've brought men to this island, only to discover that—"

"I know," Hesch interrupted, nodding sadly.

"They called me names," she went on, "and—"

"Names like 'Grot,' and 'Freak,' and—"

"All those things," She nodded. "yes."

Hesch sighed and said, "My experience was precisely the same. For all that the Earth is polluted and rotten, and yes, ugly—far more ugly than you or I—they prefer it. And I've come to understand why."

"Oh?" She looked at him.

"Maggots," he explained, "much prefer dead meat to fresh. And they also prefer the company of their own kind. The Earth is dead, where people have become like maggots swarming in her dead flesh. But this place, your island, is alive!"

"Do you really like my island, Mr., er—?"

"Hesch," he told her. "Hesch Blarzt. Yes, indeed I do like it."

"Then please stay a little longer if you wish. But be gone when I get back."

"You intend to try again then, Miss, er—?"

"Gyff," she answered. "Miss Gyffarl Twell. Gyff for short. And yes, I'll try one more time."

The Ugly Act

"I shall be gone," Hesch said, "when you return, Gyff." With which she zooped.

And so, fully intending to take his departure…soon, Hesch wandered along the beach and rolled up his trousers to splash his legs in the water. He climbed the hill to watch the clean spring water cascade over washed pebbles gleaming like jewels in the sun. He felt the gentle breeze on his skin and watched the changing pattern of dappled light under the fronds of the sighing palms. And though he hadn't intended it, still he was there when Gyff got back with a man—a young policeman with an angelic face that Hesch recognized immediately!

Hesch hid behind a thick-boled palm and watched. The cop had at first fallen on his behind in the sand, shock draining his face, but in another second he jumped to his feet. "You bitch!" he snarled, grabbing Gyff by the hair. "You must be in league with him! And I'll bet you terrorists have got something to do with the blowup, too!"

"In league with whom?" she cried, trying to free herself.

"With that Grot who damn near drowned me!" he yelled at her, snatching out his gun and striking her across the side of the head. Too dazed to do anything, Gyff crumpled to the sand. "I don't know just exactly how you two ugly shits do it," the young, handsome cop rasped, "but I'll damn well soon find out!"

With his free fist buried deep in her hair, he hauled Gyff to her feet and made to strike her again—at which Hesch came out from under the palm and shouted, "Here I am, you fiend!"

Hesch might simply have zooped the brute back to Earth, but he wanted Gyff to see how things really were—wanted her to see, as he saw, that the gulf between was truly impassable. But as the cop heard Hesch's gravelly voice he released Gyff, turned and fired all in one smooth movement. And Hesch had zooped just in time.

"Here I am," he called again, from farther down the beach. Again the cop whirled, fired off a second shot, and again Hesch zooped. "Here I am—"

But this time, as the black-clad Pretty lined Hesch up in his sights, Gyff gave a little shriek and cried, "No! No more! You…go!" And she pointed at the cop.

He went, leaving an echo, a scream that quickly dwindled into emptiness. Well, Hesch told himself, at least that whore with the pin is no longer alone…wherever she is!

"That was horrible, horrible!" cried Gyff, as Hesch went to her. And throwing herself into his arms, she shuddered and added, "It was like…like a bleedie!"

"You mean to say you fancied him?" Hesch's voice, for all that it grated, somehow managed to signal his disbelief.

"No," she shook her head. "Oh no, never—but he grabbed me while I was running through the city, and—"

"Running?"

"Yes. Oh, Hesch, you can't go back there. You must promise to stay here. The moon has exploded and the world's gone mad!"

"What? The moon, exploded? But how?"

"It must have been an accident," she answered. "It started at the refinery on Darkside, then became a chain reaction. Bits of the moon are flying through space like so much shrapnel, and the tides have gone insane. Polluted tsunami are drowning every coastal town and city in poisoned water, and it seems the whole world is destroying itself…"

"The rotten apple falls from the tree," mused Hesch.

"Hesch," she said, her sigh like broken bottles, "you seem to be so…so good! Won't you stay here with me?"

Hesch opened his mouth, closed it, shrugged, and finally said, "Er, yes. I guess so. Keeping all this going should so easy, with the pair of us working on it…if that's really necessary."

"Maybe one day," she said, after a little while, "we'll even be able to go back."

"I don't think I'll ever want to," he told her. "Maybe we won't need to go back. If the children inherit your ability to make islands, then—"

"Children?" She drew back a pace and squinted up at him. "I've often dreamed of children."

The Ugly Act

"Children, sure," he said, and shrugged. "Why not?"

And when the stars came out, then, warmed by a small fire, they indulged in their own private ugly act. Except it was perfectly beautiful. For after all, beauty lies in the eyes of the beholder…

The Beginning

Irving's Story

Her downstairs knew best, every time.

With sensory apparatus as fine-tuned as his, and little or nothing of dissonance on a typical night to detract from his accustomed nocturnal torpor, any movements however faint, stifled or furtive—but especially the latter—were ever sufficient to bring him starting instantly awake.

Thus it was on the warm summer night in question, when Her Downstairs had chosen to bestir herself and venture out into the midnight gloom...except it wasn't entirely gloomy under a hazy half-moon, and Her Downstairs' outdoor business was instinctive rather than a matter of choice: indeed, a procedure of spontaneous and all but unpremeditated necessity. She had known the time would come, of course, but without preparation or enthusiasm the business itself would be little more than an act of nature. Simply that.

And aware of the life or death importance of knowing the every move of Her Downstairs, Him Upstairs listened intently for the turning of a rusty key as she left the house and secured the door, gave her a moment to move away from the crumbling ruins of the place, then exited his corner and crept silently to the grimy window, one small area of which he kept clean to use as a peep-hole.

A moment for his eyes to adjust to the contrast between the moonlit heaps of pale yellow rubble and the deep dark shadows they cast, and then he saw her: like a shadow herself, the way she moved so surely and silently over and around the fallen walls and piled brick jumbles. She had crossed the deserted, littered street with its broken pavements, cratered and/or erupted tarmac, and was now into a wasteland (once a children's playground) of stained and tattered mattresses, broken furniture and every manner of discarded household equipage, baby carriages minus their wheels and lopsided supermarket trolleys, great sacks of rubbish and mounds of rags which might once have been items of clothing, and multiple heaps of anomalous refuse so rancid they actually steamed in the wan moonlight.

But among all the poisons there was life there, too: rats aplenty, feral cats, even a great wild half-mad dog, but nothing that Her Downstairs feared or tried to avoid; for if out of curiosity or by accident such creatures should come too close she would simply pause and vibrate at them until they went scurrying away, sometimes in pain, depending on her mood and the potency of her oscillations.

There were no paths or markers to follow but she knew the way well enough and proceeded with confidence, halting briefly here and there to look, listen, smell, feel or otherwise *perceive*, the while holding so still that she became more nearly one with the shadows before moving on again.

The wasteland she traversed consisted of several acres of a once-grassy field, long since interred under all the aforementioned dross and garbage from the crumbling ruins of this most desolate quarter of a moribund city. At the back stood a high, sturdy, mainly intact wall which in its time had formed the rearmost boundary of a pleasing landscape of swings, slides, roundabouts and climbing frames, none of which entertainments were any longer visible except for a rusted iron spine or ridge-pole rising over a set of buried swings.

Her Downstairs' route across this potential, in places virtual quagmire, however circuitous due to the avoidance of more obviously corrosive or cankerous areas, nevertheless brought her shortly to a perimeter wall in the lee of which, in a bygone decade, children from a neighbouring district (for at that time there had been no children in this desolate region) had built a ramshackle den by resting a single large sheet of corrugated asbestos atop the wall and wedging it there, and making fast its declining inward edge to a buckled framework of springs and slats that once was a large iron bedstead.

One end of this shack had been closed off with planks that somehow remained in place however loose and rotten, while the other was hung with a heavy black canvas. Inside, a filthy and reeking couch whose splayed castors permitted of little movement, was the only piece of furniture, while a frayed, badly worn rug decorated the mainly uneven floor. As a once playhouse or secluded snug for adventurous children this makeshift but sturdy hut had been adequate; now, as a refuge or nest of sorts for a prospective child or fledgling of an entirely different stripe ... well, it was similarly, satisfactorily inconspicuous. No one but Her Downstairs, and the watcher at the window upstairs, had ventured out there in a while...but now:

He believed he knew what she was about, and despite that she was almost out of sight in the debris-cast shadows of wasteland and wall could well imagine her business out there. After all, this wasn't the first time that something like this had happened, or was about to happen. Him Upstairs had been there himself upon a time—several times in fact—but obviously *never* while she was there; no, definitely not! For having watched her even as he watched her now, he had ventured out much later each time to see what she had achieved; and in a way what he, too, had achieved. For after all, was he not privy—had he not been a party—to its inception? Indeed, without his seminal participation there would have been no act for Her Downstairs to perform.

However, as he now concentrated on gazing through his peep-hole such matters scarcely stirred his mind...

Near the shack's canvas-draped entrance, those long ago children had constructed a sort of barricade or lesser wall, no doubt in order to mask and further disguise the den's presence. And as Him Upstairs sharpened his gaze on that otherwise unremarkable area of wasteland, he continued to observe the stationary upper half of Her Downstairs where she stood before the canvas awning, her lower parts hidden behind the lesser wall. And fascinated he watched the commencement of her transformation: by no means a permanent metamorphosis but one which was nevertheless prerequisite to the imminent maturation of her condition and the alleviation of the intense physical stresses with which she even now burdened herself.

For Her Downstairs appeared to be shrinking away like a rapidly melting candle, decreasing in height and disappearing behind the lesser wall as the trembling outlines of her head and thorax changed and relinquished the semblance—indeed the *precise likeness*—of a human female. Her head was flattening; it grew a spiky black crest, antennae, and more than two globular, multi-facetted eyes. And beneath that now insect head a black, furry, spindle-thin thorax was sprouting twitching twig-like appendages as it settled into the upper surface of a descending, suddenly bulging silken abdomen. Another moment and the transfigured ensemble sank down entirely out of sight as Her Downstairs disappeared behind the low wall, where evidently she squatted in the performance of her travail.

Him Upstairs waited, trembling with excitement, anticipation, as time passed and moment by moment the night deepened. Until eventually, slowly, she thrust up again from behind the wall, her false human-female identity reinstating itself and taking shape complete with its accustomed, flexible and loosely attached tegument in the likeness of the blowsy, skimpy attire generally considered most suitable by certain ladies of the night. This was how she had left the house (it was her guise against the discovery of herself as something other than a woman) and it was how she would return when her work was done—which was not yet, not quite, but shortly.

And cradled in the arms of Her Downstairs, at last the peeper at the window caught a glimpse of that which he had known he would see: the end result of her efforts, not to mention his:

That dully glistening rectangular parcel, carrying which she brushed aside the canvas awning and, hunched over now and more than ever furtive-seeming, bore out of sight into whatever comfort and protection the den could offer.

As for what it was: Him Upstairs knew that well enough. It had become his habit each time she performed this routine and when she was done, to let a day or two pass and then—perhaps in early morning light, or then again in the evening but well before dark—to make his way by a yet more circuitous route to the hidey-hole under the wall. His reason for such secrecy, such caution, when he might follow a more direct path that perhaps matched or closely paralleled hers...

...Ah, but no! It could scarcely be considered a safe, sound practice to follow as a shadow in the steps of Her Downstairs! His pheromones—little more than territorial markers, deterrent to other males of his kind for all that he had never yet confronted such a rarity—would transmit a weak but lingering spoor to such as Her Downstairs, conjuring images of prey in her sensorium ... and more than likely pangs of hunger in her belly.

Yet despite dangers real or imagined, but more likely the former, he would run the gantlet, and not just the once but several times during the coming period of maturation. And so for a starter, tomorrow or the day after, he would take another indirect route to the den on the far perimeter of the wasteland to see what he knew he would see, keeping it in mind against the not so distant future. As for what it was:

An egg-case of sorts: a resilient protective parcel or capsule in which the young of certain species come to maturity. In one of Him Upstairs' unused musty rooms there was a bookshelf, and on the shelf a handful of limp, abandoned books for young children. One of these was a damp, grimy so-called children's encyclopedia, which had long since lost its boards and spine, and consisted of pages of colorful illustrations with brief explanatory texts. The printed words meant nothing at all to him, who could not read, but one of the full-page glossy illustrations in itself told something of a tale without words, so that he could ignore the otherwise meaningless legend: "In a Tidal Pool."

There, pictured in a shallow seaweed-draped pool on a rocky beach, were many living creatures—limpets, winkles, tellins and the like, and the silica and lime remains of such molluscs—along with tiny fishes, crabs, a small lobster, starfish and anemones. But that which had most drawn the attention of Him Upstairs, when the book had fallen open one time at the page in question, was a dull yellowish "Mermaid's Purse," further described (to no avail) as "The egg-case of a skate or shark." For in *almost* every detail other than its dimensions the capsule was the very image of Her Downstairs' occasional deposits at the wasteland shack. As to that last:

From the additional image of a female child seated on a rock at the edge of the pool, Him Upstairs had derived the approximate size of the egg-case as four by two inches, with a thickness of something less than an inch and a half. In other words it was approximately one fifth the size of Her Downstairs' egg-cases, though just like them at each of its four corners it was equipped with a tangle of vestigial byssal filaments. This last probably hinted of some obscure ancestral connection, but Him Upstairs had no real knowledge of that; any reckoning he did was mainly instinctive and self-preserving.

Finally, the pool's illustrated egg-case was semi-opaque, displaying no more than the merest outlines of its foetal contents…. Which was where any further comparison with the issue of Her Downstairs' had come to an abrupt end. For while features suggested by certain vague bulges and curves half-imagined, half-observed through the rubbery, flexible amber skin of the pod in the pool formed *acceptable* outlines of an as yet undeveloped creature of a recognizably earthly nature, the oddly disturbing configurations that Him Upstairs had thought to discern in the capsules in the wasteland shack…quite simply did not. No, not even to Him Upstairs.

Perhaps that was why he felt driven to follow the development of those capsules: as a means of reckoning the approximate time when they would have matured sufficiently to hatch.

Which might be a very good time to stay as far as possible out of the way…

———————

He was Irving or just Irv to the men of one of the demolition teams working on the outskirts of town, something over a mile but less than a mile-and-a-quarter from the derelict area where "he" lived upstairs from "her" below. The men of the team considered him a retard or some kind of throwback—perhaps even a low-grade mutation of sorts—but nothing so bad as to require action by "the authorities." There were lots of twisted kids around these days. And anyway he was strong as a horse and often laboured long hours for next to nothing.

Fortunately his protean cells, like those of her below, allowed for a degree of variability. He passed for human, however imperfectly, and must wear an uncomfortable corset that irritated and compressed the chitin-cased legs of his lower-thorax into his upper abdomen, but for as long as was necessary his shape-changing DNA could cope with just about everything else. His multi-faceted eyes had been the only other real difficulty, which he had resolved by wearing dark glasses with wide side-piece supports. And so, while he accepted that what must be must be, he was always glad to get home of an evening, upstairs and out of sight, where he could remove these accessories and relax into his proper form.

As for what the demolition men were doing there on the edge of town: they were reducing to rubble those buildings considered too far gone to be worthy of further occupation. The blast of the so-called "conventional low-yield nuke" that had destroyed the town centre some twenty-seven years ago had utterly wrecked its entire infrastructure and threatened the integrity of the housing as far out as the furthest suburb, where now a majority of the buildings stood like stacks of badly balanced dominoes ready to topple at a moment's notice—or even without one.

Likewise the lone and slightly leaning structure that housed Him and Her, which had barely survived the bomb and now offered meager shelter. There was no power and no water but what the rain brought, which sufficed for their needs. As for food—well, that was why Him Upstairs worked: in order to buy meat and sugar (and beer, of which he was inordinately fond,) and why Her Downstairs, with needs of her own, was a prostitute.

The wreckers had been here, obviously, but that was a quarter century ago, when they'd been obliged to work against the clock by virtue of the lingering radioactivity. Then too a handful of kids from

70

the closest habitable region had built their den against the wasteland's rear wall, which they'd been obliged to leave to the elements when the radiation warning signs went up on the perimeters of all the contaminated areas.

This area, in fact, hadn't been too badly poisoned, though initially and closer to ground zero—where Him and Her had evolved—conditions had been quite deadly. The town centre was on the coast, for this had been a touristy, seaside place seventy or so years ago, before the nuclear power station was built only a few miles away. That was what The Enemy had targeted throughout the entire length and breadth of the country: all the major power sources, as well as the cities, and the centres of industry and finance. However, some radioactivity had been leaking from the power station into the sea for a great many years before the brief but terrible war with its additional toxins … which probably explains something of the eventual emergence of such as Her and Him.

Him Upstairs had a friend among "the wreckers," as the men of the demolition team called themselves. Jim Salmon was the one who drove an ancient Toyota right through the wasteland area most mornings on his way to work. And whenever he saw Irv walking in his jerky fashion along the ravaged, littered road, he would stop and give him a lift. "Gonna make yourself a little cash today, Irv? Buy yourself some cigarettes, a six pack of local brew, maybe a woman?" And then his catarrhal laughter, for no reason that would have made sense to Irving: "Har! Har!"

"Money for bacon, sssugar, beer," Irv had told him, nodding and trying to control the sibilant, sometimes plangent buzz of his delivery. "No womansss."

"'Cos you can't find one who'd be interested in a freak like you, eh? Not even the one who I get ter see every other Friday night? You musta seen her, might even know her; she has ter live around here somewheres. I usually pick her up from where she's standin' on one of the corners hereabouts, and she fixes me up in the car. Usually jus' a hand or blowjob, you know? Actually, I prefer the hand. Tried the mouth once...Jesus, like stickin' it in a fuckin' big pencil sharpener! Offered her money for a proper fuck, but for what I was willin' ter pay she wouldn't wear it. And anyway I couldn't wait around that long—me missus would get suspicious—Har! Har! And *anyway* anyway, on the strength of that blowjob, it would be like shaggin' a cement mixer! Har! Har! Har!" And of course it was big fat Jim with his toothless, warty face, tiny squinting eyes and gangly apelike arms who had been the first of the men to call Him Upstairs a freak!

"Not know her," Irving had been wise enough to shrug and shake his head. "Not sssee her." Which had signaled the end of their conversation as Salmon returned his attention to avoiding the road's heaped debris and yawning potholes...

There were maybe a dozen wreckers on the job in the district where Him Upstairs performed casual work, which consisted mainly of fetching and carrying: "Bring me this," or "Take this over there," stuff. In his workmates' terms Irving was given nothing too complicated for his "retarded brain" to comprehend; but still this had been sufficient in *his* terms that over a not inconsiderable period he had garnered a basic cache of words—a mainly elementary assemblage of grunted commands and their meanings—into his spongy sensorium.

In the early days he had worked for almost nothing, simply hoping to be rewarded in terms of cash or credit in order to acquire the one or two things he needed or enjoyed; he didn't have enough of Her Downstairs' audacity to press for more, despite that where physical effort was concerned he worked at least as hard as any of the wreckers. Then again he didn't need more, but after a while the gaffer had taken pity on him anyway and jokingly put him on the payroll as a "tea lady," in order to justify paying him his pittance; this despite that Irving had never brewed a cup in his relatively short life and never would, and was anything but a "lady"—or even a human being for that matter!

On evenings at five o'clock, when the wreckers knocked off, Jim Salmon would offer "the retard" a lift and Him Upstairs would accept, only to dismount from the rusting Toyota a crafty quarter mile from home, continuing on foot and unobserved to his and one other's dilapidated abode. Then, entering the house through a hole in the wall at the rear, he would creep as quietly as possible upstairs.

Oh, if she was home Her Downstairs always heard him, of that he felt sure, and there might even be some indefinite, anomalous movement—a shuddersome *stirring*—in the deeper, darker indoors shadows, but she rarely bothered him except on certain few and far between occasions when she required him to become…an accessory.

Now, as the weeks lengthened into months following her latest *deposit* in the shack on the wasteland's rim, Him Upstairs shrank from the likely imminence of another of those infrequent "requests" for his assistance; an invitation which, lured by her pheromones, he had never been able to refuse, even though instinctively—

—He dreaded it…

And sure enough, the next Friday evening saw Him Upstairs' calculations—more properly his instinctive forebodings—proving themselves well-founded.

The first warning came when riding home with Jim Salmon in the latter's antique Toyota. "Well, Irv," said that one, "tonight's the night!"

And while ordinarily Irv wouldn't reply—would not engage in common or garden conversation except to answer as best possible well-defined questions—this time Salmon's obviously excited statement at once galvanized his curiosity. "What happensss tonight, Jim?"

"I'm seein' *her* tonight," the other replied. "That's what 'appens!"

"Ssseeing her?"

"Yers, the woman. The one who pumps me piston. Or maybe I'll risk another blowjob, 'cos when it 'urts it's sometimes that much sweeter—know what I mean? No, you probably wouldn't. Anyway, 'ow does a bloke like you get your jollies, Irv? Self-sufficient, are you? Har! Har!"

And: "Ssself-sssufficient," Him Upstairs had answered with a nod, hoping his reply would suffice without being at all sure what Salmon had meant other than he'd asked a question. But as for the rest of their conversation—Salmon's talk of "the woman" and of "tonight"—oh, Irv had understood that well enough.

For tonight was Friday, one of those "every other" Friday nights...

———————

Later:

Him Upstairs had stayed alert, awaiting the unmistakable clatter of Salmon's old banger as it drove slowly past the house, and aware of Her Downstairs' not quite so passive, indeed impatient bumping around in the ground floor's shadows. Normally she would be up and about shortly after dark—especially every other Friday—but tonight, like Irving himself, she'd been listening for the banging and rattling of the Toyota. She had not wanted to venture too far from the wasteland, not tonight, because it really wouldn't any longer matter if Salmon met her close to her decaying old refuge or even caught her emerging from it; he wouldn't after all be talking about it, and the closer to the wasteland shack they met the better.

So that just a few seconds after Salmon's old car with its shaky dipped headlights had gone jerking and clanking past the front of the house, Her Downstairs' unusually anxious-seeming activity had abruptly abated as she moved to the foot of the stairs. And her colloidal secretions were undeniable where they wafted up to Irv, coaxing him from his cluttered corner roost to the landing on the upper floor, where he waited with the equivalent of bated breath as she told him:

"I wisssh you to attend. Do you undersssstand?" Her Downstairs' physical speech was as sibilant and plangent as his own, but enhanced by a series of subtly symbolic bodily motions—however poorly he perceived them in the building's gloom—and reinforced by the potent, near-hypnotic pheromones she employed, her wishes could neither be misinterpreted nor denied. And:

"I understsssand," he replied shakily from the landing.

"Then go there now, at once!" she commanded. "Go there, to where he fightsss the fabric for hisss freedom!" And:

"I go!" he replied, but stayed glued to the spot until she had gone out into the night. And only then did he move...down the creaking stairs and out of the house, and across the old rubbish tip of a playground—this time by the shortest route—to the shack under the wall. And there, making no attempt to enter the elsewise deserted den, he hid himself in the rubble nearby and *heard* (or more properly perceived) the scratching and the scrabbling from where: "he was fighting the constraining fabric of his egg for his freedom"…and for whatever else he craved; but most obviously, as Him *from* Upstairs remembered from his own birth, for nourishment, victuals—food!

And oh, Irving's hunger had been vast and undeniable! Only the all-powerful *she* had been safe from such newborn savagery, yet even *she* had taken no chances but had brought her burgeoning child that with which to stave off his craving: a human customer of hers who she had been grooming especially for his birthing, even as she now groomed Jim Salmon. And with her help, her instruction by performance or perpetration, such shrieking initial *pabulum* had sufficed until in a while Irving had developed tastes and preferences of his own…

But that had been then and this was now, when shortly, as he crouched naked in the wasteland rubble down to his natural, unmodified arthropodal chitin and uncorseted spindle-legged furry abdomen, he heard or sensed something other than the efforts of the would-be hatchling in the shack: Her *from* Upstairs with her victim Jim Salmon, on their approach across the surrounding desolation.

"Why out here?" Salmon was asking her. "Why in this place among all the garbage, when we could be comfortable in that ruin you came out of, or even in the car? What the hell is different about tonight?"

"It's different, yesss," she replied. "Because it's ssspecial!"

"Special? But it's just a hand job! What's special about that?"

"You'll sssee, you'll sssee…" And Irving could see them now, where they arrived at the den.

"Wait here for jussst a moment," she continued speaking to Salmon, as they paused behind the low wall in front of the canvas awning, "Jussst a moment, yesss, while I fix thingsss inssside."

75

But as she vanished behind the canvas she called silently to Irving: *Come now! Ssstrike him down, bring him insside and asssissst me!* None of which was new to Irving.

At the last moment Salmon heard Irv's low buzzing as he crept upon him, looming out of inky shadows into wan moonlight. Then he saw Irv—as he really was and in his entirety! And:

"Arghhh!" Salmon gurgled, staggering drunkenly and flailing leaden arms as he tried to ward off this man-sized crustacean or cockroach-thing. And: "Huh?—Huh!—*Arghhh!*" once again, as he stumbled and Irv seized the opportunity to cosh him with nine inches of rusty iron pipe. Down he went, but before he could hit the compacted debris underfoot Irv had him by the collar of his overcoat and was dragging him into the den through the awning held open by the female thing.

"Good! Good!" she approved of Irv's efforts, buzzing feverishly and blowing bubbles from her clashing mouthparts as he hoisted Salmon's heavy, inertly sagging body up onto the couch. "And now you mussst help me with thisss." For having completely cast off her human guise she was down on all sixes, tearing at a tangle of byssal filaments at one of the corners of the hugely expanded, throbbing and jerking egg-case.

Unable to refuse—with his receptors swamped by pheromone emissions that numbed every instinct with the possible exception of self-preservation, and weakened even that—Irv joined her on the worn carpet and went to work with his forelegs and mandibles on the bundle of filaments furthest from hers, a diagonal distance of some four and a half feet now that the softened, less than opaque parcel had stretched under the growth and frantic struggles of its contents. And no sooner had Irv added his efforts to the task of freeing the larval creature than the overtaxed capsule ruptured, splitting apart along one end, corner and side, releasing from within a sticky, thorny, voracious infant.

But there are infants, and there are infants.

If Irv, when alone upstairs, had leafed a little further through that forsaken so-called "Child's Encyclopedia" on the rickety bookshelf, he might have come across pictures of a different sort of pool—a freshwater pool—with creatures in many ways unlike the saltwater variety. And whether he had understood or not, among these he might well have seen images of dragonfly larvae: those merciless killers and devourers of lesser pond life, even younger, smaller members of their own species!

For in a certain respect Nature's creations—even those born of accidental nuclear mutation, which after all has been part and parcel of all evolution since the first primordial life came into being—are limited, despite their multiformity, by an apparently restraining design which decrees that at birth they will all hunger, indiscriminately and cold-bloodedly, and attempt to feed on whatever presents itself, be it a nipple, a leaf or another caterpillar. Many infants, of course, are helpless to feed themselves, while other newborns like the dragonfly and greater water-beetle larvae…are not.

Half-in, half-out of its egg-case, the monstrous *issue* of Irv and Irv's mother at first attacked the latter, biting at her currently slender abdomen. Buzzing loudly (with parental pride? Possibly) she nevertheless thrust it aside. It immediately attacked Irv, clamping its mandibles on one of his spindly thorax legs and biting right through it close to the first chitin-clad joint. At once reacting to the pain and realizing something of the damage the thing had inflicted, he managed to hurl his son up and away from him, so that the spiny, slimy, wildly flailing thing landed on the figure lying prone on the couch. And as Irv backed away on his uninjured lower legs, stumbling blindly into the canvas awning and tearing it down, thus allowing yellow moonlight to flood the shack—that was the moment when Jim Salmon chose to regain consciousness.

He woke up, saw the nightmarish thing sitting on him, opened his mouth to scream…and issued a mere grunt, little more than a gurgle, as the horror thrust pincer-like mandibles into his gaping mouth and nipped off his tongue at the root, while claw-tipped forelegs hacked at his face and throat, almost at once unhinging his lower jaw. And as the rest of the hatchling's legs clutched Salmon's jerking body in a vice-like grip, so the starveling thing broke into his skull and began eating him from the brain down.

Irv didn't wait to see the rest, whatever that would be. For even as it ate, so the thing's eyes—his son's (and brother's!) multi-faceted eyes, with a myriad moons reflected in them—were foll-owing his every movement, watching him oh so intently! As for its mother: having for the time being exhausted her pheromones, she no longer tried to command Irv's attention, his obedience, but was buzzing loudly and *almost* continuously as she joined in the terrible feasting. And she too, between taking sucking, bloody bites from Salmon's lower body, was watching Irv in what seemed to him to be a very speculative, even anticipatory manner…

In another moment he fled—running on all limbs bar the missing, lesser one, whose twiggy stump trailed a thin stream of ichor—across the wasteland and debris-strewn road, in through the hole at the back of the house, up the stairs and into his corner. And lacking orders or instructions, lost as to whether and where to hide himself away, (and what then?) in the spongy core of his sensorium Irv felt the shame of his counterfeit disloyalty and feared its consequences…

In too short a time, however, there were new and very different chemical effusions drifting in from across the wasteland. Pervading the atmosphere, they spread however invisibly like ink spilt in water, and Irv's apprehensions, slowly at first but soon gathering pace, evaporated away…

For until now Her Downstairs' had been satisfied to hold Him Upstairs in thrall, demanding his compliance with those colloidal emissions designed to render him submissive, but making no effort to assist him when he was attacked. And he remembered how it had been when *he* was born: how she had stood off, signaling and buzzing her approval as he savaged to death both his father and the unfortunate human being she had provided for him. The memory had grown dim, for after all he had been newborn, with everything still to learn, but now it sprang to mind as if it had happened only yesterday: he had fed, then fled, scampering away across the wasteland, only to return before morning and burrow in the debris to escape the light and heat of the rising sun.

As for the rest: that had been instinct. As day followed day, becoming weeks and months, Irv had matured, and as he ripened he had first felt what he was feeling now, which from the beginning had served to draw him back here: the lure of Her Downstairs' seductive secretions, her prurient promise of sexual delights that only a single remaining shred of instinctive self-preservation caused him to doubt. For he more than suspected that he had fathered the *next* father, and would father no more.

And again the urge was on him to flee, put distance between himself and her whose only care was for the survival and continuity of species. Had she birthed a female creature things might be different; but no, the half dozen young Irv had fathered with his mother had all been male, with not one female among them to take over when she was done. Perhaps it was his fault: a genetic disorder in a species so recently evolved that its future was not yet secure; but whatever, Him Upstairs had had chances enough.

Also, while it was not unusual that Her Downstairs would be sexually receptive at this time, Irv had never known her to be so quick off the mark following a grand banquet at the birth site; normally she preferred to rest, sometimes for weeks, after eating her fill. Which was why he had felt—albeit briefly, as her pheromones perverted his sensorium—the urge to flee.

But no longer, because now she had seduced him yet again, and as she approached from across the wasteland Him Upstairs trembled with arthropod passion as his reproductive system prepared a packet of sperm. And creeping from his corner to the landing he waited to hear the squeal of Her Downstairs rusty key as she let herself into the house. She entered, shed the human form which she had reestablished against being observed in her original likeness, and without pause came to the foot of the stairs. There she turned her back on the stairwell, lifted her tail and issued her lustful scents in increasingly extravagant volume, the while buzzing a song of lying, dissolute craving. And unable to resist her, Him Upstairs fell for it.

Except he didn't fall but jumped, with his grasping limbs outspread and his organ extended—descending as a parachutist descends before pulling his rip-cord—and all to no avail. For midway in his flight Her Downstairs flipped over onto her back, her scorpion stinger uppermost and rigid, her pincer claws eager to clutch...and no way Irv could slow his fall or even deflect it.

As he slammed down on her she stung him, transfixed him, and before Irv's writhing could damage her stinger, used her vibratory function to hold him still as he rapidly stiffened and far more slowly died. And all the while as he died she buzzed him a sad song of farewell.

She would eat him later, or perhaps save him for their son when he returned—as she knew he would, of course—to initiate the next phase of the cycle...

The Running Man

It may be true you can run—but as for finding a place to hide...?

Chapter I

Now? Now, I wouldn't even fool with a Ouija board, not for my life. You won't even catch me reading a ghost story! But at that time...

I was a teacher—mathematics and associated subjects, especially geometrics—at a school in North London. A bit boring, really. Not much call for triangles and circles in North London, not even then. But of course in those days the word "square" only meant a parallelogram with four equal sides and four right angles. It would be another-twenty odd years before it became slang for anything else.

Those days—the mid '30's—before The War. So long ago, and still the thing preys on my mind and probably always will...

In my spare time I had become interested in the work—or the pastime—of a small but dedicated group which called itself the Society for the Higher Resolution of the Unquiet Dead. SHROUD for short. Londoners all, we termed ourselves "psychic investigators", and, on long weekends or holidays, would go off and sample the spectral atmospheres of England's ancestral haunts.

Not that the house in Cambridgeshire (standing almost at the junction of three counties: Cambridgeshire, Lincolnshire and Norfolk) was well known for its phenomena; it certainly wasn't "listed". But we were interested anyway, for our own reasons. More of that anon...

There were five of us in our particular group; we'd all chipped in, and the estate agent had been glad to get the place off his hands, even as a few days let...it was that unpopular! Harkness, one of our group, had gone up the weekend before and secured it; he'd been on a business trip for his boss but got back to attend SHROUD's monthly meeting at *The Waggoners.* Cocooned in a corner away from the rest of the crowd, Harkness told us all about it:

"Got the rooms for a song!" He was jubilant, grinning from ear to ear. "Has to be something wrong with a once-grand old place like that when you can get it mid-season for a few quid!"

"What's it like?" asked Jackson, our self-appointed leader, who once actually (or allegedly) had seen a ghost. I had heard his account several times, and... Frankly, I doubted it. But he was the sort that has to be the star attraction or life has lost all meaning. He was surly, too, and occasionally aloof when speaking to those less "psychically inclined", which probably accounted for my dislike.

"Does it have any amenities?" I wanted to know.

Harkness read from notes he'd prepared. "Toilets, two up and one down; bathrooms likewise; two rooms with showers, I got them both. Both a bit dated but in reasonably good order. Ground-floor kitchen half-modernized, but both need a gas cylinder for cooking; not guaranteed but the proprietor will sell us good unused ones if we need 'em. Bedrooms galore, but only two double beds in each. Musty old mattresses but dubious sheets, blankets or pillows, so it's a sleeping-bag job... Well, for me anyway. A massive open fireplace downstairs, which we won't need—if we do, there's a great pile of wood stacked out in the gardens. Oh yes, and no lights! They won't switch the juice on just for a few days. There are two old oil lamps, which I fixed up while I was there."

"A dump!" commented Jackson, sourly.

But I felt obliged to say: "What do you want, a haunted house or an all mod-cons overlooking the bay?"

Jackson turned his cold gaze on me. "You're new to this game, aren't you?" He was maybe thirty, slim, had a habit of staring unblinkingly through his small specs. His hair was going a bit thin and his cheeks were slightly hollow. He liked to think of himself as cadaverous, bookish, erudite—I considered him a poseur.

I shrugged. "So? I mean, we're going up there to investigate paranormal phenomena—not for a seaside outing! This is my first one, yes, but I'll probably spot anything weird just as quickly as you."

He sniffed. "That remains to be seen."

"What about supplies?" George Ainsworth spoke up. He was our youngest, maybe twenty-three, short and blocky and scruffy as hell. A rough diamond, there wasn't an ounce of malice in him. And he was an expert photographer. "Is the village close by? I don't want to cart a load of photographic kit up there if it's right on our doorstep."

"Village? Village?" cried Peter Harkness. "Hey, I'll tell you about a village!" He was around thirty-five. Enthusiastic, but big, slow-moving and watery eyed, and so eager to please that people tended to lean on him a bit. He always seemed to buy far more rounds than his turn; chief beneficiary, Graham Jackson, of course.

"Shh!" cautioned our fifth member, urging restraint. Clive Thorne was our oldest and world-wisest. He'd served a long term with the Army, and not quite settled down yet. But he was strong and inspired confidence. He was maybe five feet eleven, and all muscle. "Calm down," he said. "Half this lot at the bar will be up there with us if you're not careful!" SHROUD's several cliques guarded their finds fiercely.

Harkness lowered his voice. "Village?" he whispered. "Well, there's Guyhirn just a couple of miles away. But across the fens toward Crowland is a *real* find. It's not on the latest maps, except maybe Ordnance Survey—but haunted? Lord, even if the Oaks wasn't there, it would still be worth visiting *that* place! It was a village four hundred years ago, but now it's done, decayed, falling apart. I spotted it from a dormer window at the Oaks; a spire out across the fens. Only a few miles as the crow flies, but it seemed like ten. The road winds like a snake; you come through a copse…and there it is! Two tumbledown

streets crossing each other at a disused church, and a corner pub called
The Running Man."

"A pub, eh?" Thorne smacked his lips. "But not a hotel, right?"

Harkness lowered his voice a little, and said: "No, sorry about
that—but we'll be all right for a pie and a pint when we're up and
about! And anyway, this pub's got a whole lot more than that going for
it. "Its sign is the weirdest thing I've ever seen. In fact you won't believe
it! My eyes are fine long distance, but lousy close up, so I couldn't make
out the finer details. But there's this ragged bloke on the sign, and
he's…"

"What, running?" Jackson cut in, with a derisive snort.

"…*And* he's bleeding!" Harkness continued. "I mean, he's wild-
eyed and his clothes are torn, and he's got blood dripping off him!
Horrible!"

"You're sure it's not a slaughterhouse?" I chuckled, trying to
brighten things up a bit.

"It's a pub!" Harkness actually scowled at me. "I found my way to
it, went in and asked about the sign. The barman told me it's from a
legend almost as old as the village. How one night a man, all torn and
bleeding, had gone stumbling through the streets pursued by three
cowled figures in black. No one helped him, because there'd been
rumours of plague…He might be a plague carrier, and the cowled men
would be priests trying to help him. But they weren't! A woman in her
cottage saw them catch him, take out carving knives, *and cut him up into
little bits!* Which they put in sacks and carried away, back the way
they'd come."

Throne grunted, said: "Certainly sounds weird enough!"

"Anyway," Harkness finished it off, "then the plague came. The
village was hard hit—people thought it was the punishment of God—
the land around turned barren and the survivors moved out. Came
decline and decay. Now there's only the crossroads, and a few tottering
old houses…"

"I'm convinced," I broke the silence. "Even if the Oaks doesn't come up to scratch as a base to work from, visiting that ghost town will make the trip worth it. Especially *The Running Man*."

Ainsworth said: "And I've *got* to get pictures of that old pub sign!"

"Better still," Harkness nodded, "pictures of the *original* sign! The old boy at the pub has it, keeps it locked away for its value. The one outside is a copy. He didn't have the time right then, but he said next time I was in I could see it."

After that we settled down to drinking, made the rest of our arrangements, passed a pleasant but otherwise unspectacular evening. A pity I can't say the same about the time to come...

Chapter II

Monday morning bright and early, we were on our way north in Clive Thorne's people-carrying banger, Harkness' boss' car in a garage having "turned nasty" at the end of his recce. It was an A1 motorway ride at first, more than halfway to Peterborough with Thorne at the wheel, Jackson sitting up front with his pipe, and myself in the back with the others thumbing through our so-called "literature": books and pamphlets on famous haunted houses and other parapsychological cases. On the way, Jackson had poisoned the atmosphere, puffing on his evil pipe and boring us silly yet again with the interminable story of his ghost, embellishing it just a little bit more each time he told it.

"So there I was," he finished off on the approach to Peterborough, "left all cold and clammy, and this shining, spectral *thing* drifting off into the woods. For all I know, it's still there, but I've had enough of that one" (as had we) "and never been back..."

"Anyway," said Thorne, who had been dying to change the subject for what felt like a good many hours, "that was then and this is now. So, what about these disappearances from *The Oaks*, eh? Here we go, off to investigate this poor old house—which might well be entirely innocent—all on the strength of a few people vanishing in or around it! It was you who stumbled across the connection, wasn't it, Graham?"

Jackson, puffing away, answered between puffs: "Well, I've a sharp eye for that sort of thing. I was doing some newspaper research, came across some interesting facts. Summer of '32, young London couple on the run, heading for Gretna Green. They detoured and ended up at The Oaks, hired it for a fortnight. Alas, the girl's father had put an ad in the papers and offered a reward for word of their whereabouts. A local spotted them in the village, and the game was up. Daddy came rumbling up from the family hearth; him and a couple of burly lads broke down the door and burst in. The kids' clothes were there, their sleeping things and other personal belongings—but no sign of them! Not then and never since…"

"Interesting," Thorne nodded. "Suicide pact, d'you think?"

"Well if it was," said Jackson, "they probably made the pact in that abandoned house. Second case: two years ago an old tramp breaks in, lives there for a couple of days. The police get wind of it, and since they're looking for a burglar or petty thief, they pay him a visit. But it's the same story: his things are there—not that he'd ever possessed very much—but he's not."

"On top of which," Harkness broke in, "there's the atmosphere of the place. Wait and see for yourselves…But you wouldn't find me staying there on my own, I can tell you!"

"Well, you're not on your own," said Thorne, "so stop worrying about it. And anyway, that's what we're here for." Following which, we were all pretty thoughtful and quiet…

Coming through Guyhirn toward The Oaks, in an outlying huddle of fairly ancient houses covered in ivy and flaking paint, we passed a square-towered old church. Opposite stood the local pub and restaurant—not *The Running Man*, but to Clive Thorne a pub was a pub! "A pie and a pint!" he cried jubilantly. "We'll dump our stuff, nip back here for lunch."

Then Guyhirn was behind us, and Harkness directed Thorne down a third-class road for several miles to the lonely old hotel, *The Oaks*.

And if we'd had our doubts before, just seeing that old place told us we'd been worrying needlessly. Or, on the other hand, worrying with good cause, depending on your point of view…

The proprietor of the place was waiting for us with the keys. We were right on time and paid cash there and then, which pleased him no end. He wasn't much of a one for hanging about; seeing us inside, he gave us a few hurried dos and don'ts and was on his way in less than five minutes. We'd have liked to start exploring right there and then, but Thorne's suggestion about feeding ourselves seemed a good one. So we dumped our stuff and drove straight back to the pub.

George Ainsworth had a half-pint with the rest of us at *The Two Coaches*, then excused himself; he wanted to photograph the church. He liked to rub brasses, too, so churches interested him. He came back fifteen minutes later with the verger and introduced him: Mr. Applebury. Applebury was small, round and friendly, quite extrovert and not averse to throwing back a pint of best beer. He ordered, smiled and said: "George says you're staying at *The Oaks?*"

"That's right," Jackson eyed him down his nose. "A very atmospheric place, we believe."

Applebury nodded. "Yes, you've picked a good one there—if ghosts are your game. Myself, I'm not a believer—in ghosts I mean!" He chuckled. "But if I was, I'd have to believe they're here. At the house, the church across the road there, this whole area."

"You know the history of the region, then?" I invited him to sit with us. Jackson grudgingly made room.

"I know the history of the church," Applebury shrugged. "A church is always a focus down the centuries. Births, deaths and marriages, records, old legends. You want to know about a place, visit its churches."

"Tell us about your ghosts," Thorne invited, "Er—that's the ones you don't believe in."

"I'll tell you something about *The Oaks*, if you like, for what it's worth—and a snippet or two of church history. The two are connected, you see. At the turn of the 16th Century, the plague was bad hereabouts, and of course the church was a haven. Somewhere in the local fields there's supposed to be a mass grave, so the dead are certainly here. But you'll have to find your own ghosts. I only deal in facts, not fictions."

"We're all ears," said Jackson dryly.

"Please go on," I urged before the arrogant sod could put Applebury off. "You mentioned the plague. What, as far back as 1340-50?"

Applebury soon set me right. "Ah, no! The Black Death was only the beginning. It raged for two years, but, after that, scarcely a decade went by without a resurgence. Right up to the end of the 18th Century. One such outbreak, called simply 'the plague', occurred here in 1596 — and the locals blamed it on a peculiar sect who at the time had their own 'church' or headquarters, at *The Oaks*."

"Three hundred and fifty years ago?" Jackson sounded skeptical. "Well, we haven't yet had a good look at the place, but I wouldn't say it was *that* old!"

Applebury shook his head. "You misunderstand me. The *present* house will be fairly recent, a hundred and fifty years maximum. But its foundations, maybe even its end walls, are as old as the church across the road; for the first house was built there about the same time — early 16th Century. It's in the records. The family didn't prosper and the last of the line moved to London about 1580. Then, for a long time, the house stood empty. Too far out from the village, and too expensive to be purchased from local purses..."

Jackson was beginning to take notice. He glanced at our rapt expressions. "What did I tell you? This is all good background stuff! I'll probably do a pamphlet on *The Oaks* for the AGM next month."

I urged Applebury to go on. "But surely *The Oaks* hasn't stood empty as long as all that? Anyway, you said there'd been a second house built on the foundations."

He held up his hands. "Whoa! Let me finish telling you what I know of the whole story." And, after a moment: "In the late 1500's, in the reign of Queen Elizabeth I, the Chorazos Cult had a chapter in

London. The cult was pagan and worse than pagan, and it's members a polyglot bunch to say the least. Originating in the mountains of Romania, there were nevertheless Chinamen among them. Africans and Arabs, Hungarians and, and as you'd expect, Romanians. Their leader 'Chorazos'—we know him under no other name—had been a gypsy. They had come to England as 'refugees', from what we don't know; possibly they'd been hounded out of their native lands.

"In 1595, they were hounded out of London, too, but we do know a bit about that. Apparently their 'Temple' in Finchley was an opium den full of whores, rife with orgiastic ceremonies and perversions. Human sacrifices—to whom and for what purpose?—were seemingly regular occurrences…

"Eventually the Queen ordered an investigation—on the advice of Dr. John Dee, incidentally, of all persons!—and the place in Finchley was destroyed. Ah, but Chorazos and his principle 'priests' had already made their exit! A year later, they turned up in Scotland where they carried on as before. Not a wise move: Elizabeth might be interested in astrology, alchemy and the like—she had a leaning toward the occult, too—but James IV of Scotland found all such practices abominations!

"Doubtless James would have acted, but in the end it was taken out of his hands. Chorazos had built his temple in the lee of the Pentland Hills. But after the disappearance of a number of village children and some young adults, the people of Penicuik rose up in a body and…that was the end of the sect.

"And now you'll ask, 'what has this to do with us, especially with *The Oaks*, eh? I'll tell you—or rather, I'll ask you: what about the missing year—between 1595 and 1596? Where was the Chorazos Cult situated then, eh?"

"They were here?" This from Thorne.

Applebury nodded. "And their centre of operations?"

"*The Oaks!*" And that was me.

"So there you have it!" Applebury beamed.

Jackson had grown skeptical again. It was plain to see that—to him—all of this sounded too good to be true. "And the connection with the old church across the road?"

"Ah! Well, that's in the church records. The parson at that time was a portly fire-eater named, appropriately enough, Goodly. He took against the sect from the first. There had been the usual disappearances, etc.—ladies of—*ahem*—dubious character were known to frequent the 'ceremonies' at *The Oaks;* and worse, when Goodly himself attempted to enquire the nature of the worship there... Chorazos roundly cursed his church and the entire area! And looking around now, at the regional decay, I'm tempted to believe that the curse is still extant!" he sighed.

"Any description of this Chorazos?" George Ainsworth wanted to know. "A sketch, or maybe a painting? Something I could photograph?"

"*Huh!*" Jackson snorted. "That's asking for jam on it!"

Applebury raised his eyebrows a little. Pointedly ignoring the obnoxious Jackson, he spoke to the rest of us. "Town records often did include contemporary sketches and paintings—you're quite correct, George—but not this time. No, the cultists were something the townspeople would rather forget—especially after they turned on them and burned The Oaks down!" He saw our expressions. "Oh, yes! That's how the people dealt with the sect in the end. So...no pictures, I'm afraid. There's a painting of old 'Hellfire Goodly', yes, but not one of them. A description, however, might be easier to come by. I think we might supply that. If you'd care to finish up here and come across the road with me to the church...?"

Chapter III

An hour later, on our way back to *The Oaks*, Thorne asked, "So, what did you make of it all?" He was speaking to all of us, but Graham Jackson answered him first:

"Black-cowled foreigners, like a monkish order? Services dedicated to some alien 'god' called Yot-Sottot? Human sacrifices?" He shrugged. "Obvious, isn't it? Demon-worship, what else? Trouble is, the idiot villagers burned the place down! I've read somewhere that ghosts don't often survive that sort of thing. It's like an exorcism. Like when they used to burn witches."

While he talked, I thought back on our visit to the church. Personally, I'm not much of a one for churches, and couldn't tell a font from a transept. Applebury had taken us down the central aisle of the huge, echoing old place to a small room at the rear. He'd hurried us along, and I'd noticed he was sweating. "Count the rows," he'd suggested, breathlessly. "Of pews, I mean. See what figures you get."

It had seemed an odd request, but we did it anyway, counting off the rows of seats to ourselves. At the door to the room at the rear, he said: "Well?"

Jackson shrugged. "I lost count," he said. Obviously he hadn't bothered.

"Twenty-six," I spoke up.

"What?" Thorne seemed surprised, glanced back down the hollow belly of the old building. "More like thirty six, surely?"

We all looked back, tried to count the pews from where we stood. But the light was poor and a dim sun, burning through high stained glass windows, struck motes of floating dust and made the place smoky and ethereal.

"Odd perspective, isn't it?" said Jackson, scratching his chin.

"Yes, it is," Applebury nodded, his Adam's apple visibly wobbling. I stared at him, decided he looked a little…afraid?

"Odd perspective…perspective…perspective…"

It was only an echo, but sharp and clear, and it came a full minute after Jackson's original statement! It startled all of us, especially Applebury. Offering up a sickly sort of look, he said: "The acoustics in here are…they're sometimes more temporal than spacial." Without explaining his meaning, he'd then led us away into the small back room.

91

As we went in I heard George Ainsworth muttering, "Well, *I* counted twenty-two rows!"

"There was a time," said Applebury, who seemed recovered now, "when this room was used as a vestry. It's rarely used at all now, and more of a library for church records than anything else." We could see what he meant.

There were a good many ledgers and folders atop the oak desks; other tomes, Holy Bibles, manuscripts, and records leather-bound into books covering many decades, were displayed on shelves behind dusty glass. Peter Harkness looked about, traced a line with his finger in the dust on the wooden arm of a chair, seemed puzzled...Much the same as me, I supposed.

I turned to Applebury, said: "You're verger here? But this place hasn't been used in...in a long time!" It was a guess, but it was correct.

"It's voluntary," he said quickly. "These days I'm more a watchman, really, a caretaker. I'm just looking after it until they pull it down. Which they will, God willing, sooner rather than later!" After that, he turned a little sour, applied himself to our business and got finished with it as quickly as possible. When we left the place and he locked up, I noticed how relieved he seemed to be out of there...And I wondered what it was he believed in, if not in ghosts...?

"Yot-Sottot," said Peter Harkness with a grimace, breaking into my thoughts. "I mean, there's a name to conjure with. I never saw that in any demonology before! It sort of, well, *feels* evil!"

"I don't know how it feels," Jackson snorted, "but it *sounded* like so much waffle to me!"

"It was all there in those old books," I reminded him. "Dated, even signed by old 'Hellfire Goodly' himself. Waffle? It was authenticated. And I'd say it *is* authentic."

"Me too," said Thorne, driving the car into the grounds of *The Oaks*. We piled out, entered the old building, began to explore and get the feel of the place. Thorne wandered into the kitchen, but his voice came back to us: "It was authentic, all right. Too much background detail not to be. 'Great Old Ones' who came down from the stars when the world was young. Kutulu and the demon sultan Azathoth, Yibb-Tstll and Shuggah-Mell, Shub-Nigguth, and…hell, half-a-dozen more I can't even remember! But Chorazos and his lot, apparently they worshipped this Yot-Sottot: a being co-terminous in all space and conterminous with all time. A thing that is every when and where, if you know the gates. But only Yot-Sottot himself *knows* the gates. Weird as hell!"

"And the leaders of this cult or sect, they actually lived here!" George Ainsworth's voice, from a downstairs bedroom, was full of excitement.

We began to congregate in a spacious sitting-room. And from somewhere upstairs came Jackson's voice. Since he couldn't put a damper on things, he'd decided to join in. "Yot-Sottot *was* the gate, and he led them all through it and down from the stars. Well, we may not have ghosts here, but we certainly have demon-worship."

"If you worship Yot-Sottot," Thorne called back up to him, "as Chorazos and his people did, then he'll teach you to change the structure of space, how to warp the fabric of time."

Jackson came down from upstairs, leaving Peter Harkness still bumping about somewhere up there. Suddenly he let out a yelp, a squawk as if from a long way away. We heard him come-clumping down the stairs, except he seemed to be coming for a long time. And he was panting and muttering to himself, "Bloody hell, bloody hell, bloody *hell!*" We went to the door of the lounge, looked out into the entrance hall, toward the foot of the wide wooden staircase.

Finally, Harkness came into view, shaking and shivering, hair full of cobwebs, pale as…as a ghost! He literally flew into our arms. "Jesus!" he gasped. "I mean… I mean, I *know* this place! It isn't as if I haven't been here before…"

"So?" Clive Thorne stared at him. "So what's wrong?"

Harkness tried to get a grip of himself, shook his head. "I thought…I thought…"

"Oh, good grief!" Jackson tut-tutted. "Get to the point, for God's sake!"

"Shut up!" Thorne shouldered him aside. "Peter, what is it?"

"I...I went upstairs, to the first floor. I mean, there *is* only one floor upstairs. But then I went up to the attic. Except—it wasn't there! Just another storey, another floor. So I thought it was my specs, or those three quick pints of beer, or I'd somehow confused myself. And then I *did* go up into the attic. I went to look out of the old dormer window, but it was grimy. At least, I thought it was grimy. But it wasn't. It was simply dark outside, as if it were night. Then I saw the moon up and the stars. God, it *was* night!"

We all looked at each other. There was no denying Harkness meant it; he was shaking like a leaf. "So I came down," he continued, his hands fluttering. "But the stairs went down and down, and...Christ, I thought I was never going to get...to get...down...again!" And he fainted!

Thorne caught him; we carried him into the sitting-room, stretched him out, splashed water into his face. After a while, he came to, sat up, looked all about. And he saw the worried expressions on our faces. "What? Did I pass out?"

"Yes, you did." I nodded.

"Something like that, anyway," said Jackson, dryly...

Chapter IV

Out of nowhere, one of those summer storms had blown up. If the old house had been gloomy before, now it grew positively dark. Outside, the rain hammered down.

"There's your darkness," I told Peter Harkness. "A storm was brewing, that's all. And the moon is often out during the day." He nodded, looked grateful—if a little doubtful.

"Light!" said Thorne. He brought the oil lamps from the kitchen, got them going. Then Jackson assumed command:

"Right! So it looks like we're confined, at least until this storm lets up. But we've got a gas cylinder to connect up, wood to fetch indoors, a fire to light. We can stow away our provisions, brew up a pot of tea, lay claim to our sleeping areas...at least attempt to make the place livable down here. Later, after a meal, time enough then to think about exploring, er, upstairs…"

Oddly, his suggestion for once found no opposition. There were things to do and there was system, order in it. And no-one, not even Thorne, actually wanted to explore upstairs—not right then. We got to it, settled ourselves in, waited for the storm to let up, which it didn't. If anything it got worse; there was even the occasional flash of distant lightening. We got a roaring fire going; Thorne cooked up sausages, eggs and beans, we opened a few bottles of beer and had a drink. Came 7:00 pm and it still rained, and now the light was really failing. Finally, Jackson said: "About an hour's light left, if you can call it light! Me, I'm for a look around upstairs. Any volunteers?"

Harkness shook his head at once. "Not me," he said. "Tomorrow in the broad daylight, maybe." George Ainsworth stayed with him while the rest of us took a lamp and climbed the stairs. There were no carpets, just bare boards, and the wallpaper was at least forty years out of date. We suspected a young couple with perhaps an aged relative had once had the house, however briefly; the bedrooms and toilet downstairs hinted as much. But as the hiring agent had told us, no-one had ever stayed very long here.

Upstairs was very similar: bare boards, grumbling plumbing, probably sound and in working order but not especially savoury. And the "perspective", for want of a better word, as in the church, all wrong. Our oil lamp burned brightly enough, but its light just didn't seem to travel right or fill the space. It was difficult to judge distances; the echoes were wrong; the shadows thrown by the lamp seemed to have moved too swiftly. Disturbing, but not what you could call threatening.

"Haunted?" Thorne looked at Jackson, his face ghastly in the artificial light.

Jackson shrugged, shook his head. "Somehow it doesn't feel ghostly," he finally answered. "Tainted, more like." And—again—he had it right. We climbed more stairs. The attic, admitting light from only one small dormer window, was too dusty and cobwebby for us to be bumping about in; we merely looked in, then called a halt for the night. I did glance out of the dormer window, but I couldn't see any moon. The storm, of course…

Back downstairs, Clive Thorne stirred himself. "Me," he said, "I'm for *The Running Man!* A pint of best will go down just great!"

George Ainsworth was snoring in a chair beside the fire, Jackson and I declined, too; but Harkness jumped at the chance to be away from the house for a couple of hours. And anyway, he knew the way across the fens. They went off together, came back an hour later thoroughly dejected. The pub was shut; proprietor away on business; *The Running Man* wouldn't be running again until tomorrow night.

Anyway, all of us were tired. Ghost-hunting could wait until tomorrow. After all, it was only our first night.

No one opted to sleep upstairs.

Chapter V

As it happened, we all slept in the huge living-room. Someone kept the fire going—probably Peter Harkness—for in the morning it was still burning down into white ash.

Around 10:00 am, Clive Thorne woke us up with tea—which was good—and buttered toast like squares of tarmac—which wasn't.

The sun was shining, however hazily; the world looked fresh outside streaked windows; now, perhaps, we could get down to it. And, in a body, we explored the house. Downstairs, upstairs, attic: normal as normal could be. Big, old, and full of echoes; a bit sorry for itself, nothing out of the ordinary…Not then, anyway. Jackson found a small card table and began to make notes for his proposed "pamphlet"; Thorne started measuring the house up and making diagrams of the floors and rooms; George Ainsworth got his cameras ready for the night, when he would set them up strategically with trip-wire "ghost-traps"; I spent my time with Peter Harkness, who was still a bit shaky.

At noon, we went into town and had a few too many at "our" local, then sauntered over to the church—which was firmly secured, and

The Running Man

Applebury nowhere to be found. We got back to *The Oaks* about 3:30 pm and settled ourselves down for an afternoon snooze, because we planned to be up and about for much of the night.

About 7:00 pm, Clive Thorne gave me a shake and said something about *The Running Man*. I opened my eyes, saw Thorne and Ainsworth standing there, George with his box camera round his neck. Jackson was still asleep and snoring in his sleeping-bag across the room, and I still felt groggy. That's how beer gets me.

I declined Clive's offer, promised I'd have the fire going again when they got back. They tip-toed out—probably because they didn't want Jackson's company—and Peter Harkness went with them. He didn't fancy being the only one awake in the house, not with night coming on. I heard him say that as they went out, and I think that's what kept me awake…

Anyway, I finally got up, washed, made the fire. And by then Jackson was awake, too. He made coffee, grumbled that the Primus store was leaking a bit. He could always find something to grumble about…

About 7:45 pm we finished our coffees; and by then, too, the house had grown very quiet. Maybe even ominously so. We lit the lamps, each of us admitting that we occasionally found ourselves holding our breath, listening intently—but to what? The sighing of the evening breeze in the branches of the great oaks in the grounds? A creaky old floorboard somewhere upstairs? We were both thinking the same thing: floorboards don't usually creak unless someone steps on them. But we were the only someones in the house—weren't we?

Jackson, pre-empting me, said: "There's only two of us." He was nervous, blinking his eyes just a little too fast.

"Two of us against what? A heavy ghost?" I didn't feel brave, but I'd been dying for a chance like this. "Well, you can stay down here if you want to, but I'm going to take a look." I took up one of the lamps, and found Jackson right on my heels as I started up the stairs.

"We really shouldn't," he said, his voice shaky.

"Why not? Whatever it is, it can't be as bad as your shiny, spectral thing in the woods!" The pleasure I took in saying that made up for my own bad attack of the jitters.

"That was...different!" he said. "I mean, I...I didn't just go walking *into* it!"

"Well, this time, we're walking into it," I told him. "Or you can go back down—on your own." And then I noticed that we were *still* going up the stairs. I said nothing, but a moment later Jackson noticed it too. It lasted only a second or two: the feeling that we'd been climbing for far too long, and then we were on the landing. At the end of the long corridor was a narrow window looking out on a black night...On a what? Middle of summer, only 8:00 pm—and it was pitch black out there!

"...I *didn't just go walking into it!*" Jackson's voice came echoing to us, as from a million miles away. "Oh Jesus!" said Jackson very quietly. "Oh my God!"

We checked looked into all of the rooms—which somehow seemed to take ages—and all the time Jackson stumbling close on my heels. The idiot: he should have brought the other lamp! The upstairs rooms were empty, but the odd "perspective" of the place was back.

"We should go down," Jackson whispered. "We should go..."

"Up!" I said. I was in a bad state too, but I could still think in a straight line. If we'd heard something and it wasn't on this floor, it could only be in the attic. I found the stairs and headed up them, with Jackson's fingers trembling on my back. We climbed and climbed. *Oh Lord*, I said to myself, *please let us reach the attic!*" But we didn't. Instead, we came out on the upstairs landing—again!

Chapter VI

Jackson flipped. "The pews in the church!" he panted. "It's just the same. We have to get out of here. I have to get out!"

The Running Man

He grabbed the lamp and it nearly came apart in our hands. I had to let go of it. And he ran off with it like a hare back downstairs. To hell with *me*, the coward just ran! And I admit it, so did I.

Down, always down. A headlong, flying, floating flight in near total darkness, without ever seeming to get anywhere. The upper floor landing, and again the upper floor landing!

And Jackson's gibbering floating back to me, and the light of his lamp always just too far in front, its distance distorted and all perspective altered. Yot-Sottot: a being who could change the structure of time and space, and us trapped somewhere along the warp...

It was like an unending nightmare. "Out, out, out, out, *out!*" he was babbling; and other voices, mine and his, saying: *the pews of the church*, and *up, up, up!* I would soon crack and I knew it. Landings and stairs, landings and stairs, landings and stairs and...

...And Jackson coming back up, his face hideous with fear in the flaring light of the lamp! His eyes bulged and there was froth on his lips. "On the stairs!" he shrieked. "In cloaks, cowls, knives! They're here, do you hear me? *They're here!*"

"What? Who?" I tried to grab him. Mad as a hatter, he bore me before him backward up the stairs. We hit the landing and almost collapsed there, but that was when I noticed the shadows coming up the wall. Cowled shadows.

I got behind Jackson, put a hand over his babbling mouth, dragged him along the corridor. Almost exhausted, he made no protest. I took the lamp from him, put it in a room, quietly closed the door. We stood in the utter darkness of the corridor, me hissing in his ear: "Be quiet! For God's sake, *be quiet!*"

They came up onto the landing, looked this way and that. Two of them—cowled, yes, and strangely hunched. If they'd turned our way...I don't like to think about that. But they went the other way, disappeared into the weird distance of the place. I counted up to ten, let go of Jackson and regained the lamp, tip-toed breathlessly for the landing. I felt my hair was standing on end; I hadn't known it could do that, but it did. And what about Jackson, now that he'd had a breather?

I shouldn't have asked it, not even of myself! He came leaping and gibbering at me, snatched the lamp again and went bounding down the stairs.

This time the descent seemed normal—or nearly so, considering that there might be a pair of cowled cultists on our heels—or would have done if not for the cabilistic, esoteric and erotic designs painted crudely on the walls in red and white. But I had no time for the latter as I sought to catch up with my raving colleague. And then, at last, we were down on the ground floor. That was when I tripped, went flying. Jackson raced ahead, toward the hall and the main door of the house—but skidded to a halt as the door opened and two more cowled figures entered. They didn't see me where I lay sprawled in the dark at the foot of the stairs, but they did see Graham Jackson...For he had the lamp!

He cried out; an inarticulate, mad, rising babble of sound, threw open the living-room door and hurled himself headlong through it. In there...I can't swear to what I saw. Candles? An altar or some such? A circle of cowled heads, all turning in Jackson's direction as he sprawled and the lamp was sent flying? All these things—perhaps. But one thing I did see was Chorazos, and I make no mistake when I say *thing!*

It could only be him: taller than the others, officiating at the alter. His hood was thrown back and beneath it...I don't know what that horror had for a head but its face was a writhing, shifting mass of worms! I lay frozen with terror, none of my muscles even attempting to obey me.

The two cultists who had come into the house from the outside were after Jackson in a flash, and as they followed him into the living-room, so they took out long, curved knives from under their cassocks. But I have to give Jackson his due: he wasn't just going to stand and take it. Flames from the lamp had taken hold on hangings and esoteric tapestries; the demon priests were converging on him; he ran, tripped over the altar and sent candles and priests alike flying, then made a crazy, hurtling leap for the window. Knives rose and fell as he bounded away from them, but then he was out through the window in a crashing of glass and wooden lattice-work, out into the garden's dark surroundings…Which seemed to me a very good idea!

I had got my second wind, got my senses back, too. And as several of the cowled cultists in the living-room went out though the shattered window after Jackson, I up and made for the door. Going out, I slammed into Clive Thorne and George Ainsworth. Peter Harkness' white face stared at us out of the car's window. Thorne and Ainsworth saw my condition and the look on my face. And I saw the looks on all *their* faces.

"The house," they said as one man. "Look at the house!" I scrambled into the car with the rest of them when Harkness yanked the doors open, and only *then* looked back at the house.

"It's not…not *The Oaks!*" said Harkness, his voice hoarse as a croak.

I continued to look, began to understand. "Oh, it is," I gulped. "But not in this century…"

The gaunt old structure reared, different in every stone from the one we knew. Thorne backed the car away, threw it into a gravel-crunching reverse turn. And it was then we say the villagers with their torches. They were setting fire to the old place, shouting and screaming their hatred, hurling their torches in through the door and broken windows. And their massed cries like a thin keening wind, and their figures insubstantial as smoke. Our ghosts at last, they wore the garb of the late 16th Century!

Down the drive we went and out through the gates, and when suddenly I came to my senses I cried: "What about Jackson!" The others, staring hard at me but said nothing. "Graham's out here somewhere, running, bleeding," I continued. "Pursued by, by…" And still they looked at me. "But surely you saw him come bursting through that window?"

Thorne said, "Tell us later what happened in there. Right now we're going to find a police station. But we'll say nothing about…about this. Only the "facts" about the leaky gas cyclinder, the old lamps…And maybe later about Jackson being missing."

"But he isn't," I insisted. "He isn't…missing?"

George Ainsworth switched on the car's interior lights and passed back a photograph which someone had carefully tinted. I understood later it had been given him by the proprietor of the pub they'd revisited. I glanced at it, looked harder, then stared with bulging eyes. A pretty good shot of the original pub sign from *The Running Man*, the descriptions of contemporary witnesses must have been given the artist vivid accounts. There was no mistaking him; his clothing in tatters, bloodied limbs, face and hands. It was Graham Jackson, of course...

I looked back again, and in the near-distance the night sky was shot with black smoke and red, roaring flames...

Somebody Calling

The only way she could. He simply had to listen harder.

I'm telling my story now, after all this time, because it's not one which would have been accepted earlier without its bringing about my incarceration, and that was something I couldn't allow for reasons which will become apparent. But even as I make this statement of "confession" I feel it's worth pointing out that I don't in any way consider myself a criminal, or that the action I took those many years ago was anything other than just...and that's the other reason why I now put pen to paper: so that the police may finally close their files on a case that's lain open for far too long.

Not that this record is entirely altruistic, for in making it I also hope to salve my conscience (professionally speaking, at least) in that it was never mine to take lives but to try to protect, preserve and extend them. What a great shame that not all lives are worth the effort, and that there are others which should never have been brought into being in the first place.

So, here we are in the early winter of the year, certainly in the winter of my years, and in the last few hours remaining to me—my genes and my mother's nuclear legacy having finally caught up with me—it's time I told my tale....

––––––––––

A doctor, I entered the profession at the age of twenty three; which for reasons my mother and I both understood well enough, was what she had always intended for me. And it's as well that she saw her wishes in that respect fulfilled; just a few years later she was dead from problems related to a lifetime of work at the atomic research establishment.

"Huh!" (As she had used to complain so bitterly toward the end.) "It was either that—the radiation—or those pills for depression that I'd been taking for twenty years…or perhaps both! Do you remember thalidomide, John? Remember reading about it in those medical books of yours? Well, terrible as that stuff was, it was no worse than aspirin compared to the poisons I was taking! If only I could prove it, but too late for that now."

And in fact too late for anything.

I missed her, of course, but life goes on—life and work, and death, eventually, and taxes always—as they are wont to have it.

Anyway, being single and of necessity solitary in my ways—even more so now that she was gone—I kept myself to myself; and despite that my workload had increased proportionally with her death, I carried on at the practice while somehow managing to cope with the additional chores at home. Life was tasteless but tenable, at least until that night a year later, when the snow lay frozen on the ground and the roads were icy black.…

Having driven home to where my Victorian house stands secluded at the edge of extensive woodlands, as my car's tires crunched on the gravel of the drive inside my gate, so I sensed—more than sensed, saw—that something was wrong. I get my mail at the surgery and no postman ever visits my home; what's more, I seldom have visitors of any kind, and never uninvited. So that the footprints already iced over in my drive's thin blanket of snow might well have induced a degree of concern on their own, let alone in combination with that light in the porch, where I never left one burning!

Switching off my car's headlights and motor, I sat still, silent in the darkness. Senses alert, I listened, hearing only my own rapidly beating heart and nothing else. And the silence—the utter, unusual silence—was terrible.

Somebody Calling

Quickly I entered the house through a front door that had been forced and left standing ajar, and as quickly realized my worst fears…or perhaps not quite the worst. My study was in a state; it looked like a small whirlwind had gone through it. Several personal items—items which had sentimental value if little else—were missing. And the main living rooms were the same: all had been disarrayed, ransacked.

Upstairs, too, where in my bedroom the intruder had shown his total contempt by defecating on the Oriental car pet at the foot of my bed. Utterly appalled, again I paused to listen…and once more heard nothing. Only that same terrible silence.

Back downstairs I flew, to that place which from the first I should have investigated if I'd dared accept the concept of a worst possible scenario. And all the while I was hoping against hope that wherever else he'd been, the intruder had not discovered the small room behind the bookshelves in my library at the back of the house…but hoping in vain.

I found the door in the shelving opened up, and behind it the secret place revealed.

Inside, the light was on. The computer keyboard lay flat, apparently undisturbed on its swivel arm in front of the empty chair. The computer was working—at least it was switched on—its screen showing nothing of any importance. But other than these things and a few less important mechanical adjuncts, the room was empty, monstrously depleted.

I reeled against the wall in what little space there was, grasped my head in my trembling hands and concentrated hard on my listening. I concentrated and concentrated…to no avail. There was only the silence, and, beneath my straining fingers, the smooth, cold feel of the titanium plate under the skin at the back of my skull.…

When I had calmed down a little I considered my options, only to discover that I didn't have any! My material losses—those one or two precious personal items that had been taken—well, I could do without them. I would have to, for there was no way I could report this matter

105

to the police. Or I could have, but that would have meant all sorts of questions, gross intrusions into my privacy, oh, and difficulties galore. Which meant that the problem was mine and mine alone, and the sooner I got down to work on it the better. But where to start?

I decided the best thing to do would be to sit still with a drink and wait for somebody to call me. For even if the call was distant and indistinct, still I might get some idea of the direction. Fortunately my drinks cabinet and its contents were intact; I poured myself a drink (as it soon would transpire, a little too much drink), and settled down to put my plan to the test...

...only to come awake with a start at 11:00 p.m., to find the remains of my drink spilled in my lap, while the house and the atmosphere were as still and as silent as ever.

Or perhaps not.

Was that a whisper I heard? Was that what had awakened me, a whisper from out there? Had somebody called?

Outside it was bitterly cold...all the better to rid my head of brandy fumes, bring my mind to bear on the job in hand. The stars glittered like ice chips in a sky where the moon was a wafer-thin crescent; the wind too was thin, cutting where it came hushing out of the woods. And yes, I thought it carried a message—a sound that went all unheard, except inside my head—the sound of somebody calling. A mayday call in fact, a cry for help, from the far side of the forest.

All very well, but if I was to make a sweep of the region beyond the woods I must first refuel my car, and I knew that at this hour the local garage wouldn't be open. Nothing for it but to wait until first light. And knowing that I wouldn't be able to sleep, still I went back into the house and tried...

————————

In the still of the night somebody was calling. I remembered it the next morning when I came awake with a terrific headache. It had seemed like a dream, but my headache told me otherwise. And I certainly hadn't consumed that much brandy! But it came as no great surprise that somebody had called during the night hours; for there's nothing to get in the way at night, when everything is still and quiet.

I fueled my car, armed myself with a small scale road map of the area, and skirted the woods to their far side. And while it might have been my fevered imagination, it seemed to me that during the journey I twice heard somebody calling. On the first occasion it was the merest whisper, but on the second it was so clear that I felt sure I was closing in on the source.

A mile or two beyond the woods lay a small country village with which I was unfamiliar. External to the city's suburbs, it lay outside my area of responsibility; and, since I was more or less tied to my catchment area, by professional and personal commitments both, there had never been any need to venture this way before. Yet it was here that the second and clearest of the two calls (if, out of sheer desperation, I hadn't imagined them both) had seemed to sound so sharply on my inner ear. But as I drove along the main street toward the far end of the village, that sensation of nearness gradually receded. And I knew it was time to stop, consult my map, and get my bearings.

By then my head was aching again—as much from fear and frustration as from concentration—and for a moment or two I massaged my scalp, applying pressure to my subcutaneous plate. Then, in a while, after I had calmed down, I was able to study the map.

Obviously I had overshot the source of the calling, which had to lie somewhere between my present location and the woods farther back along my route. It couldn't be here in the actual village for the simple reason that if I had passed as close as that then of course I would have been aware immediately of its presence. It wouldn't have been that I strained to "hear" some distantly whispered SOS, rather that I would have been capable of more tangible communication…of sorts.

So, back along the way I must go, retracing my steps. But at least I knew now that the place I was looking for wasn't by the roadside but must be set well back from it.

As for my method: well, you couldn't exactly call it triangulation! More trial and error, actually. But with my map to help me, I was certainly making progress.

The map:

Two miles back, midway between the village and the woods, I had noticed a crossroads. It was there on the map: an unmetalled road, more properly a track, crossing at right angles the road down which I had driven. In both directions, east and west of the main road, several properties stood well back in marked isolation. I suspected they'd be neglected farm buildings; the land here and the people who worked it were not much known for their productivity.

And so I drove back to the crossroads, pulled to the side of the road, and sat there with my window rolled down, cool in a wintry breeze. And I concentrated, concentrated, until—

—There!

Somebody was calling! I felt my head almost inadvertently turning to the east, and then knew for certain that my way lay in that direction, that somebody was there.

And now my fear had turned to anger, and my anger in turn was building and my scalp tingling as I drove slowly along the track toward a clump of near distant, dilapidated buildings. I could actually feel somebody drawing closer moment by moment—yet nevertheless gave a start when suddenly I "heard:"

John! I feel you now. I feel you near. Come for me, John.

Come quickly!

———

There was a paddock behind a leaning gate, stables with sagging roofs, and a farmhouse with several boarded windows—but smoke wafted from a chimney in the end wall, and a battered white van stood in what was once the farm yard. I drove off the track into the cover of a copse and went the rest of the way on foot. And:

John! somebody called again, clear as spoken words now. *He has a weapon!* And the picture of a shotgun formed in my mind.

Somebody Calling

I paused behind a lean-to full of rusting farm implements. Is he with you now?

No, I think he must be sleeping. He was…he was sort of busy last night.

Busy? The short hairs at the back of my neck prickled, but I just had to ask. How, busy?

He was…he was doing things…three times, but I'm not hurt.

I glanced at my watch. It was 8:45, still quite early, and if he'd been (I couldn't help but shudder) "doing things" last night, then it seemed highly likely that somebody was right and he'd be sleeping it off.

I edged up to the door of the house, put my ear to the old oak panels and listened. Silence. Good. The door was locked but just a few paces away a sash window lifted at my touch, its dry pulleys squealing a very little. Heart pounding, I was over the sill in a moment, the sash falling shut behind me but this time silently. And brushing aside the rags of moth-eaten curtains, I paused again to listen…and was thankful to hear nothing.

In the sickly yellowish light from the grimy, flyspecked window, I looked round the room. It didn't appear to be in use. A few sticks of furniture were thick with dust and cob webs, and the old, mold-stained wallpaper was peeling in several places.

The air was tainted, stagnant. A door on my left led to a corridor, the main passage into the house from the front door. And somewhere in or just beyond the passage, a dim red glow pulsed on and off with mechanical regularity in the gloom.

My first thought was that perhaps the house was alarmed—that in opening the window I might have initiated some sort of security system—but if that were so, then why had the house continued to remain as quiet as a tomb?

Crossing carefully to the door, I looked into the passage and saw a second room on the other side. Its door was standing open, with an area of its interior visible, so that I was able to make out the source of the pulsing light—a computer console, with a screen that was blank except for a small red light whose steady winking indicated the computer's standby mode.

Breathing just a little easier, I slid across the corridor and into the room of the computer...and saw at once that this place was very much the center of the house. It was tidy if not too clean, with one wall that was shelved floor to ceiling, and another that had been whitewashed over to serve as a screen for the combined video/CD projector that was situated near the computer console. The wall shelving was full of labeled cassettes and discs, but right then I wasn't able to study the subject of this considerable collection.

I did, however, pick up and break open the double-barreled shotgun which I found standing in one corner near the door. The gun was loaded; easing it shut again, I balanced its comforting weight in the crook of my arm. As might be imagined, from then on I felt a lot more secure as I continued to explore the rest of the house.

Downstairs there wasn't very much more to see: a kitchen, toilet, and small living room, where the last few embers of an open fire glowed in a grimy grate. But as well as the doors to these rooms there was another, far stouter door in the passage...and it was locked. All of the rooms were in a filthy state and I didn't linger in any of them, but as for the locked door in the passage—that was where I was most aware of somebody's proximity, and knew that some body must be aware of mine. Knowing what I was about, however, she made no comment that might startle or disturb me.

She, yes.

Forgive me. This was the only way I could do it: by telling the story my way, by building to where I've left myself no choice but to reveal everything—this secret I've kept these many years—which even now I'm loath to divulge. But give me a moment...I need a moment to compose myself, also to compose the rest of this, and then I'll get done....

I found him upstairs in one of the bedrooms.

Somebody Calling

Having heard me climbing the creaking stairs, he was out of bed, stumbling around the room and trying to dress himself. I saw stained, dirty underclothes, a gross, hairy body, a fat red face full of stubble, set with a large, loose-lipped mouth and little piggy eyes that glared their hatred and fear. And: "What?" he grunted, fastening his belt buckle. "Who?" as he reached for a stained shirt draped across a bedside table. "Don't bother," I told him, aiming the shotgun. "You can forget the shirt, the vest will do. Downstairs, and don't try anything silly. I'm not a very good shot, but with this thing I don't need to be."

"My shoes," he grunted, reaching for them where they lay on the floor beside his bed.

"No shoes." I shook my head. They were something he might try to throw at me.

And now he began to bluster. "Who the fuck are you? What do you think you're doing, breaking into my house like this?"

"I'm arresting you," I answered.

"Arresting me? For what? In civilian clothing…you're no policeman." Now that he was awake, he was beginning to look a lot more dangerous.

"I'm Detective Inspector John McKenzie," I lied. "I don't wear a uniform. Now get downstairs, and quickly. There are one or two things we have to talk about."

Squat and waddling, breathing heavily and muttering under his breath, he started down the stairs, pausing just once until I was obliged to prod him in the back of the neck with the twin barrels of his gun. And in the living room I sat him in a chair before moving over to a set of drawers.

Rummaging in the top drawer I found what I wanted: a roll of adhesive tape. And before he could give it too much thought I moved around behind him. But the way his eyes swiveled this way and that, like a trapped lizard's, I could see what he was thinking: that I would have to put the shotgun down in order to tie him up…and he probably wondered why I was bothering to restrain him in the first place.

So I did put the gun down—I put its butt down, hard, on the crown of his head. Then, while he lolled to and fro, half stunned, I taped his thick wrists to the chair's arms, his fat neck to its headrest, and his dirty feet to its legs. And when he looked like he could speak again, I said:

"She's in the cellar, isn't she?"

"She?" he mumbled in return. "I don't know any she." "Well, then," I said, "somebody is in the cellar, right?" To which he answered, "Fuck off and die!"

I put the barrels of the gun against his ear and said, "If you don't tell me where the key is, I'm going to kill you. This gun—both barrels—should take your head right off those ugly sloping shoulders of yours."

"Huh…huh…who the fuck are you?" His voice was only a whisper now, or more properly a thin croak.

"I'm her brother," I told him. "Her twin brother."

And it was true—it is true—that I'm somebody's twin brother, her Siamese twin.

We were born back-to-back, joined at the back of our heads, even sharing a little brain stuff. We both had our own brains, but there was joining stuff, too. When they separated us, they said I stood a chance but somebody would probably die. I think they wanted her to die, but our mother didn't. Mother was one of those pro-lifers, also an untouchable. She'd never been to prenatal, never been examined, never been X-rayed or anything of that nature. But even if she had been it wouldn't have made even the slightest difference; she was pregnant, determined to deliver, and even more determined to care for her child…in fact, her children.

So she'd taken us home—both of us—and cared for us, and somebody hadn't died.

When we were five we had our plates fitted (mother paid a specialist for somebody's plate; she paid for his silence, too, because by then my twin was supposed to have died), and I got a new one when I was seventeen. Somebody hadn't needed a new one because her skull was already full-grown when she was five, or at least it was as big as it would get.

112

But let me go back a little. So they'd separated us, yes, but not entirely. What I mean is, some kind of tenuous connection remained. Tenuous at a distance but much stronger when we were close. Telepathy? Well, I know it sounds like it, but no, not exactly. It was awareness rather than knowing, and feeling rather than hearing. And yes, it was loving, too. I mean, how can you fail to love someone who you know loves—relies upon, depends upon, would really die with out—you? And after all, I was only doing what our mother had wanted me to do: being a doctor, then a carer, someone to tend to somebody's needs, if or when she was sick.

As for her name:

She'd never had a proper name, was never christened. And when we'd tried to give her one, my mother and I, she wouldn't accept it. Even as a child, an infant, she'd known that people had names. And somebody had never considered herself a person. But then, apart from her mother and brother, nor would anyone else consider her a person—ever.

She had thought of herself as nobody, and it had been up to mother and me to convince her that she was some body, which finally she'd accepted. She'd allowed herself to be somebody, with a small "s" that loaned her the anonymity she craved.

And now somebody was downstairs, in the cellar…

The key was on a narrow dusty ledge above the door frame. But as I unlocked the door somebody said, if not in so many words, John, I'm very cold. It was more that I myself gave an involuntary shiver as I felt her mind touch mine. And then finally I went down to where somebody lay in a cobwebbed corner under a dirty sheet on an old stained mattress.

I wrapped her in my coat, bundled her upstairs and along the passage, kicked open the front door and went to my car. I put her on the front passenger seat, turned on the engine and the heater, and asked her, "Will you be all right? Just for a minute or two?"

Yes, John, she answered, and made familiar sucking sounds with the blow-hole-cum-feeding orifice in the side of her face. I'll be okay now. Please be careful.

With only one thought, one intention in mind, I went back into the house. But I'm not a killer by nature—anything but—and first I had to know something more about my burglar. The answer I sought might be there in the room of the computer and projector. And for the next fifteen minutes I played discs and tapes of the utmost depravity onto the whitewashed wall screen.

Men with dwarves, with other men and amputees, with grotesquely obese women and emaciated, almost skeletal girls; also with animals—pigs, dogs, sheep and ponies. Bound women with running sores, scar-tissue for breasts, and shaven lice-ridden heads; one such lying on her back, drinking the urine of three men through a tin funnel.

As for the loathsome being I'd left tied to a chair, well he featured in far too many of these…these what? Entertainments? They went on and on, seemingly vying with each other to be the most repulsive, each of them worse than the last. Twice I threw up before shutting everything down and returning to my captive.…

———————

He was struggling like a madman to free himself from the chair, rocking from side to side, forward and back. And when he saw me come into the room he redoubled his efforts.

"Do you want me to hit you again?" I asked him. "Fuck you!" he gasped. "You and that fucking thing."

"She's my sister," I said, "my twin, and you must be made to pay for what you've done."

"I didn't mean to…to take her," he panted, exhausted from his struggles. "I was after money, jewelry—anything I could sell for a few quid."

"But you did take her," I answered. "And what's more, you *have* taken her!"

"You don't know anything!" He blustered. "I know everything," I told him.

"I'm no worse than you!" He yelled hoarsely. "Her brother? Well, that's as may be, but nobody would keep a thing like that if he wasn't fucking it!"

I almost threw up again, then put the shotgun to his head and said, "You…are a very sick man. But you're right about one thing: I'm not a policeman, I'm a doctor. And I think that maybe I can help you."

He saw what he thought was a ray of hope, decided to play it for all it was worth, licked his lips and blinked his piggy eyes at me. And then he said, "Do you…do you think you can cure me?"

"Oh, I'm really quite sure of it!" I said, squeezing both triggers and recoiling a little from the blast…

———————

After that—

—I tossed some sticks of furniture into the sitting room, tore down moldering curtains to drape haphazardly through all the downstairs rooms, and laid a trail of torn newspapers from the hot embers in the grate to the curtains, the furniture and all. Then I waited until I saw the first flames come creeping, and with that it was done.

It was snowing fairly heavily by the time I'd reached the main road, but back there in the near-distance the dense black smoke was already rising to the sky.…

———————

Later, back home with somebody, I washed and fed her, examined her for bruises and…and whatever. But apart from her obvious weariness she seemed no worse for wear. So I let her sleep the morning out in her cot, and before I went off late to work returned her to the small room behind the bookshelves.

And that's where I left her, as always, in the cushioned chair from which she could reach her long feeding straw on the left—reach it with the hole in her face—and the computer's swiveling keyboard on the right, with the three-fingered hand on her only limb, a solitary elbow.

For that was where somebody felt happiest, or at least as happy as she ever felt: in control of her own little window on a world she would never see or visit except like this, through the plain oblong shape of her computer screen. There again, at least the screen had a recognizable shape…

———————

It was all a long time ago, but now it's over. My genes and/or mother's nuclear legacy have caught up with me, caught up with somebody, too, and it's time to end it all. No big deal—just Big "C"—and in a way we welcome the end, somebody and me.

We'll fade away together, in touch as always, as sweet as I can make it with a sharp needle and the very gentlest drugs. And if I believed in God, why I might even look forward to it, much as somebody does. Oh yes, for my sister is convinced that however we look in life, our souls are ravishingly beautiful.

But more than that, she also believes that after her soul is set free, finally she'll be Somebody.…

Vanessa's Voice

Both beautiful ... and deadly!

I still can't believe that it happened that way. I get this feeling that I must have missed something, that I was mistaken; an earthquake, perhaps, or some other perfectly normal and explicable *physical* phenomenon, as opposed to...

And yet — well, I have Jim's letter, and I have evidence of my own five senses, which I've always believed to be sound enough.

The letter (more a note, really) is quite a simple thing, delivered to me by a solicitor — afterwards. Jim knew what was coming, I think. Certainly he had a good idea. But of course he had lived with it, with the growing manifestations which only he recognized, with the guilt. Perhaps, (I keep trying to convince myself) that's all it was: a guilt complex that got out of control, that took over. But that hardly explains the end of it all, what I saw and heard — or rather, *didn't* hear — and the medical evidence...

I've known Jim always; he was the type of person you seem always to have known. He was there at school; clever enough but nothing outstanding, played the recorder and two-finger piano. He was there in the town — at all the dances, a good-dancer and looker; in the pubs, a witty conversationalist. He never had a lot of money, but sufficient. Charm, for want of a better word, was Jim's forte. If he'd been Italian, then Jim would have made a damn good gigolo (but he was English and usually the soul of sincerity); if he'd been a politician, then you'd vote for him. He was "a nice person." No teacher ever caned him at

117

school; no girl ever refused him a dance; no one ever interrupted one of his funny stories; and not even the bums tried to impose upon him. Yes, he definitely had something. A combination of Prince Charming without a princedom, and Frank Sinatra without a voice. But…

Vanessa had the voice.

I didn't know Vanessa when first they took up with each other. Jim had a flat in town, sufficient for a bachelor, always upside down but clean; the type of place you would take a friend for coffee (or a last drink after they'd called time) without feeling embarrassed. Jim didn't pay much for the place; he got on well with his landlord and there hadn't been any trouble in the five years he'd been there.

I first learned of Vanessa when I noticed how *much* neater Jim's place was. Immaculate? — well not quite that, no, it was just a flat all said and done, but what a woman does for a house Vanessa had done for Jim's flat. I said nothing (at that time I knew nothing) but I guessed there was a woman somewhere. Why not? He'd had girlfriends before, through none had ever made her presence so plainly known as this one.

Then one evening Jim 'phoned and asked me out for a drink. He wanted me to meet her. I went, I saw, I didn't like! They say opposites attract: well then, things were as they should be, for this girl was surely Jim's opposite.

She was blonde, blue-eyed and beautiful, and she knew it. She could sing, and she knew that too. That first night I got filled up to here with it; with her singing, I mean.

Now I don't know opera from rock-'n'-roll — I might just be able to tell you the difference between Gigli and Chuck Berry, or Ray Charles and Chopin — but that night I learned things, or at least I *should* have learned things if I'd been at all interested and if it hadn't all been layered on so sticky and thickly.

Vanessa was excited, Jim explained, because she'd just been "sent for" by "someone big" in the "music" world down in London. Which was as far as he got, for that was where Vanessa took over. Her voice needed "exposure," she told me. She'd had enough of these "one night stands" at local dance halls. She needed "a manager," a well-organized "tour," or even better, a "recording contract." After all, well, "ballads" were okay, and the occasional sentimental "pop number," but she had a "near-opera voice" and she didn't want to ruin it. And so on for three solid hours with every musical term or name in the business thrown in for good measure.

What amazed me was that Jim seemed to lap it all up like so much spilled honey; he savoured every word of it, every beautifully formed word from Vanessa's beautifully formed mouth. If he wasn't in love with her, he was in love with her love of her! And…I don't know (perhaps it was because he was such a good listener) but whenever she stopped to sip her drink or light a cigarette Vanessa seemed to find Jim almost as fascinating as she found herself! He had plainly "charmed" her, but it was patent he was no less charmed himself. She was a year or two older than his twenty-five, possibly more mature, too, despite her blatant vanity.

I asked myself if this affair could last: and I answered that it couldn't. A girl so very much in love with herself needed no such love from a man, certainly not from Jim. I knew he didn't have sufficient drive anyway to keep up with her demands. For Vanessa would require more than love. She would require admiration for breakfast, dinner and supper; and while love's young flame burns brightly, still it invariably burns down the candle. There would be others, I guessed, with longer candles than Jim, who could wait him out until his love and admiration might seem to Vanessa to be on the wane, and then step in armed with refreshing flattery to drive him out.

All this from a first drink with a girl, one I had never met before? I have always prided myself on being able to read characters. But I could never have foreseen the end of it…

Next spring they were married. In between I hadn't seen much of them. I knew, though, that before they married they had been hard pressed to find any time to spend together; Vanessa's singing had been taking her all over the country. That was why Jim had quit his job to become her manager proper. It had worked quite well, it seemed, and their engagement had followed quickly.

It was only after the wedding that Vanessa decided she needed a manager with a bit more acumen, someone with a real "in" in the business. And of course being Jim, her husband stepped aside and agreed; and they went on, with success following success for Vanessa and Jim being ever the more pushed back, out of things and, I guessed, beginning to feel just a bit sorry for himself.

I hadn't known, however, that he'd taken seriously to booze. The first I knew of it was when I heard how Vanessa had missed out on what had looked like being a good contract with a small but established recording company.

Jim had apparently been to blame. He hadn't liked the way one of the company's executives had seemed to have more than a merely speculative eye on his wife. After a late-night party, at which Jim had consumed far more than his fair share of alcoholic refreshments, there had been an argument and the said executive had lost some teeth. Later it came out that Jim's apprehensions had been quite without foundation; the man he had hit was queer as a nine-bob-note, quite harmless. His manner towards Vanessa had meant nothing; he was 'that way' with every girl who worked for him—and with the men too, only with them he meant it!

Vanessa had been furious, but Jim had managed to win her over by telling her that she would only be wasting her talents with such a piddling little company anyway. And of course, knowing how good she was and that therefore he must be perfectly correct, she had forgiven him.

A year went by; Jim's drinking got worse as he was pushed more and more into the background; their quarrels grew more frequent. And yet at better times they still seemed to find a mutual fascination, though such times were now few and far between.

Came the time, about fifteen months after their marriage, when Vanessa appeared to have reached her musical ceiling and was on a rapid decline. She had also begun to morbidly bewail her fate and blame her failures on Jim. After all, hadn't he been responsible that time for ruining what could have been her big chance? And didn't he live off her, like a leech, following her all over the country and drinking what few pounds she picked up just as fast as she earned them?

Truth to tell, Jim had lost a lot of his charm. In just a year his drinking had taken a heavy toll. Vanessa, on the other hand (though she had also started to argue with her manager) was still very beautiful and her voice was better than ever. With the right breaks...

Which finally came one night on a stage in a dance hall in the Midlands. For some time (it later came out) an agent from one of the big companies had been following her about, just listening. In the dressing-room he finally approached and asked Vanessa if she could talk to him. He was going to a party, would she come along? He wanted to talk business. Vanessa agreed. She was delighted. She knew that her voice had been in very good form that night. Moreover she had argued again with her manager—something to do with Jim's drinking—and her manager had promptly ripped up her contract and walked out on her.

At the party, held at a large private house on the outskirts of Nottingham, Jim had tinkled the piano and thrown back the gin while Vanessa sang blues and ballads to the delight of the guests and in particular the handsome agent, Tony Hanks, whose eyes never left her.

Perhaps it was the way Hanks watched her, his open admiration — and not only for her voice—and certainly the drink had much to do with it, but Jim soon began to sour, and his piano-playing, too. The trouble started when Hanks went over to the piano and laid a hand on Jim's shoulder.

No one heard what he said for sure; something like: 'Okay, move over son, I'm still sober. Perhaps Vanessa can follow me—she certainly couldn't be expected to follow you!'

At least, that's what Jim told me Hanks said when I met him later. Of course he had flared up, tried to land one on the agent's nose, and Hanks had spread him all over the piano!

When Jim came to he found himself lying on his back in the shallow water of the fish pond in the garden. The party was over and the last guests were straggling home. A cartoon drunk with a balloon told him that Vanessa had gone off in tears with Hanks right after the "fight."

And though they later patched it up between them, that was really the beginning of the end. Jim came back to his flat in town here, where eventually I heard all his troubles out, and he stayed for a week nursing his injured pride. But at the end of that first week he wrote Vanessa a letter which she answered, and within a month he went off again after her.

By that time, though, she had signed a touring contract with Tony Hanks and the agent had become her manager and closest companion. There was no funny business between them, you understand; but now, though the money was starting to roll in thick and fast, Jim seemed to find himself in the background even more than before. It seemed as though he was never able to spend a minute alone with his wife, and always he lived with the knowledge that her money was buying his booze.

And so, after a time, it was decided that he should come back to the Midlands to live. Jim and Vanessa, they had made a sort of "pact" between them. I met him a few weeks after he got back. He was a very different man to the one I had known only a few years earlier. Gaunt and showing all the symptoms of a seasoned alcoholic, Jim nevertheless was at last making a try of it. He had found work, forced himself to cut down on his drinking; he was saving his money and gradually drawing about himself the trappings of former pride and strength—what little he'd ever had.

He told me about the "arrangement" that he and Vanessa had come to. They would give themselves time to think things over. Jim would come back to his flat; she would follow her career; at the end of a year they would see what was to be done about things, they would see how things stood between them…

No, all was not quite over between them, not yet, but note "quite," and Jim's working and self-imposed sobriety was his way of showing

Vanessa's Voice

Vanessa that he could still make a go of life, and that therefore they could make a go of their marriage despite differences of ambition, character and personality.

It was not very long after this that Vanessa bought the house between Leicester and Loughborough, a lonely old place not far out of Woodhouse. From then on, whenever she had a weekend to play with, she'd spend her time there with Jim. Plainly she, too, was trying hard to make a go of it. But of course her career, her voice, always came first.

And always, sooner or later, the time would come around when she must be off chasing her career. Hanks would pick her up in his big car and her husband would be left alone once more in the rambling old-fashioned house, for he had again given up his flat to move in there. When she was with him at the house things were good for Jim, and I visited once or twice. At such times Vanessa's personality and ego dominated all, but Jim seemed happy, even if he was back to his drinking—and anyway, who was I to complain or comment?

All too soon came the time when Vanessa had to be away for what looked like being the better part of a year, and that hit Jim badly. Plainly he was very much in love with her. Nevertheless the year went by, and towards the end of it Vanessa's first record boosted her to stardom overnight. Within a few days of the long-player's release she was appearing on popular television shows as regular as clockwork; her beautiful voice could be heard on every juke box in the country. And then Jim was invited to her big success party.

You would think that by then he'd been long warned off parties, wouldn't you?

The celebration was to be at the home of Vanessa's parents in Harden on the Northeast coast, a small town perched upon the cliffs and overlooking the North Sea. This (if things worked out) was to be their venue for the reunion proper, as they had planned it more than a year earlier. In all that time, though their letters had been pretty regular, the pair had spent no more than half a dozen or so weekends together, and in the last four months they had not been together at all.

The big day came round at last and Jim caught a train for the Northeast, but he missed his evening connection in York and so got into Harden more than an hour late that night. Vanessa's parents were quite well-to-do, of old Harden stock, and it looked to Jim as though the whole town was in attendance at their big house on the cliffs. Music played, guests laughed and chattered in the gardens, and in the party rooms lights blazed and accentuated the gaiety.

A summer breeze brought the tang of ocean to Jim as he got out of his taxi and walked down the lighted path to the house—and it also brought the sound of Vanessa's voice.

Never had he heard her sing so beautifully, a soul-rending ballad of unrequited love, and as she came to the end of her song on a high sustained note, Jim paused in the door of that room where the guests of honour were gathered to hear Vanessa sing. Tony Hanks was at the piano, and Vanessa sat beside him looking as lovely as Jim had ever seen her.

And just as she looked up to see him standing there, so her handsome manager leaned over to kiss her on the cheek.

I suspect that it was more a feeling of hurt in his heart than anger—though certainly there must have been a lot of frustration there too—but whatever it was it sent Jim striding across the room to yank the agent from his seat at the piano and smack him soundly all about the room. Jim was sober this time, and now the memory of the indignities he had suffered at the hands of this man, real and imagined, rose up in his mind to sting him again. Too, the element of surprise was on his side. Hanks stood no chance but bounced from wall to wall in the disarrayed room, until Jim ended it with a beautiful punch to the agent's jaw.

It was only then, when the scene was over, all bar the recriminations and the clearing up, that Jim noticed Vanessa, shocked and weeping, standing alone in a corner of the room and tenderly holding her throat. During the fight she had tried to separate the two men, and a wild blow from her husband had caught her in the throat.

Some reunion…

Vanessa's Voice

What could Jim say?—what could he do? He had won this round of his own personal battle with Hanks but had completely lost the last round of his fight with compatibility; Vanessa could see now, quite clearly, that they could never hit if off—not while she had her career, her voice…

Jim came back yet again to the Midlands, this time to pine his heart out and write letter after letter—with no response, no answer, and eventually no hope. It seemed that Vanessa just did not want to know.

Then he found out about her voice. Jim found out?—the whole country found out!—through the medium of the daily newspapers. To Vanessa's credit she managed to keep the true story quiet. The public only heard about her "accident;" how she had somehow hurt her throat, the fact that her voice might never be the same again.

And it never was.

Within the space of another month Tony Hanks had her to the best specialists in Europe, to no avail. Her vocal chords were irreparably damaged; she would never sing again. And from then on the end came very quickly.

The final phase began when Vanessa's parents wrote Jim at the old place near Woodhouse. He was still living there, hoping against hope that his wife would show up sooner or later. The letter begged him to go up to Harden on the coast and talk to Vanessa. She was suffering terribly from depression—acting and talking wildly, threatening suicide—continually restless, living on her nerves. Hanks, cutting his losses, had finally walked out on her. Her parents believed that if only Jim could get her to come back to the Midlands with him everything could be smoothed over. She often mentioned his name out loud in her albeit confused and very troubled dreams. Jim *must* come up to Harden! The way Vanessa was going, well, she would probably end up in a refuge!

And so off Jim went again to the Northeast; and to tragedy. He was with her—in fact, close to her, too close to her—when it happened.

Again the newspapers carried the story: that of a woman tormented by the collapse of her career, a collapse incidental upon a personal, tragic accident; how she had been "unable to bear the thought of a life without song," and how she had taken that life in a wild leap from the high coastal cliffs at Harden...

After the funeral Jim came back to the Midlands to stay, this time permanently.

At first he appeared to be the very epitome of heartbreak, and it seemed to me that in only a very short time he had become the merest ghost of a man. The house was his, now, and an expensive affair it would prove to be. Vanessa had left no will; her money (what little was left following her tour of the finest European throat specialists) was tied up with the recording company.

Money or none, Jim made no attempt to return to work but spent his time wandering about the large, lonely house and through the ancient streets of nearby Woodhouse.

Occasionally he would come to see me in town. On those very rare occasions I would get the impression that he wanted to tell me something, but he never did. He did ask me something once, though, something which, looking back now that it's all over, I find very relevant. At the time I thought nothing of it.

"What do you think," (he'd asked me) "about the next world?"

"Eh? You mean life after death? Well, you know me, Jim. So far as I'm concerned it's all worms and dust. No life after death, because there's simply nothing left for life to exist in—and no reason why it should. No, when we shake off this mortal coil we shake off life past, present and future. The world goes on... but the dead are gone!"

He seemed strangely relieved. "Who said that—that last bit?"

"I did!"

He laughed, but I thought his laughter was awfully dry and strained. In fact that was the last time I ever heard him laugh.

I saw him in town only once more after that, and he looked so ill on that occasion—so haunted—that from then on I hardly let a day pass without I would talk to him on the telephone, just to be sure he was all right.

Vanessa's Voice

I have said that he was ill, that he looked haunted, but in addition he seemed to have developed a nervous tic, a stressful twitch that pulled the flesh spasmodically at the corner of his mouth; and he seemed always to be listening for something, something no one else could hear. I began to hear it put about by people we knew that Jim was pretty weird these days: "*funny*, you know?"

I didn't agree, but I couldn't disagree either. For that last time I saw him in town—in a café in broad daylight, over coffee and in the middle of a perfectly ordinary, routine conversation—he had suddenly silenced me with a raised finger to whisper: 'Listen!—*Shhh!*—You hear that? But other than the chatter of people conversing over coffee and biscuits, the clinking of cups, and the traffic noises from outside—there had been nothing.

Then came the day of his telephone call. He was hysterical on the other end of the line, screaming into the 'phone, pleading with me to go up to Woodhouse, to the old place at once. "It's getting worse!" he screamed. "Can't you *hear* it—even over the 'phone? Dave—Dave, I think I'm going to go out of my mind!"

I told him to hang on, stay right where he was, I would be there immediately. And then I drove out of town like I've never driven before or since. The god of motorists must surely have been on my side that day, for the wonder is that I didn't get picked up for speeding or jumping red light; but whether the gods were with me or not I was soon out on the country roads, and then I really put my foot down.

Why I should have been in such a panic personally, I still don't know—unless it was his voice, Jim's plainly terrified, trembling voice when he asked: "Can't you *hear* it—even over the 'phone?" All I had heard was his hoarse, panicked breathing and, in the tinny distance, a crackling of faraway static...

After skidding to a halt in a spray of gravel chips, almost vaulting the garden gate and rushing up the path to the house, I discovered the door to the old place to be open. Not bothering to knock or announce my arrival in any way, I quickly let myself in.

The place was as I had previously known it. A little unlived-in perhaps (as well it might seem in the absence of Vanessa's great energy and aura); and at first I thought it was empty, that Jim had managed to get a grip on himself and had gone out. Then I heard the wind — at least, it *sounded* like the wind!

Or the ghost of a wind — a keening, eerie wail that went on and on monotonously — a sound which finally I traced to the library. It was Jim, kneeling on the carpeted floor by the old piano, head in hands, eyes glaring in a dead white face, rocking to and fro, to and fro in a lunatic rhythm. He saw me and keened all the louder, froth dribbling from drawn back lips.

I crossed the room and took him by the shoulder. "Jim, what the…?"

"*Now!*" he screamed, slapping my hand away. "Now, d'you hear it?" His glaring eyes burned into mine for a moment before he returned to his wailing and rocking.

I felt the hair on my neck abruptly stiffen and glanced over my shoulder in spontaneous apprehension. Empty, the room was empty of life except for myself and my poor friend — and yet…

Could I hear something? A distant voice, lifted high in a malevolent magnificently sustained note? No, of course not, my alert imagination and nothing more; but then a tremulous tinkling drew my disbelieving eyes to the ornate chandelier depending in glittering glass tiers from the centre of the ceiling.

The chandelier was vibrating, its multifaceted baubles thrumming visibly, resonating in sympathy with — but with what? And wine glasses, too, in their rosewood cabinet across the room, humming and moving, dancing to some unheard rhythm, giving testimony to an unseen presence. An earthquake, obviously.

The chandelier, the wine glasses — my gaze moved jerkily from one to the other and back again, comprehending yet almost refusing to believe. A sharp splintering sound yanked my head round to the windows. A diagonal crack had appeared in one of the panes, and even as I stared an adjacent window shivered to fragments in its frame. A succession of sharp explosions sounded from the cabinet of glasses, but these were almost drowned out as Jim's keening became a high-pitched scream of purest agony.

"The singing!" he screamed. "For God's sake—can't you hear her voice?—*Her beautiful, awful voice!*" Sweat burst out in glistening globules on his parchment forehead and face, and he pressed his hands even tighter to his head. Still I could hear nothing but the continuous disintegration of protesting glass, and now glass fragments were flying in all directions from the wildly gyrating chandelier.

"She thinks I pushed her, Dave!" Jim babbled on. "And in a way I did, oh God, I did! But I didn't mean to. I'd lost sight of her, and when I finally found her she was standing there on the very rim of the cliff. I knew what she was thinking: that she was going to jump! I called out to her… She turned and saw me…saw me reaching to grab her and took a backwards step… And then… Then she was gone…!"

"She was gone, Dave! And she blamed me! She *still* blames me…for everything! *And this is her revenge!*"

While he had spoken, or raved, the crazy shuddering of the house — which I had mistaken for an earthquake, for what else could it be?— had diminished. But then, as Jim gave a wild shriek and clapped at his head, his ears, it started up again. At which he clapped even harder, clapped so hard I thought he must crush his head between his palms! He did this three or four times, an expression of indescribable pain etched in acid lines upon his wetly gleaming features, and as the chandelier finally shook itself free from the ceiling to crash down onto the carpet, his eyes popped almost from their sockets and he toppled over like a felled tree, to lie motionless at my feet.

His eyes continued to stare madly, but they were quickly glazing over. And the house was suddenly, dreadfully still. And whimpering, which I admit unconditionally, I fled at last, leaving Jim's lifeless body behind me where it lay.

———

A week or so later a letter came from his solicitor, telling how the police now believed that Jim had probably pushed Vanessa from the cliffs that night when she had asked for a divorce, asking me as his close friend not to defend him any longer but stay neutral or silent in any further connection with the case; or, perhaps I might reconsider certain unresolved aspects and want to speak to the investigating police about them. Her parents after all had been completely mistaken; she hadn't needed Jim at all, hadn't wanted him. In fact she had grown to loathe him. Her mind had finally focussed upon him, and had identified him as the cause of all her disappointments and (not unreasonably) the personified destruction of all her dreams.

Certainly she had called his name in her sleep on those occasions when she stayed with her parents, but they had also heard the curses that sometimes accompanied those cries for Jim's help and understanding—but also their contrary condemnation of him—in the night. And only a few days or so later, despite that he stayed at a hotel in the village and only came to the house in daylight hours, it had been obvious that their marriage was finally over. Then, on that fatal night when Jim had run after her, tried to accompany her, attempted one last time to console her when she ran wildly, desperately from the house and from him... when he had almost caught up with her, then he had "seen her make that wild, mad leap" to her death.

Such had been his story, but after much soul-searching, and after her parents had found Vanessa's letter—a suicide note, possibly, under a pillow in her bedroom—it had seemed more than feasible that she had indeed done away with herself. Such had been her frustrations that *they* had driven her over the edge, as it were, and not poor Jim.

Personally, well, I still refuse to believe in any kind of life after death, but if the will is strong enough, and if there is a purpose...perhaps *something* lingers on, for a while at least.

But that it should have happened *that* way...

I haven't been to the police yet, and this is the first time I ever refused to come to the aid of Jim. It couldn't do anyone any good to know the whole story—it could only serve to blacken a dead man's name—and in any case I know that he's been punished enough.

Vanessa's Voice

I believe Jim's story as he told it to me; and for the record there was no earthquake. There was however an autopsy, which showed Jim's death to have been caused by a bursting of the brain. His eardrums were little more than tatters, and every membrane of his body had been ruptured...

The Vehicle

Some might think of him that way, others as a dyadic personality?

I.

Power-cells weakened in an accidental emergence from hyperspace too close to one of the void's ultimate omnivores, a Black Hole, then almost completely drained in a further desperate jump to avoid the Hole's awful attraction, the Hlitni craft flickered back into reluctant three-dimensional being a few moments and several thousand light years later within Sol's system of eight planets. Brakes straining to capacity, it whipped in past the third world's satellite, drilled through the planet's atmosphere without raising a single blister on its completely heat-resistant skin, finally slowed and hovered six feet above the muddy bank of an English stream in a densely wooded area.

It hovered for only a second or so, then the cells gave up their last spark of life and the spaceship fell with a plop into the mud. It landed a few inches short of the water, close to the bank's spiky tufts of grass, and lay there static and half-submerged. Inside the cone-shaped ship the crew was at emergency stations, separated—by human standards of comparison—by distances of hundreds of yards. All of this within the six-inch spike that was the ship.

Their communication system—basically telepathy, boosted mechanically by a device totally independent of the main power cells—was still working, permitting Hlitni conversation:

"Sarl, Klee? Are you two functioning?"

The Vehicle

"*Yes, Inth,*" Sarl came back. "*I'm functioning.*"

"*Me, too,*" reported Klee.

"*Good!*" Inth said, then asked: "*Sarl, what's the damage?*"

"*None that I can scan. We came down fairly soft.*"

"*And Klee, how's power—or shouldn't I ask?*"

"*You shouldn't ask, Inth. We're drained...?*"

There was a pause, then: "*That bad, eh?*"

"*That bad, yes,*" Klee answered, "*but perhaps not desperate. It depends.*"

"*There are many power sources on this world, yes!*" Sarl, the youngest member excitedly reported. "*Before we fell I scanned tremendous energy expenditure!*"

"*We all did,*" Inth said. "*But the nearest source was at some distance—and we no longer have a vehicle...*"

Immediately, fearfully, Sarl and Klee scanned the ship's vehicle where it hung suspended in its cocoon. As Inth had so bluntly pointed out, the vehicle was dead. The cocoon's life-support system had depended upon energy bled off direct from the power-cells. Within it a creature like a tiny butterfly—only half-an-inch long but still many times larger than all three crew members together—lay with its wings and body contorted, grotesque in rigor mortis.

Finally, after a pause to let the implications sink in, Inth continued: "*There you have the problem in a hyondle—and it certainly doesn't look any too good. But we're not finished yet. Look, lets get together and see what we can scan.*"

"*Where there's a force.*" Sarl added, trying to sound cheerful but not quite making it, "*there's a function.*"

"I do believe, Sarl," said Klee dryly, "that if your antennae started to fray and your carapace developed cracks, you'd still be optimistic!" Nothing more was said until they convened some minutes later in the recreation room.

II.

When Harry "the Hit" Coggin saw the police roadblock up ahead, he attempted to do a graceful, unconcerned, controlled left turn off the road onto a farm track. Which would have been fine except the track gate was tied not quite fully open, and Harry's "borrowed car" was just a mite too wide.

The police had spotted him in any case, and as he threw open the door of the car—its nose now deep in a ditch, along with the shattered wooden frame and bars of the gate—three of them set off at a run in his direction. Harry had no gun, or he might well have stood his ground and attempted to shoot them down before they could tackle him. They were unarmed, but that wouldn't have bothered Harry Coggin. Instead he set off along the track as fast as he could go, heading for the woods which started just beyond the small farm at the track's end.

He was still wearing the drab grey garb of the prison, but that was no handicap; compared with the smart uniforms of the policeman, Harry's loose-fitting prison clothes gave him ample freedom of movement. Truth to tell, the men pursuing him were not too eager to catch up with him. They were putting just enough effort into it to satisfy their superiors back at the roadblock. And their hesitancy was hardly difficult to understand.

Harry "the Hit" Coggin stood seventy-seven inches tall and weighed two hundred and forty pounds, not one of which was wasted. For two years a rare combination of native intelligence and sheer brawn had made him undisputed king of the underworld, and during that time he had earned his nickname many times over. Then his luck had run out: he was caught red-handed and jailed for life for a double-murder of extreme savagery. Since then, at a top-security prison, he had indulged almost fanatically in athletic exercise, and his constant displays of strength and physical agility in the exercise yard had kept warders and fellow prisoners alike gaping in awe.

No, his three immediate pursuers were hardly putting heart and soul into their task, but why should they? No doubt Harry would hole-up in the woods, and then the dogs would be brought in, and that would be that…Completely painless, for everyone except Harry.

The Vehicle

By now the fugitive was past the farm end entering the woods. He paused to get his bearings, catch his breath, look back. It looked pretty good. Even if those three coppers caught up with him they could do nothing. He was in tip-top condition and full of grim determination; he didn't intend to be taken again, not easily at any rate.

He clenched his fists and gritted his teeth. It would almost be worth letting them catch up with him… But no, however enjoyable the prospect, that would be a waste of precious time. What he had to do was find a decent hideout until nightfall, which was only a few hours away, and then make his way to one of the three neighbouring villages. It wouldn't be easy, and doubtless before very long there would be a cordon with dogs, but Harry Coggin was no fool. He had friends up north, friends who were expecting him. If he could only lay his hands on another car…

He plunged on into the woods, altering the course of his flight to take him more nearly north. The woods, he knew, were almost five miles through at this point. In less than an hour he should be through to the opposite side. The law would be there, too, and long before him, but he would see them first. Then it would be touch and go until the fall of dark. It would help if he could find a decent place to hole-up. With this thought in mind he came out of the trees onto the bank of a long, narrow pool. Reeds grew tall and lush at the water's edge; the place would be a haven for moorhens. It would also be a good spot to throw the dogs off the trail.

Without hesitating he waded out through the reeds and mud and struck out across the pool. The water was cool and it freshened him up a bit. On the far side he quickly squeezed his shirt and trousers as dry as possible before moving on. Way back at the edge of the woods, Harry knew that the enemy would be calling up reinforcements: police dogs, trackers. But right here and now he was alone. Completely alone in the heart of the woods, with only the cooing of wood-pigeons and leaf-dappling rays of penetrating sunlight to keep him company…So why the hell did he keep thinking someone was watching him?

III.

And in fact someone was watching Harry "the Hit" Coggin, three someones—or somethings. Inth, Sarl and Klee were scanning him closely, trying to make something of him. Quite obviously Harry was not a power source in himself—not one that the aliens could tap, anyway—but he could doubtless take one of the Hlitni to a power source, and then he could be made to bring the source back to the ship.

For of course to them Harry was simply a vehicle, far vaster than any they had ever come across before in their galaxy-spanning voyagings, and far more intelligent. And thus handling him or any other of his kind would be a far different hash of khrumm to handling the simple vehicles they were used to. But they were equipped for it; it should not prove impossible or even.

In fact they admired Harry, for certainly he was a very powerful vehicle indeed. Oh, they had scanned other potential creatures in the woods, hundreds, thousands of them, and all apparently controllable. But Harry was fast-moving, extremely strong, and unlikely—they thought—to fall prey to natural enemies.

Then, as they continued to scan him, he started to veer away from them at an angle that would take him past them at too great a distance. There was only one thing for it. Perhaps the three of them together could exercise a measure of external control. With one of their own vehicles there would be no problem, but with this one...?

They would have to see...

———————

Harry was most surprised to find his feet going contrary to his mind. He had made up the latter, just a few minutes earlier, to skirt the steep, heavily overgrown hill in front by diverting slightly north-west. Indeed, he had already begun to change his course to circumvent the obstacle. Yet now—why!—here he was scrambling up through gorse, saplings, bracken and tall ferns, leaning forward to maintain his balance as he negotiated the steep slope, having returned almost without knowing it to his original course. Now what the hell…?

The fugitive paused for a moment—just a moment—letting the creases in his forehead deepen. Then he shrugged, gritted his teeth and carried on climbing. It must be sheer, animal instinct, he told himself. And he trusted his instincts. Come to think of it, the hill was quite a high one; from the top he should have an excellent view of the woods to his rear.

A few minutes later Harry gained the crest, but by then he had apparently forgotten all about his plan to use the high place as an observation point. He had almost forgotten about the policemen, too, who might be hot on his trail…but not quite. Obviously, (he told himself) it was the sure knowledge that they were back there somewhere that drove him on, ever faster, through the woods. And yet (strange, unaccustomed sensation) it seemed almost as if some mind other than his own now guided his powerful piston legs. Again Harry frowned, and again he gave a mental shrug. He was going in the right direction, wasn't he?

IV.

"Klee," Inth said in his most casual manner, which was a sure sign that something was bothering him, "have you by any chance scanned the ship since we came down? Have you studied its buoyancy, perhaps?"

Klee fractionally relaxed his part of the trio's telepathic control on the still distant fugitive and prepared to scan the ship. Inth stopped him short: "*No, don't waste the effort. Allow me to tell you that we are sinking. Slowly but very surely, we are going down into the mud, and unless we can appreciably increase our prospective vehicle's speed…then our chances of ever leaving this backwater world are slim indeed.*" He paused to let that last sink in, then added: "*Of course, the biped can be exerted to the full— expended in an all out effort—once we get Sarl astride his brain…*"

137

"Then we'd better start scanning for the nearest compact power source,"
Klee nervously answered. "And we'd better start hoping that our vehicle,
when we've got him, is strong enough to carry that power source back to us.
It would be too bad for us if Sarl burnt him out before we got the job done!"

———————

Harry was down the hill now, and his stride lengthened as he bounded between trees and crashed through thickets. In the back of his mind somewhere a voice kept asking him if he was crazy, and dully, knowing that he was talking to himself, he kept answering that he must be! But he was still headed in the right direction, and he was certainly covering ground faster than any policeman could. So why was he worrying?

The answer was simple, and when it occurred to Harry he deliberately grabbed at the bole of a tree and halted his headlong flight. For a moment the fog lifted from his brain, allowing him to see things clearly. He was worrying because this wasn't the way he'd planned it, and also because for some reason he couldn't remember exactly *how* he'd planned it—except that he knew this wasn't it. Look at him: racing like a crazy man through the woods, like a maniac, all caution thrown to the wind. His legs were bleeding from brambles, his feet aching from the pounding they were taking, the muscles in his legs tightening up fast.

"I have to take it *easy!*" Harry told himself desperately, the thought barely out of his head before he was off again, legs driving like pistons and heart pumping, sweat rivering off his chin and down his neck, stinging between his legs and under his arms. His eyes were bugging now, partly from the unaccustomed straining, partly in horror of— what-the-hell-ever it was—and his chest rising and falling faster and faster. With the air beginning to burn in his lungs, he felt that all of his exercising, of which he wasn't sure he was the author, hadn't prepared him for this.

Then he saw the stream up ahead. Water! Dragonflies hummed like tiny helicopters over the cool water. He plunged on toward the stream, went down on his knees at the bank—but he didn't drink. In the mud there, something shiny. Harry reached out a hand...

It was like his brain had received an electric shock. He reeled and clapped his hands to his head, sucking air until the pain went away. Then, through eyes that were stinging and blurred, he looked again at the Hlitni spacecraft. A tiny dark patch grew on the silver, an opening. Something slender emerged and glinted in the sunlight. Harry snatched back his face instinctively, and that was the second last instinctive thing that he ever did.

A tiny projectile—trailing a wire so slender that the world's smallest spider might have difficulty spinning anything of a narrower gauge, yet strong enough to swing a brick—flashed up to strike Harry between the eyes, penetrating the bone. As he leaped up to his feet with a cry of outrage and shock—the *very* last instinctive thing he ever did— the projectile rapidly reeled in its wire, at the end of which sat Sarl in his pinhead capsule. The whole thing took little over a second.

Harry staggered stiffly at the stream's edge for a moment, then stood stock still. In less than fifteen seconds as he stood there, his heart slowed down to normal, his respiration quieted down, his eyes stopped bugging and took on a peculiar glaze. Then he moved, wading slowly out through the stream, being especially careful to avoid the Hlitni ship, splashing for the far bank in water up to his knees. He stepped up onto the bank and tried out his arms, swinging them. He turned his head left and right, focused his eyes, drew air into his lungs until his chest swelled out.

Then he started to run again, slowly at first but picking up speed and coordination as he went. Harry "the Hit" Coggin was in gear, engine running—but Sarl sat at the steering wheel and it was Sarl's foot on the accelerator. The Hlitni had their vehicle...

V.

"He had me worried there for a moment," said Klee. *"When he reached out to touch the ship."*

"Yes," Inth answered. *"With the power-cells drained he could easily have crushed us. It is fortunate that we didn't stun him when we all three pressured his mind together!"*

Klee offered a mental nod, and this too was communicated to Inth. Then, after a moment's silence, he said: *"I believe we are still sinking."*

"I was about to suggest," answered Inth, *"that we attract two of the small, four-winged flyers, just in case we have to evacuate. They scan out a very short life-cycle, but we could always transfer later if the need arose."* And as an afterthought, he added: *"They are quite fast—could take us to Sarl in no time at all."*

"How's he getting on?" Wondered Klee, using his magnet mind to snare a dragonfly and pull it, unresisting, to hover over the gradually settling vessel.

"By now he should have mastered his vehicle completely," answered Inth. *"Let's see how he is going, shall we?"*

Sarl was doing very well indeed. Harry's body functioned as never before, at maximum efficiency. Mindless, operating solely at Sarl's direction, he plunged through the final fringe of woodland to arrive at the edge of the fields beyond. In the distance smoke curled upward into the late afternoon sky from unseen cottages; skylarks sang high overhead; the bark of a dog at play carried on the still air from afar. Sarl noticed all of these things but immediately put them aside. This was no time for studying an alien world through alien eyes; there was barely sufficient time to get through with the job in hand. He sensed Inth and Klee the moment they scanned him.

"How am I doing?" he asked.

"Dead on course." Inth answered.

"The power source is presently situated in that clump of trees on the hill up ahead," directed Klee.

"Thanks for the confirmation," said Sarl gratefully. *"I was a fraction disoriented. He handles beautifully, but it's a bit difficult to control him and stay right on course at the same time."*

"Hey!" Inth came in again. *"I scan a pair of bipeds in those trees. They are right beside the power source. Is that odd, I wonder?"* His mental voice, boosted by the communicators, frowned. *"I don't think I quite like this..."* he paused, then quickly went on: *"And Sarl, you'll have to get moving faster. The ship's going down into the mud quite quickly now."*

VI.

Constables Williams and Brown had driven their police car up a grassy incline to park it in a lone clump of trees bearding the southern slope of the hill. The hill stood between the nearest village and the woods proper, and under the cover of the trees they would be hidden from the view of Harry if he chose to make a break for it within their radius of responsibility. Such would be most unlikely, of course; the woods formed a front some miles long, of which each police sector was only a fraction.

There were eight more cars spread out about the woods; sixteen more constables in all, not to mention a smaller number of plainclothes men. Several of the latter detectives were armed; it was generally accepted that Harry "the Hit" Coggin wasn't going to come quietly. Still, and where constables Williams and Brown were concerned, the odds were about eight to one against him coming out of the woods just here. He certainly wouldn't do it in daylight...

Which was why Williams almost dropped his binoculars when, from out the woodland fringe and plainly unabashed, in no way attempting to hide his presence, Harry Coggin ran into the late sunlight of the open fields. The fugitive stood for a moment, turning his head left and right, then seemed to gaze straight up the grassy slope of the hill at the spot where Williams stood with his binoculars, not quite hidden in the shade of a clump of trees. For a moment Williams stared directly into the other's eyes, and he couldn't help but notice, even through the glasses, how strangely vacant those orbs were.

"Well, I'll be…!" he excitedly whispered, passing the glasses to Brown who quickly put them to his eyes, and murmured:

"Yes, he's here!" Then, while Brown kept a close watch on Harry, Williams went to the car parked a little deeper in the clump and quietly, urgently passed on the news.

Meanwhile, drawn as if by a magnet to the hidden police car, Harry came across a field and up the hill in an unerringly, unnaturally straight line. His clockwork legs drove him forward and up; his strange eyes were fixed unflinching upon trees near the hill's summit.

Brown, previously complacent, quickly became nervous. Still watching the approaching runaway, he called out to the returning Williams: "'Ere, George. This bloke's reckoned to be dangerous, ain't 'e? But just look at the *size* of 'im! Through these glasses, 'E's bleedin'…'uge!"

"It's okay, Fred. There'll be more of the lads here in no time. They're on their way now."

"But 'e's supposed to be after a car, ain't 'e?"

"He'll probably run…" Williams answered uncertainly, "as soon as he sees us." But after a moment's thought he added: "Of course, we could always jump him. We can hide and hit him as soon as he pokes his head in here."

"Listen," Brown insisted. "I've 'eard about this bloke. 'E's not the kind you jump—'e's a killer, 'e is!" He immediately searched around and found himself the short, club-like branch of a fallen tree. Williams, feeling suddenly naked, did the same.

And on came Harry, veering from his immaculately straight course only to avoid obstacles in his path: a thick patch of gorse bushes, a boulder, a lone tree. And his speed was such that the blue-clad watchers in the trees knew he would surely reach them before the help they had called for got here. The plan had gone sour. Harry "the Hit" Coggin hadn't waited for nightfall; he had not even tried to stay under cover, out of sight. His approach was almost insolent, mechanical…it seemed to Williams and Brown that he knew exactly what he was about. But all they could do was hide and wait.

Then, from the direction of the village, the constables heard the welcome growl of a car's engine, and knew as soon as they saw its black bonnet nosing up through the grass of the hillside that it contained plainclothes men, detectives who would probably be armed.

———————

"Trap!" Inth's telepathic warning sounded sharp in Sarl's receptors. *"Those two bipeds in the trees are waiting for you, I'm sure of it!"*

"But what—? How—?" Sarl began.

"No time for questions and answers. Just concentrate on what you're doing," Klee came in. *"We need that power source. It's our one chance. You have your vehicle, Sarl, and it's a powerful one. It should make a powerful weapon, too. Use it!"*

VII.

When young, up-and-coming detective-inspector Rimbolt climbed out of his car, it was to be met with a scene of savagery. His driver, as young as himself and less experienced, was similarly awed. Constable Williams, his skull laid open to the bone, was writhing on the ground in the shade of the trees, shouting unintelligibly and moaning between shouts. Constable Brown was in the act of battering Harry "the Hit" Coggin with the branch of a tree; Coggin held up his arms before him and deftly fended off the blows. Then Brown's club struck the fugitive's shoulder and there was an audible crack. The stricken shoulder slumped, but at the same time Coggin brought Brown a back-hander that flattened the policeman's nose and hurled him down in the leaves and earth.

At that, with a shouted command, detective-inspector Rimbolt snatched out his police automatic and leveled it at the fugitive. Coggin took absolutely no notice but stooped, scooped up Brown's unconscious form, tossed it like a rag doll at the newly arrived pair. The two of them were knocked off their feet, Rimbolt's gun discharging harmlessly in the air.

As Rimbolt climbed to his feet there came the sound of rending metal. He could hardly believe the evidence of his own eyes. There stood Coggin, wrenching at the bonnet of the white police car, tearing it open with his bare hands—no, with his bare *hand*, for his right arm hung almost uselessly at his side!

Even as the wide-eyed detective watched, bolts sheared and metal creaked. Finally the dented, twisted bonnet flew up with a crash and Coggin leaned forward to tear at the car's heavy battery. Blood flew from fingers lacerated on sharp metal edges as he straightened, tucking the battery under his good arm.

Then the blue-clad form of Rimbolt's driver hurtled out from the shade of the trees, striking Coggin in a rugby tackle as the fugitive turned from the car. "Good man!" Rimbolt shouted, searching desperately for his fallen weapon. Then, as he found the gun and turned back to the scene at the car, there came a sickening crunch—and a brief gurgling sound.

Harry "the Hit" Coggin kneeled over the young policeman's body, holding the battery high in one huge hand. With brutal force he brought it down into the already crushed and bubbling pulp of the young man's face. Aghast, Rimbolt cocked his weapon and fired it at Coggin from a distance of no more than fifteen feet. He missed, squeezed the trigger a second time…Nothing happened, dirt had choked the firing-pin.

Then Coggin looked up from his bloody work and saw him.

Rimbolt froze. The look in the killer's eyes was indescribable: not madness, neither that nor hate, nothing like Rimbolt had ever seen before. He backed away from Coggin, stumbling backward through low shrubbery, his mouth open and dry, eyes wide in fear. Then the fugitive climbed lopsidedly to his feet, turned away and began to run. Back down the grassy slope toward the woods he went, the battery tucked under his good arm, swaying and stumbling like a badly balanced robot.

Rimbolt's nerve returned. He quickly cleaned the firing-pin of his gun and kneeled against the bole of a tree. He aimed two-handed at the raggedly running figure and squeezed the trigger. The bullet hit Coggin somewhere low in the rear right of his body, probably his kidney, Rimbolt thought, spinning him through three hundred and sixty degrees. He fell, tumbling head over heels down a steeper part of the slope.

"Got you—you bloody black-hearted bastard!" Rimbolt shouted. Then his jaw dropped and he shook his head in utter disbelief. Coggin had climbed to his feet, was hobbling now with a queer, lurching gait, and still he carried the battery. Before the detective-inspector could take aim again the fugitive had disappeared into the trees.

VIII.

"I'm in trouble!" Sarl fearfully reported, *"each part of this creature's anatomy seems to rely more or less on its neighbouring parts—very much like the Gvries of Sapha-sapha VII. Right now parts of the system are trying to close down, the mind particularly. I've deadened the pain areas but that's had little effect. He's lost a lot of efficiency; he's losing essence, too, where he was shot. He's leaking like a pitted power-cell!"*

"Are you going to make it?" Inth remained comparatively calm.

"Oh, I'll make it—providing there are no more interruptions!"

"Yes," Inth told him. *"I was just about to mention that…"*

"Eh?"

"Klee and I have been scanning the area where we first picked up your vehicle. There are a lot more of them closing in—bipeds like him. They have quadrupeds with them. Symbiotic, at a guess. It looks serious. After the reception you got when you went for the power source, we have to assume…"

"I'm not a complete Yhinn!" Sarl heatedly protested, not waiting for Inth to finish. *"They saw us come in: they probably know what we're up to; they're trying to stop us!"*

"You could very well be right, yes."

"Can't you two throw them off, send them on a false trail?"

"We've already tried that," Klee came in, a little less calmly than Inth. *"After all, we're no more Yhinnish than you, Sarl—less Yhinnish, most of the time. The bipeds we could probably confuse a little, even though there are several of them, but the quadrupeds are particularly single-minded. They are tracking your vehicle and show only a passing interest in the illusions we've thrown at them. If we had more time, more experience of this world's life-forms—and if we knew exactly…"*

"If, if, if!" snapped Sarl, quite insubordinately. *"Forget it! Just maintain tracking contact with me, that's all. I've trouble enough without worrying about anything else. I'm doing my best to control a careening, damaged, barely functioning vehicle—and the trees in this wood all look alike to me!"*

"Temper, Sarl!" Inth snapped right back. *"How can you hope to control any vehicle when it's plain you can barely control yourself? Just make sure…"*

"Trouble!" came Klee's boosted warning, cutting off Inth's rebuke. *"There are two more bipeds hot on you trail, Sarl! They're closing with you fast. You'd better get that big vehicle of yours moving faster."*

"Do you want me to burn him out? He's badly damaged—and he's already going as fast as I can push him. Anyway, I'm nearly home. Be ready to take me aboard."

———————

Plainclothesmen Carter and Dodds had witnessed at a distance some of the action atop the wooded hill, and they had tried to take steps to cut Coggin off if he made a run for the woods again. Possibly they would have been successful had their car not bogged down in marshy ground to one side of the hill.

They had not thought for a moment to climb the hill in the tracks of the other two cars; there were already four policemen up there, one of them armed, and Coggin was, after all, only one man. When their car

146

got stuck fast they had scrambled out of it in time to see Coggin knocked down by Rimbolt's shot, his fantastic recovery, finally his hobbling escape into the trees. They had known something of the man's unenviable reputation, but nothing of his near-invincibility!

Immobilized by astonishment for a few seconds only, at last the detectives had set out after Coggin on foot, their weapons cocked and to hand. He had not been difficult to follow: where he'd passed, the ground and foliage were splashed with blood. He certainly wouldn't get far with a wound as bad as his must be.

Following the fugitive's scarlet trail—made doubly easy by the sounds of his crashing through the underbrush somewhere ahead— they moved as fast as they could. They were eager to put an end to this thing. Neither of them doubted for a single moment that the wounded man would surrender as soon as they had him cornered; his wound and their weapons permitted of no other possible conclusion. Suddenly Dodds caught his colleague's arm, dragging him to a halt.

"What's up?" Carter asked, his voice hushed in the wood's green shade.

"Listen...you hear anything? No? I think he's gone to ground. Either that or he's keeled over. Come on, let's get him!"

IX.

A minute later, entering an area of the wood where the boles of stout oaks towered high, as Carter ran past one such pillar, Sarl was waiting. He had his vehicle in gear and ticking over, with his foot on the clutch, and as Carter came into view he gunned Coggin's big motor and released the man's coiled muscles.

Right behind Carter, Dodds saw the massive, bloody fist strike out and clout the side of his colleague's head, knocking him clean off his feet with its force. Quite definitely Carter was out cold, if not dead, and now Coggin swung to face the second of his pursuers. For a split second Dodds looked into eyes that were utterly empty—then he

147

squeezed the trigger of his gun and Coggin was blasted back, arms flung wide, into tangled briars.

Knowing he had hit the big man in his right breast and guessing quite reasonably that he had done for him, Dodds put his gun away, stepped forward and leaned over Coggin's spread-eagled body. The empty eyes flicked open and stared at him; the terrible left hand whipped up and grabbed his throat, pulling him down. Dodds made several ugly, gurgling sounds as his windpipe was crushed. Then the big hand left his throat, bunched into a club and drove into his forehead. Finally his body was tossed aside and Coggin staggered upright. His hands, trunk and legs were covered in blood that pumped and splashed from his wounds. He swayed, picked up the battery awkwardly from where it lay nearby, then turned and moved on into the woods. Astride the man's dimly flickering brain Sarl grimly urged the last dregs of life out of his crippled, dying vehicle.

X.

"They have released one of the quadrupeds," Inth's message boosted into Sarl's mind. *"It's coming in this direction, and its coming fast. It could be after you—after your vehicle—or it could be after us! There's no way of knowing. Controlling their bodies is a very different hash of khrumm to reading their alien minds. We have tried to get into this quadruped's mind, but no use. So you'd better hurry, Sarl, hurry!"*

"I'm here," Sarl answered, desperately fighting to keep Coggin's bloodied almost-corpse aloft, *"already at the stream—and I see the quadruped!"*

Bruce, a big black Alsatian, always unruly and excitable, had slipped his leash when his handler stumbled on a root. That had been immediately after the party skirted the boggy area about the pond. With the quarry's scent strong in his nostrils and ignoring his master's commands, Bruce had bounded off into the trees and bushes. Apart from his unruliness, Bruce had one other problem: an unwillingness to let go until his target stopped moving! Once the target, or quarry, was down and disarmed, a police dog could usually be called off—but not Bruce. That was why his handler was sweating now as he raced through the woods after his runaway dog. If Bruce caught up with Coggin alone, he'd simply kill him out of hand!

Driven almost to a frenzy as Coggin's scent grew stronger, the dog had quickly covered the last half mile. Now he broke from the cover of the trees onto the bank of the stream. Ears erect, nose eagerly sniffling the air, Bruce's dog eyes took stock of two separate items. A bright shiny thing lay low in the mud close to the bank, and across the narrow strip of water a man lurched drunkenly, almost falling as he splashed out into the stream. The shiny thing was immediately forgotten; Coggins scent was so strong now that Bruce could almost taste it. With a whine of fury building to a snarl in his throat, he sprang to the attack.

Coggin's eyes were glazing, sending blurred pictures to Sarl. Nevertheless he saw the dog bounding across the stream toward him, saw the leap that brought the furry horror snarling for Coggin's throat. If Sarl's vehicle should be knocked off his feet now, the Hlitni driver knew he'd never get it up again. He directed all of Coggin's departing strength into his left arm and hand, swung the battery in a deadly arc. Brain and fur went flying as Bruce's final leap ended in crunching death.

As the dog's body went floating slowly downstream, Sarl pushed Coggin a few more paces forward, tossed the battery to land on the bank eight feet ahead of him, said:

For Great Hilta's sake…!"

The corpse went down on its knees in the water, swayed from side to side. The lights behind its eyes went out…and something flashed across the distance between the tiny spacecraft and Coggin's brow. A second later, as the corpse toppled forward, the rescue capsule was reeled in again and Sarl was back in the ship. Coggin lay face down in the stream, anchored by reeds, bobbing gently with the current, staining the water red.

Fifteen minutes later, as velvet evening started to settle and yellow lights in local village streets began to come on one by one, the spaceship's silver spike hovered over high tension cables where they stretched between great pylons. Briefly, causing no one the slightest concern, the lights in the villages dimmed and distant generators felt a momentary draining. Then the lights brightened again and curious observers might have noticed a tiny meteorite that traced a line of fire *upward* across the dusk of England. The Hlitni had departed, leaving behind a mystery that no man would ever solve satisfactorily.

Out into the spaces between the stars they sped, hurdling the light years that separated them from their destination. And in its cocoon in the bowels of the ship their new vehicle cool and asleep and uncaring, hastily commandeered against some yet unseen future need, pollen of the flowers of Earth still clinging to its legs. When they a wakened it, for however brief a time, it would serve them no more complainingly than had Harry "the Hit" Coggin, and…who knows? Perhaps, when they had replaced it with a vehicle more to their liking, it would then go on to buzzing away its lifespan exploring the strange flowers of some alien world's warm jungles.

Perhaps one day, hybrid blooms would burn beyond Orion…

PART 2

The Novellas

Mandraki

Take care who you lie down with … and where!

There is no sensible explanation for what follows—no sensible or scientific explanation—or if there is I've failed to find it. Not that I've really looked. But then again, where would I start? I feel that I'm in a nightmare and can't wake up. But I know that in fact it's real, for I've seen it all before. I've seen it before and didn't believe it then; and now it's happening I would definitely prefer not to believe it! It was like the Lorelei, I know: a myth or legend, but it lured me: the weird mystery of it. And anyway, it's too late now for I'm wrecked on the rocks. Or wrecked in the pebbles, the dirt, the boggy soil.

What a jumble!

So let me start again, at the beginning. That way I won't be jumping any fences before I come to them…

―――――――

Unlike other children, I wasn't a believer in…well, things. Even Santa Claus only lasted until I was three or four. Maybe I lacked imagination, but as a youngster I never considered myths and legends as anything other than old fireside yarns translated into books to amuse and entertain; they were without foundation. Or maybe someone had explained it to me that way early on in life; my father, perhaps, who was a very much down-to-earth type. Whichever, to my young and perhaps unimaginative mind old-wives tales, adages and slogans, catch-words and phrases, they all fell within the same category: I knew

153

that akin to folklore and fairytales, they had been created to suit situations.

My mother, from Yorkshire, was full of these things: "Red sky at night, shepherd's delight; red sky in the morning, shepherd's warning. Where there's muck there's brass. The grass is always greener on the other side..." etc. Imparted as words of wisdom—or maybe in a cautionary context prior to my putting some seemingly shaky plan or other into action—or delivered with a sad slow shake of the head when things didn't work out; or with a smile broad as sunshine on those occasions when she was able to correct something before it went wrong—"a stitch in time saves nine." In this way my mother, like most mothers, could be wise before and after the fact.

Nowadays, however, I'm more inclined to look for sources—for the meaning behind the myth—or maybe just for answers. And for all that I've discovered "there's no smoke without fire," still I have failed to "let sleeping dogs lie." With the result, of course, that I've been bitten. A pity I didn't pay heed to that other one: "once bitten, twice shy..."

Do you know the story of Pandora's box? Of course you do. And haven't we created a box of our own—a sarcophagus—in Chernobyl? And isn't the African jungle just such a box, where mutant viruses we haven't even heard of may be waiting to leap off monkeys onto us? That last is simply Nature in one of her ugliest guises, I agree, but surely the *real* boxes are in the laboratories, where scientists study, store, and even *make* such lethal imps. "Back to Nature!" people cry. But is that really the answer?

Diseases that transfer from animal to animal to people. An awful *thing* that moves from sheep to cows and mutates along the way, and won't die when you cook it, so that eating a hamburger you risk turning your brain to a sponge. Poisons in the air and the soil and the sea, and in all manner of creatures: *natural* poisons, that is. A jellyfish whose living sting causes convulsions and death, bats that carry rabies, brightly colored Amazonian frogs whose sweat is a poison as deadly as any we know. And these are only a few of the things that we *do know* about.

Mandraki

But what about those we don't know about? And those we've forgotten or that we ignore, that came down to us as myths and legends?

What about the green things? Poison ivy and stinging nettles, and mushrooms taken in small measure that will cause you to hallucinate (and eaten freely kill you in a minute) sprouting in harmless earth; and indeed *all* of the green things that flourish in mire and decay. The ingredients for witches' brews. I remember my mother had a beautiful scented rose bush...one that sprang up where my pet kitten was buried...

People complain (rightly, I suppose) about the destruction of the rain forests, but I can't help wondering. Oh, I know: we seem to delight in murdering species that aren't even catalogued as yet, and there may be rare cures in some of them to balm the ills of the world. But what of those that aren't so beneficial? Are there potential ills in the earth and in the forests that are beyond Man's cures? For it seems to me there's always a balance: for day there's night, for black there's white, and for good there's evil. So what about penicillin...?

Ebola? Or is that just for starters?

Myths and legends. What *really* happened to the people of Sodom and Gomorrah? Some prehistoric form of AIDS? Something they got from their animals and passed on to each other? Whatever it was, it sucked all the moisture out of them and turned them to pillars of salt. And vampirism and lycanthropy? Superstitions and nothing more—or were these the olden names for rabies before we knew what hydrophobia really was? Hydrophobia...is that why the monstrous blood-suckers of so many worldwide legends were, or are, afraid of running water?

Premature babies die from fungal infections in hospital units—and the cause is found to be wooden spatulas used as tongue depressants in throat examinations. Say "Ah!" and die. Other babies suffer amputations where spatulas have been used as splints on their tiny limbs. And these...these *lollipop sticks* are just dead wood! But the fungus in the wood wasn't nearly dead, obviously.

Poisons, Catalysts, and Other Biologically Transmissible Hazards: Animal-to-Man, Plant-to-Man. Or: *Flora, Fauna, and Associated Fears: the Biological Interface. (Are We Returning to Our Roots?)* I could write a book on it. For God knows I've read enough about it…

What I'm saying is, things that would have been put down to witchcraft or demonology three hundred years ago—things that rheumatic old ladies would have been burned at the stake for—now have scientific explanations. Well, Some of them.

And so might this. But I doubt it.

The witches of the Old World knew of these things, and so did its priests. They had to, to fight fire with fire. And I'm sure that a handful of them, in certain places, still do.

But God, what a jumble! And my story still untold. Because I've been putting it off…

A few minutes ago the Greek Orthodox priest noticed me scribbling in my book. I saw him yesterday down on the beach, well away from the salt flats and marshy margin. He seemed unusual, I thought. But he was friendly to a girl who must be the skimpiest-clad Greek female I have ever seen in the Mediterranean. Or maybe it's simply that the place was isolated from the more touristy areas; or she could be from the mainland, Athens perhaps, which is cosmopolitan and far more tolerant.

Anyway, the girl had been swimming around the rocks of a reef close in to shore and she'd brought back a wire basket of large black spiny sea-urchins, echinoderms. I didn't know they were edible, but she in her tiny bikini and the priest or monk in his tall black capstan of a hat and ankle-length black robe sat on a slab of rock cracking them into a basin and squeezing lemons onto them, eating them raw and with great relish, washing them down with weak, local retsina.

As I passed close to them, between the narrow dark strip of sand that passed as a high-water mark and the pitted white rock where they sat, the priest squinted at me and cocked his head on one side. Smiling, he said, "Guten Tag?" His greeting was also a question.

Mandraki

I shook my head but agreed, "Pleasant, isn't it? Not too, er…*zesti?*"

"English!" he grinned, and his teeth were extremely rotten. The girl, stunningly beautiful, glanced at his teeth and tried not to shrink away. And I couldn't help thinking—*with teeth as bad as that, his breath has to be bad, too.*

There was something about him; I couldn't smell him like the girl *must* be able to, and so didn't mind, well, looking at him—I was somehow *drawn* to look at him. And I saw how old he was: probably a grandfather. Wrinkled as an olive that fails to fall from the tree. And I remember asking of myself: *why do they wear black? Why, in all this heat?* For even on a relatively cool day it must have been hell under that black robe.

But by then his smile had fallen away, and frowning, he seemed brought up short; almost as if he believed he knew me from somewhere but couldn't remember. And as I made off along the beach, kicking at the shingle to uncover a few bleached shells, his yellowish gaze had followed me. I could feel his eyes on me…

In the shade of a walnut tree whose branches made a tent and hid me at least partially from view, I seated myself on a gnarly root, looked back at the beach, and wondered at the paradox of this apparently incompatible pair. And after a while a sleek white motorboat came speeding into view from behind the jagged headland and sliced towards the beach, unzipping the sea like a pair of blue jeans. The girl waved, and wonderful bronze creatures lounging behind the rail of the sundeck waved lazily back. They had come to pick her up.

A moment later, she was saying her goodbyes to the old man and running for the water. A dive took her from shallow to deep water as the boat slowed to a crawl inside the reef and settled on its bow wave. Swimming with easy, practiced strokes the girl reached the boat; hands that glittered with gold and doubtless expensive watches reached down for her; her lithe body streamed water as she was drawn from the sea. And I was jealous of whoever it was who patted her backside as her feet found the deck.

Then the boat revved up and leaned over a little as it turned for the open sea, and I saw that the old priest was already heading back my way. He was still a way off, however, so I managed to avoid him—to not notice him—and returned to the village. I had avoided him, *then* at least, but not the second time, two days later, though why I should have wanted to avoid him at all is anybody's guess.

Or maybe not. Perhaps I was afraid to discover what I was searching for…

———————

So now, two days later—

—I'm writing this back in my room in town. It's not yet noon, so I can calculate how early it must have been when I saw the priest again, in that place, this morning. Maybe that's why he came to talk to me: because he wondered why I was there and so early? Or maybe he still thought he knew me.

That place:

I emphasize it without even thinking about it; but I had better explain *what* place I'm talking about, and try to say why I was there; why it's so important I had found it as close as this to the village, and why the old Greek priest or monk thought it might be better if I hadn't found it, or returned to it, at all…

My father had been there, too, as a Special Forces Commando in World War II—oh, thirty-five years ago—when some of the islands were crawling with invading Nazis. To this day many of the Greeks despise the Germans, despite the fact that they live off their tourism. As to which island or islands *exactly*…it doesn't matter. You really don't want to know. Or if you do, I'm not telling. Unlike my father, I don't intend to leave so many clues. Curiosity killed the cat.

So why am I writing this down, if not for posterity? Perhaps it's for the old Greek priest, or monk. Maybe I'm telling him about this Pandora's Box of his, or of theirs, whoever the other guardians are. But I suspect there's nothing much I can tell him that he, or they, don't already know. For the box was opened during the war. Opened *again*, that is.

158

Mandraki

And it was then that my father was here.

He was a young or youngish man then, only twenty-five or so. Me, I wasn't even born, and wouldn't be for another ten years. But when he started to come back here—in my early teens—he had to bring me with him because my mother believed he was seeing another woman out here. This was after she had developed her photophobia; the Mediterranean sun would have killed her. So if not for another woman, why else would my father, knowing her deadly condition, insist on spending all his holidays in the Greek Islands? Anyway, it was only a year or two after he'd started on this Greek thing of his—this odyssey?—that Ma died of cancer. And I remember he said it was a mercy. But what was a mercy? What did he mean? The fact that her cancer had taken her so quickly, or that she had been spared what was still to come?

An odyssey: we wandered from island to island, visiting all the places he still remembered from the war. As a spy, in the guise of a Greek, he had served in a lot of places, and we revisited them. This was during my holidays from school, these being the only times he could bring me with him, therefore the only times Ma would let him come. And she stayed home in England, in her dark glasses, in her shady room. And she probably fretted about his fidelity, while he was fretting about something else entirely. Fretting and…stiffening up.

…I'm stiffening, too. I tell myself it's the Greek Islands: the heat. But it isn't. Or if I drank ouzo maybe I could blame it on that. The owner of a taverna saw me easing my neck, slowly cranking my shoulders—all my painful movements generally—and asked if I drink much ouzo. I asked why? He told me if you don't drink it with water it drains the oil out of your joints. Then he pointed out the old men: their rheumatic joints; their shuffling about wearing gnarled, weathered-leather, pained and patient expressions. And: "Ouzo!" he declared, with the emphasis on the "z". "When they were young, they drank it too much. They drink thee ouzo without thee water." Well, maybe they did, but I don't.

This island was the last one we came to. I suspect because he was avoiding it. I suspect because he knew, as I now know, that this place was the one. And he was putting off the inevitable…

He had taken to drink (not ouzo, but just about everything else), soon after we lost my mother. I know now that it was just to ease the pain, the stiffness in his joints…or mainly so. His room was next to mine, and one night I woke up to the sound of his moaning. Thinking he was nightmaring about Ma, I went in and sat on his bed.

He had been drinking and didn't wake up, but I heard him say, "Don't sleep with the mandrakes, John." That's me, John. I stayed a little while but eventually, as I left him and tiptoed to the door, he said it again. "Don't sleep with the mandrakes! They whisper their warnings, John, but even they don't understand. They have forgotten, as I shall soon forget. They would scream, but they've forgotten who to scream at. So don't sleep with the mandrakes…" His voice was full of shudders.

And in his study all sorts of botanical books, clippings, photocopies from rare library sources, vegetable vagaries. But this was a man who loathed gardening! And there were maps, too, all of Mediterranean shores and islands.

But: "Not a single Mandraki," he said to me one time. "Oh, the locals know the name—the term?—well enough. There are Mandrakis every-bloody-where, as frequent as St. Paul's bloody Bays…except on the maps! The closest we get to acknowledging it is in Rhodes: Mandraccio Harbour, where stood the Colossus. The rest of it is all myth and legend—like vampires on Santorin, the volcano island. You know our saying, John: don't take coals to Newcastle? You know its meaning? That it's pointless taking coals to Newcastle because Newcastle has enough of its own? Well of Santorin they say don't take vampires! And of mandrakes they won't speak at all!"

I scarcely knew what he was talking about, not then. But I did know that he was a down-to-earth man who had never had a lot of time for myths and legends. Never *used* to have, anyway. "It's as if," he said, sighing his frustration, "I wasn't supposed to remember. But I do, and I know that it's important."

There I go, jumping about again. It's not easy to remain lucid. My bones ache…

———————

"Important!" said the old priest, puffing and panting where he clambered towards me over a heap of weathered stones that might at one time have been a wall.

…But I was going to explain about the place—if not its actual location, an idea of its topography. Little or no use as a guide; there are a million places just like it.

Inland, a range of low but jagged mountains. Green but by no means lush. Scrubby, let's say. And a white dot way up there that could be a monastery. Closer, vague grey foothills falling down from the mountains, their spurs reaching out to the aching blue Mediterranean. A quarter-mile away, above the beach, something of a church. Oh, very well, a church…but some of the Greek Island churches are little more than shrines, tiny little things. And this is one of them.

Four walls with a high frontal facade bearing a white cross. Inside, a whitewashed room no bigger than your living room, with arched niches or recesses in the walls that house icons. And medieval paintings on the walls depicting Jesus, angels, one or two saints with haloes, demons, and sea-beasts. When priests come down from the monastery, they probably pray there. Or they use it to keep watch…?

Then the land sloping down to the sea, and in between this jumble of rock-piles and a few scattered ruins, not ancient but just primitive fishermen's houses; I'm told there was a village here before the earthquake. But which one? The islands have had lots of earthquakes. Finally there's a handful of untended, ancient olives that might even have been a grove at one time, and a disused path leading through them to the deserted sand and shingle beach. Obviously it's off the beaten track.

At one end of the beach where the ground dips and the sand turns to mud there's a boggy place, a swampy margin that smells bad when the wind is from that direction. The ground behind is flattish, only gradually rising, and between the marsh and the church the vegetation thickens up a little. A few gnarly olives, spiky bushes, spitefully sharp grasses, some wild-flowers, various weeds, and a lot of Greek pod-plants—squirting cucumbers?—that *pop!* and spit weak acid at you if you brush by them too close. And mandrakes: *Mandragora officinarum.*

"Or perhaps thee different, er, sapecies?—ah, yes, *species!*—thee different *species* altogether, but mandraki anyway, of a sort, yes," the old priest told me, with a decisive nod. Then asked, abruptly: "Was you father German, perhaps?"

"You don't like them, do you." I said, knowingly.

"Thee mandrakes? Thee Germans?" He cocked his head on one side in that way of his.

"Either…. Both!" I said with a stiff shrug, from where I'd chosen a flat rock for a seat. I was surrounded by mandrakes, sprouting in the rich, swamp-fed soil. "But…the Germans?"

"Ah, thee Germans!" he answered me shrug for rather more thoughtful shrug. "Now is too late, not liking them. I not believe in this thing, thee sins of thee fathers. You know? I not *want* believe…"

"And thee mandrakes?" (I was picking up this peculiar person's manner of expression.) "And this 'sapecies' in particular?"

"Thee necessary evil," he replied, almost without thinking. But then he *did* think, and quickly corrected himself: "Er, Thee *samell*—thee stink. Thee flowers—sickly, when is too many of them …like here. Nasty samell, yes?"

"You keep watch over them." I was direct.

He chose not to understand, frowned and looked back at the church. Between the church and the scrubby ground, a few leaning stone crosses and headstones within a low-walled area spoke mutely of an ancient graveyard. "Over *them*," he said, "yes. Men who died in thee war. Local men. Thee resistance."

"In England there would be some kind of memorial," I said. "A monument. And every year people would come to remember. Here the people seem to have gone away."

162

"Some come," he said, looking at me curiously.

"And then you are here, to *keep* them away," I said. "or to make sure they are simply visiting the beach. Like the girl you talked to the other day."

"Thee girl?" And then he remembered. "Ah, thee girl! With thee, er, thee black, er—"

"—The sea urchins. Echinoderms?" I prompted him.

"Thee *echini*, yes! She has thee lover. She want be alone a little moments, for thee thinking."

"But it's a bad place to do your thinking, eh? Your dreaming?" I said. "I mean, too close to the mandraki?"

Then he knew that I knew. His eyes went wide, and leaning closer he said, "You know of me, of us, thee brotherhood—but do you know *me*, myself?"

"The sins of the fathers," I said. "No, I don't know you, but I think my father might have."

And then he knew for sure. "You father!" he gasped. "So, I was right. But not thee Germans. Thee *English* captain! Thee soldier! You are looking so much like him—*ah!*" Followed by silence for a long while. And I took the opportunity to think back, back...

My father, the English captain. He had been one of several officers who organized the islands' underground resistance. Loners mainly, they spoke Greek—looked Greek, under a Mediterranean suntan—fished during the long summer days, and created mayhem at night. So he'd told me, on one of those rare occasions when he told me anything.

...After Ma died, he refurbished her old greenhouse to cultivate them. Mandrakes, I mean. And now I wondered: You know the old myths, the old legend of the mandrake, don't you, old priest, or monk, whatever you are? Oh, I know *you* do! But I'll tell you what *I* know anyway. See if I get it right, okay?

They were well known in Biblical times...well of course they were! As long as there have been shamans, witches, witchdoctors, alchemists, occultists—as long as there have been myths and legends—there have been mandrakes. They are said to have aphrodisiac properties. Maybe that explains Solomon in Song 7: 13…"The mandrakes give a smell, and at our gates are all manner of pleasant fruits, new and old, which I have laid up for thee, 0 my beloved." He was a horny one, Solomon. "Come smell the mandrakes, while I get my leg over." That's what he was really saying.

And then there's Genesis 30: 14-16…the story of Jacob, Reuben, Rachel, and Leah. What woman needs another woman's man when she can chew on the fruits of the mandrake? Or bring herself off with its root.

And the smell…narcotic? "When perfectly developed the fruits lie in the centre of a rosette of dark-green leaves, like yellowish bird eggs in a nest. They have a peculiar but not unpleasant smell and sweetish taste, and being principally an emetic, purgative, and narcotic, are mildly poisonous. The plant was much employed in dubious medicine in the olden days, mainly due to superstitious regard of its thick tap-root, which has a passing resemblance in shape to the lower limbs and quarters of the human body…"

That's what one book says of it. But that's one of many books and mainly botanical. Other volumes are more concerned with the superstition itself. Look for the mandrake in Josephus, and in Pliny, and in the "Lost Books" of Solomon himself…if they weren't, alas, "lost." but since they treated of magic, King Hezekiah destroyed them, "lest their contents do harm."

The mandrake—the *baharas*—the Zauberwurzell or sorcerors root… as in the German.

My father used to kill Germans. And then the Greek monks had to dispose of the bodies.

"They had wagons," my father recalled one time. "Nothing motorized, you understand. Just donkey-hauled carts with wooden or very occasionally rubber wheels. Traders hauled fish, fruits, kerosine, oil, hay, between villages. The priests had to come down out of the mountains for all their provisions, even for water when the rains were late. At least, that was the excuse they used for always being around. But if we were up to a bit of sabotage and a German patrol came on the scene, we weren't afraid to take them out. We could always count on the brotherhood to be there with a cart. I can't tell you how many motorcycles got dumped in the sea where the cliffs fell sheer into deep water, or how many German bodies were hauled away in those donkey-carts. The monks weren't much bothered by German checkpoints or patrols, you see? Not at first, anyway. I mean, for supposedly religious types they were the blankest-faced liars I've ever come across! And the bravest. But oh, there's at least one thing about them I still don't know."

"You don't remember where all this happened?" I said. It was a guess, but I was right. "It was life and death, but still it escapes your memory?"

"We were active on many islands," he told me. "It's as if it has all merged into one. As if I'm not *supposed* to remember it!"

"But it's important?"

"Very! What did they do with the bodies?" he said. "That's what I keep asking myself. What did they do with those bloody bodies! Where—*how*—did they dispose of them? I mean, those German patrols simply disappeared. So completely that for a long time the officers in charge must have begun to believe they were dealing with deserters! Which wasn't unthinkable, because by then they were on the losing end of things. And they were watching the harbour, all the small bays and other suitable landing places, checking that their young soldiers weren't simply running away to the mainland and putting distance between."

"What is it that's drawing you back?" I asked him. "Is it just to get it out of your system—the horror of it, I mean?"

"The horror of it? Of the war, the killing?" He shook his head. "Horror, yes, of something. But not of that. That was my job…"

"And you never did find out what the monks were doing with the bodies of the Germans you killed?"

"No." He shuddered, despite that it wasn't nearly cold in the greenhouse. "Yes, I did…I think, but I'm not sure. And that's what's driving me. I have to be sure."

"Oh?" I tried to keep it light, because this was the closest my father had ever come to the root of it. My God…*to the root of it!*

"One night," he told me, very quietly, "one night when my party of Greek resistance fighters had blown up a small ammunition depot and melted back into the hills, I talked to one of the priests. He asked if he could help, but I said no, there was nothing to dispose of this time. Which was when I thought to ask him what they did with the bodies. He was a young man, but perhaps not so young as myself, and very mild-seeming. But, 'Ah,' he told me with a grin you wouldn't believe—an almost fiendish grin that opened up a mouthful of gapped, uneven, broken teeth and savage satisfaction—'the bodies of the Germans, yes? Well, don't you worry about them. They will never be found. Not a trace. They are no more. They sleep with the mandrakes…'"

"His broken teeth?"

"Some German had hit him in the mouth with the butt of his rifle. Nerves were fraying and their brutality was on the increase. Also, a group of priests had been rounded up and shot along with the young men of one of the villages. It was as a reprisal for the loss of one of their officers."

"And this sleeping with the mandrakes thing?"

"I took it to mean they were buried. Like this Sicilian thing about sleeping with the fishes—when they dump a victim's weighted body in a lake or in the sea. That's what I *took* it for, anyway…"

———————

"But you…I not understanding," said the old monk, breaking into my memories. "Him, you father, I understanding that. But not you. Why *you* come here?"

"You understand about my father?" I said, eagerly if achingly, and more than a little wearily. "Then you know why he did it, why he slept with the mandrakes—actually *slept* with them, here—there." I twitched my stiff neck, indicating the ground behind me, the coarse Mediterranean shrubbery, weeds, and mandrake rosettes in their dozens in the damp earth at the edge of boggier ground.

Mandraki

"A mistake," the old man told me. "He not know…thee accident! Thee Germans, they were ready for leaving thee island. Your father do bombs, sabotage on their boats. They hear him on his radio: he will be picked up from thee beach. But which beach? Thee Germans not know. They cover thee one road, thee donkey tracks, and thee beaches. Your father, he must hide. He is—how you say—pinned down, yes? He stay here, thee whole long night, hiding. But *here*, in this place! Mandraki!"

"And he slept. Lying low. On the ground. With them."

"He was—how you say?—exhausted, yes. He cover him with some bushes, and he sleep…"

––––––––––––

Exhausted, and he slept. Like me that time when I was with my father in the greenhouse. I was exhausted by the tension and the continual mental tug-o'-war. We were sitting opposite sides of a garden table. Suddenly he got mad with his useless memory—or with the memories that wouldn't let themselves be remembered—and he brought his left fist down on the table. His little finger made a dry cracking sound, and broke off at the junction with his hand. It just broke off!

He looked at it lying on the table, then at the stump. No blood. It didn't bleed. It was grey, fibrous, like a piece of rotten dowelling; there was maybe just a suggestion of moisture, like an old carrot when you snap it. Useless and unfeeling, his entire left hand was more or less the same. He could scarcely bend the rest of his fingers. This was the first time I had noticed this infirmity, because he'd kept it hidden. But no longer.

And I thought: leprosy! I knew there were colonies in the Greek Islands, though the disease has been on the decrease ever since World War Two. But he had been *in* World War Two! Was that what this was all about?

He reeled out of the greenhouse and I sat there paralyzed thinking he was going to get help, see a doctor.

Exhausted, yes…emotionally exhausted. And I fell asleep.

I slept with the mandrakes.

When I woke up I was in my chair…but my feet were three or four inches down into the dry earth, as if it were a bog in there! I pulled them out, and that made a sucking sound. Then I pulled up the mandrakes—dragged them up by those horrible forked roots which are so like the bodies and legs of a man or woman—all of them. But though I half expected it, (for I had been reading my father's books), not a one of them screamed.

Of course not, for they *were only* mandrakes! They had *only* been nourished with water, and maybe a little plant food. They were plants, with no dreams of their own.

His scribbled letter said goodbye; he was going back to the islands. I would not see him again. Whatever he left behind was mine. And whatever else I did, I must never sleep with the mandrakes…

Too late.

When I removed my shoes, they had been eaten right through the soles. They were as soft and as riddled as Gorgonzola. And I wondered: some acidic poison in the plant food, maybe?

But I thought not…

———————

"You missed him," I told the old monk, whom I now knew to have been my father's monk. "He came back. He was—he is—here. But you didn't stop him. Why not?"

"I hear them," he said. "Mandraki! In my dreams I hear them! It is like thee—how you say—thee *excitement!* Thee whispers! But not for thee longest time. Then last summer I hear them again. But I think is *only* a dream. I come down from thee monastery anyway. But they are quiet again. I not know, but perhaps…"

"…Not perhaps," I cut him off. "Definitely. That was my father." And I held up my father's watch, stainless steel, all crusted with dirt, as I had found it in the soil where I slept with the mandrakes. He had always been a solid, very much "down-to-earth" type, my father. *Hah!*

I'm sure that the old monk couldn't understand my humourless grin when I told him: "The strap—a single corroded link of the strap—was sticking up out of the earth. Where there's muck there's brass, you see, or sometimes chromium-plated steel…and sometimes much more that that." By then he had brushed by me to go stumbling about in the mandrakes, his mouth gaping—working in a sort of silent, violent, biting horror—snapping at the air with those blackened fangs. Because suddenly he knew that I had been sleeping…sleeping there, with all those mandrakes. And yet I felt sure there was something other than horror in him, some grotesque curiosity, something habitual, almost an addiction.

There in a den of squirting pod-plants, which he set popping and hissing as they jetted off like small aerial plums to spread their seed, he found my bed. A place where the soil was indented in my shape; more than indented, *compressed*, to a depth of some eight or nine inches.

"But why? Why *you?*" he finally mumbled.

I could have told you then, old monk, that it was probably in my blood, or that I had picked up my "habit" in England, in my mother's old greenhouse. But I didn't bother. I knew that it was irreversible, and that eventually you'd be reading this. Oh, yes, for I know now that this is for you.

Still, I was a little anxious and angry. You may remember I asked you: "Why haven't you destroyed them? Is it…*Godly*, or priestly—or even monkish—that they're allowed not only to exist but to flourish here?" And your answer:

That the mandrakes had been here in Mandraki before you, and before every invader, and that they'd always been used for the same purpose. That there are Romans down there, and Asiatic Huns, Knights Crusader, Turks, Italians, and goodness knows who or what else! "Their screams, they would be making thee brotherhood deaf—or mad!" you said. "Thee whole world might be make deaf, or mad!"

"They scream?" I didn't believe…until I remembered my father's nightmares. *They would scream* (he said), *but have forgotten who to scream at!*

"In our dreams," you explained, you old Priest of the Mandrakes. "In thee dreams—and in thee *minds*—of men!"

"But mainly in the dreams of the brotherhood? The Brotherhood of the Mandrake?" I nodded my understanding. "A Pandora's box, which you daren't destroy."

"And besides," you said, "thee Turkey man is always thee threat, even today…" Followed by that terrible grin of yours that my father saw, for like me you had accepted the inevitability of *my* lot. And you had simply shrugged it off! With that grin, and a smell like raw sewage from your rotten mouth—you oh-so-false-priest you—you'd accepted that I was lost! And I knew you would do it again, if you thought it was necessary. You and your *un*orthodox brothers, in their high white monastery somewhere in the mountain heights, would start it up again if or whenever your bloody island was threatened!

And then, quietly I asked you, "Do they know? Did any of them other than my father know? Tell me: are they down there thinking, *knowing*, even now? And…and does it hurt? I mean the change? Does the change hurt?"

But you could only shrug that fateful shrug of yours, for you didn't know. And it seemed to me that now you had accepted *my* fate, you didn't really care…

You didn't know if it would hurt, couldn't say if there would be pain, because the ones *you* had lain to rest with the mandrakes were already dead. (All of them, I wonder?) But like my father before me *I* am still alive. And by the time you read this, old man, I *shall* know! But *un*like my father, I shall remember everything. And it will be that much faster for me, for while he did it only once, I've slept with the mandrakes night after night!

And because it will be faster, I won't have time to forget, I shall remember! And tomorrow or the day after—or the night after that, or next year—but definitely while I'm still able, I'll come back here. And I *swear* that I'll remember, for everything will be written here in my book. Then, when they take me, I'll not merely sleep with them but *talk* to the mandrakes, explain it all. And then *they* shall know and remember, too.

Mandraki

Yes, and then they'll know how to scream and where to *direct* their screaming! Good luck to you and your bloody brotherhood then, you old false priest…!

––––––––––

The girl from a speedboat, where it lolled oh-so-gently on a sea blue as the sky, spied the old monk on the steep route to the monastery with her binoculars and sighed her relief. He was the same one who had spoken to her before, she felt sure. That had been what, a year ago, two? She felt glad that she hadn't been here while he was still on the beach. But no, this time he was already climbing a track between stunted olives, and he seemed to be in a hurry. That was good; she hadn't much cared for him; his entire aura—especially his breath, his teeth—was horrible! But he was a priest, or a monk, and so she had shared her catch with him. This time, however, the beach was deserted. Odd, that every time they'd sailed by it was always deserted. But this time her entire party had decided to come ashore, and she had been first in the water.

The boat was anchored on a surface flat as a mirror; and this lovely girl, towing her things in a waterproof bag, prided herself that she'd beaten the rest of them to dry land. But now here they came, their golden bodies arrowing lazily into the shallows. She glanced at them now and then; but suddenly felt an urge to once more focus her binoculars on the old monk.

What on earth was he doing?

He had come to a halt; he stood stock still on the rocky goat track, then gave a little leap—and then another! And now he was tearing something up. A book? Scraps of paper went fluttering, like a flower shedding petals. His weird dance continued. He cavorted, his body twisting and whipping, his black cassock swirling, billowing. And for a moment—a brief moment as she twisted a knurled knob to bring him into clearer definition—she saw his face. Those bulging eyes; that yawning rictus of a gape. And his ravaged teeth that she remembered only too well! Then his tall black capstan hat went flying; he appeared to be slapping his open palms hard against his ears, as if to crush his head between his hands!

Some kind of ritual? Or was it simply a bad toothache? But that agonized look on his face… why, she believed she could even hear his screams, or somebody's screams, from here! Such a powerful image — like *The Scream* by that odd artist fellow, Edvard Munch, wasn't it? Or maybe he was insane. They must be very lonely up there, somewhere higher on the mountain. But she had twisted the knob too far and the priest had suddenly blurred to a lurching black blob.

Then, once more remembering his smell, she shuddered and put the binoculars down. For despite that he was a priest, or monk, or whatever, his memory was an offence to the tranquility of the place. This forgotten little patch of beach, that for some reason or other no one ever came to visit. This place, known only as Mandraki.

A tranquil place, yes.

But high up in a monastery in the mountains, everything was other than tranquil. Everything was bedlam…

Two-Stone Tom's Big T.O.E.

Yes, except he was an entire science heavier than that!

The distinction between past, present, and future is an illusion, although a persistent one.

Albert Einstein

Adam Tempest drove furiously through the city's almost empty, early morning streets cursing himself, or more properly a too-tightly wound alarm-clock, for the "lateness" of the hour. Late in that it was already a few minutes to six a.m., when old Two-Stone Tom's experiment was set to commence; or to "go off," as a certain junior member of the team—a self-appointed if somewhat morbid court jester—had had it, in something less than (a hasty glance at his watch) five minutes' time.

Two-Stone Tom, yes. Better known—and to his face rather more deferentially—as Thomas Fotherington Wright: a scientist and, more especially, a distinguished theoretical physicist and cosmologist; also, and far more importantly, the lab's director and leading light. The latter in light of the fact that it had been his millions, or his banker father's before him, which in the main had built "the lab," the massive complex where one of his pet theories was about to be put to the test. Two-Stone Tom and his Big T.O.E.: his Theory Of Everything.

"The Lab," Adam mused, ignoring the speed limits. But that was a poor, indeed totally inadequate description of the place where he, also a physicist, worked. It definitely wasn't CERN, no not by a long shot, but neither was it a mere laboratory. A huge cube of a building some three blocks square in landscaped grounds on the city's rim, with its own numerous "labs", workshops, test-beds, offices and studies; with its powerful computers, rest rooms and quiet area—the latter in an extensive soundproofed library—a kitchen, and even an open—air smoking and strolling gallery; not to mention a retractable section of the roof fitted with a variety of telescopes…it was indeed a complex.

The car park had been a last—minute addition to the place's main building; narrow and featureless, a five-level tower with a spiralling interior ramp, it accommodated the vehicles of the sixty-odd people who worked there. The ground floor was for the menials—the cleaners, cooks, a handful of clerks—while the four upper levels had been set aside exclusively for the use of the staff: the white-coveralled notables with their (allegedly) superior IQs.

As Tempest fought centrifugal force and navigated the final bend in the road on complaining tyres, so the complex came into view less than half a mile away. At perhaps half that distance, there was another car on the road in front of him, which he was rapidly catching up on. But as he glanced at his watch for what must he the tenth time Tempest saw that he was most definitely going to be late; and, damn the man, Thomas Fotherington Wright was a stickler for punctuality—he wasn't about to be sitting on his backside twiddling his thumbs, and waiting patiently for Adam Tempest!

Grinning however sourly, grimly as he considered Fotherington Wright's nickname, how it had come into being, Tempest gave way to the inevitability of a ticking-off and eased up a little on the accelerator. It was quite clever really—if irreverent—of that selfsame self-appointed court jester to have thought of it: Two-Stone Tom's passion for Einsteinian quotes, for example that one about time being illusory. It was Einstein's name: in English translation "One Stone." Hence Fotherington Wright's transition into "Two-Stone Tom": Albert E's loyal disciple, who occasionally appeared to consider himself the original genius's second coming. Well, relativistically speaking. And again Tempest grinned, this time at his own cleverness.

Two-Sone Tom's Big T.O.E.

As for Fotherington Wright's T.O.E.: it was simply, or perhaps not so simply, his goal to finalize what Einstein and every scientist since him had attempted—and failed—to achieve: a Theory Of Everything, from the invisibly tiny to the infinitely massive, from theoretical quantum conditions to observable cosmic enormities.

"The universe," Fotherington Wright was fond of repeating, "is not only bound by space but by time: it is indeed a space-time continuum. Wherefore if time is but an illusion, then what of space? Is the future, like the past, already established both in time *and* space? Not so much a continuum but an immedium? Let us take a small item—say a glass bead, exactly the same today as it was yesterday and will be tomorrow—and see if we can't dislodge it from the NOW into some other alleged space, another WHEN. We won't he smashing its atoms but merely relocating them intact within the apparent impermanence."

As to how the test would work, or not:

"I haven't yet calculated whether the shift will be to what we call the past or to what we imagine as the future; that will be determined as a result of the initial experiment. Its mechanics are simple: the bead will be released to roll down a groove on a gentle test-bed incline, where at a predetermined central area of the groove the power shall switch on automatically for just one second. Then, assuming my figures are correct and the power flows true and steady, the bead should disappear and relocate immediately to where it was ten seconds earlier—at its point of release!

"Similarly, or possibly contrarily—depending on a number of as yet unresolved factors—the bead may vanish and at once *advance* ten seconds in alleged 'future time' to reappear, stationary, at the buffer at the lower end of the groove. And regardless how it goes, forward or back, if we are successful the 'where and when' of it will be that we have proved that the entire concept of space, inseparable from its temporal accomplice, is just such an illusion as Einstein refers to however cryptically. Moreover, at last we shall have made a giant leap forward toward the formulation of a viable T.O.E.!"

Genius or lunacy? The two are balanced on a knife-edge, allegedly; and with a final, fruitless glance at his watch Tempest slowed down more yet, shrugging resignedly as he turned off the road onto the narrow driveway toward the car park's arched entrance. As for the driver of the car in front—probably another member of Fotherington Wright's team, though Tempest didn't recognize the car—he was driving far too slowly, and the vehicles were now nose to tail. And again softly cursing, he saw that it was exactly six a.m. as both cars entered under the sign with a figure ONE indicating the ground floor level…which was when events began to go strangely if not yet horribly awry.

Things blurred.

It was simply that: for no more than a second or two there was this visual distortion, a sort of physical wrenching which Tempest not only saw but felt, experienced within himself—a drunken twisting and weird *lengthening* of the way ahead into an indeterminate if not infinite distance—like sitting in a barber's chair looking down an apparently endless chain of mirrors. As for the glaring fluorescent lighting in this claustrophobic, concrete mausoleum of a place: however momentarily the tubes in the ceiling had flared up biliously where they curved away into an impossible region that looked like nothing so much as a cosmic wormhole or black hole's interminably spiralling whorl, and Tempest was left feeling sick and dizzy despite the transience of the anomaly.

But even as he slammed on the brakes and shook his reeling head, then reached up a hand to rub furiously at his apparently lying eyes, so the crazily elongated chaos ahead quit its inexplicable writhing and stretching and. concertinaed back to normality like an elastic band stretched beyond its capacity. Which occurred almost simultaneously with the ceiling lights suddenly blinking out—all of them, leaving only gloom and silence and emptiness behind.

Emptiness…well of course.

Naturally the car park was empty on the ground floor level: the menials wouldn't begin to arrive for another ninety minutes at least. But upstairs the rest of the so-called inner circle's vehicles—all seven of the other team members' cars — would he in their parking bays; would have been there for perhaps an hour or even longer as the experiment was set up and the equipment checked out. Adam Tempest's part in that, the final delicate adjustments to the lasers: that would have been handled by someone else. Which in turn would mean grovelling apologies all round; to Two-Stone Torn, obviously, and to whoever had stood in for Tempest, and then to the team as a whole…damn it to hell!

As for what had just happened, he rationalized as he started up the car's stalled motor and switched on its headlights: well, it was clear he'd been pushing himself too hard. A lousy night's sleep, then skipping breakfast, finally driving like a madman with his nerves on edge: it was a wonder he hadn't suffered a heart attack — or a stroke? Was *that* what happened when you had a stroke? Had he in fact had one, a small one? God, he hoped not! Not that! And all because of a faulty clockwork antique he called an alarm clock. Jesus!

Anyway, it had left him more than a little shook up. And as for the ceiling lights: well, shit happens. It had to be that a fuze had blown somewhere, causing the failure. Or maybe the experiment itself had sucked the juice out of the lights. Was the lab's entire electrical system connected up, including the car park, Tempest wondered? He doubted it. Surely not. But even so, Fotherington Wright's calculations would definitely have taken such as that into account…

Wouldn't they? Wouldn't he? Well of course he would!

And annoyed, irritated by his doubts and shrugging them off, Tempest drove the car slowly toward the first up-ramp. Say what you like about old Fotherington Wright, his was an intellect to be reckoned with. Oh, indeed!

Two-Stone Tom: the very definition of an absentminded professor, or perhaps a mad scientist? No, neither one. Just a very determined, eureka-obsessed man, who tended to ignore the mundane facts of existence — and possibly the laws of physics — in favour of the scientifically exotic. Such as his Big T.O.E.

And right now in the heart of the lab the team, minus one, would be either jubilant or dismayed at the success or failure of Fotherington

Wright's experiment in space and time, both of which concepts were illusory according to him — and perhaps to Albert E.? But then, who in his right mind would care to argue with the latter?

The team minus just one, yes; because the car ahead of Tempest didn't belong to some other late team member after all but a menial, (an unfortunate term), who was even now parking it in a bay near the up-ramp. Had it been a second member of the team such as Tempest had hoped for, that might have reduced the pressure he was feeling in respect of his own tardiness.

For "tardiness," or worse still "indifference," was how Two Stone Tom would surely see it; the hell of that being that actually Tempest was as eager as anyone else on the team to learn the result of the test! With which thought supplanting previous concerns about his health, he pursued the lancing cones of his headlight beams and glanced just once at the other vehicle and driver as he drove past and steered his car onto the up-ramp.

That brief glance at the other early-bird arrival left Tempest with a vague impression of a confused- or worried-seeming female face in profile: possibly a clerk, or perhaps an office gofer in one of the support departments...

The arch over the second level greeted him not only with a big white number TWO, whose paint was flaking, but also a peculiar, even eerie feeling of loneliness. Moreover, he noticed for the first time the cobwebs draping the entire length of the ceiling and the inch thick drifts of dust in the parking bays. Someone, some alleged maintenance man, was obviously sleeping on the job here. Not merely empty, the entire level actually looked deserted! Where, for instance, were the tyre tracks of the cars that had occupied these bays six days a week every week for several years now, and would occupy them again in just an hour or so's time?

And once again Tempest found himself rationalizing:

These apparent incongruities could only be an effect of the headlights, he felt sure; he'd never before had occasion to use them in the car park, and only rarely if ever at night. He didn't much care to drive in the evening or after dark, especially not at dusk. To his understanding at dusk things were very similar to what he was experiencing right here and now. Dusk, yes: universally accepted as the most dangerous time to be out driving, when visibility is so poor that things are rarely as they appear to be and nothing may be taken for granted.

So then, that had to be it: it was his headlights, illuminating things that appeared alien to what he was accustomed to. And believing he'd discovered the culprits, he now noticed that one beam was a fraction too low, and the other a mite too high. They needed adjusting, which should have been done at the car's last servicing and certainly would he at its next!

As for feeling lonely…but in this empty place in odd or unusual circumstances like these, surely that was only natural? And yet, as the loneliness settled on him more heavily yet, and beginning to feel a certain nagging anxiety without fully understanding why, Tempest chewed on his bottom lip and steered the car into the jaws of the second up-ramp…

Curiously, the next level's THREE was in good order, clean and bright as if freshly painted. And there was no sign of dust or cobwebs. All was as it should be, and Tempest felt inordinately pleased, even elated, when he saw two cars parked in their respective bays. Two of the team's cars, obviously — middle-ranking members of the team, as indicated by the allocation of bays on this level — with five more cars to go if their owners had arrived here with time to spare; that's if *their* bloody alarm-clocks were in good working condition! They would be on levels four and five, of course. Three of them on four, and Two-Stone Tom's and one other, his crony John Stockton's, on the topmost level five…well, "naturally."

The rest of the spaces up there were for the senior heads of the lab's various supporting departments.

Tempest's bay was on level four, a fact of which he'd been quite proud…but probably not for much longer. Lateness for such as today's experiment—and a Fotherington Wright experiment at that—had to be classed as a cardinal sin, tantamount to mutiny at the very least. But no use crying over spilt milk, or space- and time-teleported glass beads for that matter.

Beginning to relax a little and letting some of the tightness, the strain that he had scarcely realized was there, drain from his shoulders, Tempest dropped a gear and turned onto the up-ramp to the fourth level; his level, together with three of his colleagues. But as his car climbed the ramp, so the tenseness in his neck and shoulders came back again—in spades.

That was because the bright white paint of the FOUR sign over the arched entrance at the top of the ramp was no longer bright or white; it was faded, flaking, and streaked with dirt or maybe mould. Worse still, it wasn't a FOUR but a THREE! And even as Tempest, his eyes starting out and his bottom jaw falling slack, drove under the sign and onto the level, so his car passed through a fine cobweb curtain that billowed up to drape the windshield.

Now what in the…?

Tempest's heartbeat picked up alarmingly. Was it his short-term memory? Or that stroke thing, maybe? Or could it simply be a lack of concentration, the temporary confusion of a mind preoccupied with so many other abnormalities?

A confused mind? The hell you say—maybe he was losing it altogether! What, Alzheimer's, at his age? Well whatever it was it was steadily getting worse.

God Almighty!

For having only just arrived on what a majority of his five senses didn't want to believe was a second level three but *must be* the actual level four, and as he dropped another gear to let his car advance slowly down the dusty central aisle (while automatically avoiding shattered glass and metal debris from fluorescent lighting fixtures that had long since crashed from the ceiling,) so his slightly misaligned but acceptably functioning headlights seemed perversely intent on lighting up the same two cars, parked in adjacent bays, that he knew he'd seen less than two minutes earlier on the floor below this one!

But…*were* they the same?

Tempest brought his car to a jerky halt opposite the parked vehicles. His windows, despite being draped with a fine network of dust and cobwebs, were scarcely opaque, and switching on his sidelights he was afforded an astonished, terrifying inspection of what looked like a pair of rotting antiques in their utterly neglected parking bays.

Terrifying, yes. Because for all that these ancient wrecks where they squatted low on bowed, rusting wheel rims and flattened tyres, with their licence plates and fenders dangling and their headlights leaning from their sockets—and for all that at their apparent age, in their condition, they couldn't possibly belong to any colleagues of Tempest's—still he believed he recognized their once-sleek outlines. And despite that their plates were mottled and flaky with rust, and if Tempest's wide-eyed disbelieving gaze and cobwebby side window weren't playing tricks on him, the plates of the car on the right were undeniably *last year's*, less than nine months old! Why, he remembered when Allen Johnson, one of the team members and a close friend, had bought this latest model and drove him home in it when his own car was in the garage being fitted with a new exhaust! (And when it *should* have had its headlights adjusted.)

But…this was impossible! All of this was utterly —

—Impossible?

Unless he was dreaming or out of his mind.

But he didn't feel at all insane. Only afraid, scared half to death. Because he could no longer rationalize; because suddenly the truth hit him like a bolt of lightning; because beyond a doubt there could be only one answer. It had to be the experiment: Fotherington Wright's messing about with space and time.

What the hell had the man done?

Now Tempest remembered all the doomsayers when the boffins at CERN started smashing elementary particles together at near light-speed: they were only trying to understand conditions way back at the Big Bang, the birth of the universe, but some crazy people had been sore afraid they might cause another, even Bigger Bang…or perhaps those people weren't so crazy after all. And then there was the lab's so-called court jester, one of his comments about the imminent experiment: "They tell us we're all made of star-stuff," he had said. "Well, okay, but personally I prefer to think that when my time is up I'm going down into the ground as a big smelly worm-fest, not back out into the void as a rapidly expanding cloud of instant star-stuff!" At which he'd laughed and shrugged. "Anyway, why worry? At least it should he painless—Ha-ha!"

And finally, there was what Two-Stone Tom himself had said on at least one occasion: "I haven't yet calculated whether the shift will be to what we call the past or to what we imagine as the future." And with an introspective, rather uncertain frown, he had added: "Then, always assuming my figures are correct and the power flows true and steady, everything should be well…"

What, "always assuming…?" *Assuming*, for God's sake!

And what about that: "true and steady power flow…?"

And then, Jesus Christ: "everything *should* be well…!?"

But what if his figures weren't correct? What if the power flow wasn't true and steady? What if everything had worked out anything but well?

Now, in Tempest's mind's eye, he saw once again Fotherington Wright's frown as he had mumbled comments such as those he now so vividly remembered. And suddenly he knew the reason for the introspective frowning…which was because Two-Stone Tom really wasn't sure—hadn't really known—just exactly what to expect!

Jesus! Had scientist indeed! Or was he just so absentminded it made little or no difference? Except now it appeared it made all the difference in the world! But…the world? Tempest got a grip on himself; at least he tried to. What was he thinking? The entire world? Surely not. Just how big could this thing be?

At least there was a way to find out, and quickly. Or so he thought…

And churning up what could well be a century of dust as he hit the accelerator and went fish-tailing toward the down ramp, Tempest felt the first trickles of cold sweat on his spine and forehead and shivered, but not from any kind of normal cold. It was the sweat of fear, as when he sometimes jerked awake from a really bad nightmare. Except he knew now that he wasn't dreaming, that this was as horribly real as it could get.

Down one level he went, to an utterly pristine level three; this time an empty level three. And without pause down to level two (thank God!) And on down to…*another* two! And gasping—making dry-throat sobbing and grunting noises, and scraping the walls of the down-ramps causing sparks to fly in the spiralling rush of his descent—to yet another two, another, another, and another, as he descended, descended, descended.

A seemingly endless continuum of twos, and not one of them exactly alike!

Some of them appeared to be under construction, the walls as yet unrendered or the white paint still wet where it marked off the parking bays. Others were full of rotting cars and the debris of a defunct, rusted, sagging lighting system. The sign that said TWO was hanging from one ancient screw as he gave up trying for the exit and took an up-ramp. Which was at the same time as he glanced at his fuel gauge.

God, he was driving on fumes almost! And he'd intended to fill her up, would have done so this morning if he hadn't been rushed and driving so furiously. But on the other hand, and as it turned out, maybe he hadn't been late enough, that he would be a lot better off not making it here at all! But at least he *was* still here—wasn't he?

Where or whenever here was!

He forced himself to calm down. Okay, so however bad this was there was little or nothing he could do about it. He could always try to reach the ground floor later and let himself out, if there was anything out there to let himself into, but maybe his best bet right now would be to find a way in: into the lab itself.

That was why he was on his way back up. Up there on levels three, four, and five there were elevators that would take him to a single in-between level and a door directly into the complex.

That's if the elevators were working, of course. If not in this time, then perhaps some other?

Tempest's mind reeled! He didn't know *when* he was, or might end up being! His watch said the time was—almost six-twenty. But in what day, year, decade, or century? A month ago or fifty years in future time? *If* there was such a thing as a future and not just some insanely concertinaed NOW!

The new level two was in good order, as fresh as yesterday and half full of parked cars. It all looked so normal, so very ordinary, that Tempest felt his heart give a great leap inside him. It was simply the notion of the closeness of other people, of not being entirely alone, despite that there was no one actually here in the car park. Well okay, whenever this was, sometime in the "past," he hazarded a guess, they'd all be at work in their offices.

But in the next moment his heart gave another surge at the sight of another car descending the down-ramp from level three. Then as it went past him on the other half of the central lane, and going in the opposite direction, of course, he saw that the driver was the same girl or woman who had parked down on level one. Patently she'd been doing the same as him, driving up and down through various time zones...which would make some kind of sense if "time" was indeed illusory and of a oneness! As to how they'd missed crossing each other's paths until now: Tempest hadn't the foggiest idea!

She had looked at him as she drove past—her mouth open, eyes staring, hair all over the place as if she'd been yanking on it—but it was like she hadn't even seen him. She must be in shock. And why not; Tempest was in shock, too, despite that he had the dubious benefit of knowing something of what was going on here.

Two-Sone Tom's Big T.O.E.

Damn! He had to get after her! Troubles shared are troubles halved, or something like that. And at least she'd be company.

His tyres squealed as he jerked the car around in the central lanes, a hurried three-point turn, and took off after the unknown woman whose vehicle was already entering the down-ramp.

And a few seconds later he was descending the same ramp—

—To an empty level three, and no sign of the other car! Space and time were fluctuating, the oneness of each dimension overlapping for both Adam Tempest and the half-crazy woman. He supposed she must be that way by now if she'd gone through what he was going through.

But now he had to bring himself under some kind of control; his nerves were jumping, heart pounding, and sweat was drenching his shirt.

"Adam, my lad," he told himself out loud and breathlessly, "this hole you're in is hellish deep, so for Christ's sake *stop digging!*" And: "Keep your cool," he went on, forcing himself to breathe slowly, deeply. "For if you don't you could very easily overheat, crash and burn! And not only physically but your mind too!"

Okay, fine…now, what had he been doing before the other car came into view? He'd been trying to reach the upper levels. Well, and here he was on three. Objective achieved! So now park up, go see if the elevator's working, try to get into the lab.

And after that?

Whoa! Hold your horses, Adam! One step at a time. For let's face it: you mightn't like what could be waiting for you in the lab…

––––––––––––

The elevator wasn't working. No, of course not; no electricity, no lights, no way. Not on this level anyway.

Tempest went back to the car, started her up and glanced at the gas gauge; only a glance, because in fact he really didn't want to discover the worst of it. And in any case the gauge had let him down far too often in the past—or in what passed for the past…? But the number of times he'd tapped on that glass to make the needle jump: they were uncountable.

And so on up to level four. And oh joy!—or at least something of relief—as he rode up under a pristine FOUR sign into the marvellous glare of fluorescent lights, and saw at a glance that the level, his own level, appeared in working order! Moreover, he immediately recognized the three cars that were parked close together in their allocated bays. These were the cars he had expected to see from the onset: the properties of a trio of his team colleagues.

Tempest didn't bother to park in his own bay—though he'd almost done so until it dawned on him how ridiculous that would be in the circumstances—but prompted by a sudden idea, something he had seen on many a police procedural show, he drove up level with the three parked vehicles, got out, and went to each car in turn to lay trembling hands on their hoods.

He was attempting to find out what time it was, the recent "past" or some not so very far off "future"; whether it was his NOW, or some overlapping WHEN. The working lights had suggested it was his NOW, and while the first two of the parked cars were stone cold, the hood on the last one—Jim Houseman's vehicle, which had managed to retain just a bare minimum of its engine's warmth—appeared to corroborate it.

Houseman must have been the last of the three to get here; he wasn't the most reliable of the lab's technicians and, like Tempest himself, might well have overslept. In which case, and also like Tempest, he'd have been pushed for time and in something of a hurry. Which would account for his car's still-warm engine. In any case, it appeared he'd at least made it in time for the experiment.

God! That word again: "time." It kept cropping up, despite that it was rapidly losing its meaning! But if Houseman had indeed arrived here recently, then maybe he'd also managed to use the elevator to make his way into the lab. And if so, then perhaps the elevator was still working.

Tempest ran down the length of the central lanes to the wall housing the elevator, and skidded to a halt in front of a pneumatic metal door within its shallow arched recess. The door was not quite

186

shut; seven inches of trousered ankle and a foot wearing a sock and a leather shoe were protruding through a five or six-inch gap. Lying there on the floor, trapped by the automatic door, or possibly having itself caused the door to malfunction, the motionless foot, or rather the sight of it—but more especially the *smell* that accompanied it, a stench that presumably emanated from the elevator—caused Tempest to shudder.

Leaning forward and crouching down a little, he stared hard at the shoe. He recognized that shoe: left-footed, it was extra wide with a heavily built up sole and heel. Which told him that the extremity inside it had to be Jim Houseman's club-foot.

Putting his right arm and shoulder into the gap, he forced the sticking door open a few extra inches—and almost wished he hadn't bothered. But he'd wanted to know, to be sure of what he suspected. And now he knew.

The rest of "limping Jim," as Tempest had always thought of Houseman, though never in jest or unfeelingly, was sure enough in there—mostly rotten and liquescent, what was left of him.

At which point all of the level's fluorescent lights failed startling Tempest and causing him to jump a foot, and the elevator's door gave a single spastic jerk and stood still again…

———————

Holding his nose, Tempest squeezed into the elevator and, hope against hope, tried the single button that would normally carry him between the upper levels to an automatic interior door accessing the lab.

Nothing happened, and with his ex-colleague's corpse lying soggy and stinking underfoot, and darkness all around, Tempest had to get out of there. His lungs were running out of acceptable air and he no longer had any reason to stay. Shaking like a leaf, he squeezed back out through the gap into the car park proper…

His car's headlights, still issuing their cones of light, guided him back along the central lanes. This time he couldn't run but walked, however unsteadily, because his legs were feeling about as soft as jelly.

But at least he was able to think, which was when another idea occurred.

Tempest's car was almost out of gas, but his three ex-colleagues' cars were parked where he'd left them; "ex"-colleagues, yes, at least for the time being, because for all he knew they might have suffered fates similar to Houseman's. But whether or no, it would make perfect sense right now to siphon off some of their fuel into his own tank…

Except he didn't have any flexible tubing, and the caps on the other cars' gas tanks were locked.

God, nothing seemed to be working in his favour! The fates appeared to have it in for him, even as badly perhaps as they'd had it in for poor Jim Houseman. But as Tempest leaned dizzily against his car, still badly shocked but slowly recovering—more readily accepting the unacceptable as the innate instinct for survival began to surface in him—suddenly he heard the thunder of another car's engine reverberating in the otherwise terrible silence.

A moment or two more and the vehicle, the half-mad woman's car, came hurtling from the down-ramp, fish-tailing toward Tempest where he ran into the oncoming lane, frantically windmilling his arms to flag it down. Then he stopped waving and froze, because she was almost on him and it didn't look like she'd be able to stop!

"Jesus Christ!" he cried, drawing his arms in, elbows down, forearms and hands covering his face and chest. Then—

—The screeching of brakes savagely applied, and the car's fender actually brushing his pants below the knees as the vehicle slewed to a halt.

Now Tempest's legs really were jelly as he stumbled to the driver's door and looked in through the open window. And: "God *damn!*" he shouted, more out of terror than rage. "Lady, I know you're scared, but you almost ran me down!"

Wide-eyed, white as a sheet, hair a total mess, she bit her lip, which he saw was already bleeding, and mumbled: "You don't understand. I can't…*I can't get out!* And I think I'm losing my mind!"

"Well that would make two of us," Tempest told. her, steadying himself. "But listen, we haven't gone mad. It's the lab. An accident in the lab. And what's happening here in the car park, and maybe elsewhere, this is the result. I haven't been able to get out either, so we're stuck here until we can work something out. Hey, two heads are better than one, right? And at the very least two's company."

"I'm not…not going crazy?" she said, her eyes beginning to focus. "An accident you say? But what kind of accident could do this?"

Tempest studied her more closely. She was maybe twenty-six or seven, not at all bad looking, despite her currently pinched features, but scared half to death. She probably wouldn't understand if he told her what he knew of it, but any kind of explanation had to be better than nothing. If he spoke professionally it might steady her up, let her see he was a responsible, reliable authority—not that he felt remotely authoritative right now! But taking charge of things might also help him get a grip on himself.

"It was a spatial, temporal experiment," he began. "Some of the lab's physicists—top men, or so they thought—were trying to move a small object around in space and time. As for myself, I was supposed to be part of the team but I didn't arrive here until it was too late. They went ahead and carried out the experiment without me. I'm not sure if that was a bad or a good thing where we are concerned, but in any case it must have gone wrong." He shrugged helplessly.

She obviously had understood, nodded and said, "It was you I saw in my rearview. You followed close behind me into the car park, and that was when it happened, right? I saw, even *felt* it happen! And it happened again after you drove by me and went up to level two. Suddenly I was no longer down on level one; I was up there on two, but there was no sign of you! Since when everything has been…just weird! But will they be able to correct it? Just how long will we be stuck in here?"

Before Tempest could attempt a reply that wouldn't frighten her more yet, she went on: "I'm all tensed up, cramped and aching. I've got to stretch my legs. I only cane in early to catch up on some work I had to do, and now I feel like I've been driving for hours!" With which she got out of the car.

What she'd said about driving for hours reminded Tempest of something, and he asked her: "How much gas do you have? I'm all out and we could be here for—I don't know—quite some time."

"I'm almost out," she told him. "Perhaps a tenth of a tank? But I can't be sure. Enough for a few more miles, maybe?"

Tempest groaned inwardly. But concealing his disappointment as best possible for her sake, he said, "A few more miles? Well, that might be okay. But like I said, I'm afraid it might take a while to find the exit."

"It's already been *quite* a while!" she replied, moaning her relief as she straightened and stretched her aching limbs. Then she began to giggle hysterically, her face twisting, eyes rapidly blinking, coming very close to tears before managing to control herself and asking: "But is this truly level four? You see, all this time I've been trying to get *up* here—until now I've got *down!* This place is like...like some mad gardener's hedge maze or something—but a maze with no route to the exit! And I really did think I was going insane!"

Tempest nodded. "Yes, it could do that to anyone who didn't understand. I *do* understand—something of it anyway—and it very nearly did it to me!" Then he frowned and said, "You know, I've seen you come down from level three once already. I was on level two when you came down and drove by me. Anyway, why would you want to get up here in the first place?"

She shook her head. "I remember seeing you," she said, "but I didn't come down from three: I came down from two! *All* of the levels were twos at that time! I couldn't escape from them. Oh, and by the way, I just came down from two *again*, not from five, as you might think." The very thought of that made her begin to giggle again, only to pause and take a long, deep breath before continuing: "I'm sorry, but I think I'm still a bit shook up."

Tempest blinked and thought: *What, only a bit shook up? How was that for phlegmatism?* Well she'd be a damn sight more shook up if she had seen what he had seen, or if she knew how serious things really were. All of that could wait, however, while once again he asked: "And you wanted to get up here, because…?"

"Because I knew that on levels three, four, and five there are elevators to a door that connects with the lab. But down on level two the elevator only takes you down to the ground floor, and you have to walk round to the front of the building and get checked out by Security before you go in. Of course, that's if two's elevator is working, which it isn't. I've tried it maybe five or six times, and on five or six *different* level twos!"

Tempest nodded. Yes, he understood how she felt. The whole damn mess was maddening. But now:

"Look, let's talk as we go. Do you mind if I drive?"

"No," she replied. "In fact, I'm delighted I won't have to! Sooner or later I was going to crash into something." And then, with a nervous toss of her head, "Except I'm not going anywhere for the moment, not until I've tried the elevator."

"Er, not a good idea." Tempest took her arm. "And anyway, I already tried it. It's not working and it's…not good."

"Not working?" Her face fell.

"No electricity, no lights—no elevator."

"And you said it's…what, not good? What can that mean? How is the elevator not good?" She backed off from his hand on her arm.

Tempest thought: *Ah, well. This can only make things worse for her but we might as well have done with it from square one.*

And so: "You see," he began, "there's this man in the elevator, someone who used to be a colleague of mine…" At which he paused in order to find the right words.

"A man in the elevator?" She frowned. "Who *used* to be your colleague?"

Hell with it: there were no right words. "He's dead!" Tempest blurted it out. "What's more, he looks like he's been dead for some time, maybe weeks. I figure he got in the elevator at the precise moment they activated the experiment, and—"

"Wait," she cut him off. "Dead for weeks? How can that he?"

"Time is shifting," he explained. "Space, too. The time is no longer now—or rather it is—except it's every NOW. Space is the same: we can be any place at any time. That's within the radius of the experiment affected area, of course."

"Within this car park, you mean?"

"And inside the lab building itself," he replied. "And just possibly—but I repeat, *possibly*—everywhere else! But that's all guesswork and right now I don't want to even begin thinking about it."

They got into her car, Tempest taking the driver's seat and checking the fuel gauge. Having slumped into the passenger seat beside him, she said: "I still don't understand. How is it your friend or colleague was so...well, so very dead? I mean, like a long time dead. And how come we haven't been so badly affected?"

Heading for an up-ramp, Tempest glanced at her and thought: *What do I tell her to ease her mind? And how about own mind? On the other hand, talking things through can't make them worse and might even help clarify the situation.* And so:

"Well, I can perhaps hazard another guess," he said. "Which is all it will be: a guess."

She nodded. "So go on, please hazard away!"

"Maybe we were right on the perimeter when they pressed the buttons," he said. "Perhaps the closer you are to the source of the problem, the worse it affects you. In which case we have to consider ourselves damn lucky that we were on the edge! It appears we're static in here—I mean stuck in a mutually cohesive space-time stream— while everything around us is fluctuating.

"As for Jim Houseman, my dead colleague in the elevator: it could be that when the experiment went wrong he was very badly, physically affected; maybe he had a heart attack or something. You remember how we felt, what we saw and sensed just as we entered the car park? Well, maybe it was that much worse for poor Jim; so much so that it killed him. As for the condition of his corpse: it must have been some *future* Houseman's corpse I saw—just like we've been seeing past and future levels of this damn car park! I mean, if we were to go to the elevator right now we might see Jim in a yet more distant future condition: a pile of dust, bones, and rotting rags. On the other hand, we could find him freshly dead, with the door of the elevator swishing to and fro, to and fro, against his trapped foot! That's about as much as I can say…"

"But enough," she answered very quietly, "and maybe just a bit too much!" And starting to chew on her lip again, she huddled down into herself…

The sign at the top of the up-ramp was as pristine as if freshly painted and read FIVE. The woman gasped, laid her hand on Tempest's arm and said, "Thank goodness! I was sure it would be another level two…anything but what we would want it to he!"

But Tempest only thought: *Sweetheart, all I want is out!*

"And look!" she cried. "The lights are still working!" But in the next moment, gazing out of her window, she gave a sharp little cry and clutched his arm that much more tightly.

Out the corner of his eye Tempest caught a glimpse of what she'd seen and yanked on the steering wheel, causing the car to swerve violently as a rust coloured, howling thing soared clean across the hood, clearing it by no more than an inch or two.

"Oh—my—*God!*" the woman gasped, releasing Tempest's arm and squeezing down in her seat as he brought the car to a halt. "What in the name of…?"

"It's a dog," Tempest answered shakily, getting out of the car. "Just a dog. And he goes by the name of Planck."

"What? Are you sure?" Leaning across the driver's seat she pulled the door shut, then wound down the window a few inches.

"Oh yes, I'm sure," Tempest told her. And crouching down a little, he called out loudly, "Planck, hey Planck—here boy! Where the hell did you go? Ah, there you are!"

At which a reddish, lanky Afghan hound, tail down between his legs, came skittering out from behind a concrete stanchion where he'd taken cover. At first nervously he approached Tempest's crouching form; then, as he recognized a friend, his tail lifted a little and began to wag uncertainly, until finally he stopped whining and came at a trot, tongue lolling.

Now the woman, who by now Tempest was beginning to think of more as a girl—but a very frightened girl—also got out of the car and came to join him. "Plank, did you say?"

"Uh-uh," Tempest answered, thought about it and shook his head, then said: "Yes, but not how you may think. Same sound, wrong spelling. Planck with a 'c' before the 'k'. Named after Max Planck, the German physicist who originated quantum theory. But please don't ask me why because where brightness is concerned he doesn't have two photons to rub together; in fact *thick* as a plank would more readily describe him! He belongs to Thomas Fotherington Wright, the fellow who's—"

"—The lab's head man? I've heard of him, of course. I've seen him but never met him. And this is his dog?"

"Yes." Tempest nodded. "It's his lab, too! Might as well be Fotherington Wright's world where mere mortals like us are concerned!"

"His lab?" She repeated him. "You mean he's the director?"

"It's his *place!*" Tempest replied. "He owns it. Lock, stock and barrel."

"Oh, I didn't know that."

Planck was whining again, half worriedly, half in pleasure at having his head and floppy ears rubbed.

"So if Fotherington Wright's that important," she frowned, "what made him bring this poor frightened creature here—and then leave him here?"

"Planck's probably got himself lost," said Tempest. "Like a couple of other poor frightened, animals I could name—that's if I knew your name, of course. So perhaps we should introduce ourselves. I'm Temp, or Mr. Tempest. Professor Tempest, actually, but my friends call me Temp. It's more or less appropriate since my speciality is time—er, temporal conditions?—while a majority of my colleagues prefer the other three dimensions to mess around with: you know, like the cosmos and 'everything out there.' But with me it's time." He shrugged. "You wouldn't think so, since I'm nearly always late, but that's me. And in any case they go hand in hand…space and time, I mean."

She stared at his outstretched hand for a moment, then offered him one that was still shaking more than a little and answered: "I'm Marie Longhurst—and not very pleased to meet you, not in the circumstances." She managed a forced smile.

"Understood," he told her. "So, may I call you Marie?"

"Oh, please do." She shrugged. "That's…what I go by."

A rather odd answer—until she held up her right hand for his inspection. Her wide silver bracelet was inscribed with her name thus: "E. Marie L."

Ethel? Edith? Elspeth? Whatever, Tempest had to agree that to his taste Marie was far more acceptable. But in any case he was concentrating on rather more important things. And: "Look!" he said. "That's what Planck is doing here."

Her head turned, her gaze following his pointing finger to where two cars stood side by side in their bays some twenty or so yards away. And Tempest continued:

"The closest of those cars is Fotherington Wright's. Sometimes he brings Planck in to work with him. It wouldn't be the first time he'd have to send someone out here to rescue Planck from the car. He's what you call absentminded." And to himself: *Or maybe as mad as a bloody hatter!* "Let's see if he's left his keys in the car. Because sometimes he does that, too."

She drew back a little. "Shouldn't we first try the elevator? It's right there on the other side of the ramp, closer than those cars."

"We will," he answered, "but I'll admit it right now: I'm a bit leery of elevators! So we'll check the cars out first…"

————

Fotherington Wright hadn't left his keys in the car, but one of the back seat windows had been wound down.

Tempest nodded. "That's how come Planck's here: his master forgot him. He also forgot to wind up the window, and it looks like Planck got out of the car too late to follow him into the lab—which was either sheer good fortune on the dog's part, or maybe the only clever thing he's done in his entire life!"

"And now can we try the elevator?" She was impatient, which Tempest readily understood.

"I suppose so," he answered, licking his suddenly dry lips. What he had told her was the truth: he wasn't at all sure about using an elevator, neither on this or any other level. It could be that the closer they got to the lab—the very center of the space-time disturbance—the worse things would be affected. So that even if the elevator was working, the lab might not be the safest place in the world. To visit.

But on the other hand—

—Since NOW was obviously sometime in the recent past, and since Two-Stone Tom's and his long-haired crony John Stockton's cars were the only vehicles up here, NOW was most probably only a short while before the experiment was due to take place—the experiment that had caused, *or was yet to cause*, all of this!

At which, as that very thought struck home, Tempest gasped, grabbed Marie's Longhurst's hand and started to race toward the elevator.

Almost jerked off her feet, she yelled, "What's wrong? What are you doing?"

"If we can get into the lab," he shouted back, "we can maybe stop the experiment dead in its tracks. You see—it hasn't happened yet!"

What was more—and damn it to hell—on one of those level twos he'd been on, the one in good order with all those cars on it, it hadn't happened then either! That could have been weeks, months, even a year ago…plenty of time for him to stop this crazy thing. But was that even possible? No, it probably wasn't, because that way he might have bumped into himself!

Well then, was *that* possible?

But what the hell difference did it make now? For that boat had long since sailed, and Marie Longhurst was asking him:

"It what?"

"This has to be some time before six a.m. That's why Planck is here and only two cars, and why the lights are working. This bloody nightmare hasn't been set in motion yet! Come on, run!"

"You mean we've gone back in time? But that's…why, it's crazy! *You* are crazy!" And suddenly fearful again—perhaps of Tempest now—she dug her heels in and almost brought him to a halt.

"Haven't you heard a word of what I've told you?" He hauled harder yet, making her jump and skitter. "It's not just the car park that's moving in space and time, it's you, me, Planck, and every other damn thing! So if you want to get out of here, stop holding me back and start running! We have to get into that lab before six a.m.!"

Unconvinced, she glanced at her watch, anchored herself yet more firmly, and cried, "But it's already quarter to seven!"

Well of course it was, but only according to their watches! Tempest gave up on her, released her and turned to run the last dozen or so yards to the elevator in its recess. But even as he got close, with his outstretched fingers reaching for the call button, so the door slid open with a pneumatic hiss!

Windmilling his arms, Tempest uttered a small, choking cry and took two or three staggering paces to the rear. But it was only short, fat, balding John Stockton standing there, preparing to step out of the elevator. But…what on earth was this? *Balding?* John Stockton, who only yesterday was wearing his hair on his shoulders, as he'd worn it for as long as Tempest could remember? Stockton, yes, looking equally taken aback but by no means afraid or disturbed. And:

"Adam Tempest!" the fat man said. And then, sarcastically, sneeringly: "So very glad you could make it! But what on earth are you doing up here on five? And dressed like…like *that?* Maybe you'll explain yourself later. But for now tell me: have you perhaps seen Planck? F.W. thinks he may have left him here, stuck in his car."

Still off balance and babbling incoherently, Tempest backed off more yet before finding a measure of self-control. But finally: "Stockton?" he gasped. "It is you, right? Well, thank God for that! But you can forget about Planck. We've got to go back into the lab, *stop the experrrrrrrriiiiiiiiii—*

"—ment!"

Too late! Not enough time! Or perhaps too much time! Everything was elongating—even his words—warping, bungey-jumping away from Tempest and bouncing back. It was like a small earthquake, not only under his feet but in his body, his head, too! Stockton blinked out of existence and the elevator door turned red with scabs of rust as it suddenly leaned outwards from the yawning emptiness of the shaft behind it. At the same time the lights went out and a cobweb curtain draped itself smotheringly over Tempest's head and shoulders; while from close behind him Marie Longhurst gave out a nerve-shattering shriek that echoed deafeningly in the suddenly, incredibly *ancient* car park!

Galvanized by her scream, Tempest spun around, saw her sprawled on a pile of broken tiles, chunks of rotten concrete and rusted electrical fittings, in the rubble of what was once the roof of the building. Beams of dim daylight filtered down through thick cobweb layers and galaxies of drifting dust motes, making visible directly overhead and along the entire length of level five a great many gaping holes with sagging saw-toothed edges, where parts of the ceiling and roof had long since caved in.

Marie's hand was to her mouth, her eyes wide and terrified, her entire body shaking. But as Tempest made stumblingly toward her she finally found her voice.

"Wh-wh-what just happened? Wh-where are we?"

Ne are where we were," he helped her to her feet. "But not *when* we were. But look! The car—your car—is still with us, and untouched, just as we seem to be. Probably because we were furthest away from ground zero when all this happened."

198

"And Planck?" Dazedly swaying while he steadied her, brushing mostly imaginary grit from her blouse and skirt, she looked all around through utterly disbelieving eyes. "Where's Planck?"

Tempest nodded, then grimaced as he shrugged a veil of cobwebs from his head and shoulders. "Planck was here—right here—when it all went down. He's still here, but not right now. If he was here now…well, even his bones would be dust."

"Are you still guessing?" Now she swayed toward him, clung to him, looked for assurance, confidence in Tempest's eyes and found nothing. He didn't want her to see how afraid he was but couldn't help himself, and so looked away. And:

"It's *all* guesswork," he said. "Just like bloody Two-Stone Tom's theories, especially his Big T.O.E.!" Then, squinting in the dim light, he continued, "One thing for sure, the light is fading. Wherever, or more properly *when*ever we are, it's going to be night before too long. We don't want to he stuck up here in the dark."

And shuddering, her hand seeking her mouth again, she whispered, "God, no!"

"But getting off this level," he went on, fighting back his own fears, "that may prove something of a bumpy ride, what with this debris and what all. I just hope your car is up to it!" *Or at least that it's in better condition than I kept mine…*

———————

The beams of light from above were shifting, growing weaker as somewhere out of view the sun dipped towards the horizon. Then, as the pair clambered away from the rubble-strewn area towards Marie's car, they simultaneously sensed movement in the darker corners of the ceiling where as yet it remained intact.

In the next moment they both froze, their eyes straining in the gloom, gazing upward at the source of the seemingly furtive activity. And as the outer fringe of that soft, mobile darkness crept more surely into view first a dozen—then a hundred, and possibly a great many more—pairs of glowing feral yellow eyes opened, every one of them fixing their avid, unblinking gaze on Tempest and the girl.

"Bats!" said Tempest.

"But the *size* of them!" she replied. "Surely we don't have fruit bats in our country?"

"Well we didn't have," he answered. "At least, once upon a time. And they certainly wouldn't have been…Jesus, so inquisitive!"

That last because several of the creatures, with wingspans of some thirty inches, had spread veined, leathery pinions and were swooping down to circle the human intruders.

As Tempest waved his arms, batting defensively at the air around his head, the tip of a beating wing—in fact a clawed, grossly extended finger—raked across his forehead drawing a thin scratch hung with tiny beads of blood. At which the horde on the sagging ceiling set up a mass chittering and, almost as a single entity, swarmed aloft in a flight that wasn't so much inquisitive as inimical.

"Fruit bats?" Tempest gasped, still batting at the air with one hand while trying to shepherd the girl towards the car with the other. "Hell, no! Fruit bats don't attack people—not that I ever heard of! These are something else, mutations from three thousand years in the future for all I know."

"My hair! My hair!" she cried, as two of the bats clutched at her tresses, their wings beating at the air as if trying to carry her off.

Tempest swiped at them, felt a wing crack under his attack, saw one of the bats spin off and crumple to the debris-littered deck. At that the rest of them, an aerial horde that was shutting out the light and even the air, or so it seemed, backed off a little but only a little; barely sufficient that the fugitive humans were able to get to the car and scramble to something of safety within.

Then for a while, no more than a minute or so, the cloud of great, chittering bats flew in a fury all around the stationary vehicle, so that even if Tempest had tried to drive he couldn't have seen the way ahead for their soft-furred bodies and fluttering wings. But at last the ugly, ridge-snouted creatures flew up in a spiral, disappearing out through the gaps in the ruined ceiling and roof into a rapidly darkening dusk, where the first stars were just becoming visible…if not in any easily recognizable constellations.

The future? Well perhaps. But Earth's future? Tempest could no longer be sure. And: "This could be even worse—maybe a lot worse—than I thought," he muttered to himself, barely conscious of speaking his mind, but loud enough that Marie Longhurst had heard what he said.

"Worse?" she whispered. "But what could possibly be worse?"

Gritting his teeth, Tempest started the engine, sprayed the windshield and got the wipers going, then engaged the gears and rolled carefully forward.

"I said—" she began to repeat herself.

"And I heard you!" he snapped, and at once relented. "Look, I'm sorry. Just let me get us off this level, and then I'll try to explain. But please remember, it's all—"

"Yes, I know: guesswork, right?"

Which, other than a single nod of his head, hardly required any answer at all…

———————

Negotiating the fallen debris along the length of level five to the down-ramp at the far end seemed an almost interminable process, and the ramp itself was in a very poor condition. Tempest couldn't even be certain that under the sliding scree of rubble from above it was still intact; on two occasions as the vehicle bumped and slithered downhill, he felt rotten concrete shifting under its weight.

As they proceeded—however slowly, carefully—so he tried to explain why things could indeed "possibly be worse."

"The thing is…well, did you notice anything odd, peculiar, about the way that bald man in the elevator looked, before he—"

"—Disappeared?" she cut him off. "I didn't recognize him, if that's what you mean. But his clothing was rather strange. I mean, I don't think that I've ever seen a suit like his before. There was no collar on his jacket, and his trousers were flared and brightly chequered. He looked more like…like a harlequin than a scientist!"

Tempest nodded. "Right, I remember seeing those things too, but they hardly registered because I *did* recognize him, except the last time I saw him—and that was only yesterday—he was dressed like a mortician and his hair was as long as a girl's!"

"Is that supposed to mean something?" she queried. "Perhaps he had his head shaved; or he's ill, having some sort of treatment? Maybe the last time you saw him he was wearing a wig."

"No, I don't think so," said Tempest, his voice barely audible. By which time they were down onto a level four as ancient but by no means as devastated as level five.

In the dim, eerily green glow of an unknown source of illumination, the pair could see that the ceiling was badly cracked but holding up; while the floor ahead, though inches thick with dust, appeared to be reasonably stable. To one side, about halfway along the level, three oblong heaps of rust rose a foot-and a-half off the floor. Despite that they were completely unrecognizable as cars, still Tempest knew that was exactly what they were or had been. For after all, this was the third occasion on which he had seen them in the same place, different times: once when they'd looked comparatively new; then as junk-yard relics; and currently in the penultimate stages of decay, before finally they'd blow away as so much red dust.

Tempest brought the car to a halt. Stunned by the thought—the very idea—of knowing where they were but not when, except that it was a long, long way from home, he could only shake his head numbly and sit there for several silent seconds, trying to accept the weirdness, the absurdity, of their situation.

Absurd, yes: because if it wasn't so terrifying it would be oh so bloody funny…

Marie leaned over and touched his arm, causing him to jump. "We're a pair of strangers," she said, keeping her voice steady though not without a deal of effort. "Strangers adrift in time, apparently, with only a few miles worth of gas left in my car's tank. And though I really don't want to know, you still haven't told me what could he worse than this."

Two-Sone Tom's Big T.O.E.

Tempest gave himself a shake. She had succeeded in bringing him out of himself, freeing him from what might easily have become a state of panic-induced immobility. He took a deep breath and licked stick-dry lips, then said: "In short—even if we're able to get back to our own time and place—it may not be *our* time and place." And before she could query that:

"I don't suppose you know the theory of parallel or alternative universes?"

"Oh but I do!" she replied. "I had a boyfriend once who was a huge Science Fiction buff. Which meant, of course, that I had to suffer all those old Star Trek reruns with him. But…what has that to do with…anything?" Seeing the look on Tempest's face, suddenly her eyes were very wide. "Just what are you trying to tell me?"

"Another of Two-Stone Tom's far-out theories," he answered, barely able to keep his voice from giving out. "That at the Big Bang, the newborn universe had multiple choices. A finite speed of light? Gravity, drawing everything together, or anti-gravity pushing everything apart? And, what the hell, why just *one* universe? Why not a multiverse, or rather, multiverses? Why not new universes springing from each and every event?"

"And you think—?"

"*God damn that bloody idiot!*" Tempest thumped the steering column and accidentally hit the horn, its single blast of sound booming and echoing in the car park's greenly-glowing confines. "Why couldn't he see—why couldn't *we* see—what might happen? For it's not only space and time that he's unified with his Big T.O.E., it's everything! He's taken over from God and recreated entire universes in his own image, the way he's always believed things should be! It was only supposed to happen in the laboratory, but like some kind of Frankenstein monster it's escaped!"

Marie tightened her grip, grasping his arm in tense, steely fingers. "But you can't be sure, right? I mean, it's still just so much guesswork…right?"

And just like that she gave him hope, albeit the straw that the drowning man clutches, but at least something to hold on to. For what he had told her was, after all, just so much guesswork John Stockton, dressed like a harlequin—or perhaps a man from a parallel world?—querying the way Tempest himself was dressed? Giant bats like nothing seen or heard of before, attacking and injuring people? Yet still it might be barely possible that there were simple explanations for these anomalies...mightn't it? Tempest could only hope so.

Sighing and letting his tense shoulders slump a very little he finally replied: "Guesswork, yes. The parallel universe part at least. But as for the rest of it, what we've seen and experienced on these various levels..."

Which was as far as he got before—

—*Ping!*

Something fell from above, hit the windshield, bounced and went skipping away across the bonnet, finally rolling to a halt on the level's dusty floor. But Tempest had seen it: that small red sphere, maybe half an inch in diameter. Moreover, he'd seen its like before: a glass bead that had been intended for use in a lab experiment.

In *the* lab experiment...

Ping! Ping! Ping! Three more glass beads.

Then ten, fifty, innumerable glass beads! Hitting the windshield, hammering on the car's roof like so much hail, bouncing and skittering along the entire length of the level and sending up puffs of dust wherever they landed. Until Tempest was unable to stay in control a single moment longer.

And: "Jesus Christ!" He cried then, knowing that it was no longer guesswork, that this was the result—or part of it—of a thousand, or hundred thousand, or million, so-called "experiments" in an equal or possibly infinite number of parallel laboratories!

———————

"We've got to get out of here!" Tempest yelled over the din of falling beads. And crouching down in his seat behind the steering wheel, wincing from the assault on the roof, the windshield and bonnet, he put the car in gear and headed for the down-ramp. But the beads were everywhere and he was accelerating too quickly. The car skidded, spun sideways, straightened up again as he fought with the steering. Even when Tempest applied the brakes, still the car sped forward, its wheels locked, roller skating on beads that were piled deeper than the dust!

"What is it? What's happening!" Marie's face was white as a sheet, her large eyes starting out as she squirmed this way and that, shrinking from the battered windshield, where cracks were spreading like instantaneous cobwebs over the entire surface of the glass. "W-what are those things?"

"Our worst fears realized!" Tempest replied, still fighting with the steering, jolting in his seat, grunting a curse as the car sideswiped a stanchion, bounced off and swerved towards the down-ramp and the bounding deluge of red marbles that was rolling down it.

Then, by some miracle quite beyond Tempest's understanding, he was able to steer the car onto the ramp; following which the vehicle's motion would have been outside any driver's sphere of control. No longer being driven or even guided, it simply tobogganed down the ramp, sailed on a sea of beads across the lanes of level three, and slammed headlong into the opposite wall.

As Tempest and Marie jerked forward and back in their seats so the car's engine shut down, and for a single horrible moment they both thought the same thing: that the gas tank was finally empty. But no, having glanced first at each other, then at the gauge, they sagged in their seats, gasping their mutual relief at seeing that while the needle was firmly in the lower red, it was still hovering just above zero. It was the shock of the impact that had caused the engine to stop, that and the fact that Tempest's foot had been on the brake, not the accelerator. Moreover, the beads had stopped tumbling down the ramp and the rest of level three appeared free of the things.

"From level five to four, and now from four to three." Tempest muttered. "If it keeps up like this we may even get down to one. So keep your fingers crossed, Marie, because where there's hope..." Which was more for her sake than his own. But he could always hope.

———————

At first the car refused to start. But at the third go, just as the engine was stuttering, winding down, suddenly it burst into life again.

"Fumes!" Marie moaned. "That's all she's got left now: just a tankful of fumes. And of course it had to happen right now! I feel like a complete idiot, because for as long as I can remember I've never let the gas level get so low. Do take it easy on the pedal, won't you?"

Listening to pressured beads popping out from under the vehicle's tyres and spattering on the concrete deck, Tempest nodded and backed off carefully from the wall. And as he turned the car along the level…"Damn!" he sputtered. "Will you look at this? The lights are on and the place is empty, no cars at all! And no damage or signs of aging. It could be this morning—or some morning, or night—before the experiment. The place looks brand spanking new, certainly as new as I've ever seen it!"

With a last handful of glass beads spitting out behind the car's back tyres, Tempest took it easy on the gas and made for the far down-ramp.

Now, he thought, *if only our luck holds…*

"You're right," Marie agreed with what he had said a moment ago. "It all looks so totally normal!" Her voice was firmer now more controlled, and Tempest tried to match her.

"Perhaps the effect isn't lasting," he said. "Maybe events are—I don't know—evening out somehow? Anyway, here we go, down onto level two. At least I *hope* it's level two!" That word again. So perhaps it was true that hope springs eternal.

"Wait!" she said. "Shouldn't we try to get into the laboratory again?"

"No!" he shook his head determinedly. "There's been enough of that. It hasn't worked out and I don't think it can work out. I just want to get us the hell out of here—*right* out of here and right now—while we're still sound of mind and limb!"

And moments later, when Tempest drove off the ramp onto the level, they both breathed audible sighs of relief when they saw that it was indeed level two, even though it wasn't in the same almost pristine condition as three. For the light fixtures were dangling from a ceiling that sagged in places, and the concrete floor had zig-zagging cracks all along its length. But since it *was* level two, with only one more down-ramp to go, at least the exit and their possible salvation felt that much closer…

———————

For the first time in what felt like several ages Tempest found he could breathe a little easier, despite being aware that they weren't out of the woods — or more properly the car park — just yet. And when, *if*, they got out…what then? How would things be in the world they had been accustomed to outside?

Making no mention of his on-going fears, he avoided as best possible the cracked and occasionally rubble-strewn floor as he drove carefully down the central lanes; but as the car approached the final down-ramp he was once again holding his breath and was aware that Marie was doing much the same. She was taking in only sufficient air to allow her to mutter continuously to herself, over and over again: "Oh god! Oh my God! Please let it be…please *let* it be…oh *please* let it be…!" Until:

"Here we go!" he said, and turned onto the down-ramp, where they at once saw that the overhead sign at the bottom displayed a starkly simple figure ONE.

At which Tempest found himself echoing Marie's prayers, albeit in his own way: "Christ! — oh Jesus Christ! — please let us make it!"

And: "We *can* make it!" she burst out beside him. "We really can! Look, at the far end there, the entrance — and for us the exit — and the daylight pouring in from outside! Better still, the place looks safe, intact."

Marie was right, except Tempest had noticed something other than the daylight and wasn't sure just exactly what he had seen. In that selfsame moment, however, he knew precisely what he was feeling.

As for what he'd seen: there were strange beings here; they were firming into existence and emerging from the shadows. This went hand in hand with that other thing that was happening: the sickening twisting and elongation of the level into an apparent eternity; the sudden *wrenching* of space and time that signalled yet another evolution of the NOW into a very different WHEN and WHERE. And as rapidly as that—as the level concertinaed back into what would surely be only a temporary, transient stability—Tempest saw all too clearly that level one was no longer safe and anything but intact!

Reeling as if she was drunk beside him in her seat, physically and mentally tottering no less than Tempest himself, Marie now saw something of what he had seen: the first of the strange creatures, now fully formed or realized, as it came loping from the shadows. And as she recovered from the shock of the transition:

"What the…?" she gasped. "Is that—but how can it possibly be—Planck?"

Tempest had lifted his foot from the accelerator, applying the brakes as soon as he'd felt the change sweeping over everything. Now, examining the alien eight-foot-tall thing that was approaching the front of the car, not to mention a dozen or so others of the same species that were closing in on both sides, he could see how, at first sight, it would be easy for someone to make the same mistake as Marie.

They were long-haired, a reddish-orange in colour, floppy-eared and very dog-*like*—even Planck-*like*—but they walked upright on weird hindlegs. Also, their forelegs or "arms," with paws and dangling talons, depended below their regressive knees and hung halfway down their calves. Far worse, when they opened their black-shining leathery muzzles to snarl, Tempest saw that their jaws and scythe like teeth were quite obviously the equipage of savage carnivores.

As for intelligence: those beings on both sides of the car were already peering in through the windows, snuffling as they groped at the door handles!

Galvanized into action, Tempest managed to choke out instructions as he tried and failed to get the car back into gear: "Marie, secure your door!"

"Huge!" she gasped, snapping upright in her seat and doing as he had directed. "These things are…they're *huge!*"

"And they're not Planck," he told her, completely unnecessarily, as he ground his teeth and the gears both while fighting the gear-stick. "But they could be his mutated descendants from some far-future parallel fucking world!"

The creature at the front of the car had climbed up on the bonnet. It carried what looked like a rusted iron rod which, as it threw back its head and began to howl, it aimed at the weakened, bead-splintered windshield directly in front of Tempest.

Again galvanized, he finally got the car into reverse gear, burning rubber as he backed off at speed to unbalance the thing on the bonnet, sending it sprawling even as it's makeshift weapon shattered the windshield. Then, ignoring the shower of glass shards and ramming the car into first, Tempest caused the tyres to burn and shriek anew as he roared forward, slamming into and over the fallen monster.

And without pause he changed up and raced for the exit…or tried to.

But as Tempest had already noted, this now derelict level, once the ground floor of a serviceable car park, was no longer in good order. Much of the ceiling had caved in, and the badly gapped floor was heaped with its rubble. And as if that wasn't enough, the car's engine was once more stuttering and coughing as the last dregs of fuel—literally fumes—were sucked out of the tank.

"More of those awful things!" Marie was shouting, as Tempest bumped the car over heaped debris and swerved to avoid the wider, deeper gaps in the floor. "My God—just look at them!"

But he was already looking: at a central area of the level that was more or less clear of rubble but full of Planck creatures: a gang of them, two dozen at least! And seemingly heedless of life and limb they came loping, many of them dropping to all fours, then throwing their heads back and howling like banshees from red-haired, vibrating throats…

———————

The intentions of the creatures seemed perfectly obvious.

"It's them or us!" Tempest shouted as he hurled the car at best possible speed head-on into the slavering horde.

Hairy bodies split or burst open, and bones crunched under the lurching, clanking, battered car, as flesh and blood spattered on the last dangling shards of what had been a windshield. And it was then—with no more than fifty or so littered feet of level one left to be covered between the clattering vehicle and the glorious daylight flooding in from outside—only *then* that the final nightmare revealed itself.

Tempest felt it happening first—that sickening, dizzying shock to his faculties—then *watched* it happening in his rearview mirror: that incredible extension of the ruined level into unknown times and distances behind the car, followed by the now monstrously familiar snapping-back of space-time into a different configuration, a new reality.

Starting back there but rapidly closing, catching up with the car, in the blink of an eye Tempest saw the total disintegration of the building into so much dust, watched broken concrete slabs reverting to nothing, to their elementary particles, while the surviving dog-things simply vanished. He watched the chaos of metastatic, metamorphosing matter following after him, pursuing the car like a creature sentient in its own right.

Turning to look back, Marie had seen it too. "God! Oh God! *Oh my God!*" Her voice rose to a deafening shriek as it appeared that the devolution of space-time into nothingness must surely reach out to engulf the car. And closing her eyes, finally she buried her face in Tempest's shoulder.

The fuel tank was empty and the car had coughed and stuttered its last. But as the dying vehicle had humped and lurched its way up, over and down the other side of the final mound of debris, even as it threatened to jerk to a standstill, Tempest had thrown the gears into neutral. And hauling on the steering wheel, he had somehow managed to turn the car into the glaring daylight of the exit.

Where previously there had been a speed bump and a rise of no more than six inches into the car park, now there was a six-foot drop out of it! And as the car launched its terrified passengers into thin air, behind them the building disappeared in its entirety, as if it had never been there in the first place—which indeed it hadn't, not in the *first* place!

Yawing toward Tempest's side, and tilting forward a little, the car fell; and sensing the weightlessness—fully believing this must be the end—Marie's screams turned to sobs, muffled where she pressed her face deeper yet into Tempest's shoulder.

Briefly glimpsing what was happening, Tempest had likewise closed his eyes, only opening them as the car slammed into the ground and his and Marie's combined weight burst his door open and hurled them out and down...onto lush green grass and soft earth!

"Christ! Oh, Jesus God!" Tempest groaned then, his hand gentling his chest where the pain reassured him that at least he was still alive. "I think...think you've bust my ribs!" And then, wincing as another jolt of pain shot through him when his probing fingers discovered the sore spot: "Ow-*ouch!* Well, one of my ribs for sure!"

She unwrapped her arms from around him, lifted her head and looked all about. "But where...where are we?" She struggled to sit up, drank deep of the sweet air, and still a little breathless said: "What just happened to us? And where...where's the car park?"

"*Uh!*" Tempest grunted. "Help me up, can't you?" He held his side as she eased him into a seated position. And utterly mystified, as their racing heartbeats gradually slowed and whirling senses began to adjust, at last the pair studied their surroundings.

To one side of them: there rested the car in the long soft grass, its driver's door hanging from a wrenched hinge, and its splayed wheels axles deep in rich loam. Badly battered, a total wreck, it was destined never to move again. And beyond the car, where the concrete bulk of the car park had reared—

—Greenery, a forest! Pure and primal and...peaceful? It was the same all around them: fruiting trees and shrubs, palms, flowers, all under a blindingly blue sky. Leaves wafting in the sweetest of sweet breezes, where birds—shocked by the arrival of these strangers—had stopped singing; but now they began to sing again. Bees buzzing from flower to flower, and small harmless creatures lending motion to the grasses as they went about their business. Nearby, the tinkle of water over pebbles, where a stream sparkled in the sunlight.

And Marie said once again, "Temp, where *are* we?"

"One thing's for sure," he finally answered. "We're not in the car park, Dorothy!"

"What? Oh, Oz!" She almost laughed, however weakly, hysterically.

"Well, but for a bunch of Munchkins…" he replied, with a shrug that brought him yet more pain.

"It's …it's an orchard," she said then.

"Or a garden," Tempest answered. "But a garden run wild. A primal sort of place. Hey, I'm not complaining! Any place would have to be better than the nightmare we've just been through."

Marie nodded, and agreed, "Yes, it's like a wild garden…But then she gave a start before repeating herself: "But…a *garden?*"

And suddenly she was wide-eyed, staring at Tempest where he nursed his cracked or broken rib. "Well?" he said, staring back at her. "Is there something?"

Saying nothing, with her jaw falling open, she simply held up her silver bracelet for him to read its inscription, just as he had read it once before, what felt like a hundred years ago, in the car park. E. Marie L. And:

Ethel, Edith, Elspeth, Tempest remembered what he'd thought then. And it was like he'd been struck by lightning, electrifying, when his mind blazed up in sudden understanding.

She saw it in his face and said, "Mr. Tempest, or professor, or just Temp…except, of course, that's just a nickname, not your real name. So now will you tell me something? What *is* your real name, your first name, Mr. Tempest?"

But Adam knew he really didn't need to. And for just a few seconds he couldn't have spoken anyway, even if he'd wanted to.

Then they laughed, both of them—even though laughter hurt him—and their laughter was indeed more than a little hysterical; until finally he was able to control himself and say:

"Eve, whatever you do keep your eyes open for snakes—and don't even *think* of touching those apples!"

The Long Last Night

Was it just a myth—or a Mythos?

I

I had met or bumped into the old man on what was probably the very rim of the Bgg'ha Zone. And after careful, nervous greetings (he had a gun and I didn't,) and while we shared one of my cigarettes, he asked me: "Do you know why it's called that?"

He meant the Bgg'ha Zone, of course, because he had already mentioned how we should be extremely careful just being there. Shrugging by way of a partial answer, I then offered: "Because it's near the center of it?"

"Well," he replied, "I suppose that defines it now. I mean, that's likely how most people think of it; because after a number of years a name tends to stick, no matter its actual origin. And let's face it, there's not too many of us around these days—folks who were here at the time—people like myself, who are *still* here to remember what happened."

"When the Bgg'ha Zone got its name, you mean?" I prompted him. "There's a reason it's called that? So what happened?"

Getting his thoughts together, he nodded and said, "The real reason is that shortly after that damn Twisted Tower was raised when *They* first got here, after they came down from the stars and up from the sea, or wherever, the only time anyone went anywhere near the Twisted Tower voluntarily—'to find out what it was like!' I've heard it said, if you can credit someone would do such a thing! — the damn fool came out again a ragged, raving lunatic who couldn't do anything but scream a few mad words over and over again. 'The Bgg'ha Zone!' he would scream, laughing and skittering around and pointing at that mile-high monstrosity where it stands dead centre of things. And: 'The Twisted Tower!' he'd yelp like a dog. But he was harmless except to himself, and making those noises and a mess was *all* he did until they bound and gagged him to keep him quiet. Then his heart gave out and he died with a wet gag in his mouth and the froth of madness drying on his chin…"

"You talk too much and too loudly," I told him. "And if I really should be as afraid of this place as you make out, then what in God's name are *you* doing here?" Before he could answer I shook another Marlboro from its pack, lit it, took a drag and handed it to him. I had no reason to antagonize the old boy.

"God's name?" he turned his head and stared at me where we sat amidst the rubble, on the remains of a toppled brick wall; stared at me with his bloodshot eyes — his sunken, crying eyes that he'd rubbed until they were a rough, raw red — before accepting and sucking on that second cigarette. And: "Oh, I have my reasons for being here," he said. "Nothing to do with God, though. Not the God we used to pray to, anyway; not unless I'm here as His agent, sort of working for Him without really being aware of it. In which case you might think He would have chosen a better way to set things up."

"You're not making a lot of sense," I told him, "and you're still much too noisy. Won't they hear you? Don't they sometimes patrol outside the Bgg'ha Zone? I've heard they do."

"Patrols?" He took a deep drag, handed my smoke back to me, and went on: "You mean the hunters? And do you know what they hunt? They hunt us! We're it! *Meat!*"

He took back the cigarette, and after another drag and a sly, sidelong glance at me from eyes still bloodshot but narrowed now: "Anyway, and like I said, I have a good reason for being here. A *damn* good reason!" And he balanced a small, battered, heavy-looking old suitcase on his thighs, using his free hand to hug it to his belly.

"But as for right now—" he continued after a brief moment's pause, while the look he was directing at me became rather more pointed, "—I reckon it's your turn to state why *you* are here. I never saw you before, and I don't think you're from the SSR.... So?"

"The SSR?"

"The South Side Resistance, for what *they're* worth—*huh!*" he answered. But I wasn't really listening. Having taken back my smoke again, I was watching his veined right hand moving to rest on the gun at his bony hip, as again he asked, "So?"

"I stay alive by moving around," I told him. "I don't stay too long in any one place, and I live however I can. I go where there's food, when and where I can find it, and cigarettes, and on rare occasions a little booze."

"The old grocery stores? The shattered shops?"

"Yes, of course." I nodded. "Where else? The supermarkets that were—those that aren't already completely looted out. In the lighter hours, the few short hours of partial daylight when those things sleep, if they sleep, I dig among the ruins; but stuff is getting very hard to find. Day by day, week by week, it's harder all the time, which is why I move around. I ended up here just a couple of days ago. At least I think it was days; you never can tell in this perpetual dusk. I haven't seen the sun for quite some time now, and even then it was very low on the horizon, right at the beginning of this...this—"

"—This long last night?" he helped me out. "The long last night of the human race, and never more certainly of Henry Chattaway!"

Then he sobbed and only just managed to catch it before it leaked out of him, but I heard it anyway. And: "My God, how and why did *this* bloody mess happen to us?" Craning his neck he looked up to where black wisps of cloud scudded across the sky, as if searching for an answer up there—from God, perhaps?

"So—er, Henry?—in fact you *are* a believer," I said, standing up from the broken wall and dropping my smoke before it could burn my fingers. "And if so, what do you reckon, then? That we're all career sinners and paying for it?" I stepped on the glowing cigarette end, crushing it out in the red dust of powdered bricks.

Controlling his breathing, his sobbing, the old man said, "Do you mean are we being punished? I don't know — probably. But come with me and I'll show you something." And getting creakingly to his feet, he went hobbling to a more open area close by, once the corner of a street — more properly a mangled junction of twisted blackened ruins and rubble now — where the scattered, shattered debris lay more thinly on the riven ground, and only the vaguest outlines of any actual streets remained. Of course, this was hardly unusual; for all I knew the entire city, and probably every city in the world, would look pretty much the same right now.

And after tugging on the sleeve of my parka while I followed him and stood glancing here and there, only too well aware that out in the open at this once-crossroads we would be visible from all points of the compass, albeit dimly, my companion finally let go of me to point toward the north-east. So that even before my gaze could follow the bearing indicated by his scrawny, shaking arm, its trembling hand and finger, I knew what I would see. And:

"Look at that!" His words were no more than a husky whisper, almost a whimper. And again, more urgently this time: "*Look!* Just look at it, will you! Now tell me, isn't it obvious where at least one of those names comes from?"

He was talking about the Twisted Tower — a "mile-high monstrosity," he'd called it — where it stood, leaned or seemed to stagger or sway like a phantom heat haze, perhaps a mile and a half away, or two miles at most. But matching it in its utterly unnatural ugliness was its almost obscene height...a mile high? No, but not far short; with its teetering spire stabbing up through the disc of cloud that had been lured into circling it like an aerial whirlpool or the debris of doomed planets round the sucking well of a vast black hole. It was built of the wreckage, the ravaged soul of the crushed city; of gutted high-rises; of many miles of railway carriages twined around its fat base and rising in a spiral, like the thread of a gigantic screw, to a fifth of the tower's height; of bridges and boardwalks torn from their foundations; of a great round clock-face recognizable even at this distance and in this gloom as the face of Big Ben; of a bulge of concrete and glass that had once stood in the heart of the city where it had been called Centrepoint...all of these things and many more, all parts now of the Twisted Tower. But it wasn't really twisted; it was just that its design and composition were so utterly alien that they didn't conform to the mundane Euclidean geometry of scenery that a human eye or brain would automatically accept as the shape of a genuine structure, observing it as authentic without making the viewer feel sick and dizzy.

And though I had seen it often enough before, still I took a stumbling step backwards before wrenching my gaze away from it. Those crazy angles which at first seemed convex before concertinaing down to concavities...only to warp forth again like gigantic boils on the trunk of a kneeling monster. "That mile-high monstrosity," yes—but having seen it before, if not from this angle, I had known what effect it would have on me.

Which was why I concentrated my gaze on what lay in front of it, seeming closer by some hundreds of yards to me than the aberrant dunce's cap of the Tower, and likewise seemed to teeter or waver as in some kind of inanimate yet feverish kneeling obeisance there. Out of true, at an angle of maybe twenty degrees or so to the horizontal in the foreground of the Tower—and in place of the proud prominence of its former self, now looking like the broken half-eggshell of some unimaginably vast roc-bird lying in the uneven debris of its ravaged nest—it was that once venerable, now desecrated relic, the dome of St Paul's cathedral.

"Horrible, *horrible!*" the old man said and shuddered uncontrollably—then gave a start when, from somewhere not very far distant, there came a dismal baying or hooting call; forlorn sounding, true, but in the otherwise silence of the ruins terrifying to any vulnerable man or beast. And starting again—violently this time as

218

more hooting sounded, but closer still and from a different direction—the old man said, "The Hounds! That howling is how they've learned to triangulate. We've got to get away from here!"

"But how?" I said. "The howling is from the south, while to the north-east…we're on the verge of the Bgg'ha Zone!"

"Come with me—and hurry!" he replied. "If some of these wrecked buildings were still standing we'd already be dead—or worse! The Hounds know all the angles and move through them, so we must consider ourselves lucky."

"The angles?"

"Alien geometry," he answered, limping as best he could back down the collapsed rubble strewn canyon where we had met, then turning into a lesser side-street canyon. And panting, he explained: "They say that where the Hounds come from Tindalos or somewhere—or something?—where there are only angles. Their universe is made of angles that let them slip through space somehow, and they can do the same here. But London has lost most of its angles now, and with the buildings reduced to rounded or jumbled heaps of debris, the Hounds have trouble finding their way around. And whether you believe in Him or not, still you may thank God for that!"

"I'll take your word for it," I told him, sure that he told the truth. "But where are we going to?"

"Where I intended to be going anyway," he replied. "But you most probably won't want to go there—for which I don't blame you—and anyway we've already on our way."

"Where to?" I said, looking left, right, everywhere and seeing nothing but heaped bricks and shadowy darkness.

"Here," he answered, and ducked into the gloom of a partly caved-in iron and brick archway. And assisted by a rusted metal handrail, we made our way down tiled steps littered with rubble fallen from the ceiling, now lying under a layer of dust that thinned out a little the deeper we went.

"Where are we?" I asked after a while. "I mean, what is this place?" My questions echoed in a gloom that deepened until I could barely see.

"Used to be an old entrance to the tube system," he told me. "This one didn't have elevators, just steps, and they must have closed it down a hundred years ago. But when these alien things went rioting through the city, causing earthquakes and wrecking everything, all that destruction must have cracked it open."

"You seem to know all about it," I said, as I became aware that the light was improving; either that or my eyes were growing accustomed to the dark.

The old man nodded. "I saw a dusty old plaque down here one time, not long after I found this place. A sort of memorial, it said that the last time this part of the underground system was used was during the Second World War—as a shelter. It was too deep down here for the bombs to do any damage. As for now: it's still safer than most other places, at least where the Hounds are concerned, because it's too round."

"Too round?"

"It's a hole in the earth deep underground," he replied impatiently. "It's a tunnel—a tube—as round as a wormhole!"

"Ah!" I said. "I see. It doesn't have any angles!"

"Not many, no."

"But it does have light, and it's getting brighter."

We passed under another dusty archway and were suddenly on the level: a railway platform, of course. The light was neither daylight nor electric; dim and unstable, it came and went, fluctuating.

"This filth isn't light as you know it," the old man said. "It's bioluminescence—waste elements, or shit to you! It leaks like smoke or mist, but its tissue left behind by those bloody awful things, the Shoggoths, when they pass by or through the darker places! Unlike them, however, it's harmless, except maybe as a poison. But just look at it up there on the ceiling."

I looked, if only to satisfy his urging, at a sort of glowing fog that pulsed where it spilled along the tiled, vaulted ceiling. Gathering and dispersing, it seemed tenuous as breath on a freezing cold day, but clinging and dense as thin soup in cracks or hollow place where tiles had fallen. And:

"Shoggoth tissue?" I repeated the old fellow. "Alien stuff, right? But how is it you know all this? And I still don't even know why you're here. One thing I do know—I think—is that you're going the wrong way."

Having climbed down from the platform, he was striking out along the rusting tracks on a heading that my sense of direction told me lay toward—

"North-easterly?" he agreed, as if reading my mind. "And I warned you that you wouldn't be safe coming with me. In fact if I were you I'd follow the rails going the other way, south. And I would go now! Then, sooner or later, somewhere or other, I'm sure you'd find a way out."

"But I'm not at all sure!" I replied, jumping down from the platform and hurrying to catch up. "Also, it's like I said: you seem to understand just about everything that goes on here, and you're obviously a survivor. As for myself, well I'd like to survive too!"

That stopped him dead in his tracks. "A survivor, you say? I was, yes—but no more. My entire family is no more! So what the hell am I doing trying to stay alive, eh? I'm sick to death of trying, and there's only one reason I haven't done away with myself!" By which time the catch was back in his voice, that almost sob.

But he controlled it, then swung his small, heavy, battered old suitcase from left to right, changing hands and groaning as he stretched and flexed the strained muscles in his left arm, before swinging the suitcase back again and visibly tightening his grip on its leather handle. At which I saw in his grimace the pain quickly returning. He must be either left-handed, or maybe that arm was stronger than the other.

"You should let me carry it," I told him, as we began walking again. "At least let me spell you. What's in it anyway? All your worldly possessions? It certainly looks heavy enough."

"Don't you worry about this suitcase!" he at once snapped, turning a narrow-eyed look on me as his right hand dipped to hover over the butt of the weapon on his hip. "And I still think you should turn around and head south while you still can, if only…if only for my stupid peace of mind's sake!" As quickly as that he softened up again, explaining: "Because I can't help feeling guilty it's my fault that you're here, and the deeper we get into the Bgg'ha Zone, the more likely it is that you won't get out again!"

"Don't you go feeling guilty about me!" I told him evenly. "I'll take my chances, just like I always have. But you? What about you?"

He didn't answer, just turned away and carried on walking.

"Or maybe you're a volunteer—" I hazarded a guess, though by now it was becoming more than a guess, "—like that first one who went in and came out screaming? Is that it, Henry? Are you some kind of volunteer, too?" He offered no reply, remaining silent as I followed on close behind him.

And feeling frustrated in my own right, I goaded him more yet: "I mean, do you even know what you're doing, Henry, going headlong into the Bgg'ha Zone like this?"

Once again he stopped and turned to me…almost turned *on* me! "Yes," he half-growled, half-sobbed, as he pushed his wrinkled old face close to mine. "I *do* know what I'm doing. And no, I'm not some kind of volunteer. What I'm doing—everything I do—it's for me, myself. You want to know how come I know so much about what happened around here, and to the planet in general? Well, that's because I *was* here, pretty much in the middle of it; the middle of one of the centres, anyway. And you've probably never heard of them, but there was this crazy bunch, the Esoteric Order or some such. They had their own religion, if you could call it that, their own church where they got together. Their 'bibles' were these cursed, mouldy old volumes of black magic and weird, alien spells and formulas that should have been destroyed back in the dark ages. Why, I even heard it said that…."

But there he paused, cocking his head on one side and listening for something.

"What is it?" I asked him. Because all I could hear was the slow but regular drip, drip, drip of seeping water.

Then with a start, a sudden jerk of his head, the old man looked down at the rusting rails, where three or four inches of smelly, stagnant water glinted blackly as it slopped between the sides of the tracks. And: "*Shhh!*" he whispered. "*Listen*, damn you!"

II

I did as I was told, and heard it: the distant hollow-sounding echoes; the alien grunting, and muttering, and slapping of feet in shallow water which we had only recently come slogging through. But these inhuman grunts, these entirely outlandish sounds, were very definitely not to my companion's liking.

"Damn you! *Damn you!*" the old man whispered. "Didn't I warn you to go back? You might even have made it in time before *they* blocked your way. But you can't go back there now!"

Just the tone of his hoarse, whispering voice was almost enough to make my flesh creep. "So what is it?" I queried him again. "Who or what are 'they' this time?"

"We have to get on," he replied, ignoring my question. "Have to move faster—but as quietly as we can. Their hearing isn't much to speak of, not when they're up out of their element, the water—but if they *were* to hear us…"

"They're not men?"

"Call them what you will," he told me, his voice all shuddery. "Men sorts, I suppose…or frogs, or fish! Who can say what they are exactly? They came in from the sea, up the Thames and into the lakes and wherever there was deep water. It was as if they'd been called…no, I'm sure they *were* called, by those crazies of the Esoteric Order! But true men? Not at all, not in the least! Their males must have mated with women, most likely—or possibly vice versa, maybe?—but no, they're not men…"

Which prompted me to ask: "How can you know that for sure?"

"Because I've *seen* some of them. Just the once, but it was enough. And you hear that slap-slapping? Can't you just picture the feet that slap down on the water like that? Good for swimming, but not much good for walking."

"So why are we in such a hurry?"

And once again, impatiently or yet more impatiently, he said, "Because they can call up others of their kind. A sort of telepathy, maybe? Hell, I don't know!"

We moved faster, and I could almost hear him wincing each time our feet kicked up water that splashed a little too loudly. Then in a while we came across a narrow ledge to one side, where the wall had been cut back some two feet to make an old maintenance walkway four feet higher than the bed of the tracks.

"Get up there," the old man told me. "It's dry and we'll be able to go faster without all the noise."

I did as he advised and reached down to help him up. He wasn't much more than a bundle of bones and couldn't be very strong, but he didn't for a second offer that small suitcase to me or release his grip on it. And with me in front we moved ahead again; until eventually, this time without my urging, he continued telling me his story from where he'd left off; his story, along with that of the alien invasion or takeover—or *walkover*—which seemed to come a little easier to him now. So perhaps he'd really needed to get it off his chest.

"It was those Esoteric Order freaks. At least, that was how everyone thought of them: as folks with too few screws, and what few they had with crossed threads! But no, they weren't crazy—except maybe in what they were trying to do. And actually, that even got into the last of the newspapers: how the Esoteric Order was trying to call up powerful creatures—god-things, they called them—from parallel dimensions and the beginning of time; beings that had come here once before, even before the evolution of true or modern people, only to be trapped and imprisoned by yet more mysterious beings and banished back to their original universes, or to forgotten, forbidden places here on Earth and under the sea…

224

The Long Last Night

"Well, that was a laugh, wasn't it? As 'daft' as those flying saucer stories from the 1950s and '60s, and all those myths of dinosaur monsters in a Scottish loch and hairy ape men on Himalayan mountains; oh, and lots of other myths and legends of the same sort. But daft? Oh, really? And if those oh-so-bloody-clever newspaper reporters, the ones who infiltrated the church and saw them at their worship and listened to their sermons—along with the other religious groups that scoffed at their 'idiotic beliefs'—if they had been right, then all well and good. But they weren't!

"And when should it happen—when *did* it happen?—but at Hallowmas: the feast of All Hallows, All Saints!

"And oh, what an awful feast that was—*Them feasting on us*, I mean—when those monstrous beings answered the call and came forth from their strange dimensions, bringing thralls, servitors and adherents with them. Up from the oceans, down from the weird skies of parallel universes, erupting from the earth and bringing all of the planet's supposedly dead volcanoes back to life, these minions of madness came; and what of humanity then, eh? What but food for their tables, fodder for their stables."

That last wasn't a question but a simple fact, and the old man was sobbing again, openly now, as he turned and grasped my arm. "My wife…" He almost choked on the word. "That poor, poor woman…she was taken at first pass! Taken, as the city reeled and the buildings crumbled, as the earth broke open and darkness ruled!

"Ah, but according to rumour the very first to go was that blasphemous, evil old church! For the so-called 'priests' of the Esoteric Order had been fatally mistaken in calling up that which they couldn't put down again: a mighty octopus god-thing who rose in his house some-where in the Pacific, while others of his spawn surfaced in their manses from various far- flung deeps. Not the least of these emerged in the Antarctic—along with an entire plateau! That was a *massive* upheaval, causing earthquakes and tsunamis around the world! Another rose up from the Mariana Trench, and even one from far closer to home, an unknown abyss somewhere in the mid-Atlantic. He was the one—damn him to hell!—who built his Twisted Tower house here in the Zone. In fact the Bgg'ha Zone is named after him, for he was—he *is*—Bgg'ha!

"And there's a chant, a song, a liturgy of sorts that human worshippers—oh yes, there are such people!—sing of a night as they wander aimlessly through the rubble streets. And having heard it so often, far *too* often, dinning repeatedly in my ears while I lay as if in a coma, hardly daring to breathe until they had moved on, I learned those alien words and could even repeat them. What's more, when the SSR trapped and caught one of these madmen, these sycophants, to learn whatever they could from him, he offered them a translation. And those chanted words which I had learned, they were these:

"'*Ph'nglui gwlihu'nath, Bgg'ha Im'ykh Ia'ihu'nagl fhtagn.*' A single mad sentence which translates into this:

"'*From his house at Im'ykh, Bgg'ha at last is risen!*'

"And do you know, those words still ring in my ears, blocking almost everything else out? If I don't concentrate on what I'm doing, on what I'm saying, it all slips away and all I can hear is that damned chanting: Bgg'ha at last is risen! Ah, but since he was able to rise, maybe he can be sent back down again! And perhaps I even have...even have the means with which...with which...."

This was far more than he had ever told me before; but here he fell silent again, possibly wondering if he had said too much.

Then, as we rested for a few minutes and I looked down from the maintenance ledge, I could see how the dirty water was as much as seven or eight inches deeper here where it glinted over the rusting rails. And seeing where I was looking, my companion told me:

"Yes, there's even deeper water up ahead, and likewise on the surface *over*-head."

"Ahead of us?" I repeated him, for want of something to say. "But...on the surface?"

"Mainly on the surface," he nodded. "That's where it's leaking from. We're heading for Knightsbridge, as was—which isn't far from the Serpentine—also as was but much enlarged and far deeper now.

That too was the work of Bgg'ha; he did it for some of his servitors, the kind we heard wading through that shallow water back along the tracks. There's plenty more of them in the Serpentine, which is part of the great lake now that drowned St James's Park and everything in between all the way to the burst banks of the Thames. Which means we can stay down here for another mile or thereabouts, but then we may yet be obliged to surface for a while…either that or swim, and I really don't fancy that! I don't much fancy either choice, in fact."

"You've done this before," I said as we set off again, because it was obvious that he had, fairly often and perhaps recently. It would explain how he knew these routes so well.

Sure enough he nodded and replied, "Five times, yes. But this will be the last time. For you too—your first *and* last time."

"Or maybe not," I answered. "I mean, you never can tell how things will work out."

"Young fool!" he said, but not unkindly, even somewhat pityingly. "You'll be right there in the heart of the Bgg'ha Zone! In the roots of the Twisted Tower, that loathsome creature's so-called 'house!' And I can tell you exactly how things are going to work out for you: but I won't, except to say you're *not* going to be coming out again!"

"But *you* did," I answered him. "And all of five times…if you're not lying or simply crazy!"

He shook his head. "I'm not lying, and I'm not crazy. You're the one who's crazy! Listen, do you have any idea who I am or why I'm really here?"

I shrugged. "You're just an old man on a mad mission. That much is obvious. I may even know what your mission is, and why. It's revenge, because they took your wife, your family. But one small suitcase—even one that's full of high explosive—just isn't going to do it. Nothing short of a nuclear weapon is ever going to do it."

The look he turned on me then was sour, downcast, disappointed. And: "Have I been *that* obvious?" he asked, coming to a halt where the ledge stepped up onto an actual platform. "I suppose I must have been. But even so you're only half right, and that makes you half wrong."

The Shoggoth light was suddenly poorer, where the mist writhing on the tiled, vaulted expanse of the ceiling was that much thinner. Our eyes, however, had grown accustomed to the eerie gloom and the fluctuating quality of the bioluminescence, and we were easily able to read the legend on the tunnel's opposite wall:

KNIGHTSBRIDGE

"My God!" my guide muttered then. "But I remember how this place looked in its heyday: so clean and bright with its shining tiles, its endless stairs and great elevators, its theatre and lingerie posters. But look at it now, with its evidence of earth tremors and fires; its blackened, greasy walls; its collapsed or caved-in archways, and all the other damage that it's suffered. And…and…*Lord, what a mess!*"

A mess? Something of an understatement, that. The ceiling was scarred by a series of broad jagged cracks where dozens of tiles had come loose and fallen; some of the access/exit openings in the wall on our side of the tracks had buckled inwards, causing the ceiling to sag ominously where mortared debris and large blocks of concrete had crashed down; and from a source somewhere high above a considerable waterfall was surging out of an arched exit and spilling into the central channel, drowning the tracks under a foaming torrent.

As we clambered over the rubble the old man said, "I think that I—or rather we—are very likely in the shit!" And I asked myself: *What, another understatement? How phlegmatic!* And meanwhile he had continued: "Like everywhere else, this place is coming apart. It's got so much…so much worse, since the last time I passed through here."

Which was when he began to ramble and sob again, only just managing to make sense:

"There's been so many earthquakes recently…if the rest of the underground system is in the same terrible condition as this place…but then again, maybe it's not that bad…and Hyde Park Corner isn't so far away…not very far at all…and anyway, it was never my intention to surface here…there's water up there…too much water…but still there's a half-decent chance we'll make it to Piccadilly Circus down here in the underground...I've just *got* to make it to Piccadilly Circus...right there, under the Twisted Tower itself!"

Feeling I had to stop him before he broke down completely and did himself some serious harm, I grabbed his arm to slow him down where he was staggering about in the debris. And I shouted over the tumult of the water: "*Hey! Old man!* Slow down and try to stop babbling! You'll wear yourself out both physically and mentally like that—if you haven't already!"

As we cleared the heaped rubble it seemed he heard me and knew I was right. Shaking as if in a fever, which he might well have been, he came to a halt and said: "So close, so very close...but God! I can't fail now. *Lord, don't let me fail now!*"

"You said something about not intending to surface here," I reminded him, holding him steady and trying to divert him, if only his mind. "Something about maybe having to swim?"

At which he sat down on a block of concrete fallen from the ceiling before answering me. And as quickly as that he was more or less coherent again. "I wouldn't even try to surface here," he said, shrugging his thin shoulders. "No reason to do so. And anyway there's far too much water up there—and too many of those monsters that live in it! But we must hope that the rest of the system, between here and Piccadilly Circus, is in better condition."

"Okay," I said, grateful for the break as I sat down beside him. "Piccadilly Circus is our destination. So how do we manage it? And will it mean we have to get down in the water?"

Swaying a little as he got to his feet, he looked over the rim of the platform before answering me. "Are you worried about swimming? Well don't be. The water here isn't nearly as deep as I expected. I think it's finding some other route into the shattered earth, maybe into a recently fashioned subterranean river. So even though we won't have to swim, still it appears we'll be doing a lot more wading; knee-deep at least, and maybe for quite a while yet. So for the last time—even though it's already far too late—I feel I've really got to warn you: if you want to stand even a remote chance, you'll turn back now. Do you understand?"

"I think so, yes," I told him. "But you know, Henry, we've been lucky so far, both of us, so maybe it's not over yet. You may be sure it's the end of the road for you, but I'm not."

"I can't convince you then?"

"To go back? No." I shook my head. "I don't think I want to do that. And the truth is we all have to die sometime, whether it's at Piccadilly Circus, under the Twisted Tower, or back there where those—those *beings*—were splashing about in the water. I mean, what's the difference where, why, or how we do it, eh? It's got to happen eventually."

"As for me," he said, letting himself down slowly over the rim of the platform into water that rose to just above his knees, "it *is* a matter of where I do it, where I can be most effective. My revenge, you said, and at least you were right about that. But you: you're young, strong, apparently well-fed, which is a rare thing in itself! You probably came in from the woods, the countryside—a place where there are still birds and other wild things you could catch and eat—or so I imagine. So for you to accompany me where I'm going..." He shook his head. "It just seems a great waste to me."

There was nothing in what he'd said that I could or needed to answer; so as I let myself down into the water beside him and simply said, "So then, are you ready to move on?" And since his only reply was to lean his bony body into the effort—for the flow of the water was against us and strong—I added, "I take it that you are! But you know, Henry, pushing against the water like this will soon drain you. So may I suggest—only a suggestion, mind you—that you let me carry the case? If you want to do the job you've set yourself, well okay, that's fine. But since I'm here why not let me help you?"

He turned to me, turned a half-thankful, half-anxious look on me, and finally reached out with his trembling arms to give that small suitcase into my care. "But don't you drop it in the water!" he told me.

"In fact don't drop it at all—neither that nor bang it around—or damage it in any other way! Do you hear?"

"Of course I do, Henry," I answered. "And I think I understand. I've seen how you take care of it, and it's obvious how crucial it must be to your mission, however that turns out. Perhaps as we move along you'd care to tell me about it…but it's also fine if you don't want to. First, though, if you don't mind, could you get my cigarettes and lighter out of the top pocket of my parka?" For even though we were well above the water level, still I was hugging the case to my belly with both hands. And I explained: "The water's very cold and a drag or two may help to warm us up—our lungs, anyway. So light one up for yourself and one for me." And when he had managed that: "Thanks, Henry," I told him out the corner of my mouth, before dragging deeply on the familiar smoke.

He smoked, too, but remained silent on the subject of the suitcase: in particular its "secret" contents, as he seemed to consider them.

As already more than hinted, I thought I might know about that anyway but would have preferred to hear it from him. Well, perhaps there was some other way I could talk him into telling me about it. So after we had waded for another ten or twelve minutes and finished our cigarettes:

"Henry, you asked me a while ago if I had any idea who you might be," I reminded him. "Well no, I don't. But it might pass some time and keep our minds active—stop them from freezing up—if you'd care to tell me."

"*Huh!*" he answered. "It's like you want to know everything about me, and I don't even know your name!"

It's Julian," I told him. "Julian Chalmers. I was a teacher and taught the Humanities, some Politics and—of all things—Ethics, at a university in the Midlands."

"Of all…all things?" Shivering head to toe, he somehow got the question out. "How do…do you mean, 'of all things?'"

"Well, they're pretty different subjects, aren't they? Sort of jumbled and contradictory? I mean, is there any such thing as the ethics of politics? Or its 'humanity', for that matter!"

He considered it a while, then said, "Good question. And I might have known the answer once upon a time. But then I would have been talking about—God, it's c-*cold!*—about human politicians. And as for ethics: well, since the actions, or the *mores majorum* of the human race may no longer be said to apply—"

At which he had paused, as if thinking it through. And so:

"Go on," I quickly prompted him, because I was interested in light of my own standing; and anyway because I wanted to keep him talking.

"Well, the invaders," he obliged me, "and I mean all of them—from their leaders, the huge, tentacle-faced creatures in their crazily-angled manses, to the servitors they brought with them or called up after they got settled here—all the nightmarish flying things, and those shapeless, flapping-rag horrors called Hounds, and not least the scaly half-frog, half-fish minions from their deep-sea cities—not one of these species seems to have ever evolved politics, while the very idea of ethics might seem as alien to them as they themselves seem to us! But on the other hand, if you're talking *human* politics, human ethics—"

"I don't think I was," I said, quickly dropping the subject as another maintenance ledge came into view around a slight bend.

We couldn't have been happier, the pair of us, to get out of the water and onto that ledge. And more than mildly surprised, I was relieved to discover that a welcoming draft of air from somewhere up ahead was strangely warm!

"Most places underground are like this," the old man tried to explain it. "When you get down to a certain depth the temperature is more or less constant. It's why the Neanderthals lived in caves. It was the same the last time I was here, which I had forgotten about, but this warm air has served to remind me that we've reached—"

HYDE PARK CORNER

The Long Last Night

He let the legend on the tiled wall across the tracks finish it for him, albeit silently.

"So, what do you think?" I asked him, as we moved from the ledge onto the underground station's platform. "How are we doing, Henry?"

"Not good enough," he answered. "We should be doing a whole lot better! My fault, I suppose, because I'm not as strong as I used to be. I'm just too frail, too weak, that's all, and I'm not afraid to admit it. It's what happens when a man gets old. But that's okay, and I can afford to push myself one last time. Because this *will be* the last time—my last effort in this long last night."

"Hey, you've done okay up to now!" I told him. "And if this warm draft keeps up it will soon dry out our trousers. That's not much, I suppose, but it may help keep our spirits up."

He glanced at me, if only for a moment conjuring up a thin, sarcastic ghost of a smile, and with an almost pitying shake of his head said: "Well okay, good, fine!—whatever you say, er,

Julian?—but right now it's my turn to spell you. So if you'll just give that case back to me…"

Not for a moment wanting to upset him, I handed it over and said, "Okay, if you're sure you can handle it—?"

"I'm sure," he replied, as we looked around the platform. And glancing down at the tracks I saw them glinting dully under no more than twelve or fifteen inches of water. But both of the arched exits from the station were blocked with rubble fallen from above, making my next comment completely redundant:

"It appears there's no way up, not from here."

Henry nodded. "Not even if we wanted or needed one, which we don't. Next up is Green Park, and following that—assuming we get that far—Piccadilly Circus. But Green Park is right on the edge of the water, and—"

"And that's Deep One territory, right?" I cut in.

He nodded, frowned, narrowed his eyes and said, "Well yes, I do believe I've heard them called that before…"

"Of course you have," I replied. "And that's what *you* called them, back there where they were splashing about in the water behind us."

Still frowning, he shook his head and slowly said, "It's a funny thing, but I don't remember that…" And then with a shrug of his narrow shoulders: "Well, so what? I don't remember much of anything any more, only what needs to be done…"

III

And with his frown slowly fading and a last look around, he finally went on: "Well then, now we have to get back into the water. Just when we were drying out, eh? Be glad Green Park's not far from here, only one stop. But it's one hell of a junction, or used to be. It seems utterly unreal, even surreal now, like a weird dream, but there were three lines, criss-crossing Green Park in the old days. I still remember that much at least." He gave himself a shake, and continued: "Anyway, for all that it's close to the lake, it was bone dry the last time I was there. Let's hope nothing has changed. And after Green Park, at about the same distance again, then it's Piccadilly Circus. Almost the end of the line, as it were. Almost the end for us, anyway."

His comment was loaded, the last few words, definitely, but I ignored it and said, "And is that where we surface?"

Again Henry's nod. "It'll make your skin crawl!" he said. And matching his words, he shuddered violently; which I didn't in any way consider a consequence of his damp, clinging trousers. Then, when he'd controlled his shaking, he continued: "But yes, we'll surface there, right up Bgg'ha's ugly jacksy, or as close as anyone would ever want to get to it!"

I waited until we were moving steadily forward again, in water that came up inches short of our knees, and then said, "Henry, you say our skins will be made to crawl. But is there any special reason for that? Or shouldn't I ask?"

"You shouldn't ask." He shook his head.

The Long Last Night

"But I'm asking anyway." Which was just natural curiosity on my part, I suppose. And whatever, I wanted the old man's take on it; because we all see things, experience things, differently.

"As you will," he said with a shrug, and went on: "Piccadilly Circus as was is lying crushed at the roots of Bgg'ha's house. That great junction, once standing so close to the heart of a city, is now in the dark basement of the Twisted Tower, that vast heap of wreckage where he or it lords it over his minions—*and over his human captives*, his 'cattle.'"

"His cattle…" I mused, because that thought or simile was still reasonably new to me. At least I had never heard it expressed that way before coming across Henry.

"As I may have told you before," the old man said, "that's all his captives are: they're food for Bgg'ha's table, fodder for his stable."

We were moving faster now, under an arched ceiling that was aglow, seemingly alive with luminous, swirling Shoggoth exhaust. And the closer we drew to Henry's goal or target, the more voluble he was becoming.

"Do you know why I'm here?" he suddenly burst out. "I think you do—or rather, *you* think you do!"

Nodding, I said: "But haven't we already decided that? It's revenge, isn't it? For your wife?"

"For my whole family!" he corrected me. And the catch, that half-sob, was back in his voice. "My poor wife, yes, of course—*but also for my girls, my daughters!* And my eldest, Janet—my God, how brave! I would never have suspected it of her, but she was braver than me. Inspiring, is how I've come to think of it: that my Janet was able to escape like that, and somehow managed to crawl back home again. But she did, she came home to me, and then…then she died! Not yet twenty years old, and gone like that!

"She died of horror and loathing—because of what had been done to her—but never of shame, for she had fought it all the way. And it's mainly because…because of what Janet *told* me had happened to her that I've kept coming here. It's why I'm here now: for Janet, yes, but also for her younger sister, Dawn, and for their mother; and for all the other females who've been taken—*and who are still there,* maybe alive even now in that Twisted Tower!"

"Still alive?" I repeated him. "You mean, maybe they're not just fodder after all?" At which I could have bitten through my tongue as it dawned on me that it was probably very cruel of me to keep questioning him like this. But too late for that now.

Sobbing openly and making no attempt to hide it, Henry replied: "Janet was taken two months ago. They took her in broad daylight, or what we used to call daylight, on her way back home from an SSR meeting. She'd been a member a long time; she'd never forgotten how her mother was taken. A boyfriend of hers from older times had seen it happen. It was those freakish flapping-rag things, those so-called Hounds. I was always telling her to stick to the shadows whenever she ventured out, but on this occasion I'd forgotten to warn her against angles. They had taken her on a mainly intact street corner; just ninety degrees of curb and buckled walls that cost Janet her freedom and, as I believed at the time, her life too. But no, Janet's captors were working for that thing in his Twisted Tower, something I hadn't known until she escaped and got home just a month or two ago.

"That was when I found out about what goes on in that hellish place. Since when I've risked my own life five times making this trip in and out, always hoping I might see Janet's mother, or her younger sister Dawn, and that I might be able to rescue them somehow…but at the same time making certain deliveries and planning for the future…in fact planning for right now, if you really want to know. But my wife…and Dawn…that poor kid, just seventeen years old: they're somewhere in that nightmarish tower, I feel certain. But alive and suffering still, or dead and…and *eaten!* Who knows?" There he paused and made an attempt to bring himself back under control.

Feeling the need to have the old man continue, however—no matter how painful that had to be for him—I said, "Henry, before Janet escaped, did she ever actually see her mother, or her younger sister Dawn, there in the Twisted Tower?"

The Long Last Night

He shook his head. "Not once. Other girls, plenty of them, but never her Ma. But where Dawn is concerned, that's completely understandable; she was taken just a week or so after Janet found her way home in time to...in time to die! Yes, she'd got out of that place before Dawn was so much as taken in..." And then he paused for a moment or two before trying to continue.

"Now, I know it must sound like I've been pretty careless of my girls, but that's not so. And maybe it's for the best if Dawn really is dead now...because of what her sister told us was *happening* to those other female captives."

And as he broke down more yet, as gently as I could I asked him, "Well then, Henry, what did Janet tell you? What *was* happening in there, to the other female captives?"

Sobbing and stumbling along through the water—sobbing so loudly I thought he might sob his heart out—still he managed to reply: "Oh, that's something I see in my blackest nightmares, Julian, and I see it every night! But first let me tell you how Dawn was taken...

"I had left her at home while I went looking for a place to bury Janet. No big problem there...a hole in the ground, with plenty of bricks and rubble to fill it in. Necessary, yes, because there are packs of *real* hounds running wild through all the ruins. But after taking care of her, then I went rummaging for food in the debris of a corner store I'd found: canned fruit, and meats and such. But when I got back home with my haul—'home,' *hah!*—a concrete cellar in a one-time museum, a mainly buried wing of the old Victoria and Albert, I think it was...hard to tell in all that devastation. But anyway, when I got back Dawn was gone and the place had been completely wrecked. What few goods we'd had, sticks of furniture and such, were broken up, strewn everywhere, and the place was damp and stank of...oh, I don't know, rotting fish, weeds, and stagnant water. The evil stench of the Deep Ones, yes; for they, too, serve Bgg'ha, as I believe do all those damned octopus-heads..."

And there Henry fell silent again, leaving only the echoes of his tortured voice, and the sloshing of our legs through the water. But I still couldn't let it rest; there were things he had hinted at that for which I would like explanations. I wondered just how much he knew. And so:

"You said your wife was taken that first night," I reminded him, as if he needed it. "Taken as all hell stampeded through the city, and there was no defense against the turmoil, the horror. But that was a long time ago, Henry. And weren't these monsters slaughtering everyone and destroying everything in their path at that time? How could you possibly think your wife might still be alive in Bgg'ha's Twisted Tower? Especially after what Janet had told you about it?"

At which the old man seemed to freeze in his tracks, jerked to a standstill, and in the next moment turned on me, snarling: "How do *you* know what Janet did or didn't tell me, eh? And how much do *you* know about that damned Twisted Tower? Tell me that, Julian Chalmers!"

Oh, I was glad in that moment that I had returned his suitcase to Henry, and that he was carrying it with both hands. He still had that gun on his hip, and if he could have reached for it, without jeopardizing the safety of the case and its contents, I felt sure he would have done so. And who knows what he might have done then? But he couldn't and didn't, and I said:

"Henry, I didn't mean to hurt you, but those creatures in the Tower...they *eat* people, don't they? Haven't you already said as much? And they've had your wife for a very long time. Now, don't be offended, but in the light of your daughters' ages, not to mention your own obvious years, it has to be my understanding that your wife isn't, or wasn't, a mere girl; so what good would she be *alive*, to such as Bgg'ha and his minions now? I mean, him and his monsters? Beasts in their stables? What use to any of them except as...well, except as—"

But that was as far as he would let me go, and I could tell by the look on his face that it wouldn't in any case be necessary to finish my question.

"*God damn you, Julian!*" he said, turning away. "It was hope—desperate, impossible hope!—that's all. And as for...as for poor Dawn..." But he couldn't say on and so went staggering away through the sluggish, blackly glinting water, in the eerie light of the swirling Shoggoth tissue.

I gave him a few moments before catching up, then said: "I'm sorry, Henry, but you leave me confused. I know you're planning some kind of revenge—in whatever form that may take—but if you were really hoping that Dawn and your wife are still alive, might not the violence of any such revenge hurt them too, not to mention you yourself?"

Yet again he came to a halt and turned on me. "Of course it would— and will!" he said. "But far better that, a quick, clean death to them, cleaner to all of us, than what we could *yet* suffer—*and to what Dawn, if not her poor mother, must be suffering now, even as we speak of it!*" And then, before I could say anything more: "Now listen...

"Did you know they take young boys, too? Young men, I mean, of your age or there-abouts? And since you appear to be good at figuring things out, can you guess what *they* are used for?"

"No, not really," I replied, unwilling to disturb him further. "But in any case, maybe we should quieten it down now. I think I heard voices—some kind of sounds, anyway—from somewhere up ahead."

The old man's eyes focused as he looked all about, searching for recognizable signs on the old blackened walls. And: "Yes," he whispered, as quietly as I had suggested. "Your ears are obviously better than mine. We're only five minutes or so away from Green Park, which is one of the worst places for—"

"—Deep Ones?" I finished it for him, and he nodded. And from then on we stayed silent, creeping like mice, glad that the water level had fallen away to no more than an inch or two. And for the second time Henry entrusted his case to me...

IV

Ahead of us, the Shoggoth light brightened up a little, until it was about half as good as dim electric light used to be. Even so it suited us just fine, because Henry was right and four or five minutes later Green

Park's platform loomed up out of the shadily gloomy distance. By then, however, the alien, gutturally grunting voices we'd heard had faded away into distant echoes before ceasing entirely; but still there were the sounds of some sort of laborious work going on in subterranean Green Park's upper reaches. So we made no attempt at climbing up onto the platform but stayed on the tracks in the shadow of the bull-nosed wall, where we crouched down and kept the lowest possible profile as we traversed the mercifully short length of the station. And halfway across that comparatively open space, suddenly Henry paused to tug nervously on the sleeve of my parka, indicating that I should look at the platform's flagged floor.

Still keeping low but raising my head just enough to scan the platform end to end, I saw what he had seen: the large, damp imprints of webbed feet where the dusty paving flags had been criss-crossed. Then, too, I detected the stench of weedy deeps and the less than human creatures risen up from them—and possibly the hybrid ones also.

Deep Ones! Henry framed the words with his lips, both silently and needlessly. And: *Look!* He pointed.

From the mouths of the entry/exit archways, rubble had been cleared away and heaped aside. The stairs and one wrecked elevator, visible beyond the archways, were also clear of debris. But from one of the exits a thin stream of water was flowing forth, snaking across the platform and over the lip of the bull-noses, before finding its way down into the well and from there, presumably, into unseen channels that were deeper yet. But even in the moments we spent watching it, so the flow rapidly increased to a torrent, and at the same time a massed, triumphant shout—a hooting, snorting uproar, even at the distance—sounded from on high. But of course we already knew that the engineering going on up there wasn't the work of human beings.

And now Henry whispered, "Come on, let's get out of here!"

Some minutes later and a hundred yards or more into the comparative gloom of the tunnel, finally the old man spoke up again. "We were very fortunate back there, lucky indeed!"

"Oh?" I replied. "Lucky?"

He looked at me incredulously. "Why, the fact that they'd only recently gone up out of the station! You saw their footprints, where they'd probably been planning to flood the place not too long before we got there. Lucky, yes, for it they'd done it any earlier we'd likely be swimming by now! Surely you know or can guess what they were doing—what they're doing even now?"

Trudging along beside him, sloshing through inches of gradually deepening cold, black water, I shrugged. "Well, like you said: they're flooding the place."

"Yes, but why?"

"Because...because they like the water?" I shrugged stupidly.

Old Henry offered up a derisive snort and repeated me sarcastically: "'Because they like the water'? Is that all? Man, can't you see? Don't you understand? They're terraforming—no, *aqua*-forming— the underground system, similar to what we had planned on doing to Mars before those freaks in the Esoteric Order ruined everything! They're making the tube system suitable, comfortable, compatible—to them in their loathsome way of life! Now do you see it? This maze, these endless miles of tunnels, stations and levels; these massive great rabbit-holes—*and all of them filled with water*, if not now then soon! Paradise, to the Deep Ones! Submarine temples to their alien master, octopus-headed Bgg'ha, with myriad submarine connections to his central Twisted Tower like the strands of a gigantic sunken cobweb!"

Henry's thought or vision was fantastic and even awe-inspiring: the entire underground system filled with water! A vast submarine labyrinth where the Deep Ones could spawn and worship their bloated black deity for as long as the Earth continued to roll in its orbit.

Then for several long minutes we remained silent, Henry and I, as we slopped along under the swirling and gradually brightening glow of Shoggoth filth.

But eventually he said, "Well then, Julian—have you figured it out yet?"

"Eh? Figured what out?"

"Why they take young men, of course."

"You mean, if not to eat them?"

"Yes," he nodded. "If not to eat them. What other use could young men be put to, eh?"

Deciding to let him tell me, I shook my head. "I've no idea, Henry." And beginning to sob again, however quietly, he said:

"It's because young men are sexually potent, Julian. Just like horses in the stud farms as once were before *They* came. That's what my girl Janet told me, but it's also why she escaped and came home worn out, dying, *and pregnant!* The baby—not much more than a foetus I imagine or hope, poor innocent creature—he or she died with Janet. But better that than *it*, or *that other*, as may have been! And now…and now…"

I nodded and said, "I understand—I think. And now there's Dawn. Why don't you tell me about her, if you can?"

"No," he shook his head, "you *don't* understand! You haven't thought it through. But I didn't have to, because I had it from Janet, and I'll tell you anyway; or perhaps by now you can tell me? Why would a nightmarish thing like Bgg'ha—and the monsters in that Twisted Tower of a throne-room and dwelling—why would they want children, babies, from their captives?"

We both slowly came to a halt and stood facing each other; but even knowing what he was getting at I n.ade no reply. The old man saw that I knew and nodded an affirmative. "Oh, yes, Julian. In the long ago era of sailing ships, men from the west would sometimes come across cannibal tribes in the South Sea Islands, and these savage people had a term for the enemies they roasted for food. They called them—or the flesh they ate off them—'long pig,' because that's how we taste, apparently. Now I don't know if they ever tried 'short pig,' if you follow my meaning, but if they did, or do, what could be more tender or pure than—"

"—I understand, Henry," I stopped him. "So don't torture yourself any further."

"But what horrified me most," he continued, as if he hadn't heard me at all, "wasn't so much the thought of those *monsters* at their repast,

242

but wondering what the so-called human beings who fathered those babies—what those men, or for that matter those human *mothers*—could be dining on themselves in the Twisted Tower! What source of…of *food* could there possibly be in that dreadful place? And what kind of inhuman, bestial people, men and women, could bring themselves to do anything as terrible as that in the first place? Surely they would rather die than descend to depths as black as that? Wouldn't you think so?" "Yes, most people certainly would," I replied, even though I knew he meant it more as a statement of fact than a question—or a question easily answered. Or not immediately.

Henry could barely stifle his soul-wrenching sobbing as he staggered away from me. Yet in some superhuman way, and seeming more determined than ever even though he only just managed to maintain his balance, still he went splashing along the drowned, rusty tracks.

I caught up with the old man, caught his arm to steady him before he could trip and hurt himself, and said, "But there are all kinds of men, Henry. Most men couldn't deal with that, I think. But as for those who could, what choice would they have? They'd reap what they'd sown, as it were—if, in this case, you can excuse such a metaphor—and eat or starve in the absence of any other choice. But you know, Henry, some men, and some women too, are *very* adaptable; and in desperate times and situations the survival instinct in people such as these will quickly surface, and they'll soon become inured, accustomed to…to whatever. Yes, that kind of person can get used to almost anything…"

V

Yet again he may not have heard a word I said. And instead of scolding me for my "logical" reply to what he had told me—however sickening and disgusting that approach must surely have seemed to him, if indeed he had heard anything of it at all—he once again began to babble about his youngest daughter, Dawn:

"You've never seen a girl so lovely, Julian. I don't remember how old…but there again I don't remember much of anything anymore. Only just out of her teens, though. But when the world went to hell—growing up almost entirely underground, in that dark, damp basement we called home—what chance for poor Dawn, eh? Her dark-eyed, raven-haired beauty wasted in the gloom of a cellar. And all she ever saw of the outside world on those occasions, those very rare occasions when, at her pleading, I would take her into the light of day, was the sullen sky and the shattered city. And even so we could never stay for long…not even crouching in the rubble…for there were terrible things in the poisoned sky—Shantaks, I've heard them called, and faceless Gaunts—it was never very long before they would glide or slide into view, scouring the land as they searched…searched for…for what else but us! For mankind's devastated remnants! For the handful of human beings in the wandering, scattered groups, the shrinking tribes that remained!

"But my Dawn…she was everything to me…as her mother before her, and her poor sister too. But they were taken, all three, and what have I now—what's left for me?—except the hope of a measure…however small a measure…*of revenge!*" I think that's all that has kept me going, kept me alive."

It seemed to me that this time the old man was waiting for an answer, and so I shrugged and obliged him, saying, "Well since you ask, it seems you're right, Henry, for the need for revenge is a powerful driving force. You are that other kind of man: the kind who will carry on when there's no hope left for you at all to lust after the greatest measure of revenge that you can achieve. So to the bitter end you'll do what you have to. And for that matter, so will I…but not out of revenge. For I've always known that would be futile."

"You've always known…?"

I nodded and said, "You see, there's nothing much left for me either, Henry. So just like you I'll do what I have to—" And I had to bite my tongue as I almost added, "—to survive."

244

The Long Last Night

The Shoggoth light ahead of us was very much brighter now, and in order to change the subject I pointed it out to my companion. "Look there, it's almost daylight up front! Or as daylight used to be, I mean."

"I see it," he answered, as his sobbing gradually subsided, his voice hardening. "Another fifteen to twenty minutes and we'll be there. Piccadilly Circus…or ground zero, if you prefer."

"Hmm!" I said. "But I always thought that term described a point on the ground directly *beneath* the explosion—not above it."

He was obviously surprised. "You're right, yes! But since we both know what I meant, why nitpick?" Then, looking at me sideways and slyly: "By the way, you really have got it all figured out, haven't you?"

"Most of it," I nodded. "But I still don't know, can't see, how you've been able in the circumstances to build any kind of device powerful enough to make all of this worthwhile. I mean, you'd need a laboratory, and the know-how, and the materials."

Henry returned my nod. "Very good," he said, "very clever. But don't I remember saying that you had no idea who or what I am or was? I'm sure I do."

"Ah!" I said. "So this is what you were getting at. Except you never did get around to telling me. So then, Henry—who and what were you? And more importantly, what are you?"

"I am, as you know, Henry Chattaway," he replied. "But what you *don't* know is that I have an almost entire alphabet of letters after my name, and that I was three times nominated for a Nobel Prize in physics. Also that…"

He paused, and I prompted him: "Yes? And that?" For this was the one thing I had most wanted to know but hadn't dared ask him outright. And:

"Well, why shouldn't I tell you?" he said, as the first signs of the man-made cavern or excavation that was the main Piccadilly Circus underground gradually came into view up front. "For it's too late now to do anything else but see it through: the last of my dreams come true on this long last night."

And as we climbed up from the tracks onto the platform and I returned his small heavy suitcase to him, now fully in control he continued: "Julian, I was the top man—or rather, not to make too much of it, one of them—on PFDP, the Plasma Fusion Drive Project. Similar in its way to the Manhattan Project, it was very hush-hush even though no one in the scientific community gave it a snowflake's chance in hell, even as a theory. What? Abundant energy from next to nothing? You may recall reading that many, oh *many* years ago the same dream had given birth to the bombs that put an abrupt end to World War II. Not so much a dream as a nightmare, as it happened—at least until someone began speculating about the possible benefits: that maybe nuclear power could provide cheap energy for the entire world; which of course never really worked out. The fuel was dirty, dangerous, and had too many safety problems; the mutations and fatal diseases that followed on inevitably from the accidents and errors were hideous, while some of the infected radioactive regions remain hot even to this day.

"Well, history repeats, Julian. Plasma fusion was the next best hope for cheap energy, far better and cheaper, and so much easier to produce…why, men might even go to the stars with it—if it worked! But it didn't, or rather it did, except even the smallest, most cautious of tests warned of a Pandora's Box effect. Only let it loose and it could initiate a chain reaction with anything it might touch and fuse with. That's the only and best explanation I can give to a layman, especially in what little time we have left. But enough: we stopped working on it, and the world's authorities—every single one of them, recognizing the awesome power of this thing—signed up to a strictly monitored ban on any further experimentation…simply because they couldn't afford not to!"

While Henry talked, his voice gradually falling to a whisper, we had proceeded from the tunnel to the platform, then to the relatively pristine stairs and elevators. The latter, of course, had not worked since the early days of the invasion; but the stairs, completely free of rubble, had taken us to the surface, which upon a time had been a landmark, a

246

renowned open-air concourse where many streets joined in that great circus it was named for. A far different sort of circus now.

"This place," I said, letting my voice echo, "is looking rather empty. Not what one would expect, eh?"

"I know," Henry agreed in a whisper, probably wondering why I wasn't whispering too. "It's been like this each time I've been here. You would think it should be crawling, right? Which in a way it is, if not as you might expect. Not crawling with alien life, no, but with the very meaning of the word 'alien' itself!"

Crawling, yes. And making one's skin crawl, too. Even mine. It was the way it looked, its shapes and angles; its architectural features, if you could call them that; its non-Euclidean geometry.

It had four legs—or was it three? Maybe five?—all leaning inward, or was it outward? Something like the once dizzy and dizzying Eiffel Tower, but a twisted version, and what we had surfaced into was the base of one such leg that had used to be Piccadilly Circus. The rest of the legs were green-misted and vague, half-obscured by distance, submarine-tinged Shoggoth light, and the intervening shapes of anomalous buttresses, columns and spiraling stair-cases. And adding to the confusion nothing stood still but appeared literally to crawl, each surface flowing and changing shape of its own accord.

As for the staircases: some had steps as broad as landings, others with steps like frozen ripples on a pond, but rising, of course, and a third type with no steps at all but smooth, cork-screw surfaces of some glassy substance, sometimes turning on clockwise threads and other times winding in reverse. And all of them stationary, at least until one looked at them.

We were dwarfed, Henry and I—made minuscule by the gigantic scale of everything—and screwing up his face, shielding his eyes as he peered up into reaches that receded sickeningly into skyscraper heights and vast balconied levels, Henry said, "That must be where the life is: Bgg'ha's throne room, cages to house his prisoners, dwelling areas for them that serve him. The horror himself will sit high above all that, dreaming his dreams, doing what he does, probably unaware that he's any sort of monster at all! To him it's how things are, that's all.

"But as for his underlings—the flying creatures, and Deep Ones, and Shoggoths that build and fashion for him, varnishing their works with a slime that hardens to glass hard as steel—I have to believe that a majority of them...well, perhaps not the Shoggoths, who are more like machines, however nightmarishly organic—but by far the great *majority* of them, know full well what they are about."

"I think you're right," I told him. "But you know, Henry, we're not too small to be noticed. And I can't imagine that we would be welcome here; certainly not you, suitcase and all! You need to be about your revenge, Henry, and should it work—to however small or enormous an effect—then, while you will have paid the ultimate price, at least your physicist friends may be aware of your success and will carry on your work, assuming they survive it. So why are we waiting here? And why is that awesome weapon you're carrying also waiting, if only to be put to its intended use?"

It was as if he had been asleep, dreaming, hypnotized by his alien surroundings, or maybe fully aware for the first time that this was it— the end of the long last night. For him, anyway—or so he thought. And he was right: it *was* the end of the road for him, but *not* as he thought.

"Yes," he finally answered, straightening up and no longer whispering. "The others who helped me put it all together, they will surely know. They'll see the result from the skeletal roof of the museum. When the explosion takes this leg out the entire tower may rock a little...why, it could even topple! Bgg'ha's house, brought crashing down on the city that he has destroyed! And *that*, my friend, would be acceptable as a real and very genuine revenge! By no means an eye for an eye—for who has lost more than me?—but as much as I could hope for, certainly."

"The roof of the museum?" I repeated him as he headed for a recess (a jutting stanchion, corner—or simple nook?) in the seemingly restless wall. "What, the Victoria and Albert's roof, whose cellar was your home?"

The Long Last Night

"Eh?" He stared at me for long, hard moments…then shook his head. And: "No, no," he said. "Not the Victoria and Albert, but the science museum next door, behind that great pile of rubble that used to be the Natural History Museum."

"*Ahh!*" For at last I understood, and almost everything at that. "So that is where and how you and your team built it, eh? You used materials and apparatus rescued from the ruins of the Science Museum, and you put it all together…where?"

"In the museum's basement," he replied, as the wall seemed to enclose us in a leadenly glistening fold. "Those massive old buildings, and their cellars, were built to last. We had to work hard at it for a long time, but we turned the Science Museum's basement into our work-shop. And after tonight, when they've seen the result of our work, they'll make the next bomb much bigger…big enough to melt the entire fucking city, what's left of it!"

And that was that. Now I had all that I needed from the old man, all that I was required to extract from him. Wherefore:

You can come for him now, I told the Tower's creatures — or certain of them — fully aware that the nearest ones would hear me, because I knew they would have been listening out for me. But meanwhile:

We had entered or been enveloped in a fold in the irrationally-angled wall, a sort of priest's hole in the flowing, hallucinatory, alien cinder-block construction. And there in a corner — I'll call it a corner anyway, but in any case "a space" — was Henry Chattaway's device, its components contained in four more small suitcases arranged in a sort of circle with a gap where a fifth (the one we had been keeping from damage during this entire subterranean journey) would neatly fit. The cases were connected up with electrical cables, left loosely dangling in the gap where the fifth would complete the circuit; while a sixth component stood central on four short legs, looking much like the casing of a domed, cylindrical fire extinguisher. In series, obviously the cases were a kind of trigger, while the cylinder — the bomb — would have contained anything but fire retardant! And affixed to the cylinder at its domed top, standing out vividly against the metal's dull gleam, sat a bright red switch which, apart from the warning manifest in its colour, looked like nothing so much as an ordinary electrical light switch. The cylinder and its switch—a deadly however inarticulate combination, as the bomb *had recently been*—told a story all their own, but one which was now a lie!

Quickly kneeling, Henry opened his case, reached inside and carefully uncoiled a pair of cables which he connected up to the dangling cables on both sides. And now all was in order, or so he thought, and he was ready. But not for what was coming.

Screwing up his face and half-shuttering his eyes (I imagined in anticipation of a split-second's pain, if that!) he reached a trembling hand over the circle of wired-up suitcases, his index finger hovering over the red switch…until, remembering something, he paused and glanced at me. And then, to my dismay because I do have something of a conscience after all, he said:

"I'm so sorry, Julian, but I did give you every opportunity to leave."

"Yes, you did," I replied, kneeling beside him and, before he could stop me, flipping open the lid of one of the suitcases. "And I'm sorry, too," I said, "but as you can see I knew I really didn't have to leave."

His jaw fell; his mouth opened wide; he gurgled for several long seconds, and finally said: "*Empty!*"

"All of them," I nodded. "Especially the cylinder—the bomb." But even then the truth hadn't fully sunk in, and he said:

"I don't understand. No one—nothing, not a single damned thing—ever saw me here. Not once. And this isn't a spot where anyone or thing would think to look!"

"You weren't seen here, no," I replied with a shake of my head. "But you were seen *leaving*—just the once, by Deep Ones at Green Park—the last time you made a delivery. You were correct about their telepathy, Henry. Despite the confusion, the fear in your mind, or maybe because of it, they saw something of what you had been up to and a search was made. Otherwise no one or thing might ever have come in here. But once Bgg'ha had discovered your secret he wanted to know more about you and anything else you might be doing, and

250

how and with whom you were doing it. So you see, they do care about us—or shall we say they're at least *interested* in some of us—especially those of us who would try to kill them. And so I was sent out to look for you. Or to 'hunt' for you, if you prefer."

Hearing that and finally, fully aware of the situation, the old man snapped upright. His eyes, however bloodshot, were narrowed now; the dazed expression was gone from his face; his gun was suddenly firm in his hand, its blued-steel muzzle rammed up hard under my chin. I thought he might shoot me there and then, and I wished that I'd called out to *them* sooner.

"*God damn!*" Henry said. "But I should pay more attention to my instincts...I *knew* there was something wrong about you! But I won't kill you here; I'll do it out there in the open—or what used to be the open—so that when you're found with your face shot off they'll know there are still men in the world who aren't afraid to fight! Now get moving, you treacherous bastard! Let's get out of here."

But as we moved from the drift and slide of the continually mutating wall to the even greater visual nightmare of the Twisted Tower's leg's interior, and when I was beginning to believe I could actually feel the old fellow's finger tightening on the trigger, then I cried out:

"Henry, listen! Do you really intend to waste a bullet on me? I mean, *look what's coming, Henry...!*"

They were Shoggoths, two of them, under the direction of a solitary Deep One. They came into view apparently from nowhere, simply appearing from the suck and the thrust to glide toward us...at least the Shoggoths approached us, while the Deep One held back and kept his watery great eyes on his charges, making sure they carried out their orders—what-ever those might be—to the letter. But of course I knew exactly what they had been told to do.

Suddenly gibbering, Henry released me and turned his attention on the twin pillars of blackly tossing, undulating filth, slime and alien jelly as those advancing obscenities formed more huge, slithering, soulless and half-glazed or -vacant eyes, in addition to the many they already had, and came flowing upon him. He fired once, twice, three times...until the hammer clicked metallically, first on a dead round, and once again, but hollowly, on an empty chamber. And finally, cursing, Henry hurled the useless weapon directly into the tarry protoplasm of one of that awesome pair of nine-foot nightmares. Then, as if noticing for the first time just how close they were, he turned and made to run or stagger away from them, but too late!

Moving with scarcely believable speed, they were upon him; they towered over him to left and right, putting out ropey pseudopods to trap Henry's spindly arms. And closing with his thin, smoking, desperately vibrating body, they slowly but surely *melted* him, sucking him in equal parts into themselves, and burning him as fuel for the biological engines that they were!

As his agonized shrieking tapered and died, along with Henry himself, and as the smoke and gushing steam of his katabolism rose up from the feeding creatures, the loathsome foetor of Henry Chattaway's demise might have been almost as sickening as the live smell of his executioners; but *in combination*, overwhelming the already rancid air to burn like acid in my nostrils despite that I had moved well away, the two taints together were far more than twice as nauseating.

And I was glad that it was finally over, for my sake if not for the old man's...

––––––––

In backing away from all this I had come up against a different kind of body with a smell which I could at least tolerate; indeed I even appreciated it. The Shoggoth-herding Deep One looked at me rather curiously for a moment, his almost chinless face turned a little on one side. But then as he sniffed at me and recognized my Innsmouth heritage, my remote ancestry, he further acknowledged my role in these matters by turning away from me and once more taking command of the Shoggoths.

Left to my own devices I shrugged off a regretful, perhaps vaguely guilty feeling and set about climbing the stairway with the tall treads. This was hard work indeed, for I was already weary from my journey through the underground with old man Chattaway and his suitcase full of impotent batteries.

But up there, high overhead, I knew the ovens would also be hard at work. And long or short pig, what difference did that make when I was this hungry? Hadn't men eaten fish, and in various other countries frogs, too? But the word from others I had spoken to was that this ambiguity can be a problem with changelings such as myself, changelings who—while waiting for their change, when at last they, too, can go down to the water—hunt humans: that sooner or later they begin to sympathize, even empathize with the hunted.

However, and despite the greater effort, I soon began to climb faster. For also up there were the cages and other habitats…and at least one lovely girl not long out of her teens; a girl called Dawn, who may never have known a man—or for that matter a Deep One—or not until comparatively recently, anyway. A great shame, that there were others more or less like me up there, but I expected she would still be very fresh.

And, so that I wouldn't fall victim to mistaken identity on the way up, I commenced chanting: *Ph'nglui gwlihu'nath, Bgg'ha Im'ykh l'ihu'nagl fhtagn…!*" And surprising me even as I sang, there it was again: that oh-so-faint feeling of guilt!

But what the hell, and I shrugged it off. For after all, it was like I had told Henry: certain kinds of men can become accustomed—can get used—to almost anything.

Yes, and not only men…

Weird Wines Of Naxas Niss

A wizard's stolen potion is another man's gateway to
Nirvana...*maybe!*

"You pays your tond and you makes your choices!" the barker
cried. "For the price of admission only, you may sip as many
of my priceless magical wines as you're able. The measures may be
small, but the results can be totally un-be-*lievable!* Just step inside and
a variety of choices are yours. Admission is just one tond—which may
seem a bit expensive, until you realize that you will indeed be drinking
priceless wines! So I repeat, for a mere tond you enter, imbibe my
measures one at a time but as many as you can, then exit back to where
you started...perhaps to try again? Well...maybe! But one thing's
certain: you'll never be the same man again! You pays your money and
you takes your chance! But only one or two customers at a time gents,
if you please, so as not to overwhelm me..."

David Hero and Eldin the Wanderer looked at each other with
raised eyebrows, then turned their gaze back to the barker. He was a
dapper if somewhat eccentric little specimen of *Homo ephemerens*,
(which is to say, a dreamlander), dressed in a red velvet jacket, green
pants which came only half-way down his chubby calves, bright blue
socks with their tops thonged to the bottoms of his trousers, like
reversed suspenders, and tiny black high-heeled clogs. Tubby enough
to be termed rotund, he had a voice to match his girth, but in height
came up only so tall as somewhere short of the questers' shoulders.
This meant that while he was a little shorter than most full-grown
denizens of dream, it was likely that he'd also be a good deal heavier;

254

one of those rare exceptions where Eldin's cognomen (it was the Wanderer who'd first coined *Homo ephemerens*) scarce fitted the subject. No one could be less physically ephemeral than this one!

But a dreamlander he was, a showman, too, and a barker of no mean prowess to boot—as Eldin's suddenly dry tongue in his clammy cave of a mouth might readily attest. "What with all this pattering on about his damned wines," the Wanderer said, as he and Hero elbowed closer to the barker's tent, "and the sun being so hot today and all, I do believe I'm developing a thirst!"

"So, what else is new?" Hero grunted, continuing to observe the little showman and his doings.

Beneath his velvet jacket—whose lapels merely flanked the barker's chest, like the wings of a great plump rooster—he wore a grey silk shirt blazoned with the gold-glowing legend: "Naxas Niss, Exotic Wines!" Niss' hair was black as coal, grown from a single tuft in the middle of his head, plastered down in a fringe which was cropped uniformly and equidistant from its center at a point just above his bushy black eyebrows and right round to the back of his skull. If he were slimmer, he'd be like the clothes-peg men that the children of Celephais painted to look like soldiers, but being fat he looked more like a toy lead-bottomed clown who won't fall over, because when you knock him down he wobbles upright again. As for his origin: there was that in his accent which said he was probably a Dylath-Leener, but being so radically different he could in fact be from just about anywhere. Indeed, outlandish anonymity might well be his principal disguise!

All in all, a more harmless-seeming, amusing and amiable little man the questers had never seen, which was just about the last thing they'd expected; for the fact of the matter was that they were here to "bring him in." Naxas Niss was a criminal; so said King Kuranes, and being king, Kuranes was the boss around here. What's more, Hero and Eldin were his agents, and very well paid for it, too.

It was Fair Day in Celephais; which mean nothing very much, for you could find a fair somewhere in the Timeless City almost every other day of the week all year round. A surfeit of fairs, in fact. Not hard to explain, really: fairs require that people are giving, and at the same time nothing kills them off faster than inclement weather. The people of Celephais were good and giving, the climate invariably kind, and rain extremely rare. So Celephais and fairs went hand in hand. As long as Mount Aran had had its snowy crest, and palms and ginkgos at its foot, and rocky spurs reaching out and sinking into the incredible blue of the Southern Sea, just *precisely* so long had there been fairs in Celephais; which is to say a very long time indeed.

However, (and as any addict will readily attest), not all fairs are fair fairs, and some are downright unfair. For every fair with shies where coconuts may be won, there's a least one where they can't, with more glue in the cups than coconuts! And if the shies are fixed, then it may generally be reckoned that the rest of the fair will follow suit. Word soon gets about, though, and *un*fairs quickly lose their customers, move on or go broke. *Fairs* in general can be recognized by their great crowds of laughing, jostling, bright-eyed people, while *unfairs* may have large surly-looking men lounging threateningly about between the various stalls and side-shows.

"And yet," said Hero, out of the corner of his mouth, for he and Eldin were close now to the barker, "this bloke seems to be getting all the customers he can handle."

"So I've noticed," Eldin answered. "And a good many of 'em go back for more. There's one old lad I've seen go in the front of that tent and out the back three times already. At a tond a time he'll soon be broke! So it can't be a confidence trick 'cos no one gets caught on the same hook twice, and certainly not three times! On the other hand, if Niss is a thief, then what's he stealing? We've been here for half an hour at least and I haven't heard a single cry for help, nor yet seen a sign of distress or even discomfort on a single face."

They thought back on this morning's message from Kuranes, delivered to them by runner at the tiny garret where they lodged overlooking the wharves. Normally the king would have called them to his ivy-clad Cornish manor house on the city's outskirts, where a bit of Cornwall went down from the walls to the shore and became a jumble of granite, seaweed and tangled fishing nets called Fang Rocks; but the note explained why on this occasion he had not done so:

Hero, Eldin—

I have matters to attend to in Serannian, else I'd speak to you personally. Here is the problem: nakedness, imprudence bordering on madness, possible fraud and probable theft, and lots of aimless running about! It's like a plague, which despite (or because of) its various embarrassments remains hidden.

It has been brought to my attention mainly by way of the complaints of its victims' wives. And the one common factor (malefactor, I suspect) is a man called Naxas Niss in his tent at the fair. He works whichever fair suits him, only an hour or two at a time, paying a fat percentage to owners and/or organizers for the privilege.

Currently I've had it reported that he's on his way here; but I've also heard that having done his worst, he makes his escape in haste and never works the same fair on consecutive days. So if you don't get hold of him quickly you will need to track him down. And being the excellent agents you are, that is where you'll come in… Find Naxas Niss, whether he's in Celephais or wherever, get the Goods on him and bring him to book in front of your, er, "old friend" the magistrate Leewas Nith. And report to me the details when I return from Serannian…

Oh, and please stay out of trouble!
Yours, Kuranes.

Which in a nutshell explains the presence and purpose of the adventurers here, outside Naxas Niss' tiny, tassled yellow tent.

Hero was the rangy one, quite young, all blond, fond and smiling, and dressed in russet-brown; while Eldin was some years older, thicker set, long-armed, dark to match his attire and scarred a bit around the face, which made him threatening even when he wasn't. Late of the waking world, they made a living now as questers in Earth's dreamlands. They loved each other like brothers, (though like most brothers they'd never admit it); loved booze and a good fight, too, and girls even more; if they weren't such rogues then by now they'd be legends. Rogues they were, however, or rogu*ish*, anyway…but in any case they wouldn't want anyone apologizing for them. Kuranes thought they were good 'uns, which just about says it all.

"Something's wrong, though," Hero smiled, nodded and chuckled, as if he engaged the other in light and trivial conversation, "for I've been taking note of the people going in—one at a time, you've doubtless observed, and each accompanied personally by Niss—not all of whom come out again."

"Eh?" The Wanderer smiled in his turn. "No, I hadn't noticed that. But if it's so, why, then the rest are still inside!" It seemed obvious.

"What, twenty-five in the front and only nineteen out the back?" said Hero, chortling and slapping his thigh. "But there's hardly room in there for two or three, let alone six. Not and Naxas Niss to boot!"

"What I *have* just noticed, however," said Eldin, "is this: that of those who do come out, a third dash off in unseemly haste, in all directions, and all wearing queer expressions. Gone to puke, d'you think?"

Most of the crowd had melted away by now, leaving the pair right up front and quite conspicuous. "How about you, young sir?" said Niss to Hero, point his black, gold-tipped cane at him. "Can't I interest you in my wines?" I'll not be here all day—an hour more at most—so if you've a mind to try a tipple, now's the time, young sir, now's the time!"

Weird Wines of Naxas Niss

"Any my father?" said Hero, who liked to make a lot of the difference in his and Eldin's ages. "Can he come in, too? See, he's just this morning in receipt of his pension, and—"

With a low growl, Eldin elbowed him none too gently aside. And to Naxas Niss: "I'm sorry, sir, but the village, er, pumpkin here is in my care." Stepping back a pace, he made twirling motions alongside Hero's ear. "Can't let him out of my sight, if you see what I mean. He, er—he *does* things, you know."

"Does things?" Niss looked up at Hero a little warily, considered his peculiar grin, and backed off a pace.

"Too true!" Eldin replied, completely carried away. "Put bats up spinsters' knickers, piddles in the reservoir, generally annoys his elders and betters." And tone hardening, and tweaking Hero's ear: "Indeed, he *especially* annoys his—"

"We'd gladly come in, by all means," Hero cut him short, wriggling free of his ear-tweaking, bowing low and with a flourish to Naxas Niss. "And please excuse our horseplay; it was harmless, I assure you, much like my oafish companion here. But you see, we do everything—*almost* everything, anyway—together. Aye, and we'd dearly love to try out your wines, but not if you can only accommodate us one at a time." He then went on to explain about fair fairs and unfair fairs, finishing with: "And who's to say we'd not get nobbled as we stepped inside, eh? Not that I'd hint for one moment that you're such a blackguard yourself, Naxas Niss, but one can't be too careful these days. Best to be cautious, that's what I always say. And so, if my friend and I mayan't tipple together, why, then we'll simply take our thirsts to the marquee yonder, where they sell those excellent dark-brown ales!"

He and Eldin made as if to move along, but Niss grabbed their elbows. Looking guardedly this way and that, finally he said: "What? I should let you ruin your throats and burn your innards on slop like that? And never know the delights of my exotiques? Unthinkable!"

"Exotiques?" Eldin lifted an eyebrow.

"Antique and exotic both," Niss explained. "Exotique! Very well, since the crowd's thinned out a bit, I'll take the two of you together. But let's have an understanding, gentlemen. You've explained your fear of thuggery, so I'll explain mine. The reason I normally insist upon only one customer at a time is for fear of just such felons. Not that I would ever believe it of you two, you understand; but in any case, I must insist that once inside you follow my instructions to the letter. Are we agreed?"

Hero and Eldin shrugged, nodded.

"Very well, then it's this way, gentlemen, please." And leading them inside, he reversed his "open" sign to read "closed—for now!"

What the pair had expected would be hard to say, but it was not what they found. Inside the tent was…the inside of a tent; with a grass floor, a small folding table, and a large locked trunk in one corner. In front of the table stood a folding chair, and another behind it, while upon the table itself:

"Naxas Niss' weird wines!" said Niss, beaming.

Hero and Eldin stared fixedly at the five bottles on the table, and at the five tiny (oh so tiny) glasses which stood beside them. The bottles were chunky, of clear crystal, and each contained a wine of a different color. There were red, green, white and golden wines all in a row, and a black one, which stood a little apart. "Mine, that one," Niss explained. "A potion, a remedy for stomach cramps, purely medicinal, you understand."

"Right," said Eldin, approaching the table and rubbing his huge hands. "So what'll we try first, eh?"

Naxas Niss stepped nimbly between. "Caution, my large and eager friend," he said. "First your tond, if you please, and then an explanation."

"I have nothing to explain," Eldin frowned, forking out.

"But I have," said Naxas Niss.

"I see no point," the Wanderer was bemused. "Here's the wine, openly displayed, and here a bone-dry receptacle." And he pointed to his bobbing Adam's apple. "Will you explain how I must tilt the glass into my mouth? I've taken wine before, sir, I assure you."

Weird Wines of Naxas Niss

"But there are wines and there are wines," purred Naxas Niss. "Except be sure that *these* wines require something of an explanation."

Now Hero spoke up, handing over his tond in turn, saying: "Very well, so explain."

While the pair looked on astonished, so Naxas Niss commenced a very nimble jig for a creature his shape, the while singing:

"'It's a ritual,' said the little man, 'now listen and you'll see, One wine sends you where you were before you were here, And one transports you blushing where you most desire to be! I can guarantee that one wine will guarantee your return,

And the last wine tells which color fits which—Ah, and turns you color-blind in turn!'"

He quit dancing, beamed at the would-be bibers, took a seat behind his table and poured wine from each bottle into its own tiny glass, a thimbleful to each. "Take your pick, my lads," he said expansively. "For you've paid your money, and how you takes your chances."

"Now hold!" snapped Eldin at once, scowling a little. "That riddle you've just riddled seems a strange and sinister thing to me. Are you hinting there's danger in these wines?"

"Danger?" Naxas Niss drew back his head, tucked in his chin, looked pained. "How so? They change perspectives, that's all—but all very quickly reverts, I promise you. Sinister? But if my intentions were dishonest, would I warn you in the words of my song? No, of course not! Or perhaps there *is* an element of danger—to the faint of heart. But to the adventurer born…? However, (and he shrugged, perhaps disappointedly), "no one can force you to drink. And so, since you no longer desire to avail yourselves of—"

"Hold!" now it was Hero's turn to bark, as Niss made as if to pore the wines back into their bottles. He reached out and stayed the little man's hands. "We've paid our money, Naxas, after all."

"So choose your poison!" said Niss, and at once burst out laughing—and just as quickly sobered. "Why, what *is* all this? Do you really suppose I'd harm you?"

"Not if you know what's good for you!" growled Eldin.

"Ah!" said Niss, eyes narrowing, hand straying just a little toward the black bottle. "So you're a pair of bully-boys after all, eh?"

"No such thing," said Hero. "We're cautious, that's all, as I've avowed."

"Now look," said Niss, sighing, as he picked up one of the glasses—with red wine in it—which he at once tossed back! An expression of extreme delight crossed his face, and before it could fade he tilted the red wine bottle and topped up the tiny glass again. "Now tell me," He was all innocence, "would I poison myself?"

The questers studied his face for several long moments but he seemed entirely unharmed. "Red it is," said Eldin then, reaching for the same glass.

"And I'll go for gold," said Hero. "For if aught peculiar happens to me, why you'll still be around to settle the score."

"Good!" cried Naxas Niss. "We're getting somewhere at last."

They drank.

The wine was good, indeed exotique! Niss watched the tipplers with an expression like an Ulthar cat, some of which retire there from the waking world when they've spent their nine lives, notably from a place called Cheshire.

Hero said: "Excellent!" And a strange dazed look came into his eyes. "Truly excellent!" he said again, and before Eldin could stop him promptly walked out through the flap in the back wall of the tent. The Wanderer gaped, then dashed after him.

Outside he grabbed Hero, turned him about. "And where, pray, do you think you're going?"

Hero licked his lips and the vacant look receded. His eyes gradually focused. "Going?" he finally said. "Why, for another drink, of course!"

"Are you all right?" Eldin stared deep into Hero's eyes.

"Entirely," Hero nodded. "And you?"

"My eyes sting a bit," Eldin blinked, "but otherwise—"

"Thank you for your custom, sire!" cried Naxas Niss, closing the rear flap of his tent on them.

Weird Wines of Naxas Niss

They glanced at each other, gawped, galloped back round to the front just as Niss came out and reversed his sign to read, "Open." Hero grabbed him by a red velvet shoulder. "Whoa!" he said, dangerously low. "Drink as many of my measures as you can, you said. And as yet we've tried but one."

Naxas Niss looked astonished. "But...did I ask you to leave? I did not. You walked out of your own free will, and that one ran after you. Now lads, the rules are simple: enter my tent and a tond gets you all you can drink, but once you exit the contract's broken. Or...p'raps you'd care to try again?"

"Too damned *true!*" cried Eldin, dragging Hero by the collar back into the tent right on Niss' heels. And yet again the latter reversed his sign to read, "Closed—for now!"

"Now sit!" said Eldin, thumping Hero down in the chair in front of the table. "Sit right there, where I can keep an eye on you." And he stood behind him.

"I can't think why I left like that," Hero seemed genuinely astonished. "I certainly didn't want to. Indeed, I wanted nothing so much as another glass of wine!"

"No problem there," said Niss, rubbing his hands. "Your tonds, gentlemen, please." They paid up, however grumblingly. And again Niss went into his song and dance routine:

"Now listen and you'll see,
You'll go where you have been,
Or arrive in all innocence where you'd really like to be;
Or you'll lick your lips and feel the thirst—
And come right on back to me!"

"You missed out the color-blind bit," said Eldin.

Niss shrugged. "I was in haste," he explained. "And anyway, I couldn't make it rhyme."

Hero looked up at Eldin, and they both looked down at the wines, which Niss had topped up again. "Now then," said Eldin to Hero, "you had gold, and apart from acting daft—which isn't really unusual— you're OK. So—" And he reached for the *red* glass again!

Hero put his hand over the glass, stopping him. "That's red," he said.

"Eh?" Eldin peered close. "No, no—it's plainly gold!"

"What, are you color-blind?" Hero cried…and they stared at each other in amaze.

"Or…are you?" said Eldin.

And Naxas Niss grinned.

"What color are my clothes?" Hero demanded.

Eldin glanced at them, cried, "Blue, of course!"—and his mouth at once fell open. "But they should be brown. Which means—I *am* color-blind!"

"But only temporarily," said Naxas Niss.

Eldin snapped his fingers. "*Hah*! But that also means I should know which color's which. And I do! Green transports you blushing where you most desire to be, and white sends you where you were before you were here. Except, because I'm color-blind, I don't know which bottle's which!"

"But I do," Hero reminded.

"Good!" said Eldin. "So which one's gold?"

"I don't see much point in trying gold again," said Hero, "for I've already tried it and ended up back here. It guaranteed my return, d'you see?"

"True," said Eldin, "but at least we know it's harmless."

"Well if the point of the exercise is not to be harmed," said Hero, "why drink any of the bloody stuff?"

Eldin, thoroughly confused by now, said, "Eh? Why…because we've paid for it, that's why! Now then, which one's gold?"

"That one," Hero pointed at the green bottle, the while winking at Naxas Niss, who grinned on unabated. For it had dawned on Hero that there was an easy way round the problem, except he needed a guinea-pig. Or a not-quite-so-expensive tond-pig, as the case was.

Eldin picked up the green glass and stared at it suspiciously. "Gold?"

"Indeed," said Hero.

Weird Wines of Naxas Niss

"You're sure you feel OK?"

"Positive," said Hero. "Me, I'll try the white." And white it was.

"Hold!" said Eldin. "That's green."

Hero shook his head. "You're color-blind, remember? It's white."

"White?" said Eldin. "But if you drink that you'll end up where you were before you were here. Like...outside the tent again?"

"That's how I figure it, yes," said hero. "Nothing harmful in that, and all the time we're narrowing down the field."

Eldin nodded and they raised the glasses to their lips. And: "Go!" said Eldin. They quickly drank the measures down.

Now, this was Hero's plan:

They'd tried the red and gold. Red made you color-blind and gold sent you staggering about, with a great desire to return. That left green and white. Eldin had swallowed green. He would not be transported (blushing?) where he most desired to be, (which with this old pervert might be just about anywhere; Hero dreaded to think!) Hero of the other hand had swallowed white, so he'd like end up outside the tent again as Eldin has surmised—but nowhere and nothing dangerous, anyway.

The beauty of it was this: that they'd now sampled all of Naxas Niss' exotiques—except his black medicine, of course. They could probably do him for fraud, (forcing folks to come back for more), and possibly even for theft, (the way he snapped up tonds must be *some* kind of theft, Hero felt sure!) They might get him for technical aggravated assault, too, (making people color-blind and all); but for the life of Hero, he couldn't see how they could make those other charges of Kuranes' stick. What, nakedness? Gross imprudence? Aimless running about? He could only hope that all would come to light now that they'd sampled of green and white.

And of course all did come to light, and almost immediately.

Standing behind Hero, Eldin felt suddenly all a-flutter. "B'God!" he gasped, and commenced staggering about a little. Hero leaped to his feet—and started running on the spot!

"What? What?" he cried. But he was unable to stop his feet, which went stamp, stamp, stamp, stamp, like a squad of Baharna's regulators on muster parade.

Then Eldin uttered a very small "Eek!" and fizzled out—quite literally—leaving his good black leather clothes floating on air. Unsupported, they flopped to the floor, loose tonds clinking in their pockets.

"Now what's all this, Niss?" Hero snarled, but his feet gave Niss no time to answer. They marched him right out the back door of the tent, and hurried him out of the fairground, and ran him wildly across a dusty road, and raced him frantically down an alley toward the harbour. All the way home, the took him, those rebellious feet, and all the time accelerating; until finally they hurled him upstairs to his and Eldin's garret room, where at last they came to a halt, smoking and blistered inside his quaking boots. Hero would never know it, but he had done the three-and-a-half-minute mile…

———————

After bathing his feet in cold water for half an hour, and changing his boots for moccasins, Hero returned limping to the fairground. Eldin arrived a little later, dressed in a white sheet which he'd converted into a passable replica of desert raiment.

"If I thought I might attack you here and now," said the Wanderer out the side of his mouth and almost conversationally, "without losing my sheet and what's left of my dignity, you'd be dead in a trice. Or if not exactly dead, badly beaten. Unable to walk, at the very least. Likewise, when I find him, Naxas Niss, purveyor of exotiques." And he gloomed down on the square of flattened grass where recently stood the yellow tent of that last mentioned.

Hero pointed to his feet, which he could swear steamed visibly through the lace-holes of his soft shoes. "As for crippling me," he growled, "why, I'm already unable to walk! Indeed, I have feet like puddings! So as you can see—and while I admit my behavior left something wanting—I really do consider myself punished quite enough. No major harm done, however, and all wines tasted and effects observed at extremely close quarters. And so—"

They swapped experiences.

Hero's tale was quickly told, as above, but Eldin's proved far more interesting. "I drank what I *thought* was gold," the Wanderer growled, "but which I now know to have been green, and in the next moment— *Zzzip!*—there I was all naked, and maybe even blushing, in the bed of this young and buxom widow Misha Oosh, owner of the Yellow Yak, where nightly she displays here generous jigglers all bundled up in their blue silk blouse behind the bar."

Hero nodded knowingly. "So that's why we've been drinking in the Yellow Yak every night for the past week, eh? I fancied you fancied her."

"And there was Misha herself," Eldin continued, "taking her afternoon nap, right there in that very bed with me! Except...my arrival work her up."

Hero couldn't suppress a grin. "When do you go up?" he inquired. "Before Leewas Nith, I mean?"

"Eh?" said Eldin. "You think she gave a shriek and kicked me out? Well, and I thought she might, too—at first. But you say you fancied I fancied her? And so I did—except I didn't know that she fancied me in her turn! Throw me out? No, she did not. Oh, she was somewhat agog and all atremble at first, but when she saw who it was..."

"God help the poor woman," Hero signed, turning his face away and shaking his head. "She must be desperate!"

"Pup!" Eldin snarled. "Why, I've seen *you* making eyes at her!"

"Anyway," Hero changed the subject, "what then?"

"Well, we spent a very pleasant hour or so together, and then she said she must be up and preparing her place for evening opening. She loaned me this sheet, and helped me tuck it in a bit here and there, and here I am."

"She didn't find your being without your clothes a bit odd? Didn't she even want to know how come?"

"She did, and I explained all, which she accepted at once. It's handy being a quester for Kuranes. The king's much-loved you know. And likewise those who look after him. And after all, her bed *was* the single place in all the dreamlands where I most desired to be."

"So why are you so miffed?" Hero asked, acting innocent. "I mean, it seems to me I did you a favor!"

"And if I'd been unwelcome in Misha's bed?"

"But you weren't."

"*Huh!*"

"Huh, indeed!" said Hero. "And how about me when this case is cracked, eh? Oh, *you'll* be OK: free booze and all, and when the Yellow Yak turns out, all comfy and warm in the loving arms of Misha Oosh. But what of poor Hero?"

"You've girls aplenty," Eldin snorted, which was true enough. "You'll not go short."

"The fact is," said Hero, "that I really have done you a powerful favor. And it's to be hoped you won't forget it. So let's have no more of these threats on my life and limbs, if you please."

"What angers me," said Eldin, curling his lip a bit, "is this: that there are lots of other places I might have ended up, not all of them in Celephais, and *none* of 'em so comfy! I mean, can you imagine floating naked in a large vat of Lippy Unth's muth? Or finding yourself propped up, everything a dangle, at a bar somewhere in downtown Dylath-Leen? Or in some harem in Kled, with a dozen little black eunuchs after your bits with their curved, razor-sharp knives?"

"God!" said Hero. "It says a lot for your desires!"

"Never mind that!" Eldin snapped. "What about my clothes, eh? You've cost me a fine suit, shirt, shoes, and my purse to boos, which contained a hundred tonds!"

"Liar," said Hero, but without emphasis. "Kuranes' runner brought us a hundred expenses, fifty each, two of which you'd spent on Niss' wines."

Weird Wines of Naxas Niss

"Well, half a hundred, then," Eldin grumbled. "But I'll have it back again, b'God I will, when I catch up with that wretch! Except...where is he, eh!" And again he gloomed on the vacant patch of grass.

"Where indeed?" Hero nodded thoughtfully, chewing his lip. "Where indeed?"

Hero loaded Eldin eight tonds with which to buy himself new if less satisfying togs, and then split up and went their own ways, combing the city's markets and thoroughfares for sign or word of Naxas Niss. They paid for and sent out a pair of extra eyes, too, in the shape of the urchin Kimp Lootis, a waif late of the waking world like themselves. Kimp, long-haired as a girl and bright as a fresh-minted tond, however ragged, came to them that night with his report, catching them just before they could enter the Yellow Yak, in the cobbled mews which led to that estimable alehouse.

"Here, Eldin!" the waif stepped out of the shadows, came between the two and grasped their great hands in his own small ones. "I know where he is, or where he was, or where he most likely will be, anyway."

"Eh?" Eldin gazed down on a moon-silvered elfin face. "Where he is, was or will be? You're sure you've not been drinking his wines, Kimp?"

The urchin grinned. "It's worth a tond or two, I'm sure."

Hero gave a mock groan, flipped the child a triangular tond that glinted gold, silver, gold and silver again before being snatched unerringly from the smoky evening air. He knew Kimp could use the money, having neither home nor family to call his own. But: "Lord," he said, "I don't know who's the bigger crook: you, Kimp, or Naxas Niss! One tond's all you'll get. And now that you've been paid twice, less of your riddles and a little more information, if you please."

Kimp stepped back into shadows. "A caravan passed by, on its way to Nir and Ulthar," he whispered. "Naxas Niss joined it at a watering hole just outside the city. He paid a pouchful of tonds for passage and protection en route to Mir, which was his destination, and was last seen dragging his large trunk into the back of a covered cart."

"When was this?" Hero hissed.

"Three hours gone. By now they're half-way there."

"Good work!" said Hero, and went to pat what he guesses was a head, which was only a shadow. Soft footfalls fell like a patter of gentle rain in the courtyard, and Kimp Lootis was gone.

"It can wait till morning," said Eldin, turning his bearded face Yellow Yakward once more.

"No," Hero denied him, "it can't."

"What?" Eldin was alarmed, then aggrieved. "But it could if you'd a lovely creature waiting in there for you, eh?"

"She's not waiting for you," said Hero. "She's serving her customers, feeding and watering them, and she'll be hard at it till the midnight hour. By which time we'll be high over Nir. Anyway, the last thing she needs right now is you!"

"She needed me this afternoon!"

"That's as maybe, but now that you've laid...*claim* to her, as it were, what's the hurry? She'll go off the boil, d'you think?"

"Unlikely!" Eldin preened.

"Then it's business before pleasure," Hero nodded, his mind made up.

As they headed for the harbour, Eldin continued to grumble, "I mean, what's in a night, eh?"

"Twelve hours," said Hero. "More, if you had your way!"

"No, no, lad," Eldin wheedled. "I'd be up bright and early, I promise; and we could skip just as sprightly for Nir in the morning."

"*I* could skip sprightly in the morning," said Hero. "You—you'd be knackered! Love-drugged and aching in every bone, and you know it. Right now we're sharp-eyed, clear-headed, hot on the trail. So let's not slack off. When the job's done, that's a different matter. Also, the wind's in our favor; we'll be in Nir even sooner than I thought. And anyway, I've got what's left of the money." Which was the best bit of his argument. For Eldin had his pride; he knew that if he entered the Yellow Yak without the price of a pint, then that Misha'd think he was only there for the booze!

Weird Wines of Naxas Niss

Their sky-yacht *Quester* was tied up in the harbour. They boarded her, got the tiny floatation engine going, fed essence to the bags in the keel and up under the reinforced deck. *Quester* lifted off and Celephais sank below; the lights of hamlets along the coast began to come into view like far crowds of fireflies in the night; a warm, sweet wind off the sea filled out their sail and scudded them along with the clouds for Mir.

And cracking a bottle—just one, and middling stuff, for Hero's jaw was set—they toasted Naxas Niss' downfall, and laid their plans to that effect...

———————

On the outskirts of Nir they set down in a farmyard, woke up the farmer who grumbled a lot and threatened to turn his bull on them, and placated him with tonds that got scarcer by the minute, or so it seemed. He helped them haul the wallowing *Quester* into a barn, where with engine stilled she slowly settled to a bed of straw. Then they enquired the way to the house of Mathur Imniss, and set off on foot into town.

Nir was a sleepy place even on big occasions. Tomorrow was one such: Fair Day! "Oh, joy!" (Eldin's sarcasm dripped like acid.) "There'll be rip-roaring cow-milking contests, slimy-pole climbing, roof-thatching orgies—the lot!" And there'd doubtless be Naxas Niss' tent, too, all yellow and tassled and seeming perfectly innocuous, standing amidst the shies and side-shows on the village green.

Mathur Imniss was a retired quarrier, stone mason and builder, and a faithful old friend of the questers. They found his house and knocked him and his good lady out of bed, slapped backs and kissed cheeks for a half-hour and took a bite to eat, then bedded down till morning. It was fortunate that Mathur's son, Gytherik the Gauntmaster, wasn't to house, else they'd have been up talking all night.

Early awake, the pair disguised themselves somewhat and sought out Tatter Nees, a troubadour of their acquaintance who lived in the town. Tatter knew everyone and everything; he called himself a "wandering balladeer," but as Eldin was wont to have it, if he could sing better he wouldn't need to travel so much. However that might be, at least he was able to put them in the picture in re all manner of comings and goings. And indeed yestereve, as dusk turned to dark, a caravan had come; aye, and this morning there was a stall in the market, where one Naxas Niss, a dealer in used clothes, was very cheaply selling off all manner of mannish finery. In their disguises, (Eldin had grudgingly shaved off his beard, while Hero had applied one, and a foppish hat), they visited said stall.

Naxas Niss was busy as hell, selling clothes as quickly as he could hurl them out of his trunk, which he'd almost emptied by the time the questers arrived. Eldin's black leathers were still there, at least, tossed carelessly on Niss' folding table, but his shoes and coarse grey shirt had been sold.

"*Now* he dies!" Eldin rumbled, forging forward toward the inner circle of bargain-hunters. Hero dragged him back.

"No he *doesn't*" he hissed. "We're to bring him in, not do him in! You stay here—I'll get your gear." And he did, and paid three tonds for it, too. Niss, gathering up tonds like iron filings to a magnet, didn't notice him at all.

"God, we'll soon be broke!" Eldin moaned. "And I'm reduced to paying for my own stolen clothes!"

"No," said Hero, unrelentingly contradictory, "I am. But at least we now know what he does with them. Which makes it theft beyond a doubt. So now we've got him on all counts." He fished out Kuranes' letter from a pocket, read:

"'Nakedness, imprudence bordering on madness, possible fraud and probable' (no, it's definite now) 'theft, and a lot of aimless running about.' Niss is guilty of some and responsible for the rest. Add to that handling and disposal of stolen goods, and making fools of questers, and we can just about throw the book at him."

"I'd prefer to throw a fist at him!" growled Eldin; but Hero only smiled a wicked smile.

"No," said the younger quester, yet again. "Let's make the punishment fit the crime. And not just any crimes—or even all of them—but specifically his crimes against us."

Weird Wines of Naxas Niss

And so they stood well back and watched Niss flog what was left of his rags, and pack up his trestle and hire a couple of lads to carry his stuff. And off he went chirpy as a cricket in the direction of the village green. Hero and Eldin followed him, stopping for a (quick) drink along the way, and when they got to the green the yellow tent had already been erected and business was booming—or appeared to be.

"He's filling his damned trunk again!" Eldin spluttered, outraged.

"But not nearly so quickly," Hero pointed out. "Tonds are harder to come by here in cow-country, old lad. See, he's pulling the crowd, all right, but your actual takers are few and far between."

As if to emphasize what he'd said: "What? A tond a tipple?" one onlooker cried. "Man, I only make ten in a week! Too rich for my blood, Naxas Niss, or whatever your name is." Others muttered low, shuffled their feet, began to drift away. Niss didn't fit here. Nir's fair had always been a fair fair, but Niss' prices seemed just the opposite. He might sell off his second-hand clothes cheaply, but his exotiques were something else. There were only a half-dozen takers, (one at a time, of course, of whom only four emerged from the rear, two running off like billy-o and two returning for a second pass; only *one* of whom excited, and then rushed off like billy-o), and then no more. Until Hero approached, wearing his silly hat and false beard. Eldin had meanwhile sneaked round the back.

"A tond a try?" said Hero, putting on a high-pitched voice and jingling coins in his pocket. "I think I can manage that."

Niss cocked his head on one side and looked at him curiously. His eyes narrowed a little—avariciously, Hero hoped, and not suspiciously. Finally the little man said: "But don't I know you from somewhere, sir?"

"Indeed," Hero squeaked at once, "for I purchased a good black suit from you just an hour ago. And a very good buy it was! So if these—er, exotiques?—these wines of yours are up to the standard of your hand-me-downs, why, there'll be no complaints here!"

Naxas Niss chewed his lip. So far he'd taken only eight tonds and three sets of togs. He'd do this latest lump head, and maybe one more, and move on. Nir was a dump anyway; Ulthar should prove far more profitable; he'd get finished here, but a yak and cart and be on his way.

Still looking at Hero sideways and wondering where he'd seen him before, Niss ushered the quester inside and went straight into his spiel as before: "There's this ritual," the little man began to sing, doing his jig, "now listen and you'll see—"

Eldin entered silently through the back flap and crept up behind him.

Hero said: "One wine sends me where I was before I was here—"

Naxas Niss said: "*Oops!*" He turned and made a leap for his table, fingers straining toward the bottle of black, and galloped straight into the arms of Eldin. Somehow, incredibly, Niss wriggled free, grabbed up his bottle of "medicine" and took a swig. This was more or less what the questers had expected him to try—something like it, anyway—and Hero was quick off the mark. He snatched the bottle from Niss and likewise glugged, then quickly passed it on to Eldin. For if this was Niss' bolt hole, then by the many gods they'd surely bolt it for him!

Naxas Niss was already fading out, his tent, table, bottles and trunk likewise, and Hero was wavering around the edges, when the Wanderer also tossed back a little black. And a moment later they were no longer in Nir, though as yet Hero didn't know it. The tent, unpegged, began to collapse around them as Niss, unfreezing, shot out through the front flap. But Hero was right behind him, leaving Eldin floundering in yellow silk. Outside the tent:

They were in a great cave of a dungeon, and along one wall stood a work-bench supporting fifty or more bottles all of a different hue; and Naxas Niss shrieking and flying for the bottles as fast as his little feet could shift him. Alas for Niss, Hero was somewhat nimbler. The younger quester caught him by his read velvet collar, yanking and twisting at the same time. Niss went right on running, which made it look like he'd stepped on a banana skin; his feet shot up horizontal and his bubble-body spun face-down. And *thump* he came down on his belly, venting wind from both ends, while Hero jumped astride his fat back like leaping aboard some peculiar wobbly bronco.

Weird Wines of Naxas Niss

Cursing loudly, Eldin ripped his way through the billowing wall of the tent, then stood stock still and gawped all about; and in his bewilderment he almost took another pull at the black bottle. But:

"Don'!" Hero barked, from where he sat upon Naxas Niss' shuddering back. "Unless you're feeling especially adventurous, that is. Wasn't one nip enough?"

Eldin wasn't feeling especially adventurous; he crossed to the bench and put the black bottle down with all the others. And then, with Hero, he continued to gape all about.

The place they were in was literally a dungeon, and a strangely familiar one at that. It was lighted with green crystal glow stones which were imbedded in the ceiling, and with red ones piled in niches in the walls. They lent the place an infernal light. Stone steps cut from the virgin rock climbed one wall and through the ceiling; on the other side more steps descended; in the center of the floor, the raised rim of a dry well was loosely covered over with a heavy, rusty iron grid. And echoing up from below, indeed from that very well:

"Naxas Niss, is that you?" came a trembly old voice. And there was something familiar about that, too.

Eldin took a red crystal from its pile, crossed to the well, wrenched the iron grid aside and peered down into darkness. "Catch," he said, dropping the crystal. And down below, someone caught. The red glow in the well lit up a face wrinkled as a walnut, framed in shoulder-length white hair and a waist-long white beard, bearing a long white drooping moustache. Rheumy eyes peered, then widened in a glad, almost disbelievable smile of recognition.

"Eldin the Wanderer!" gasped the mage in the well.

"Nyrass of Theelys!" Eldin replied, nodding. "Reach up your arms."

Nyrass did as instructed, and Eldin clung to the wall's rim with one hand while dangling the other. And in a moment he'd hauled the ancient wizard to freedom. At which point Hero said: "All right, you two, let's have some help here. Bind this bugger's limbs, can't you, else I'll be sitting on him for the rest of my life!"

Nyrass found some rope and Eldin tied Niss hand and foot, then rolled him across the floor, propped him up in a seated position and roped him with his back to the wall of the old well. Silent now, the little crook tugged on his ropes awhile, then sat still and scowled at them all three where the ancient mage hugged Hero and Eldin each in turn. For the questers were his firm friends from a time when they'd helped him destroy Klarek-Yam, the mad First One who'd threatened to release Cthulhu and his kin into both dreamlands and waking world alike. He hugged them, and sobbed a little, too, explaining how he'd spent a three-month in the well, where Naxas Niss had kept him prisoned. As to how that had come about:

"My wizard ancestor, Soomus the Seventh of the Seventh, brewed many potent wines," Nyrass started to explain, nodding toward the variously coloured bottles arrayed on the work-bench. "Wines with a vast variety of properties, not all entirely harmless. Soomus also left a book, explaining their powers; but the book was encoded in Soomus' own runes, and I've never bothered much to decipher the thing. The wines I likewise left alone; left them down here, where they've been since those early days of dream, gathering dust and who knows what else to them. I thought from time to time I might destroy them, but even that could prove dangerous, and so I simply let them be.

"Well, one day there was a fair in Theelys, and that one," he pointed a trembling hand at the trussed Naxas Niss, "had a stall there. There was a game he played with three brass cups and a glittering diamond as big as a robin's egg, which he called—"

"Find the gemstone?" said Hero, sighing deeply.

"Indeed!" cried Nyrass. "D'you know it?"

"Oh, we know it, all right," said Eldin. "But Nyrass, d'you mean to say you were taken in by that one" Why, it's sleight of hand—trickery—a game to flinch farthings from the village idiots! And you a magician. Tsk, tsk!"

Nyrass bowed his head and eventually continued. "Well, Naxas also had a betting system called—"

Weird Wines of Naxas Niss

"Double or nothing?" said Eldin. "Aye, and we know *that* one, too. And how many times did you double your bet, eh, trying to find the gemstone?"

Nyrass hung his head even lower. "A baker's dozen," he admitted. "Thirteen times aye. Unlucky for some, thirteen, and especially me! But how could I lose every single time, eh? I'd seen the village children win, when they were gaming with Naxas Niss for sweetie-sucks and toffee-apples, so why couldn't I? Impossible that I should lose so often, and consecutively, but I did. Ah, but where the first bet cost me only a tond, the last one—"

"Cost four thousand and ninety-six of 'em!" said Hero, who was good at that sort of thing.

"Alas," said Nyrass. "I never was much of a mathematician."

"You're a daft old wizard!" said Eldin, but he put an arm round Nyrass' shoulders anyway. "What then?"

"I told him I probably had the money at home," said Nyrass. "He packed up his stall and came back with me. But when I looked I had only a few tonds, which he took, of course. But I did have goods. I offered him a cracked shewstone, not much good but better than nothing. And several books of outworn spells, and a pair of de-magicked wands. None of which interested him. But then we came down here, and that was where I made my big mistake."

"You told him about Soomus' wines," Hero could see it all now. "And they *did* interest him."

Nyrass nodded. "Apparently he has a talent for translation. He snatched Soomus' book, tumbled me down the well—wandless and all, and no runebook in easy reach—and set about discovering what he could of the wines."

"But you're a wizard!" cried Eldin. "Couldn't you levitate out of there, or conjure assistance or something?"

"I'm a very *old* wizard, Nyrass corrected him, "and the older I get, the more I forget. In fact, I've just about forgotten everything! Anyway, as for the rest of it—"

"Let me tell it," now Niss himself spoke up, his voice sour as vinegar. "Else at this rate it'll take all day. Soomus' book started to disintegrate as soon as I opened it. I could only discover the secrets of three of his wines before the thing fell to dust. But I'd learned enough to make a start, at least. So…I took away with me the go-where-you-were, the be-where-you-most-desire-to-be, and the come-you-home—that's the black one, as you've discovered. Just those three, see, for I was cautious. I must walk before I tried running. I used the wines at various fairs and they worked for me like…like magic! But it wasn't all tonds and treacle, I can tell you. When threatened by the occasional punter who'd been where he desired but really shouldn't have been, I'd sip black and come back here in a flash, even as you've seen it happen. Each time I cam back I'd feed the old fool, and attempt to decipher some of the labels on the rest of Soomus' bottles. Eventually I discovered the return-ye-here and the color-blinder; and with that last one, why, of course the rest were easy! But it was then I discovered how lucky I'd been. Dangerous? Those bottles are murder! The worst of 'em contained a liquid purple imp. Only try to sip from *that* one and he'd drag you in by your tongue, and you'd take his place! I weighted it and dropped it far out to sea, and then I reckoned I'd quit while I was ahead."

"Three months ago, all this?" said Hero.

"Forty-four fairs ago, aye," said Naxas Niss, more than a little surly now.

"And you didn't run out of red, gold, white, green and black?"

"That's another of their properties," said Niss. "They replenish themselves."

"Bottomless bottles!" Eldin gawped. "Now that's what I call magic!"

"But why hasn't anyone apprehended you before now?" Hero wanted to know.

"I've already told you," said Niss. "Whenever I smelled danger, I'd take a swig of black."

Weird Wines of Naxas Niss

"But you'd think those you'd fooled would warn their friends, at least," said Eldin.

"Oh?" said Naxas Niss. "Really? And let on what clowns they'd been? Or how they'd gone through tens of tonds by coming back for one more sip of red? Or tell whose beds they'd found themselves in, naked as babes? And believe me, a forbidden bed isn't the worst place a man can most desire to be!"

Hero nodded. "And if someone with more guts than most came back to give you a thrashing, they you'd simply sip black and slip back here—and your gear with you! Very clever."

"Too clever far," said Eldin. And to the magician: "Nyrass, I fancy you're getting too tottery to be left on your own. You could do with someone to look after you and your place both."

"A companion?" said Nyrass. "Maybe you're right."

Hero spoke up. "There's a homeless waif in Celephais called Kimp Lootis. He's a likeable lad who lives by his wits, but given a home to call his own I reckon he'd be good as gold. What say we see what he thinks of the idea, eh?"

He ripped through the silk of Niss' tent to the table and its bottles, found and held up green. Then back to the work-bench to retrieve the bottle of black. "Now you two hand on here," he told Eldin and Nyrass, pouring green into his palm and rubbing it into his jacket, pants and boots. All done, he pocketed black, took a quick swig of green and put the bottle down. "And keep your eyes on *that* one!" were his last words before he disappeared. Last to go was his finger, pointing at Naxas Niss. And…his clothes went with him!

Niss was furious. "He's not so daft, your spindly pal!" he snapped at Eldin. "Even I hadn't figured that out. Green affects only what it touches. Inside a man it transports him where he most desires to be. Rubbed on his clothes, it transports them, too!"

Eldin beamed. "Right!" he said. "And right now he most desires to be wherever Kimp is. Not so daft, you say? Brilliant, says me!"

"What's he like, this Kimp?" Nyrass was uncertain.

"A good lad," said Eldin. "Needs a father, that's all."

"Well," Nyrass shrugged, "it's true I've been feeling my years lately. They weigh on me like lead. And since I've no kin of my own—"

Hero materialized grin-first, likewise Kimp, still smacking his lips from the belt of black Hero'd given him.

Following which...

Leaving Naxas Niss bound (and double-bound) in the dungeon, the questers spent the rest of the day with Nyrass and Kimp. The wandered through the wizard's great castle and its gardens, tried fruits from a variety of trees; and all the while Nyrass performing small magics for the delight of the waif, and everyone feeling generally very light at heart. From a high turret as dusk began to settle, the watched the lamps flickering into life in Theelys, following which and as the stars also began to light, Eldin brewed tea and made them all a mighty plate of scrambled eggs on toast.

As for Kimp: he couldn't get over his amaze and delight that he now had a home and a father of his own; and Nyrass knew he'd never be lonely—or fall prey to the likes of Naxas Niss again—not with a lad sharp as Kimp around, he wouldn't.

Leaving the two to get better acquainted, Hero and Eldin went into town, came back an hour later towing a bunch of flotation bags purchased with the last of their tonds from a sky-ship's chandler. The bags were inflated, straining lustily inside a net but held down by massive lead weights in a huge wicker basket swaying at the ends of four ropes. And the questers hauled the weighted but weightless device behind them all the way to Nyrass' garden wall, where they fitted up Naxas Niss in a rope harness and forced a tot of white between his frothing, cursing jaws.

Off he went at once, heading full-tilt for Nir under a rising moon; and Hero and Eldin in the basket, (along with Niss' trunk and Soomus' wines), having tossed out the great lead weights to make room, and vented a little essence to get the balance just right. Like a rickshaw-boy Niss ran, was Eldin's opinion—though he couldn't remember exactly what a rickshaw-boy was; something from the waking world, he supposed—going back where he'd last been, however far, his feet waggling for all they were worth but barely touching the ground because of the flotation bags he towed on high. The wind, at least, was in his favor.

And along the way, every now and then, Hero or Eldin would toss a bottle overboard, happy to hear it smashing as its exotique contents soaked the starlit path; and Niss groaning with each bottle smashed, knowing now that he was done for and doomed to spend a spell (of the mundane sort, and if his legs held out that long) in Leewas Nith's Celephasian cells…

––––––––––

Mid-morning saw them back in Nir, where finally Niss collapsed and fell into a sleep of total exhaustion. He was a lot thinner now, and his clogs worn through to his puffy, pulsating feet. They transferred him to *Quester* and sailed for Celephais, where in Leewas Nith's afternoon sessions he was found guilty and sent down for a twelve-months' rest.

Later, aloft aboard *Quester*, (but tethered just twenty feet over the harbour, and safe from prying eyes), the king's agents found the false bottom in Niss' trunk and the little sacks of tonds he'd hoarded therein; which discovery was followed by a deal of hilarity, giggling and thigh-slapping, as the questers counted their considerable profits and congratulated themselves that all had turned out so well.

But after a while Hero licked his lips and said: "D'you know, I'm dry? A splash of wine would go down well."

"Let's get ashore," said Eldin at once, "and find ourselves an eatery till the Yellow Yak's doors spring open!"

"No," said Hero, "I mean right now."

"What? Here, now, aboard *Quester*? But…there's not a drop aboard, lad, you know that!"

"I know you take me for a great fool!" cried Hero, reaching out and snatching the bottle of red from Eldin's huge jacket pocket. "As if you could resist saving just one of them—*you*, of all people!" He pulled the cork and took a massive swig, said: "*Ahhh!*" appreciatively and passed the bottle back.

"Actually," said Eldin, "I was going to tell you."

"Huh!" said Hero.

"No, seriously. See it's no fun being color-blind on your own. But to tell the truth, you do look sort of cute in blue"

"Cute?" said Hero. "Cute?" He chuckled and took back the never-empty bottle, tilting more of its contents into his throat. And smacking his lips as he once more passed the bottle, he said: "Well, that's more than I can say for you—*in puce!*"

"Puce!" the Wanderer almost choked on the biggest swig of all. "Puce!" he sputtered and coughed. "The *hell* with that!" And he hurled the bottle far out over the water.

For three days and nights the Southern Sea was green and gold and sky-blue pink, and as for the fish which the fishermen brought in…why, rainbow trout had nothing on them at all!

Stealer of Dreams

Always remember, once they're gone they might stay gone!

U p there on the ocean-facing slope of Mount Aran, above the tree-line but not yet into the snow (for the snowy peak of Aran had been forbidden to men immemorially, and especially to waking worlders, and *more* especially to men such as Eldin the Wanderer and David Hero, called Hero of Dreams), up there, then, the atmosphere was thin but heady, the air cool and crisp, and the timelessness of Celephais amply apparent in the vista spread below: that same vista viewed by dreamers five hundred years ago, and one which others as yet unborn, or even undreamed, would view five hundred years hence.

Hero, on his own for once, or at least accompanied only by his handover, which seemed to him far more noisy than any actual physical companion might every be (with the single exception of Eldin, of course), appreciated the air of these higher regions and wished he could open doors in his ears, let the coolness waft through and blow out all the cobwebs, dead rats, indistinct memories and too-slowly evaporating muth-fumes, and so leave an uncluttered brain to start functioning again as brains should, instead of stumbling blindly around in his skull and tripping itself up on all the junk in there.

Hero had a telescope with him, which he used periodically to enhance the gazing of his slightly bloodshot right eye down on Celephais. Each time he did so the pain was a little less penetrating than the last time—which told him that his head *was* clearing, however slowly—but still he couldn't look for more than a second or two, sufficient only for the glitter of a spier or minaret to stab through his pupil, or for bright flashes of Naraxa water tumbling oceanward to set

283

his senses spinning; and the, groaning, he'd turn his spyglass on the sea instead.

Now normally that would be even worse, for the blue of the Southern Sea may fairly be described as a visual toothache; and Hero, who liked to do things with words (he wrote the occasional poem, and sometimes sang his own songs, too) had often wondered why no one had come up with a more descriptive color for it than simply blue. If a dark yellow stone could be described as ochre, then surely the Southern Sea's searing, indeed piercing color might better be titled acher? And by the same token shouldn't muth, so sweet on the tongue in the drinking, yet

turning that same inoffensive organ to a vile, decomposing blanket during sleep, more rightly be called moth? For certainly he now felt that he had a mouthful of them!

As is seen, and for all the on-this-occasion-involuntary humor of his thinking, Hero was not in a good mood. But he was at least able to gaze down on the Southern Sea without his brain doing permanent damage, for last night's storm had left the ocean scored with ranks of marching waves, disrupting it's "acher" to a bearable grey-green. And now we get to the other reason why Hero was here: for as well as the beneficial, purging effect of booze being burned out of his system by the climb, and the sweet, clear air of these heights to freshen his brain and lungs, there was also a nagging suspicion in the back of his mind that all was not well with the Wanderer.

Except to disguise this anxiety as Hero's "other reason" for being here is quite inaccurate; Eldin the Wanderer's welfare was indeed uppermost in Hero's mind, and all that nonsense about fresh air and beneficial climbing (?) quite spurious, or would be if he were willing to admit that he was ever at any time given to worrying about his fellow adventurer. They never did admit to such things, these two, and probably never would, but in fact they couldn't be closer or love each other more if they were twins. What's more, Hero half-blamed himself for Eldin's absence on this occasion, and knew that he *would* blame himself forever if aught had gone seriously amiss.

Stealer of Dreams

But...last night there'd been drinking, and boasting, and wagering as well; as the muth had gone down faster, so the boasting and wagering had grown wilder; finally Eldin had declared that "alone, single-handed, on (his) own, without assistance and entirely unaided," (sic) he could sail their boat *Quester* to Serannian the sky-floating city, and there drink three bars dry; and when Hero had called his bluff, wagering his half of *Quester* that he couldn't, then the dippy old duffer had gone staggering off to do just that! Since when he hadn't been seen, and there'd been this sudden, vicious storm. So Hero's real reason for being here was that these heights were an ideal vantage point from which to scan the still troubled waters beating on the strands for sign of Eldin's return. Except his return might well be in doubt. The trouble was this:

Without question Eldin could handle *Quester* on his own—when he was sober, and when the boat was in good repair. But a sail had needed mending, and a flotation bag had been lost in Baharna on Oriab at the end of a recent mission for King Kuranes, and a second bag had been losing essence for a long time now, so that the tiny engine had difficulty keeping it filled. And of course, worst of all, Eldin had been mindless on muth. And to these objections the sudden storm...anything could have happened.

This morning Hero had come awake in their garret room to find his companion's bed empty; remembering the other's boast and his own wager, which had been nothing short of a dare, and rushing down to the wharf (or more properly staggering), he'd discovered *Quester* gone. Seeing the state of the sea, and already fearing the worst, he'd sought out Tatter Nees, a wandering balladeer from Nir who'd been their drinking companion last night. Tatter, none too steady on his own pins, had tottered off to make inquiry, and Hero had borrowed a spyglass and headed for Aran. And he'd counted a hundred and more boats coming and going this morning, some from the sky and some from the sea, but never a sign of *Quester*.

Which brings us to the present.

"Hero!" came a distant cry, echoing out of the trees and up the slope of scree and outcropped stone. Hero focused his glass, found Tatter down there in the ginkgos, hands cupped to his mouth, ready to fire another salvo.

Oh, God! thought Hero, knowing he'd have to respond. "What is it?" he finally bellowed—and immediately clapped both hands to his temples, fully believing that his head had cracked right down the middle.

"Two things," Tatter shouted back, staggering, repelled by his own voice like a cannon recoiling from a shot. And Hero could almost hear his low-muttered curses.

"Hold it, hold it," Hero waved a ceasefire. "I'll come down."

He stood up, slid on his heels through the scree, kept his balance remarkably well and used half-buried boulders to slow himself down when his plunging might get out of hand. And at last he was into the trees, and finally down to where the troubadour waited. Tatter, a long, thin specimen of *Homo ephemerens*, gloomed on Hero, saying: "Never again, never again," in time-honored fashion, without shaking his head.

"Likewise, I'm sure," Hero replied, remembering not to nod. And: "What's up?"

"First," said Tatter, "the king wants to see you." He half-turned his face away, stared into the trees.

Hero could feel himself going white. "And second?" he said.

"Second...Hero, I—"

"Second?" Hero repeated.

Tatter took a deep breath, looked straight at him. "It's Ephar Phoog," he said. Phoog was an avaricious Celephasian auctioneer with the instincts of a ghoul. "He's dispatched a couple of his lads to Fang Rocks," Tatter continued. "There's a boat wrecked there, but not just any boat. There's a buzz in town that it's *Quester...*"

"And Eldin?" Hero's head was suddenly clear.

Tatter shrugged, bobbed about a bit, looked away again. "No sign of him. But that's not to say—"

"I know what it's not to say," Hero cut him short again. "Tatter, thanks. I know that wasn't easy."

"You'll go see the king?"

"Bugger the king!" said Hero, but softly. "I'll look for Eldin first." And he did. But when, in Ephar Phoog's auction house, the silently showed him a piece of shattered gunwale on which was painted *Ques*, the *ter* being lost; and when he recognized his own brush-strokes…

———————

Some hours later Hero saw the king.

Kuranes was busy with the renovation of a wing of his Cornish manor house, and artisans were running about all over the place with buckets of paint and whitewash, platters of mortar and various mixes, while masons trundled wheelbarrows of carved stone blocks to and fro. Generally, all was in a turmoil. Hero scratched his head and wondered: *is this how they achieve timelessness in Celephais? By refusing to let it fall into decay?* He was disappointed, for it would seem to take something of the magic out of things.

Hero was taken to the king in the great hall of the wing under repair, where Kuranes personally supervised the work; but when the king spied Hero he at once left off, took his arm and guided him to private chambers. There he commiserated with the numb adventurer, and finished by completing Tatter Nees' previously unspoken:

"—But that's not to say that Eldin is, or has…come to harm."

Hero had bathed and smartened himself up a little. Not only for his audience with the king but also as a means of distancing himself from last night's idiocy, which had not only caused his current unease but might yet prove to have been entirely calamitous. For if Eldin were in fact dead and gone…then Hero knew he'd never drink muth again, nor carouse, nor do any of the myriad other things they'd so often done together. It would mean an end to all that, and to a great deal more. Possibly an end to Hero himself. But for now Kuranes had summoned him, and so he must do his best to pay attention.

Seated opposite the king, looking at him across his great desk through eyes grown a little less bloodshot in a face grown a lot more gaunt, what Hero saw was this:

Under a paint-splashed smock, the Lord of Ooth-Nargai and the Skies Around Serannian was slightly built but regally robed, grey-bearded but bright-eyed. The slant of his eyes and tilt of their brows might on occasion be thought sarcastic, even caustic, but the wisdom and compassion in the lines of his face, and the warmth and steadiness of his gaze, spoke of a love for and a loyalty to his fellow men—especially those domiciled in Earth's dreamlands—which was quite beyond mundane measure. And yet there was this *realness* about him which set him apart from Homo ephemerens; rightly so, for he too was once a waking-worlder, long departed from the conscious world to become a power and permanent resident now in the lands of Earth's dreams. But his origins were stamped on him like the face on a fresh-minted coin; nor were they absent from his voice, which contained in its accents thrilling, often tantalizing reminders of days long forgotten and lives spent in worlds *outside* or on a higher plane than the so-called subconscious.

Kuranes returned Hero's gaze, and what *he* saw was this:

Hero was tall and well-muscled, yet lithe as a hound and agile as a Kledan monkey, and blond in the lands of dream as he'd been in the waking world. His eyes were of a light blue, but they could darken very quickly to steel, or turn a dangerous, glinty yellow in a tight spot. In fact he was usually easy going, quick to grin, much given to jesting; but while he loved songs a fair bit and girls even more, still he was a wizard-master of fists, feet, knives and any sword in a fight, of which there'd been no lack, as the crusty knobs of rock which he called knuckles avowed. A rough diamond, Hero, but one which nevertheless glinted exceeding bright.

Except now his shoulders were slumped and his face pale, where even the laughter lines seemed somehow faded. And Kuranes knew no less than Hero himself that if the Wanderer had indeed died last night, then that he'd lost the services of not only one good agent but probably both of them. And that was a loss he couldn't contemplate, for men such as these were hard to come by.

"Why did you send for me?" Hero eventually spoke up.

"Because I've a job for you," said the king, and he told him a little of what it was.

"Baharna, on the Isle of Oriab?" Hero's voice was dull. "But how can I leave Celephais now, not knowing? I couldn't." He shook his head.

"You can and must," Kuranes answered. "Indeed, it's the best thing in all the dreamlands that you *can* do! By the time you return we'll have found him. Or at least by then we'll know what's happened to him. It has to be better than moping around in Celephais, drinking every night and doubtless getting into trouble, and no earthly use to man or beast. You'll go and discover this monstrous Oriabian vampire and put him or it down—or I'll wash my hands of you."

This last was meant to shock Hero and stir him up, but it hardly touched him. Instead he merely looked at the king, and said: "We once sought out a vampire for you in Inquanok." And he shuddered. "On that occasion, without Eldin...I was a goner for sure."

"I know how you feel," said Kuranes.

"No, you don't."

"Very well, I don't. But listen: do this for me and strengthen our alliance with Oriab, and this is what I'll do for you. I'll have every boat in the harbor out searching for Eldin; I'll have men on every beach and cliff for twenty miles east and west of the city; each day you're away, I'll send you bulletins by carrier-pigeon, so keeping you up to date. And when you return, I'll furnish you with a new sky-yacht to replace *Quester*. Who could say fairer than that? But you in your turn must promise to discover, or do you level best to discover, the terror stalking Oriab and eliminate it. And you set sail today, without delay, just as soon as we are finished."

"But as you've just as good as pointed out," said Hero without animation. "I've no boat."

"Chim Nedlar is the master of a sloop; he's waiting for you even now, tied up in the harbor but ready to said as soon as you're aboard. Now what's it to be?"

Hero stood up and headed for the door. He hadn't been dismissed but the king said nothing. He merely waited, holding his breath. At the door Hero paused, looked back. "Oriab? Baharna? Me and Eldin, we've mutual interests there. We've had some good times there, too. And a few bad ones. There'll be a lot of memories sunk deep, just waiting to be disturbed so they can rise up again. My heart won't be in it."

"But your head will know it's for the best," Kuranes countered. "And stop talking as if he'd dead! We don't know that, and only the future will tell."

Hero nodded, however slightly. "Baharna," he said again, but thoughtfully. And: "Only the future will tell…" He straightened up a little, and the king thought that perhaps some of the helplessness had gone out of him. "Very well," said Hero, going out and closing the door softly behind him…

————————

Hero boarded the *Shark's Fin* an hour later. He chuckled inside a little (sadly, perhaps—or nostalgically, so soon?) thinking: *Now what would Eldin make of this, I wonder?*

"What, the *Shark's Fin* sloop?" the absent quester would doubtless have commented. "A boat, you say? Sounds more like some weird Oriental delicacy to me!" And then both of them would have wondered what "Oriental" meant, for memories of the waking world came and went in exceedingly brief and usually inexplicable flashes. And now, as Chim Nedlar showed his passenger to his bunk, indeed Hero did wonder what Oriental meant. Which was strange because he'd know just a moment ago. But that was the way of it.

"Get some sleep," the sloop's master told him, "for you look all in." And then he went off about his business. A little later they set sail, and since the wind blew fair for Oriab they were soon airborne and out of the chop of waves which still hadn't settled from the storm. Then, far out over the Southern Sea—with the wind whistling in the rigging, and the flotation engines softly thumping like a pair of great hearts below decks somewhere amidships—Chim came down again and gave his cargo a shake.

Hero hadn't undressed, merely stretched himself out and fallen instantly asleep. Dressed in soft, russet-brown leather, which was his usual garb, he wore a short jacket, snug-fitting trousers, and calf-boots with his trousers tucked in to form piratical bells. His jacket sleeves were rolled up to show a tanned breadth of forearm, and a slightly curved sword of Kled hung from his belt on his right hip, loosely tethered to his leg above the knee. But asleep he tossed and turned, and mumbled to himself a bit, grimacing now and then and balling his fists.

For not only had he fallen asleep but straight into dreams within dreams: mental phantasms which, for all that they were only a repetition of what had gone—or what had probably gone—before, were exceedingly weird dreams indeed. His mind was exhausted, doubtless from worrying about the Wanderer, because of which it was perhaps only natural that his dreams should concern themselves with that selfsame worthy.

Eldin in trouble, aboard a storm-lashed Quester; *Eldin hurled overboard, tumbling down through leagues of sky to the heaving bosom of the Southern Sea; Eldin sinking thorough the weedy deeps, ogled by fishes, finally feasted upon by crabs.*

And Kuranes' voice sounding harsh in Hero's mind, saying very unKuranes-like things, such as:

"He's not dead, just resting his bones a bit. Now leave him be, pull yourself together and be off to Baharna. You've a quest, remember? Seek out and slay me this vampire and I'll return Quester *to you—aye, and this dozy, drowned old duffer of a Wanderer, too!"*

"Watch who you're shouting at!" Hero mumbling returned. "And especially what you're shouting at him!"

But casting about he discovered there was no king there at all—no ocean floor or recumbent, crab-nurturing Eldin—only a windswept, mountainous place where ghosts of vanished dreamers cried out to him for vengeance.

"Sucked dry!" they moaned. "Taken in our prime! With all substance drawn off, what are we now but fast-fading memories? Give us back our flesh, David Hero. Give us back to those who mourn us, and yet fear us for the voiceless wraiths we are become..."

Voiceless? They seemed to Hero to have voices enough! He might even have ventured to say so, but in another moment—

—He stood on the gently rolling deck of a ship. It was night now; ah, but he could tell by the feel of things that the night was unquiet! And sure enough, true to his instinct, a scarcely luminous ghost came striding toward him; burly and bearded it was, a sailor, by its rolling gait. And yet the stars shone through its insubstantial outline where it paused to peer at Hero, then put up a hand to its pallid eyes to gaze far, far out to sea. Finally the ghost turned back to Hero and with a worried, puzzled expression, but quite conversationally, said: "The worst of it is, I can't seem to remember! My dreams have all been eaten up; and what's a dreamlander with his dreams, eh?"

"I—" Hero gaped, his eyes wide, astonished and not a little afraid of this conversation with a ghost. "I—"

"You?" the apparition frowned with faint-etched eyebrows. "Was it you took all I had been away from me?" Ghostly fingers—which yet felt real enough—reached to grasp Hero's shoulder and shake him. He gave a great start—

—Started awake!—sat up—saw Chim Nedlar there and gasped, remembered, then flopped down on his back again. But in a little while he once more sat up.

Chim Nedlar was a little overweight for a sailor, Hero thought, quickly recovering his wits. Somewhat puffy in the face and heavy in the frame, but jolly enough for all that. And there was that of the waking world about him, too, which seemed to add to his substance. He had loose lips, green eyes, dark hair parted in the middle and plaited down to his chubby shoulders, wore a shirt like a tent hanging loose to his shoes, which were wooded clogs with soles of rough hide to grip the decks. In height he came up to Hero's chin.

As Hero's heart quit hammering, so the other perched himself on the bunk opposite and said: "I could see you were nightmaring and so woke you up. Forgive me if I startled you."

"You did, and I do," said Hero. "Indeed, I thank you!"

Chim smiled, nodded. "So it's off to Oriab, eh? On king's business, too! I've heard of you, David Hero. Hero of Dreams, they call you, and you're a quester for Kuranes!"

Hero wasn't especially interested in conversation right now; though his dreams were fast-receding, he still had his own private thoughts to think; but the vessel's captain was only being polite, and Hero could find no fault in that. "A small thing," he answered with a shrug. "We're the king's men, aye, me and...and a friend of mine." He fell silent.

"Eldin, aye," the other answered gravely. "Eldin the Wanderer. Heard of him, too, and know that you're a pair of bold adventurers with many a tall tail to tell. And taller because they're all true! Me, I'm the wrong shape for derring-do, or maybe I'd have joined Serranian's sky-navy under Admiral Limnar Dass. But active service, me?" He jiggled his belly, gave a shrug. "Alas, no. So I sail the *Shark's Fin* here and there out of Baharna, finding what trade I can. I suppose we're a ferry, really. But I do get to meet some interesting folks, and I do like to listen to the tales they tell."

Hero yawned and at once apologized. "Knackered," he excused himself. "And I'm sorry, but I've no stories for you. Not now, anyway. Maybe we'll have a drink together some time, and then we'll see." He carefully lay down again.

Chim Nedlar seemed a little disappointed. He signed and said, "Ah, well—maybe I'll catch you in Baharna. Where do you pull your corks?"

Hero shrugged again, put his hands behind his head and suppressed another yawn. "*The Quayside Quaress*, usually," he finally answered. "*Buxom Barba's* place on the waterfront."

"Know it well," Chim chuckled. "A favourite haunt. Maybe I'll catch you there, then. The drinks are on me."

"Indeed?" Hero offered a weary wink. "Why, then you'll be welcome at my table any old time, Chim!" He closed his eyes, drawling: "Aye, and I dare say we'll meet there one night, in the old *Quayside Quaress.*" And lulled by the vessel's gentle roll, he slowly drifted back into sleep. This time, however, there were no dreams within dreams...

———————

In Baharna, via a chandler's shop in the harbour, Hero made for Lippy Unth's place the *Leery Crab*, standing squarish and squat as its namesake at the end of an ancient stone quay. Once upon a time the proprietor, Lipperod Unth, had owned another, similarly unsavoury place, which as the direct result of a night's affray was wrecked and submerged in a scummy, disused part of the harbour. The *Leery Crab*, unlike its *Craven Lobster* cousin, was built of stone, not timber, and its door was guarded by Lippy's large son Gooba and an equally impressive friend. They stood one to each side of the entrance, young, olive-black Pargans, towering like gleaming, meaty monoliths in the dusk as Hero approached along the stone-flagged quay.

Recognizing him at once, Gooba stepped forward, grunting: "You're not welcome here, Hero." And he set himself squarely in the quester's way.

"Don't talk daft, lad," Hero growled. "Why, it was my money built this place!"

"But my father preferred his *old* place," Gooba answered, showing his teeth in a snarl as he and his similarly mountainous friend fell into defensive crouches. "The one that you and Eldin the Wanderer sank!"

Hero paused only a few paces away. He carried a small sack which now he dipped into, coming out with a bomb as round and black as a cannonball, and a flint striker which he held up in plain view. He grinned humourlessly at their expressions, and low in his throat said, "Gooba, I still owe your Old Man a little something for feeding me to the scabfish. You remember? And a crab's much the same as a lobster to me — crusty old crustaceans both. Now I'm not looking for trouble, but if you don't ease up and let me pass I swear I'll light this fuse and lob all hell right in through that door."

294

Gooba and friend blinked, looked at each other, seemed to shrink a little. Creases showed in their black brows.

"I'll count to five," Hero pushed. "One…"

They stepped aside and he proceeded, or would have except now Lippy himself stood in his way.

"Lippy" as a nickname didn't derive entirely from Lipperod, nor as one might erroneously surmise from any great love of talking. On the contrary, Lippy wasn't much for talking; he was far more a man of action. But when he was annoyed, then he'd pout with his great black lips and thrust them out ahead of him like a warning trumpet; and when Lippy Unth looked like that…someone or ones was or were in big trouble! Hero had witnessed Lippy's metamorphosis from bartender/owner to incredibly destructive device on more than one occasion; he had determined never to see it again. Not if he could avoid it.

"No trouble, Lippy," he said now, studying the other's huge olive face and brown, rolling eyes.

"Ah!" said Lippy. "No trouble, you say? But it seems to me I've heard that before. And didn't I just now hear you threatening the *Crab* with sudden and quite unwarranted annihilation?" His eyes settled on the bomb in Hero's hand, mirroring it, which turned them to great black marbles that stared accusingly out of his head. "Also," he continued, "you mentioned an unsettled score."

"Only to bolster my argument," said Hero. "In fact I consider all old scores settled, and scars healed—or I will once this is over. Lippy, I'd no more enter here than dive head-first into the jaws of hell. But I'm looking for Eldin and there might well be a certain customer of yours who can tell me where he is."

Lippy let his eyes slowly wonder beyond Hero, along the quay. "The Wanderer's not with you?"

"See for yourself," said hero.

Lippy's shoulders, which had been hunched up almost as high as his head under his stained, straining shirt, now relaxed a very little. He narrowed his eyes. "Very well, you can come in—but the bomb gets dumped in the harbour."

Hero shook his head. "Call it insurance," he said. "It not only gets me in but out again—unscathed! *Then* I'll toss it in the harbour."

"Hero—" Lippy rumbled warningly, his shoulders starting to hunch again. Worse, his great lips began to pout. Hero was aware of Gooba and chum straying fractionally closer on the flanks, knew it was time he restated the stakes.

"I'm short on time," he said, his voice very dangerous-sounding. "So our little chat's over." He hefted the bomb, held his striker close to its fuse. "Now do I get in—or does everyone who's in get out?"

Lippy's lips retracted. "Who is it you're looking for?"

"The Seer With Invisible Eyes," said Hero.

"*Huh!*" said Lippy, at last standing aside. "Aye, he's here—damn his eyes!"

"They're already damned," said Hero, carefully stepping round the huge Pargan, through the door and into the *Leery Crab*'s smoke-wreathed, muth-reeking gloom.

The *Crab*, like the ill-fated *Lobster* before it, was appointed in something less than opulence. The bar consisted of a stout, square wooden framework in the centre of one huge room, from which Lippy, his wife and massive son could take in the entire place at a glance. As for its clientele: they were hard men, loners, ex-pirates, sea-captains from unknown parts on the lookout for a crewman to shanghai, seadogs and peglegs and others of a like ilk gathered to tell their tall tales, which got taller with every telling. But unsavoury? It could be downright unhealthy!

But the place did have its good points. In high season, for instance, there would never be any overcrowding down here. There'd always be room to sit at a bench without tangling elbows; you'd rarely have to shout to make yourself heard; you wouldn't be bothered by ladies of the night. The *things* that used this place couldn't be called "ladies" of any description. And the proprietor, Lippy himself, demanded and maintained good order at all times. Or at least tried his best to do so. "Come and go in peace," was his motto, "or in pieces, as you choose."

Booze? It wasn't good but it wasn't the worst. Lippy's license was still intact, anyway. The muth-dew was watered (probably a good idea), the spirits tasted fishy, or at least of the salty element in which fishes swim, the ales had ailed somewhat and you could pickle eggs in the wine. But on the other hand it was very cheap, provided you had a cast-iron constitution. Most of Lippy's customers had, for how much longer was anybody's guess.

In short the *Leery Crab* wasn't the sort of place in which you'd expect to find one of Kuranes' most trusted foreign operative, which was one of the two reasons why the Seer used it—the other being that he simply loved it! He was funny like that, the Seer With Invisible Eyes.

Funny in all sorts of ways, thought Hero, casting about in the glow of ceiling-suspended lanterns. But he very quickly found who (what?) he was looking for. The S.W.I.E. sat in one corner, with his back to the wall, hunched over a mug of muth. A good safe seat, Hero reckoned, sidling up and sliding onto the bottom-polished wooden bench behind its bolted-down table, ending up only a foot away from the silent Seer. He placed his bomb before him but kept the striker ready in his hand. Gooba came over, kept a respective distance, inquired: "Are you drinking, Hero?"

"A small ale," Hero told him. "And if it tastes even slightly weird I'll be very annoyed. When I'm annoyed my thumbs twitch, see?" *One* of his thumbs twitched, anyway, and sparks flew from the striker— some of them passing dangerously close to the bomb's fuse. Gooba went off at a run to fetch Hero his ale, and several wise patrons seated nearby stood up, blinked or yawned in their fashion, then quickly put distance between and removed to more solitary areas of the great room.

Through all of this the S.W.I.E. had said nothing. Now Hero glanced at him out of the corner of his eye. As usual, the Seer was wrapped in a bundle of rags with the hood thrown up to make a shadowy blot of his face. All that was visible of the man within this cocoon of rough cloth was a pair of scrawny wrists and claw like hands with long, sharp nails; these protruded from his tattered sleeves, trapping the mug of muth where it sat before him. He had seemed oblivious of Hero's approach, oblivious of all else, too; but Hero had noted that when he put his bomb on the table the Seer has visibly started. Now, however, he merely chuckled.

"A neat ploy, that," he commented without stirring, his voice like the scurry of mice in a bone-dry granary. "When is a bomb not a bomb? When David Hero is up to his—"

"—Neck in it, if you don't keep your voice down!" Hero hissed, out of the corner of his mouth. "What are you trying to do, get me crippled?"

The seer shrugged. "No one can hear us." And then, straight to business: "What's on your mind?"

"Eldin the Wanderer. He's on my mind."

The Seer's head lifted a little and turned fractionally in Hero's direction. For a moment light fell on his face, which was gaunt, hollow-cheeked, invisibly-eyed. The sockets where those eyes should be contained an emptiness deep as the spaces out beyond the stars, and certainly they looked just as cold, too. *Never give this one the old two-finger treatment,* Hero told himself, *or for sure you'll be left with a pair of crystallized stumps!*

The Seer winked, and for a moment one of the holes in his face vanished behind an eyelid. Then it was back again, deep and mysterious as ever. "Aye-aye!" said the Seer.

"Eldin," Hero repeated impatiently. "He's gone missing."

"And you want me to scry him out for you?"

Hero signed. "Of course!"

"Better tell me about it, then. The dreamlands are vast and I'm not omniscient. Points of reference may help narrow it down a bit."

Gooba brought Hero's ale and retreated, and when he was back out of ear-shot Hero told the entire tale of Eldin's disappearance. When he was done the Seer grunted, "*Huh*! He deserves it—and so do you. What? You're like a pair of big kids, you two. Booze and birds, that's all you ever seem to think about!"

Astonished, Hero drew back a little. "Why you callous old...this is Eldon we're talking about! He and I, we're like one person. A team. A well-oiled machine!"

"*Too* well-oiled!" snapped the Seer. "And far too often. I really can't see what Kuranes sees in you. Not even with these invisible eyes of mine, I just can't see it."

Hero showed his teeth, puffed himself up — and deflated in a vast sigh. "Yes, you're right," he said. "All that you said and more — you're dead right. But even if we don't amount to much, still I'm only half as much without him. I'll be like a machine without an engine, doing nothing, going rusty. Also, I..." He fell silent.

"You love him?"

"Hell, no!" Hero was scornful, or tried to be. But he knew he couldn't deceive the S.W.I.E. "Of course I do," he finally admitted. And quickly added: "Er, in my way. The big...*heap*!"

"A heap," the Seer repeated, nodding. He cocked his head on one side a bit. "Yes, I can see that, now that you come to mention it. But we're wasting time. Now listen: this right eye of mine occasionally scans the recent past, and the left can sometimes scry on the immediate future. So since this is all very sinister, or at least fraught, that's how we'll go — sinistrally! Now tell me, what do you see in my left eye?" He closed the right emptiness and Hero gazed deep into the other. But there was nothing there, just a great yawning void that whirled and expanded until he felt he was being sucked into it. Suddenly dizzy, he looked away, shook his head to clear it of the rush and reel.

"Nothing," he said, after a moment. "Just a whirlpool of...nothingness!"

"Good!" said the Seer, with some satisfaction. "That's how it should be. Does you no good, knowing the future. I prefer to be kept guessing. Keeps me on my mettle. Now we'll try the right eye."

He opened the lowered lid, closed the other, and Hero looked again. At first there was nothing, but then —

—The Seer's invisible right eye began to fill in, tiny pieces of indeterminate action slotting into place like bits in a miniature jigsaw puzzle, gradually obscuring the absolute void which formed the board behind the picture. So fascinated was Hero by this process that he failed at first to take note of the emerging scene; but as it neared completion all leaped suddenly into perspective, so that now he gasped out loud and peered more closely yet.

It was Eldin and *Quester*, the one aboard the other, all tossed about in a storm that spun the little sky-yacht this way and that like a torn kite caught in high branches on a blustery spring morning. Eldin, fighting with the sails, trying desperately to cut them loose before they pulled the boat apart; and a boom swinging, striking him, hurling him against the side of the tiny cabin where his arm seemed awkwardly trapped.

Then the mast splitting and leaning over sideways to port, and the roof of the cabin wrenched loose and all the ship's gear sucked out into the maelstrom. And the Wanderer cradling his (broken?) left arm, lurching this way and that and looking all about in seeming desperation. *Quester* was breaking up around him; the mast, splintered at its base but not yet broken free, swung to and fro, clearing the decks and shattering the upper strakes. With each wild sweep Eldin must leap over the lunging mast or have his legs smashed. Then the mast swinging far out to starboard and jamming there, causing the aerial wreck to list and more than forty-five degrees in that direction.

And Eldin struggling with a hatch cover, slamming back the bolts until the door burst open with the pressure of the floatation bag contained beneath. The Wanderer's ploy was obvious; he took a knife and cut through one of the two guys holding the bag in place, so that it sprang out of its bay below the deck and strained like a balloon to be free. Then, tangling his arms and legs in the net which covered the bag, the Wanderer reached down and sliced through the second tether.

That did it! He was snatched aloft while *Quester* capsized and slid stern-first out of the sky, down toward the foaming Southern Sea far below.

The picture faded, broke up, vanished, and the Seer's right eye was once again invisible.

"He lives!" Hero breathed, mainly to himself. And to the S.W.I.E.: "I'll tell you what I saw—"

"Hold!" husked that worthy, with whispery breath. "What you saw from without I saw from within. Two-way, these windows of mine. What, d'you think I can't read these invisible eyes I've been gifted—or cursed—with? That would be like giving a crystal ball to a blind man! As for Eldin living, however—" he grew more whispery yet, "—I'd not go daft on *that* theory, if I were you."

"Explain," said Hero.

"What you just saw was a day ago, during the storm. And it looked pretty perilous to me: floating off like that on a bag of mainly ethereal essence!"

Hero nodded. "Maybe, but we're old hands at ethereal essence-floating, Eldin and me. I say he lives! The question is…where?"

"You want to scry some more?"

"Can we?"

The Seer signed. "It's a bit of an effort," he grumbled. "But now that I've picked up his trail…and anyway, what's a talent for if not to be exercised, eh? Very well, look again." And once more he shuttered his left eye while opening wide the bottomless pit which as his right. More than eager, Hero licked his lips, looked—

—And strained back from the Seer at what he saw, lurched to his feet with a cry of denial forming on his lips! Before he could utter it, the S.W.I.E. grabbed his wrist in an iron claw, dragged him down again. "It's a picture!" the Seer rasped. "Only a picture floating on the surface of my mind. Damn it, I'm not always right!"

"Liar!" Hero gasped. "It's real and you know it!" But nevertheless he looked again in the moment before the Seer blinked and erased the thing:

A backdrop of crags reaching to frowning mountains; great grey peaks rearing skyward; dark clouds scudding east on some secret, silent mission. And in the foreground: fangs of rock, scree slides, projecting outcrops like looming menhirs. Aye, menhirs, indeed! They set the mood for the rest of the scene. For caught fast half-way down a sheer-sided cliff, there was Quester's *deflated flotation bag; it clung crumpled to the fractured rock, the web its rope net ripped—and empty!*

"Carried south, south-east by the storm—" said Hero, his eyes half-glazed, "—rushed along with the wind whistling in his rigging. Eldin eventually spied the Isle of Oriab. He deflated the bag a little, sank toward the island. But the wind was too strong or his judgement was off. He missed Baharna and flew on into the hinterland. Those peaks, the rocks, the mountain heights—those were the foothills of N'granek. I've seen it, been there, know the place. I *couldn't* be mistaken."

"But I *can* be!" the Seer insisted. "Did you *see* him crash into the cliff, rupture his bag and burst the net? Did you *see* him fall? No, you saw only—"

"—The *result* of that crash," Hero finished it for him. "I saw its result, and that's enough." His eyes had turned bleak, and yet moist, too. "Now I have to go and find his body, find Eldin, and deal with him before N'granek's gaunts find and deal with him. Or before he's found by other creatures of the night."

The Seer nodded, said: "*If* he's dead, and *if* you find him—what then?"

Hero frowned through his misery. It seemed an odd question. He shook his head. "I don't—"

"There are laws that govern the dead here in the dreamlands, Hero!" the Seer's voice was harsh. "Had you forgotten?"

Hero gasped as he saw the other's meaning. *If* Eldin was dead, then he'd died in an especially unpleasant manner. And those who died that way—in nightmarish fashion—all shared a common destiny: the Charnel Gardens of Zura!

"No," said Hero, shaking his head, "I'll not let that be! Zura shan't have him. Not the Queen of the Living Dead. I'll track him, find him, burn him before I'll let him go to her—and he'll thank me for it!"

He stood up again, and swayed a little from the sudden emptiness of his head, heart, limbs. "Now…now I have to look for him."

"Hero," the Seer again pulled him down, and was surprised that it took so little effort. "Aren't you forgetting something?"

"Eh?" Hero sat there cold and numb.

"Your quest?"

"What do you know of my quest?" His query was listless, automatic.

The Seer shrugged. "An hour ago, a carrier-pigeon from Celephais found me as I was on my way here. From Kuranes. With a message. I was told you might seek me out, and the king asked me what I know of this Oriabian vampire. More than that, he also told me a couple of things. And it now appears your quest's more urgent than ever. I'm sorry, lad, but Eldin will have to wait."

Again Hero lurched to his feet. "Not for any king's quest!" he blurted.

This time the Seer made no attempt to seize him but said: "Hero, do you trust me?"

Hero looked into his frozen, empty sockets and said, "Yes—no—I don't know. How can I trust someone when I can't see what's in his eyes? Trust you about what?"

"About Eldin."

Hero's face was gaunt, tortured. "I have to find him."

"Sit down and listen to me."

Hero sat—but inside his pain and frustration were churning toward anger. "Hero," said the Seer, "there are many small lights in my mind. They glow there like fireflies in a dark lane, or stars mirrored in a still sea. They are people I've met, memories of which I've retained. I don't know these motes individually, can't tell which firefly is what man or woman. But I'm sure I'd know if it if one of them were extinguished. None of them have been, not recently. A few have flickered now and then, but none of them have gone out."

"You're saying Eldin is still alive."

"I can't guarantee it, but I believe it. Now, do *you* believe *me*?"

"If I do, isn't that all the more reason why I must find him?"

"Hero," said the Seer. "This pain you feel, worrying about Eldin. Is it bag?"

Hero groaned. "He's more than a brother. I laugh with him…"

"How much worse is it then, for those families and friends beloved of this vampire's victims? Now don't look away but answer me. Eldin is one man, and they are many. And again I say to you: I believe he lives."

"But a short time ago you told me not to rely too much on my theory of him being alive."

"Because if I'm wrong I don't want your hatred!"

They stared at each other for long moments. Finally Hero said: "Very well, but understand: if you are wrong, I *will* hate you. What must I do?"

"You go about your business for Kuranes," said the Seer, with an audible sign, "and I'll look for Eldin. And who better for the job, eh? Me, with these invisible eyes of mine. But first, and quickly, let me tell you what the king told me, and also what I've learned for myself:

"Kuranes' message: the plague has spread to Celephais!"

"What??" Already the numbness was going out of Hero's brain; his mind was alert again, his grasp growing stronger. "The thing has taken a victim in Ooth-Nargai?"

"Victims!" the Seer corrected him. "Plural. Three of 'em."

"But how can hat be?" Hero's brow showed creases.

The Seer shrugged. "More than one vampire, maybe? Or a creature who can fly in the night across the sea? I don't know how it can be."

Hero thought back on what Kuranes had told him:

Healthy men—hardy, adventurous types all, and usually in their prime—had been vanishing without trace in Baharna and its outskirts. They left neither hid nor hair, bits or bones but quite simply disappeared—almost. They *did* leave gradually dispersing wraiths—ghosts! But ghosts of peculiar habits. No rattling of chains or lopped-off head-carrying for these missing and presumably (what else?) dead persons; no, they were simply wraiths that haunted their old homes, their families, favourite places and other "haunts" they'd know in more corporeal times.

Now, ghosts in the dreamlands were as rare as ghosts in the waking world. Oh, the dreamworld had its monsters and menaces, true enough, its regions of magick, mystery and nightmare, but as for ghosts...*Homo ephemerens* (the people of dreams) didn't generally have much of true matter anyway. They *seemed* solid and real enough, as most dreams do, but there just wasn't enough of them to leave a great deal behind. Dreamland's legended Enchanted Wood was rumoured to be home for several departed spirits, but actual *sightings* of specters were generally few and far between. Or had used to be.

The trouble with the troubled spirits which the Oriabian (and now Celephasian, apparently) vampire left behind it was this: that they were incredibly persistent in aspiring to ghosthood. Each and every victim had become a ghost, without a single exception. Also, instead of merely haunting, they went about like lost souls (which of course they were) in a sort of vacant, absent-minded, and yes, totally *lost* condition. Not lost like virginity or lost in sin, but lost as in not knowing where they were. And perhaps more importantly, *not remembering who they had been*!

And having revisited that conversation with Kuranes, and now with something of animation, Hero said: "It suddenly strikes me we can make a quick end of this thing!"

The Seer raised an eyebrow over nothing whatsoever, and said: "How so?"

"Isn't it obvious? Use your right eye to scry the past, find the vampire in his/her/its vile pursuit—or better still red-handed at a victim's demise—and I'll take it from there."

"Oh?" said the Seer. "Obvious, is it? But if what you suggest were possible there'd be no more crime in all the dreamlands! Can't you see that?"

"Eh?"

The Seer sighed. "I can't scry on criminal activities—not consciously, anyway. My eyes for the most part are quite blind to all matters of larceny, thuggery, arson, etc. Crimes against persons or property are therefore outside my scope, especially in a supernatural context. On the other hand—" (And he frowned, which, without eyes, was a sight to see), "—in this case there does appear to be something of an ambiguity."

"Say on."

"Well, I've said I'm not much on scrying supernatural stuff—and that's a fact, even though the scrying itself is nothing short of supernatural! Ah, but I *can* see the ghosts of this vampire's victims!"

"Indeed? And can you show them to me?"

"Certainly! For I've made some preliminary investigations, and indeed I have the power to recall some of the scenes I've seen. Now look into my eyes again—both of them this time—and I'll run a replay."

Hero looked as directed, and it was something like using the Viewmaster he'd owned as a child, except that when he thought of it he couldn't remember his childhood and didn't know what a Viewmaster was. Just another brief flash of memory from the waking world.

The scene was Andahad, a small but opulent seaport on the far side of Oriab. Hero knew it well enough since he and Eldin's lady-loves Ula and Una Gidduf had lived there upon a time with their well-to-do merchant father, Ham. As Hero watched, the picture in the Seer's eyes narrowed down to a house of some excellence standing on a hillside to the east of the town. Outside the house, relatives of the family, passers by, and curiosity-seekers in general, stood about in a small crowd, some having visited or being about to visit the others simply waiting to see what they'd see. Hero scaled faces and believed he saw one that he recognized; then the S.W.I.E.'s eyes took him through the main door and inside the privacy of the d welling itself.

There, in the main room—the sitting-room, with a wide window over-looking the ocean strand—the family of the missing-presumed-dead man sat around in great distress, wringing their hands and weeping, or else staring in astonishment at all that was left of the head of the family. His widow, the lady of the house herself, was quite distraught; wild-haired and -eyed, she all the time pleaded with the apparition, which stepped here and there about the room, peering this way and that, with an expression of bewilderment—no, of utter mystification—written plain on its diaphanous transparency of a face.

Hero was fascinated. He watched the ghost in its perambulations, how it appeared to examine this or that object or item of furniture in the room, frowning as if desperately trying to recall something it should know. And a weird comparison struck Hero: that the spectre's expression was not unlike Eldin's or even his own on those occasions when they would briefly recall some fragment from the waking world, only to lose it a moment later. Every so often, as it drifted about, the ectoplasmic revenant would deliberately move *around* a chair or table, as if subconsciously "remembering" that such items of furniture were there; but mainly it walked right through them, and occasionally people, too, even its own pleading, weeping, half-crazed widow.

Occasionally it would seem to recognize one or another of its children, stop and stare in its puzzled fashion, even begin to smile or cry; but then the three-quarters vacant, worried expression would return and off it would go again, f adding and quickening in turn, insubstantial as moonbeams where it examined and re-examined the room. Eventually, not looking where it was going, it passed into a solid wall and disappeared.

"An explorer and adventurer," the Seer informed as his eyes went blank as space again. "He mapped half of Kled in his time, that one. A great lecturer on his travels and travails in far, foreign places. When you're too old for questing, Hero, maybe you should take a leaf from his book and become a lecturer. He didn't do too badly out of it."

"Oh?" the other frowned. "Well possibly there's no connection between who he was and what he's become, but in any case it doesn't seem to me that he'd done to well! I mean, what is he now but a vacant vapour, eh?"

The Seer scratched his head through his cowl a moment, then offered: "Do you want to see more? I've looked into most of these cases as they've occurred. Since we're visiting in Andahad, as it were, you might also like to check out the shad of Shallis Tull."

"Shallis Tull?" Hero repeated the name. "Wasn't he big all those years ago in the anti-slave trade lobby? Didn't he forge links with Parg, become the blood brother of Gunda-ra-Gunda, the Pargan king, sabotage a Kledan slaver fleet?"

"The same," the S.W.I.E. nodded. "Hard as nails, Shallis Tull, but with a heart of gold. Alas, he too is now a ghost; he haunts the ship he once sailed against Kled!"

"He wasn't a family man?"

"No, not him. The sea was his mistress, and fair play for all men his goal. Care to visit?"

Hero nodded. "But make it brief; I fear for Eldin, and at this rate you'll never get after him."

Again the Seer's eyes clouded over...

So it went.

Through the Seer's invisible eyes Hero boarded Shallis Tull's sloop *The Silver Fish*, to witness that vessel's vampirized ex-captain vacantly exploring her length and breadth. There was something vaguely familiar about the ship's interior and below decks, but Hero was rather more interested in the ghost of Tull than the vessel it had chosen to haunt.

Finally he followed the blocky, bearded, bewildered and disembodied apparition back up on deck, where in a little while it passed into the wheelhouse, through the wheel and vanished into the woodwork.

Before the Seer's eyes could revert to their commonplace (?) vacuity, hero gazed through them onto the wharfside, where as before a small crowd of curiosity-seekers had assembled, all of them staring in wide-eyed wonder at the ghost-boat. And again, among the milling faces of these perversely peering persons, Hero thought he saw one which he recognized. Indeed, the same one that he'd seen outside the house of the explorer-adventurer.

After that, in short order, the S.W.I.E. showed Hero the ghost of Eelor Tush, a Baharnian vintner who'd journeyed to the edge of dream itself in the discovery of his rare wines; the spectral remains of Tark the Tall, mountaineer extraordinary, whose recent expedition on the south face of Hatheg-Kla in the stony desert had been the talk of all the dreamlands, (especially after his party, with the sole exception of Tark himself, had fallen to their deaths from the mountain's flank; indeed fallen *up* the mountain, for Hatheg-Kla is that sort of place); and finally the shade of Geerblas Ulm, fearless and fabled descanter into holes, first man to ever clamber down a rope to the bone-strewn floor of the ill-regarded Pit of Puth. And always Hero was aware that the same figure and face where somewhere present in the vicinity, mingling with the mobs come to gawp at the ghosts of this string of unfortunate personalities.

And so fascinated and involved had Hero become with these ocular excursions that it took some little time for the fact to dawn that here he was back in the *Leery Crab* (from which he'd never in fact strayed), seated beside the Seer who sipped at his muth as before. "Enough?" inquired that worthy, between sips.

"Quite enough," Hero nodded. "And I thank you for what you've shown me. What's more, I believe I'm onto something. Now make haste with that muth and get busy.

"Eh? Busy?"

"Searching for Eldin, of course, alive or dead. But alive, if you value my continued friendship."

The Seer drained his mug. "I shall proceed by yak to the western flank of N'granek, which I'll search most diligently," he promised.

"Good!" said Hero. "And when I've done with a spot of business—maybe even while I'm dealing with it—I'll make myself available for searching the eastern flank. Before we go our separate ways, however, perhaps you'll tell me: when exactly was Shallis Tull's demise?"

"Eh? Tull? He disappeared, oh, all of three or four months ago. One of the vampire's first victims, as it happens."

"And *The Silver Fish*? What become of her?"

"Sold in auction, the monies going to Tull's old shipmates."

Hero nodded and asked no more. They stood up and the Seer left a small (a very small) tip on the table, and in single file they took their leave of the place. Or would have, except that Lippy Unth was waiting just beyond the door.

"Hero," said the huge black man rumbling. "I'll take that, if it's all the same to you." He glanced warily at the bomb in Hero's hand. Behind him stood Gooba and friend, along with a goodly number of scarfaced patrons.

Without pause Hero struck sparks and lit the fuse, which at once commenced sputtering and smoking and of course burning down. Everyone except Lippy, who seemed nailed to the quay's stone flags, burst into furious activity, diving this way and that like so many trapped rats, taking cover where such might be had. Some went so far as to dive headlong off the pier into the scabfish-ridden scum of the harbour. Lippy, as stated, merely teetered on his heels, his olive features somehow contriving to turn a dark grey.

"This?" said Hero, innocently, holding up the smoking bomb in plain view. "Take it by all means!" And he tucked it into Lippy's wide trouser-band under his bulging belly.

Finally Lippy unfroze, snatched the device from his trousers, lobbed it out across the greasy water. In doing so he noted how light it was; noted too, that when it splashed down it didn't sink but bobbed — *exactly* like the green glass floats which the fisherman used to buoy their nets! What's more, there was a smudge of fresh black paint on Lippy's hurling hand...

"*Hero!*" he howled a moment later, when he'd had time to draw sufficient breath. But by then Hero and the S.W.I.E. both had quite vanished away.

———————

Hero decided he'd carry out an aerial search for Eldin, and he knew exactly who he'd enlist to aid him in this venture: someone with a skyship, obviously. Night had settled and the *Quayside Quaress* was alive with music, lights and laughter as he hurried along the dockside.

At the door he bumped into the very man he sought, Chim Nedlar himself, master of the *Shark's Fin* sloop.

"Ahoy there, cap'n!" Hero called out, in a voice darkly jovial.

The other peered at him a moment in the gloom, then chuckled. "Ahoy, Hero! So we get to have a drink together after all!"

"Later maybe," said Hero. "But right now I've need of your boat."

"Eh?" Nedlar seemed uncertain. "But I've given my lads shore-leave for the night. Whatever it is, I'm sure it can wait till morning."

"No," Hero shook his head, "it can't. My friend and fellow quester Eldin the Wanderer is wrecked somewhere on N'granek, where the foothills meet the mountain. I've come here, to the *Quaress*, to borrow a bit of gear, and then I was on my way to find you. By being here you've saved me the trouble. Don't worry, I'll pay you well for your time and the hire of your sloop. As for being short-handed: how many crew do you carry?"

"Myself and two—when they're there," said the captain. "She's easy in the handling, the old *Shark's Fin*."

"But built for speed!" said Hero. "Which is what's required. And the wind's dropped, and we're both of us sailors. Man, I reckon we can handle her well enough on our own. Now look, while I get me an aiming-lamp, maybe you'd like to pick up a bottle or two? Then while we search we can pull their corks, eh?"

Chim Nedlar brightened a little. "And perhaps you'll tell me a handful of your tall tales?—er, while we search, I mean?"

"A deal's a deal," Hero nodded.

As Chim made his way to the bar to buy booze, Hero's eyes narrowed a little. He watched the other's broad back disappear into the crowd…

Then someone tugged at his elbow and a foul, familiar female voice blasted in his ear: "Hero, by all that's unspeakably clean and healthy!"

"Buxom Barba!" he returned, recoiling from her breath.

Gigantically bosomed, gap-toothed from many a fist-fight, and beaming very unbeautifully, Barba grabbed and hugged him. He felt his ribs give a little and fought free. "And Eldin?" she said, punching

Hero mightily in the shoulder as she glanced this way and that/ "Now where's my favourite boy?"

"Lost," said Hero, and he explained the other's possible plight. "That's why I'm here, to borrow one of your stage-lighting devices."

She went and brought one for him: a lantern with a curved lens, to throw the light in a beam. Onstage, the amazon Zuli Bazooli's dance was made that much more sensuous where now only five lights played upon her gleaming body instead of the customary six. "My thanks, Barba," said Hero. "I'll not forget you."

"When you find him drag him back here for a drink!" she shouted, as he hurried toward Chim Nedlar waiting at the door...

———

After that it took ten minutes to get aboard the *Shark's Fin*, cast off and climb up into the night sky, and in a little while the gentle breeze off the sea was hushing them inland toward N'granek. Hero fixed up his searchlight in the prow, and Chim let his vessel drift along silently under half-said, crossing Baharna's hinterland plateau toward the central peaks. Then the captain joined Hero where he scanned the way ahead, and each pulling a cork they drank a little wine. The stuff went straight to Hero's head, which in the circumstances was perhaps to be expected.

"The engines are off, bags three-quarters full, altitude steady," said Chim. "Twenty minutes or thereabouts and we'll be over the foothills. Then we can start hallooing and hope your friend hears us, and your searchlight can double as a depth-gauge. There are fangs aplenty I wouldn't care to bang into. Closer to N'granek I'll start up the engines, gain a little altitude, head for the eastern flank. If Eldin the Wanderer's there he should see or hear us. I still think it would have been better by daylight, but—"

"But he's lived through one night out there already," said Hero. "*If* he's still alive. So by now he'll be a bit desperate—especially if he's hurt. That's why it couldn't wait till daybreak."

"Of course, of course," said Chim, falling silent and thoughtful.

"Oh?" said Hero in a little while. "Is there something? Did I perhaps snap at you just then?"

Chim shrugged. "Only because you're under stress," he said. "But I suppose in the circumstances you'll not be much for recounting your adventures. A shame. For it's my hobby, you know: listening to swashbuckling yarns. And with such as you aboard...why, to hear first-hand accounts of *your* adventures would be...but probably not at a time like this, eh?"

Hero looked at him sideways. "I've nothing against it," he said. "Indeed it might help pass the time." At which...it was as if a chill breeze blew on the back of Hero's neck, so that the short hairs stiffened there and made him shiver. He looked to see what had caused this sudden, icy gust, and there—

—Not three paces away, there stood a burly, bearded figure, peering in a puzzled fashion across the gunnel and out into the night? At first Hero almost cried out, for he thought it was Eldin. But then he saw that for all its burliness the figure was ephemeral as fluff, less than a shimmer on a hot day. Rightly so, for it was the not entirely unfamiliar ghost of Shallis Tull! Its familiarity had two sources. One: this was one of the apparitions that the S.W.I.E. had shown to him; and two: it was the ghost he'd seen in his dreams during the crossing from Celephais to Oriab. What's more, it seemed to Hero that the spectre was a warning...

"Ah!" said Chim Nedlar, "you see him, do you? From where I'm standing he's the merest outline. You see, it's all in the angle. Well, nothing to be afraid of. He's perfectly harmless. Give you a start, did he?"

The ghost quit its peering, wandered off along the deck and into the wheelhouse. Its face looked out for a moment through a window, and then gradually faded away...

"Eh?" said Hero, shaking himself. "A start? Aye, a bit of a one." He looked hard at Chim and his eyes had gone a fraction glinty. "Though why that should be I can't really say—since this was once his ship! P'raps I should have expected him."

Chim nodded. "Oh? And you know all about him, eh? Aye, the old *Shark's Fin* was once *The Silver Fish*; I thought it wiser to name here anew. I mean, it's one thing to be haunted but quite another to advertise the face! How much trade d'you think I'd of if my customers knew this was Tull's old vessel?"

"Not much, I suppose," said Hero. "But doesn't it—he—bother you? Aren't you a bit chary of him?"

"He's a ghost," Chim shrugged. "And gradually fading as all ghosts do. I see less and less of him. Another week or two and there'll be nothing left of him at all!"

"But he's the victim of a vampire," Hero was coldly logical. "I mean, what of the legends? What if he should come back in vampire guise and vampirize you?"

"*Hah!*" Twaddle! Stuff and nonsense!" Chim snorted. "Superstitious clap-trap!"

"Oh?" Hero feigned a look of surprise. "You're not a superstitious man, then:"

"Me? No, of course not."

"And yet you admit that your boat's haunted…"

Chim narrowed his eyes. "I—"

"Indeed, it *is* haunted, for just a moment ago we both saw the ghost."

Chim sputtered. "A common or garden ghost is one thing," he declared, "and a vampire quite another. The first I believe in, not least because I've seen it, but the other—"

At which point the *Shark's Fin* bumped shudderingly into something, and from down below there came the rumbling echo of falling boulders. "Crags!" Hero cried, aiming his searchlight down into darkness.

"Fangs!" Chim leaped to the wheelhouse, got the flotation engines going.

They'd been lucky, merely brushed a pinnacle and blunted its stony tip. But sure enough they'd drifted well into the foothills, and southward rose the central peaks, where N'granek was lord and master. Gaining altitude, the ship bore them up above the danger zone.

"East," said Hero a little breathlessly. "Tack east now, while I sweep with my beam and we both call out as we go. If Eldin's somewhere down there he'll see and/or hear us."

East it was, searchlight flashing, voices calling, and down below a thin mist crawling on the crags and in the hollows. But never the sight or sound of Eldin the Wanderer. And after a while: "Let down your anchor," said Hero gruffly. "It's dawned on me that if he's hurt, he may well be gathering his strength to make reply. I'd hate to overshoot him and leave him cold and broken in the mist."

Chim Nedlar did as instructed; the *Shark's Fin* swung gently at anchor some thirty-five feet over the crags, with frowning N'granek as backdrop, shrouded in a mist made yellow by the rising moon. And for an hour Hero aimed his lamp this way and that, until its oil was all used up; and all the while the two men bellowing their lungs out—to no apparent avail. "I'm hoarse," Hero finally admitted.

"Me too," replied the other.

They drank wine, Hero perhaps a little too much.

Then the *Shark's Fin*'s master spotted a tear in the inside corner of the quester's right eye, and another forming in the left. He nodded his understanding, said solemnly: "You think he's a goner, right?"

Hero looked away.

"You've adventured a lot together, you two," Chim prompted.

"Aye," Hero's voice came gruff from where he averted his face. Then, with more animation: "Adventured? *Hah*! That's not the half of it! How many men have been to the moon, Chim? We went here, got turned to moon rock there—almost, and returned to tell of it. What do you know of Lathi and Zura? They've been enemies and allies both—until now I don't quite know what they are! We've chased horned-one pirates abroad Admiral Dass' flagship, burned old Thalarion to the ground, sailed dreamland's skies on the life-leaf of a Great Tree. Adventure?"

"Go on," Chim Nedlar urged. "Tell me more. Only paint a fuller picture, Hero. These are mere scraps you're tossing me."

And so Hero began to talk.

It was the wine, his grief, the misty night. It was his loneliness. And of course it was Chim's urging. The man was a good listener: he was like a sponge, soaking up all that Hero told him. But he was much more than a mere sponge.

Hero told of his part in the destruction of Yibb-Tstll's avatar idol in the Great Bleak Mountains; and of how he'd lulled the eidolon Lathi with a lullaby, thus enabling her hive city to be razed to the ground. He talked of the aerial plank-walk he'd taken, with Zura's zombie-pirates' swords at his back, and of his rescue from that miles-high tumble by Gytherik Imniss' night gaunts; and he hold of the time he'd been vented from the bowels of Serannian in a great gust of scented flotation essence, when again Gytherik's grim of gaunts had plucked him from gravity's "fell" clutches.

And as time passed and his tales grew more detailed, so their telling became an almost automatic process; it was like siphoning water: one suck to get the thing going, and that's your lot 'til the lake's dry. Tonelessly, with neither affection nor detestation, he told of trials both titillating and terrifying; and all the while it seemed that he unburdened himself, that a great weight was lifted from him as each tale was told. And strangely, *as* each tale was told, so he forgot it— utterly, so that it didn't even cross his mind to wonder why—as he went on to the next story.

Worse far, however, than the mental depletion taking place in Hero, was the physical one. He was g rowing…flimsy! The more he divulged of his life and loves, his adventures and misadventures, his windfalls, pitfalls and pratfalls, his lucky and losing breaks, the less of *him* there seemed to be. It was as if Chim Nedlar were absorbing his *substance* as well as his words. And yet, once started, there was no stopping. His life came out in an endless stream, like a vein slashed through. And the water of a tepid tub turning pink, then red, as the poor doomed soul lies back and oh so gently expires. But there was no blood, no pain, and very little of conscious awareness of the murder taking place. Of Chim Nedlar's murder of David Hero, Hero of Dreams.

No blood, no—for Chim was not that sort of vampire.

But a vampire he was, be sure.

"More! More!" he gloated—and bloated as he fed on Hero's heroics. "Except…tell me more about Eldin, too, and Limnar Dass, Gytherik, Kuranes, oh and all the others you've known. I want to know all of their adventures, too!"

Hero looked at the other through eyes that swam like small fishes in a bland bowl ocean. Chim Nedlar, grinning, drooling, his fat face full of spittly teeth, his eyes pin-pricks of passion in a puffy mass of dough. Chim, all swollen with Hero's stories. No—with Hero's life!

And now Hero knew (however dimly) what he'd more than half-suspected anyway. Except it was too late to do anything about it. And anyway, did he *want* to do anything about it? This way there'd be nothing of him left at all for Zura. And certainly it was painless enough. But what would the worlds of dream have been like without Eldin? It was something he hadn't intended to discover.

Maybe there were dreamlands ulterior to this one, and maybe he'd meet up with Eldin again in one of them. Why not? They'd named the old lad "Wanderer," hadn't they? A ways to wander yet, perhaps. Now *there* was a thought!

"More! *More!*" Chim demanded, his voice a gurgle.

"One last tale," Hero whispered, the merest shadow of a man where he sat with his pale head lolling on the gunnel, his barely opaque hand listless where it tried to grasp and lift his bottle, but wasn't quite solid or strong enough to manage it. "The last one, Chim—for it's *this* one!"

"This one?"

"Aye," Hero nodded, "the story of how I came to Oriab in search of a monster—and found him!"

"Ah!" said Chim. "Ah! But discovered him too late!"

"I've known for some time," Hero sighed, his dying searchlight's beam beginning to show through his flesh. "Not the how of it, until now, but certainly I suspected the who."

Chim nodded. "That's as it may be; it detracts not at all from my enjoyment. Out with it,. then, this last tale. Tell it all—and then you're done. And me? Glutted, I'll first sleep if off, then live on your fat dreams for quite some little time before I'm hungry again."

And Hero, unable to resist, began to comply:

"It started with drinking," he said, his voice very ephemeral now, "and with boasting, and of course wagering as well. As the muth went down faster, so the boasting and wagering grew wilder. Mine and Eldin's of course. Finally the great buffoon declared that 'alone, single-handed, on (his) own, without assistance and—'"

The anchor chain rattled and Chim gave a start. Beneath his ballooning shirt the great mass of him quivered. His piggy eyes left Hero's fading face to scan the dark deck. There was a streamer of creeping mist; there were shadows, splashes of yellow moonlight. Nothing else.

Chim faced Hero again. "Go on," he said.

"No!" came a gruff, grim, croaking voice from the darkness of the wheelhouse!. "No, lad, say no more. For it strikes me you've damn near talked yourself to death already!"

Shallis Tull's ghost came lumbering, bearded and burly. Except it wasn't Tull but Eldin!

"Gah!" said Chim Nedlar, who knew the game was up. "*Gah!*" He drew a long thin knife from its sheath sewn into his shirt. Eldin disarmed him with a lunge and a twirl of his great straight sword. And, "Gah!" the soul-stealer said again, shrinking against the strakes.

"Eldin!" whispered Hero, unable to rise. "Eldin!"

"The same," said the Wanderer, his own voice scratchy as sandpaper. he reached down, took up Hero's bottle, drained it in one massive gulp.

"Did you hear?" Hero was thin as water, blurred at the edges, gradually going gaseous.

"Enough," Eldin nodded. "I've been clinging to the anchor chain for some little time, waiting to be sure I knew what it was all about. Now I know." He placed the point of his sword on a spot a little below Nedlar's fat, bobbing Adams-apple. "Now tell it back," he order... "All of it, exactly as you heard it."

"He told the stories of his own free will!" Chim Nedlar babbled.

"And so will you," said Eldin, grimly.

"What? At sword point?"

"You have a choice: untell the things, and unspell Hero—let out those tales of his which you've somehow trapped—or I'll let *you* out all over the deck here!" He pressed harder with his sword and the other's throat was indented, where the tiniest prick of red showed.

"I'll do it," the vampire gulped.

He retold Hero's stories. In the telling, his bulging shirt subsided a little and some of the puffiness went out of him; Hero put on flesh, or rather his outline began to fill out and look less like that of a jellyfish in the sunlight. Soon he was able to stand up. He looked more his old self, and yet still a little vague.

Chim Nedlar had come gaspingly to a halt.

"Did he retell all:" Eldin was suspicious.

Hero scratched his head. "How'm I supposed to know? I re-remembered everything he said, but how can I say he said everything?"

"Lathi?" said Eldin, and Hero nodded.

"Zura? Kuranes? Gytherik? Serannian?" Nods to all.

"The Mad Moon? Yibb-Tstll—"

"Eh?" said Hero. "Yibb-who?"

"*Hah!*" Eldin prodded again.

Chim Nedlar, looking very pale, gave a little shriek and quickly spilled the rest of the beans—spilled the rest of Hero's memory and being back into him. And: "That's it, that's all, I swear it!" he finally cried.

"Not by a long shot," said Hero darkly, entirely entire again.

Eldin didn't understand.

But Chim Nedlar did. "You're out to destroy me," he whispered, his lips aquiver.

"Too true," Hero agreed, "one way or the other. My turn, Eldin." He unsheathed his slender, curved Kledan sword in a steely whisper, held its keen edge to Nedlar's windpipe. "Let's start with Shallis Tull," he said.

Weeping and babbling, and cursing a lot between stories, the vampire retold Tull's tales, and so re-vitalized the man. In a little while something more than a ghost came bowling up from below decks, beard bristling and eyes ablaze—with astonishment, with joy! "It's coming back!" Cap'n Tull cried. "*I'm* coming back!"

And as he in turned filled out, so Chim Nedlar continued to diminish.

After Tull, in short order, it was the turn of Eelor Tush, vintner extraordinaire; but he did not materialize here but in Baharna, no doubt. Then Tark the Tall, mountain man, who probably came back clinging to some pinnacle somewhere. And Geerblas Ulm, doubtless fattening out in one of his favourite underworlds; and so on, and etcetera...

Finally Chim Nedlar was a wisp. Toward the end he'd been unstoppable (the siphon principle again) and simply spilled all the life he'd taken in back out into dreamland's ether, through which it had sped back to its rightful dreamers. They knew when he'd told all, for his eyes—about as invisible now as the S.W.I.E.'s—suddenly went extremely vacant.

He floated to his feet, leaving his voluminous shirt and empty clogs behind, and looked this way and that without recognizing any-one or—thing. Then, seeing Hero, Eldin, Shallis Tull, perhaps he did remember something. He backed off from them, passed through the ship's strakes and stood for a moment on thin air over misted, unknown chasms of night. Then he began to fall, and falling dispersed entirely.

A thin, thin cry of empty frustration and lost longing drifted back to them. Or maybe it was only the wind rising in the crags, blowing the mist away in tatters which vanished almost as quickly as Chim Nedlar…

———————

Sitting in sunlight upon a pile of nets where they dried on the wharfside, Hero and Eldin watched Shallis Tull painting out *Shark's Fin* on the upper outside port strakes of *The Silver Fish*. He'd promised to sail them back to Celephais, but not until his vessel bore her rightful name once more.

Meanwhile, Eldin had told his own tale, which Hero hadn't stolen but merely listened to: Told how he'd crashed among the crags and his flotation bag was bust; how he'd clung to a ledge while his numbed arm regained its strength and feeling; how then he'd yelled himself hoarse, yelled till he had no voice left to yell with, for the better part of a day and night. But when the mist had thinned a little he'd seen his way clear to climb up from the chasm, to where the S.W.I.E. had found him hungry, thirsty and a bit banged about, but otherwise well, and helped him up onto the back of his yak.

Then, on their way down to Baharna, they'd spied the *Shark's Fin* and heard Hero's and Chim Nedlar's shouting. Following voices and fading searchlight beam both, soon they'd come to the place where the sky-ship was anchored. By then all was silent.

Eldin would have called to those aboard but couldn't: he had no voice. And anyway, the S.W.I.E. had cautioned him: "Something's wrong here! I can smell it!"

Following which Eldin had shinned soundlessly up the anchor chain…and the rest is known.

"Who was he, d'you suppose?" now the Wanderer wanted to know.

Hero shrugged. "Someone from the waking world, I should think. Somehow, when his time was up, he found his way here. Maybe he was the kind who lives on the glories of others. You can find his like in any bar you choose: poor souls whose own lives are so drab they may only colour them with the lives of others—whose nature it is to bask in the glow of adventures they've never experienced for themselves, except as recounted by their heroes. And in his transition from waking- to dream-worlds, his dependency grew strong while his will weakened. Until he emerged here as a weird sort of vampire, as—"

"A stealer of dreams?"

"That's my guess, anyway." Hero nodded.

Eldin said: "Hmmm!" and changed the subject. "Well, lad, it strikes me I've saved your life—again."

Hero snorted. "It was you put it at risk in the first place!" he accused. "You drunken old—"

"Not so much of the 'old,' if you please!" Eldin cut him short.

"And that's the end of *that*, too!" said Hero, threateningly.

"Eh? End of what:"

"Boozing! We've done much too much of it. It's what started all of this in the first place."

"*What!*" Eldin was aghast.

"No more muth," Hero declared.

"You're joking! What about wine?"

"No," Hero pursed his lips, shook his head. "*All* booze is out—as of now."

"Immediately?" there was a frog in Eldin's throat.

(A moment's silence.) "Tomorrow."

"Good!" the older quester's grin split his face. "'Cos right now I've a hell of a thirst on. How about a pint?"

"I could murder one," Hero sighed…

About the Author

Born in County Durham, he joined the British Army's Royal Military Police and wrote stories in his spare time before retiring with the rank of Warrant Officer Class 2 in 1980 and becoming a professional writer.

In the 1970s he added to H. P. Lovecraft's Cthulhu Mythos cycle of stories, including several tales and a novel featuring the character Titus Crow. Several of his early books were published by Arkham House. Other stories pastiched Lovecraft's Dream Cycle but featured Lumley's original characters David Hero and Eldin the Wanderer. Lumley once explained the difference between his Cthulhu Mythos characters and Lovecraft's: "My guys fight back. Also, they like to have a laugh along the way."

Later works included the Necroscope® series of novels, which produced spin-off series such as the Vampire World Trilogy, *The Lost Years* parts 1 and 2, and the E-Branch trilogy. The central protagonist of the earlier Necroscope® novels appears in the anthology *Harry Keogh and Other Weird Heroes*. The latest entry in the Necroscope saga is *The Möbius Murders*.

Lumley served as president of the Horror Writers Association from 1996 to 1997. In March 2010, Lumley was awarded Lifetime Achievement Award of the Horror Writers Association. He also received a World Fantasy Award for Lifetime Achievement in 2010.

Bibliography

Psychomech Trilogy
Psychomech
Psychosphere
Psychamok

Necroscope® Series
Necroscope
Necroscope II: Wamphyri!
Necroscope III: The Source
Necroscope IV: Deadspeak
Necroscope V: Deadspawn
Vampire World I: Blood Brothers
Vampire World II: The Last Aerie
Vampire World III: Bloodwars
Necroscope: The Lost Years, Volume I
Necroscope: The Lost Years, Volume II
Necroscope: Invaders
Necroscope: Defilers
Necroscope: Avengers
Harry Keogh: Necroscope & Other Weird Heroes
Necroscope: The Touch
Necroscope: The Möbius Murders

Dreamland Series
Hero of Dreams
Ship of Dreams
Mad Moon of Dreams
Iced on Aran

Other Novels and Collections
A Coven of Vampires

Beneath the Moors
Beneath the Moors and Darker Places
Brian Lumley's Freaks
Dagon's Bell and Other Discords
Demogorgon
Earth, Air, Fire, and Water
Fruiting Bodies and Other Fungi
Ghoul Warning and Other Omens
Ghoul Warning and Other Omens… and Other Omens
Haggopian and Other Stories
Harry and the Pirates
In the Moons of Borea
Khai of Ancient Khem
Maze of Worlds
No Sharks in The Med & Other Stories
Screaming Science Fiction
Short Tall Tales
Sixteen Sucking Stories
Sorcery in Shad
Spawn of the Winds
Synchronicity, or Something
Tarra Khash Hrossak
The Burrowers Beneath
The Best of the Rest
The Caller of The Black
The Clock of Dreams
The Compleat Crow
The Compleat Khash: Volume One: Never a Backward Glance
The Fly-by-Nights
The Horror at Oakdeene and Others
The House of Cthulhu
The House of Doors
The House of the Temple
The Last Rite
The Nonesuch and Others
The Plague-Bearer

The Return of the Deep Ones and Other Mythos Tales
The Second Wish and Other Exhalations
The Taint and Other Novellas
The Transition of Titus Crow
The Whisperer and Other Voices

Curious about other Crossroad Press books? Stop by our website:
http://crossroadpress.com
We offer quality writing
in digital, audio, and print formats.

Subscribe to our newsletter on the website homepage and receive a
free eBook.

Printed in Great Britain
by Amazon